PENGUIN CLASSICS

PERSIAN LETTERS

CHARLES-LOUIS DE SECONDAT was born in 1689 at La Brède, near Bordeaux, into an eminent family of *parlementaires*. His mother died when he was ten and Charles-Louis was sent to Paris to be educated and completed a law degree in Bordeaux in 1708. He returned to Paris in order to finish his education, staying until his father died in 1713. In 1714 he became a councillor at the Bordeaux Parlement and a year later married a Huguenot lady, Jeanne de Lartigue, probably for her money. They had three children. A year after their marriage Charles-Louis inherited the barony of Montesquieu and the post of *président à mortier* at the Bordeaux Parlement, and five years later, in 1721, he published anonymously in Holland the *Persian Letters*, which ran into ten editions in one year. From 1721 to 1725 he lived in Paris frequenting fashionable society and conducting several love-affairs. He sold his post of *président* in 1726 because of financial difficulties, was elected to the French academy in 1727 and spent the next three years travelling in Europe (he stayed about eighteen months in England and became a freemason). He returned to France working mainly in Paris but occasionally travelling to the south-west to look after his estates and wine business. During this period his persistent eye-troubles got worse and he gave up freemasonry because of the Church's disapproval. In 1748 he published his most important work, *The Spirit of Laws*, which made an immediate impression and caused a lot of controversy. Montesquieu died in Paris of a fever in 1755. In 1751 *The Spirit of Laws* was placed on the Vatican Index and likewise the *Persian Letters* in 1761.

CHRISTOPHER BETTS was born in 1936 and is a Senior Lecturer in the Department of French Studies at the University of Warwick. He has written books and articles on eighteenth-century French fiction and thought and has also translated Rousseau's *The Social Contract*.

Montesquieu

PERSIAN LETTERS

*Translated with an
introduction and notes
by C. J. Betts*

Penguin Books

PENGUIN BOOKS

Published by the Penguin Group
Penguin Books Ltd, 27 Wrights Lane, London W8 5TZ, England
Penguin Books USA Inc., 375 Hudson Street, New York, New York 10014, USA
Penguin Books Australia Ltd, Ringwood, Victoria, Australia
Penguin Books Canada Ltd, 10 Alcorn Avenue, Toronto, Ontario, Canada M4V 3B2
Penguin Books (NZ) Ltd, 182–190 Wairau Road, Auckland 10, New Zealand

Penguin Books Ltd, Registered Offices: Harmondsworth, Middlesex, England

This translation first published 1973
Reprinted with an updated bibliography 1993
5 7 9 10 8 6 4

Printed in England by Clays Ltd, St Ives plc

CONTENTS

Contents

Contents

7

Contents

Contents

Contents

Contents

Contents

Contents

Contents

Contents

Contents

INTRODUCTION

FOR the general reader, Montesquieu will be better known as a political theorist than as the author of the *Persian Letters*; it could scarcely be otherwise, with a man whose analysis of the English constitution produced a famous theory of the 'separation of powers' which had a deep influence on the constitution of, for instance, the United States. But the *Persian Letters*, his first book, published in 1721, has too often been treated as merely a forerunner of the political treatise, *Of the Spirit of Laws* (1748). Looking for signs of what was to come, critics have extracted passages from the *Persian Letters* piecemeal, and virtually ignored all the other bright ideas, humour and satire which fill the pages of this work of Montesquieu's youthful maturity. In the literary field there can be no doubt that it comes first: it may be less weighty, but it is more varied in style, probably wittier, and just as wide-ranging and perceptive. It contains more satire than theory, being perhaps the finest French work (the other contender is La Bruyère's *Characters*, (also in Penguin Classics) of a great period of satire, the period which extends, in France, from Molière to Voltaire, and includes in England such figures as Dryden, Pope and Swift. The nearest English equivalent is Addison and Steele's *Spectator*. Montesquieu's Persian pair are spectators of the French scene, detached but not indifferent, with their own set of 'Persian' values, which turn out – despite a rather obvious split between Usbek's principles and his practice – to be those of a rationalist critic of established institutions, a liberal, or at any rate a believer in liberty and justice, and a utilitarian.

Seen in its immediate historical context, the *Persian Letters* is generally agreed to convey more faithfully than any other work the atmosphere of the Regency of Philippe d'Orléans, from 1715 to 1723, following the death of Louis XIV. The memory of the dead king, one of the magnificent despots of modern times, pervades Montesquieu's book. The vivacity of the reaction against him, the outburst of high spirits after the gloomy, ritualistic and religiose decline of the 'great century', the extension of interest to lands and

17

customs outside the limits of Versailles and France, the taste for experiment in public affairs as in science, the frivolity and calamities of Regency life are all to be found here. The book also inaugurated that eighteenth-century phenomenon known as the Enlightenment, a literary and intellectual movement which, in the name of freedom and humanity, attacked almost every traditional value in sight.

The creator of the two travellers through France, whose enormous popularity helped to engender a large number of later imaginary oriental critics of European affairs, had been born in 1689, into an eminent family of the Bordeaux region. Their eminence was due to their distinction in the legal profession, or more exactly to their tenure of various important posts in the Bordeaux *parlement* – under the French *ancien régime* this meant an institution which administered the law as its main function, but also retained vestiges of a political power which in the past had been considerable (and was to be revived during the eighteenth century). The *parlements* also enjoyed the prestige of the noble status which accompanied many of their functions. Montesquieu's mother died in 1696. He was given what was presumably an excellent education in a college run at Juilly, near Paris, by the Oratorians, a forward-looking religious order, and went on to study law. It was of course intended that he should follow the family career, and on the death of an uncle, the then head of the family, Montesquieu inherited his title, his position in the Bordeaux *parlement*, and the name by which he is now known. Until this year, 1716, he had been Charles-Louis de Secondat. A year earlier he had married; his wife, Jeanne de Lartigue, bore him a son and two daughters, in 1716, 1717 and 1727. Her role in life appears to have been to provide an heir and some money, in the form of her dowry, and to look after the estates when her husband was away.

Montesquieu had helped to found the Bordeaux Academy of Sciences at about this time, but this is the only indication that he had any interests outside the law. There was nothing to suggest that he was to become the author, with the *Persian Letters*, of one of the main anti-Establishment works of the early eighteenth century. The *Lettres persanes* was published anonymously in Holland – standard practice when there was a risk of official disapproval. One of Montesquieu's friends told him that it would 'sell like hot cakes', and the forecast proved to be correct; there were at least ten editions within a year. It seems to have changed Montesquieu's life: from being an intellectual gentleman of merely local importance he becomes a society man in Paris, the then centre of the civilised world, and appears to have spent some time after 1721 enjoying social and amorous success. He finally abandoned his legal career in 1726, making some money out of the sale of his *parlement* position, and in the next year got into the French Academy. The story is that the cardinal-minister, Fleury, had opposed his election on the grounds of the twenty-fourth Persian Letter.

For a while Montesquieu followed the example of Usbek and Rica and travelled round Europe, including England, where he stayed for about eighteen months, and making voluminous notes. In about 1731 he settled down to write his more serious works – first some *Considerations on the causes of Roman greatness and decadence*, published in 1734, which disappointed a public hoping for more Persian Letters, and much later, after a struggle with increasing blindness and financial worries, *Of the Spirit of Laws* (De l'esprit des lois). This study of political and social structure immediately made a profound impression with its attack on despotism, its claim to prevent despotism by the separation of the executive, legislative and judicial powers of a state, and its analysis of the relations between such varied aspects of the social situation as government, religion, geography and education. The book could not avoid being controversial in a period when the conflict between the Church and its opponents was becoming more acute, and Montesquieu, now a grand old man of French letters, spent much time in his last years defending himself against accusations of irreligion. In 1751 the *Spirit of Laws* was put on the Vatican's Index of Prohibited Books and the *Persian Letters* also came under attack, from one Abbé Gaultier; ten years later it too was to go on the Index. Montesquieu, however, knew nothing of this, for he died of a fever in Paris in 1755.

IT is not easy to describe the *Persian Letters*: their most obvious characteristic is variety. We occasionally find a sequence of letters on one subject, such as L. 10 to L. 14, which contain the parable of the

Troglodytes, or L. 133 to L. 137, on literature, or the final fifteen
letters which conclude the story of Usbek's harem; and there are also
several groups of two or three letters forming miniature debates – L.
16 to L. 18 on religious purity, L. 76 and L. 77 on suicide, or L. 105
and L. 106 on the value of technological advance. But the vast
majority of the letters are arranged higgledy-piggledy, metaphysics
next to social satire, historical speculation about the Ottoman Empire
next to a reprimand from Usbek to one of his wives for philandering
with a eunuch. In time the letters range from the Creation to the day
before the letter is written, in place from China to Sweden or Reunion
Island. Even within a single letter it is often hard to see any real
coherence. L. 40, for instance, consists of four short paragraphs on
funeral orations, the lugubrious rituals of the death-bed, human folly,
and a strange custom from India. There is a certain connection
between one paragraph and the next, but the whole seems to lack
unity. Montesquieu wrote, in 'Some Reflections on the Persian
Letters', of a 'secret chain' between all the letters, but many readers
will find it so secret as to be invisible.

Now this fragmented chaos cannot be put down merely to caprice
or carelessness. For one thing, it must be related stylistically to the
contemporaneous rococo movement in the visual arts, with its dis-
jointed lines and abundance of varied decoration; for another, it
provides a contrast to the prevalent mood of the work, which is of
rationality; it avoids pedantic orderliness, and in this respect is firmly
within the great French tradition of moral comment since Montaigne,
a tradition represented more recently by La Rochefoucauld, La
Fontaine and La Bruyère. Montesquieu takes all fields of intellectual
interest, and every aspect of human life, for his subject-matter: a
methodical treatment would have been impossible. Instead, we have
the charm of diversity, with its attendant risk of superficiality;
though Montesquieu's habit of being witty makes the risk worth-
while.

In the circumstances, to classify the 161 letters written (mainly) by
and to the two Persian travellers in Europe is bound to result in dis-
tortion, but it seems desirable to provide some guide-lines, and what
follows is intended to indicate roughly what is to be found in the
work. Formally, the book consists of a large central section, chiefly

on French life and society, but punctuated by reports of the goings-on in Persia and expeditions to far-off parts such as Russia or England. This is preceded and followed by two Persian sections, the departure of Rica and Usbek to seek enlightenment in Europe, and the eventual collapse of discipline in the harem Usbek has left. The mood gradually darkens: the beginning is optimistic, full of the affection of Usbek's wives and the idealism of the Troglodyte parable, while at the end France is suffering from the financial disaster of Law's 'System', and in Persia love has been replaced by enmity. We start with ironies about a virgin birth and finish with the tragic suicide of Roxana. The shift from comparatively humorous to comparatively sober can be measured by comparing Rica's blithe witticisms on his arrival in France with Usbek's lengthy assessment, in L. 113 to L. 122, of the causes for what he supposes to be the depopulation of the world.

According to Montesquieu himself, in the 'Reflections', one of his book's most popular features was the harem story. A modern reader is unlikely to find it appealing as fiction – there is no plot to speak of, the characters are not differentiated, the psychology is stylized. The interest of these letters lies rather in their combination of the exotic and the erotic. In the early eighteenth century the East was beginning to be opened up to Europeans; travellers' reports, the occasional real oriental, as in L. 91, and translations of such works as the *Thousand and One Nights*, increased knowledge and curiosity. Montesquieu helped to build up the fascination of the East by concentrating on the cruelty or strangeness of Persian customs, often adding to the effect by means of what was then considered to be a flowery Eastern style, as in L. 16 or L. 42. He also used the Persian scene as a point of comparison with the French, notably on the subjects of politics, religion and women; Persia is sometimes horrifying, sometimes admirable. The eroticism is equally prominent. The sexual frustrations of a society of women and eunuchs are discussed at length; an example of the sort of topic that recurs is provided by the career of the slave Zelid, who in L. 4 and L. 20 appears to have a Lesbian relationship with first Zephis and then Zashi, and in L. 53 is about to marry a white eunuch (appropriately enough, it may be thought). Nor does Montesquieu neglect more normal sexual questions, as can be seen from L. 3, L. 7, or L. 26; he adopts a style full of innuendo, which at times verges on the prurient. The line between this and what appear to be objective attempts to describe feminine sexuality is difficult to draw. L. 141, for example, the tale of Anaïs in Paradise, seems to be part'y an investigation of what sexual experience means for a woman. It is also partly an answer to the question about the nature of heavenly bliss posed in L. 125 – Paradise here is the perfection of eighteenth-century social and sexual pleasures.

The letters about Persia also provide something resembling a sociological analysis, but in imaginative terms, of the unnatural situation in the harem, which is characterized by tensions between wives and eunuchs and, from the eunuch's point of view, by the difficulty of keeping discipline when there is no focus for affection and loyalty (L. 9, L. 22, L. 64, L. 96). As the story develops it takes on strong moral overtones. In Montesquieu's words, 'disorder increases': initially the wives are frustrated, though still loving; then misdemeanours and misfortunes occur (L. 20, L. 47, L. 64), while Usbek's mood becomes more and more sombre (L. 22, L. 65). In the hectic ending everything is disrupted, and order can be restored only by ruthlessness (L. 147 to L. 161); for Usbek himself the future is without hope (L. 155). The message, as one of the eunuchs implies in L. 96, must be that rule by force alone, or despotism, will fail. The only way to justify Usbek's position of domination is by his presence and love, but his nine-year journey makes it impossible.

The subjects of women and marriage, which account for so much in the harem letters, also figure largely in the letters about France; probably more space is devoted to them than to any other subject. The purpose of the harem is to ensure wifely virtue, that is to say, chastity, by over-protectiveness. In France the different situation of freedom, or what appears to the Persians to be so, is combined with habitual infidelity, as in L. 55 and the remarks such as those in L. 28 about actresses who, off-stage, are 'approachable'. Furthermore, husbands lack authority (L. 86), and it is women who pull all the strings in public affairs (L. 107). Rica, who is readier than Usbek to accept Western ideas about women (L. 63), discusses them in L. 38. He reports the pro-feminist opinions of a 'very chivalrous philosopher', but concludes hesitantly on the masculine side.

Marriage on harem lines is an extreme, but it is the logical outcome of the claims of male authority and female virtue. However, when Montesquieu is thinking about procreation, as in L. 114, he comes up with an attack on harems, and in L. 116 he strongly recommends divorce. The *Persian Letters* also contain an ideal of family life which is very different from the harem situation: the virtuous Troglodytes, in L. 12 and L. 13, continuously exemplify this idea, which is described with the warm, sometimes sentimental effusiveness known in eighteenth-century literature as 'sensibility'. The brother–sister marriage of L. 67, like that of their parents, is another example. A belief in the sanctity of the family is suggested also by such diverse passages as Rica's disapproval of the revelations about family life that are made in lawcourts (L. 86), Usbek's indignation with the Don Juan of L. 48 and his pleas for paternal authority at the end of L. 129, and the denunciation of Law's 'System' in L. 146 for causing the ruin of so many families. It seems paradoxical that this feeling for the family should coexist in the same work with a permanent implication that women are unchaste (there is only one exception to this, in France: the wife of Usbek's host in L. 48 – unless we prefer to believe the insinuations of the Don Juan character in the same letter). A resolution of the paradox can be found by following the hints in L. 104 about the basis for all forms of human association. The theory is that the basis must be mutual gratitude between the members of a society; although the context here is political, it is a theory which can be applied in the realm of personal relationships too. The Troglodyte families, like their society as a whole, are united by mutual generosity. There seems to be a similar relationship between the brother and sister of L. 67, as is shown among other things by their willingness to sacrifice themselves for each other. Even within the conventions of the harem, a perhaps not quite serious idea of how gratitude can form a social bond is conveyed by Zulema's story of the two Ibrahims (L. 141): the false Ibrahim, superhumanly virile, can satisfy all the wives who had been neglected by the original, cruel Ibrahim, and they are thenceforward not only happy and free, in the Western style, but also faithful – presumably out of gratitude for his prowess. All these examples of happy marriage are of course highly unrealistic; the combination of romantic love and family affection found with the Gabars of L. 67, or less obtrusively with the Troglodytes, who regard themselves as one family, seems destined to remain on the level of the ideal.

The many letters, predominantly satirical in style, which describe and comment on people and institutions in France, are the most immediately attractive feature of the book and seem likely also to leave the most lasting impression; on them is founded Montesquieu's reputation for wit, although they do not have a monopoly of it. For the modern reader one obvious source of interest is the picture they provide of life at that time for a member of the educated upper class. But Montesquieu's purpose must have been to moralize rather than to document, as is indicated by the device of seeing everything through the mock-innocent but unforgiving eyes of the two Persians. The favourite method is the portrait, a technique of describing character and behaviour simultaneously, which had been perfected in La Bruyère's *Characters* of 1688. The subjects are both individuals and types: they appear in scenes similar to those found in novels, but they exemplify either particular social groups, such as judges, old soldiers, or aristocrats, or else moral qualities such as vanity or licentiousness. The Persians often contribute their own sharp opinions to point the moral. The 'decisioneer' of L. 72 and the bishop of L. 101, where the skilful use of repartee and exaggeration produces a brilliant effect, seem to me especially good specimens of the genre.

It is noticeable how often Montesquieu caricatures quirks of conversation or of intellect, things of great importance in the refined salon society of the eighteenth century, where success awaited anyone who could talk intelligently and well. In L. 54 we overhear two would-be wits planning their campaign; L. 128 describes a mathematician whose calling renders him incapable of judging the real significance of anything; in L. 59 a variety of old people can do nothing except lament the passing of the good old days; in L. 48, which consists of a succession of portraits, there is a poet who is criticized for his bizarre talk. Foolishness, a quality of the judge in L. 68, the bishop in L. 101, the alchemist in L. 45 and most French writers in L. 66, is never spared; nor is the habit of wasting time on trivialities, which is satirized in the intellectuals of L. 36, arguing about Homer, the newsmongers of L. 130, who speculate tirelessly about public affairs of which they know nothing, and both the Sorbonne and the French Academy, in L. 109 and L. 73.

The fault which Montesquieu seems especially to dislike is vanity. L. 144 contains a eulogy of its opposite together with an onslaught on two kinds of conceit, and attacks on self-importance are very frequent elsewhere; almost all the characters I have mentioned already betray some variety of it. The egotistical bore of L. 50 illustrates it at length, and L. 44 castigates the French, mankind in general, and a brace of kings on similar grounds. The theme is so prevalent that it requires explanation. I would suggest that Montesquieu's denunciations should be interpreted, in general terms, as a version of the propaganda for that ideal of civilized, somewhat conformist behaviour typified in the seventeenth and eighteenth centuries by the 'honest man' ('*l'honnête homme*'), a type who observed the social conventions with elegance and never paraded his individuality. According to La Rochefoucauld, he 'is never conceited about anything'. L. 74, which satirizes an aristocrat whose only claim to attention is his arrogance, is especially significant in this respect, since, at an earlier period, it had been the aristocracy whose code of flamboyant, self-glorifying individualism had set the tone in society and literature (notably in Corneille's plays). Now, after the emasculation of the military nobility by Louis XIV, Montesquieu's Persian gentleman comments that any pride in nobility must be based on having carried out a patriotic duty to the state, that of leadership in battle. The military role of the nobility remains the same, but their pride derives from their social utility rather than their personal worth or position.

The nobility is also the subject of a trio of letters, L. 88 to L. 90. They begin with epigrams about the current uselessness of the nobles, contrasting this with what Usbek alleges to be the case in Persia, go on to interpret the traditional noble ideal of 'glory' as a socially useful phenomenon, because it encourages the Frenchman to expose himself willingly to danger for his country's sake, and finally criticize the code of honour developed in feudal times, and still flourishing in the seventeenth century, for being irrational. In L. 78 noble pride is again satirized, the more freely perhaps because the setting is Spanish. It looks as if Usbek, the Persian equivalent of a nobleman, is in fact an early spokesman for what is now termed the meritocracy, to judge by the definition of Persian nobility in L. 89.

Because of Montesquieu's reputation as a political theorist, it is natural to treat the *Persian Letters* as a precursor of the later work and to look for ideas of political significance, especially since even apparently irrelevant letters may have political overtones, as with the implications about the use of authority in the harem letters. In the *Spirit of Laws* the fear of despotism is very prevalent; Montesquieu considers it to be a permanent threat in a monarchical government, which for him is the normal kind, and his most famous and influential theory, that of the separation of powers, arises out of the effort to forestall it. In the *Persian Letters* the fear of despotism is evoked in what is said in L. 102 of the savage punishments inflicted by Persian rulers and in L. 8 of the risks awaiting Usbek at court. When he arrives in France, he reports, in a masterly euphemism, that Louis XIV too is despotic: 'he possesses in a very high degree the talent of making himself obeyed' (L. 37). The assertion of the contrary value of liberty is found much later, in L. 131, on the origin of republics. The term does not here mean something essentially different from monarchy, but a monarchy in which the king's power is limited, by that of citizens or lords. L. 136, ostensibly a review of history books, develops the theme of liberty by saying that the modern European states were originally free, though barbaric, and lost their freedom ('the sweetness of liberty, which is in such close concord with reason, humanity, and nature') through the growth of absolute power – the power, presumably, of the medieval and Renaissance monarchs, or rulers like Louis XIV. Taken together, Montesquieu's remarks add up to an assertion of liberty against royal authority; but it must be said that, as with many other ideas in the work, indirect expression and the distribution of relevant passages among different letters mean that the assertion becomes somewhat oblique. Moreover 'liberty' appears to imply especially the rights of noblemen or other important citizens.

Given the strict surveillance of the eighteenth-century book trade, it is not surprising that Montesquieu was circumspect. His disapproval of Louis XIV is expressed merely in the surprise felt by his Persians at the 'contradictions' of royal policy; in this manner L. 37 insinuates criticism of Louis' militarism and of the fear he had of over-capable subordinates, among other things. More openly, L. 124, developing a couple of remarks in L. 122, parodies a royal decree, contrasting the money spent lavishly on effete courtiers with the impositions laid on more useful members of society. In L. 85, Louis' religious policy of enforced conformity is transposed into an incident from Persian history which parallels the Revocation of the Edict of Nantes, the harshest measure taken against the Huguenots, and this device enables Montesquieu to argue directly against intolerance.

The treatment of the political history of the Regency is more complete than that of the reign of Louis XIV, but Montesquieu's comments are often less far-reaching. From a fragment he left in note form (see Appendix, p. 288) it is clear that he thought poorly of the Regency; but he was favourably disposed towards the regent. This may be because Philippe d'Orléans restored the dignity of the Parlements, the juridical institutions staffed by the 'nobility of the robe' to which Montesquieu's family belonged; he refers to their impotence under Louis XIV and to the regent's manoeuvres in L. 92, and celebrates the traditional view of the social function of the Parlements in L. 140. Towards the end of the book, it becomes almost a commentary on current events – victories over the Turks, the Cellamare conspiracy, the death of Charles XII and the abdication of the Queen of Sweden (L. 123, L. 126, L. 127, L. 139). Often Montesquieu concentrates on the moral, rather than the political significance of his subjects; thus L. 126 concludes with some reflections on feeling compassion towards the great, and L. 139 sees the queen's action in terms of personal morality.

Much the same is true of the letters about the most sensational event of the Regency, the collapse of the 'System' of the Scottish banker John Law, who attempted to create a system of credit based on the prospects of colonial exploitation in the New World, and for a time succeeded well enough to be put in charge of financial policy, in 1720. However, confidence waned as a series of decrees altered money values almost month by month, the opposition of the established financiers whom Law had supplanted became too great, and the result was chaos. While the System lasted, enormous fortunes were quickly made, and lost, by speculation on the changing values of currency and the shares of Law's West India Company; the most obvious effect was rapid inflation. Montesquieu represents the essence of the System in an allegory about John Law in L. 142, where he is a son of the god of wind and sells balloons, an image of inflated share values that is not without effectiveness today. In L. 138 the complaints about financial policy are twofold: it fluctuates, and it permits the acquisition of great wealth for no good reason. (L. 98 makes the same sort of remark about the wealth gained in what was then a more conventional way, by the private tax-farmers.) The bitter denunciation in L. 146, another example of the use of an Eastern disguise, is based on a moral objection to the System: the minister has corrupted the nation by making it legal to pay debts with money that has depreciated in value; profiteers, taking advantage of his decrees, have brought ruin to many unfortunate families.

There is little of the more abstract type of political theory in the *Persian Letters*. L. 80 has a famous definition of the best sort of government: 'the one which attains its purpose with the least trouble'; this suggests a general theory, but the sequel of the letter shows that Montesquieu is thinking of a limited subject and advocating a policy of moderation in dealing with political offences (by contrast with despotic Persian policies). L. 104 contains a fragmentary theory of social contract, basing it on gratitude, which, as has been mentioned, is important in the context of Montesquieu's views on the family; but the issue in L. 104, the right to rebel, is again somewhat limited, and presupposes that the form of government is monarchical. However, this letter does propound fairly strongly the opinion that a king should govern for the benefit of his subjects; otherwise, 'the basis of obedience is lost.'

The significance of the letters on the Troglodytes is perhaps chiefly political. According to one interpretation, that of Crisafulli mentioned in the bibliography on page 35, they represent a reaction on Montesquieu's part against the political psychology of writers such as Hobbes, whose conception of the natural human state as 'the war of every man against every man' is realized in L. 11 with the description of the first generation of Troglodytes: their unrestrained pursuit of self-interest leads to mutual destruction. The virtuous second generation, indoctrinated by their parents, show how cooperation leads to universal prosperity Despite Montesquieu's rhapsodic style, the later

Troglodytes cannot be regarded as wholly saintly, since their happy unity rests on sound economic foundations; they are scarcely less self-interested than their brutish ancestors, but, having learnt that 'the individual's self-interest is always to be found in the common interest' (L. 12), they are able to achieve material affluence more efficiently than by individual enterprise. In L. 14 and a final letter which Montesquieu left unpublished (see Appendix, p. 286), the Utopian comes nearer to the realities of eighteenth-century life, with discussions of the ethics of money under a monarchical government. Montesquieu suggests that in these circumstances individuals will pursue money for itself, instead of producing goods cooperatively for the whole community (the Troglodytes have not used money before). These warnings about the risks of money, although put into an unreal setting, are not far away from the criticisms of ill-conceived financial policy that Montesquieu was to make when writing of Law's System.

Two letters of a religious and metaphysical turn discuss the basic ethical value of justice, which is related to the 'virtue' of the Troglodytes. L. 83, the more important, affirms that justice is the most fundamental value of all, more basic than the existence of God (the way in which this is put does not suggest that Montesquieu did not believe in God); the passage closely recalls a remark of Mirza's in L. 10, that justice is as 'proper' to men as their existence. L. 69, debating a standard problem of theistic metaphysics, the question how men can be free if God knows everything, including all men's future actions, attempts to reconcile divine omniscience and divine justice, but it becomes apparent that Montesquieu is readier to sacrifice the former than the latter.

God, then, in the *Persian Letters*, is a god of justice; and to be religious, it appears, is to obey his precepts – L. 69 ends with the remark that 'we know him properly through his precepts alone.' These are essentially of social rather than spiritual importance, as is shown by L. 46; it contains in various forms a short credo concerned with 'the rules of society and the duties of humanity', and also uses a satirical technique of comparison between the externals of different religions – in other words, it puts forward the deistic notion that elements of social or moral usefulness, which are common to all

29

religions, matter more than their diverse rituals and dogmas. In L. 57, it is because of this belief in ethical or religious rules that Usbek is so angry with a casuist, whose trade, he says, is to devise ways of excusing men from obedience to God's commands; similar remarks about bishops in L. 29 are less flippant than they might seem.

For further indications of Montesquieu's doctrinal beliefs we have to make do with hints. This is particularly true of the question of the soul, which, together with that of the existence of God, was one of the great religious problems of the time. There was in any case a long tradition of agnosticism on the subject. The first letter on suicide (L. 76) suggests belief in some kind of survival of the soul, but Heaven in L. 141 involves delights of a distinctly bodily nature; together the two cancel each other out. Although Usbek is against the doubter whom he describes in L. 75, Montesquieu's own attitude is scarcely more definite. We are reduced to supposing that his deism contains little positive except the belief in God, seen as the guarantor of social and moral values. At any rate, a letter left in Montesquieu's notebooks (see Appendix, p. 294) contains an attack on an atheist, couched in rather stronger terms than the affirmation in L. 83 of belief in God.

The letters criticizing various aspects of established religion are clearer, even outspoken considering the official and unofficial constraints that then limited the expression of opinion. This is in line with eighteenth-century religious thought generally, which is rather more notable for its critical than for its constructive achievements. The attitudes prevalent in the *Persian Letters* are anticlericalism and indifference to religion. Montesquieu does not attack the lower secular clergy, the over-worked and underpaid *curés*, who came from the lower classes, but chooses his targets among the regular clergy and the dignitaries, bishops and the Pope. Nowadays, indeed, his remarks about the latter, in L. 24 and L. 29, may appear extreme. They can be explained as the expression of Gallican feeling, the view that the French Church should look after its business without interference from Rome. This feeling was strong among Montesquieu's own class of the legal nobility, who also favoured Jansenism, a religious movement which occasioned the major internal Catholic controversy of the time. Jansenism was an uncompromising Augustinian movement which dated back to the 1630s. It had been treated as heretical by Louis XIV and the Jesuits, and a number of harsh measures had been taken against it, with progressively less success. In L. 24 and L. 101 the event to which Montesquieu refers indirectly is the bull *Unigenitus*, which Louis, in his last years, had persuaded the Pope to promulgate against Jansenism. Montesquieu interprets the bull, however, as the result of papal influence over the king, to which he seems to object perhaps rather more than to its anti-Jansenist nature. In L. 29, too, the charge against the popes is that they have had undue power over kings.

Montesquieu writes with equal vehemence about monks, notably the unfortunate Capuchin berated by Rica in L. 49 and an Indian equivalent, the bonze of L. 125. An atmosphere of disrespect is also fostered by the beginnings of some letters (L. 57 and L. 82) and by the derisive impertinences of some of the letters to Persian holy men ('men of Law') such as L. 16 or L. 93. The latter, together with L. 123, shows that Montesquieu was well aware of the traditional religious justification of a life of contemplation and prayer, but he either considers it useless or provides a moralizing, rational explanation of it. Weightier arguments against monasticism are given in the letters on depopulation; L. 117 describes monasteries as 'abysses for future generations to be engulfed in'. In all this Montesquieu is typical of the advanced utilitarian opinion of his day.

The subject of religious strife is crucial in the tension between religious and social values: fighting about religion is an obvious example of anti-social behaviour, and one that was then much to be feared, the past being full of religious wars since the Reformation, and the present dominated by bitter, though unarmed, conflict between Jansenists and Jesuits. Montesquieu's opposition to the Pope might suggest that he would support the Jansenists, but he appears to be more concerned with the fact of conflict itself rather than the rights and wrongs of it. One blunt sentence in L. 29, about the civil wars in Christendom, is adequate condemnation; its converse is to be found in L. 123, a hope for peace among the Muslim sects. L. 46 and L. 75 also make the accusation that religion means strife, adding that Christians, despite their belligerence, are not truly attached to their faith. At the end of L. 36 the ability to quarrel over religion is claimed to be a necessary qualification for theologians, while the civilized cleric of L. 61 complains that contentiousness seems to be inseparable from his profession. A judgement on the Jansenist controversy is conveyed by one of the mock prescriptions of L. 143; others among them satirize Jesuits and Jansenists more or less impartially. The conclusion of L. 85, one of the strongest passages of the book, attributes the blame for religious war to the spirit of intolerance – here it seems to be war, rather than intolerance as such, that arouses Montesquieu's indignation.

Throughout there is resolute indifference to everything in religion that is not socially or morally beneficial – ritual in L. 46, proselytism in L. 85, L. 61 and L. 49, prayer, theology, and monasticism. In L. 61, the cleric himself ends by being almost contemptuously indifferent about a distinguished predecessor. Equally, whatever in religion can be said to be of value in some more or less utilitarian way is viewed with favour, notably the moral aspects emphasized in L. 46, L. 61 and L. 85, letters which combine tolerance, indifference, and secular values in a way which shows how closely these attitudes are linked. It also seems that when Montesquieu criticizes the Church, he does so on the grounds that it ignores those socially valuable precepts which, in his scheme of things, it should be inculcating; this is what underlies, for instance, the epigram about monks and their vows at the beginning of L. 57.

To conclude by trying to define what dominates the work: it is in my view the group of concepts centring on law and justice. It is not merely that there is much discussion of legal questions, now rather more dated than other things in the book – laws concerning the family and marriage in L. 71, J. 86, L. 116 and L. 129, the law against suicide in L. 76, punishments for political crimes in L. 80, L. 102, and L. 103, sanctions in international law in L. 94 and L. 95, the French habit of borrowing their laws in L. 100, the factors involved in making and changing law in L. 129 – but in addition legal concepts such as justice or equity are transported into other spheres, mainly those of religion and ethics, and there become the supreme values. L. 83, on justice, and the letters on the Troglodytes, whose code is one of equity, have been mentioned already, as has the idea that religion is obedience to God's precepts, which are not far from being laws. What are now usually classified as political matters are often treated as questions of law, as in several of the letters listed above. Montesquieu says little about scientific laws, but L. 97 contains a eulogy of them, with an ironical attack on sacred texts for being less useful. The importance of the letters on depopulation is not, of course, in the conclusions they reach, which can seem ludicrous, but in the effort to find some constants of social behaviour by which to explain the presumed phenomenon of depopulation. He was later, in the *Spirit of Laws*, to be one of the first investigators of whatever laws may be discerned in human affairs; L. 89 and L. 90 sketch out an analysis of the code of honour that foreshadows the later book in this respect. This belief in, or quest for, fixity is in marked contrast with the appearance of confusion that the *Persian Letters* itself presents, and very often we seem to be far from anything fixed when one of the Persians throws up his hands in amazement at the illogicality of the French. But the surprise of the rational Persians is in fact occasioned by the absence of anything resembling a law, as with the diatribe against fashion in L. 99; here, Rica's exasperation is due precisely to his inability to find any principle which will explain the absurd changes that he observes. The same is true of the paradoxes which strike the Persians when they consider Louis XIV and his policies in L. 24 and L. 37, or with the series of contradictions to be found in Spain, in L. 78. Indeed, one common technique of Montesquieu's satire is to emphasize irrationality, by way of reaction against it. Changeableness is frequently derided, in love (L. 55), religion (L. 75), and finance (L. 138), as well as in such things as fashion. To return to L. 40, which was mentioned originally as an example of apparent disorder: what Montesquieu is protesting about is that men's emotions, and the ceremonies which incarnate them, seem to follow no fixed principles; this lack of reason is reflected in the disjointedness of the letter. Montesquieu, unable to explain the phenomenon, resorts to denunciation. There are, certainly, other features of the *Persian Letters*, such as its utilitarianism, which may be independent of the theme of law, but it seems to me more pervasive in the work as a whole than any other element that I can distinguish. It is perhaps no more than was to be expected from a man whose background was the legal profession and whose later great work was entirely taken up with various sorts of law.

FURTHER READING

THE following selective list of books and articles mainly in English includes works on Montesquieu and his background generally, but not the many studies which concentrate on *The Spirit of Laws*. A full bibliography of the *Lettres persanes* to about 1986 is to be found in Louis Desgraves, *Répertoire des ouvrages et articles sur Montesquieu*, Geneva, 1988, pp. 166–85. Besides the editions listed on p. 301, there are currently (1993) good French paperback editions in the Folio, Livre de poche and Garnier/Flammarion series.

P. Barrière, 'Les éléments personnels et les éléments bordelais dans les *Lettres persanes*', *Revue d'histoire littéraire de la France*, 51 (1951), 17–36.

C. B. A. Behrens, *The Ancien Régime*, London, 1967.

C. J. Betts, *Early Deism in France*, The Hague, 1984 (Chapter 11).

—, *Montesquieu: Lettres persanes* (Critical Guides to French Literature), London, forthcoming 1994.

Theodore Braun, '"*La Chaîne secrète*"; A Decade of Interpretations', *French Studies*, 42 (1988).

Peter V. Conroy, jnr, *Montesquieu Revisited* (Twayne's World Authors Series), New York, 1992.

Alessandro Crisafulli, 'Montesquieu's Story of the Troglodytes, Its Background, Meaning and Significance', *Publications of the Modern Language Association of America*, 58 (1943), 372–92.

Charles Dédéyan, *Montesquieu et l'alibi persan*, Paris, 1988.

Joseph Dedieu, *Montesquieu, l'homme et l'oeuvre*, Paris, 1943.

Louis Desgraves, *Montesquieu*, Paris, 1986.

Peter Gay, *The Enlightenment*, 2 vols., New York, 1966–9.

F. C. Green, *The Ancien Régime: A Manual of French Institutions and Social Classes*, Edinburgh, 1958.

Jeanne Geffriaud-Rosso, *Montesquieu et la féminité*, Pisa, 1977.

Ronald Grimsley, 'The Idea of Nature in Montesquieu's *Lettres persanes*', *French Studies*, 5 (1951), 293–306.

Ahmad Gunny, 'Montesquieu's View of Islam in the *Lettres persanes*', *Studies on Voltaire and the Eighteenth Century*, 174 (1978).

Norman Hampson, *The Enlightenment*, London, 1968.

Mark Hulliung, *Montesquieu and the Old Regime*, Berkeley, California, 1976.

Frederick Keener, *The Chain of Becoming: The Philosophical Novel, the Tale, and a Neglected Realism of the Enlightenment: Swift, Montesquieu, Voltaire, Johnson, and Austen*, New York, 1983.

Pauline Kra, 'Montesquieu and Women', in Spencer, Samia I., ed., *French Women and the Age of Enlightenment*, Bloomington, Indiana, 1984, 272–84.

John Lough, *An Introduction to Eighteenth-Century France*, London, 1960.

J. Robert Loy, *Montesquieu* (Twayne's World Authors Series), New York, 1968.

Haydn Mason, *French Writers and Their Society 1715–1800*, London, 1982.

Sheila M. Mason, *Montesquieu's Idea of Justice*, The Hague, 1975.

Roger Oake, 'Montesquieu's Religious Ideas', *Journal of the History of Ideas*, 14 (1953), 548–60.

Orest Ranum, 'Personality and Politics in the *Lettres persane*', Political Science Quarterly, 1969.

Nick Roddick, 'The Structure of the *Lettres persanes*', French Studies, 28 (1974), 396–407.

G. L. van Roosbroeck, *Persian Letters before Montesquieu*, New York, 1932.

Robert Shackleton, *Montesquieu, a Critical Biography*, Oxford, 1961.

—, 'The Moslem Chronology of the *Lettres persanes*', French Studies, 8 (1954), 17–27 (also in his *Essays on Montesquieu and the Enlightenment*, D. Gibson and M. Smith, eds., Oxford, 1988).

Tzvetan Todorov, 'Réflexions sur les *Lettres persanes*', *Romanic Review*, 74 (1983), 306–15.

Aram Vartanian, 'Eroticism and Politics in the *Lettres persanes*', *Romanic Review*, 60 (1969), 23–33.

Mark Waddicor, *Montesquieu and the Philosophy of Natural Law*, The Hague, 1970.

—, *Montesquieu: Lettres persanes* (Studies in French Literature, 31), London, 1977.

D. B. Young, 'Libertarian Demography: Montesquieu's Essay on Depopulation in the *Lettres persanes*', *Journal of the History of Ideas*, 36 (1975), 669–82.

Persian Letters

THIS is not a dedicatory epistle: I am not asking anyone's protection for this book. People will read it if it is good, and if it is bad I do not care whether they read it or not.

I have detached these first letters so as to see if the public will like them; I have a large number of others in my files, which I may publish later on.

But this would be on condition that I remain unidentified, for if my name were to become known I should keep silent from that moment on. I know a woman who walks quite gracefully, but she limps as soon as anyone looks at her.[1] The book's defects are enough in themselves, without exposing my own to criticism as well. If it were known who I am, people would say: 'His book doesn't match his character; he ought to use his time on something better; such things aren't worthy of a serious man.' Critics never fail to make remarks of this sort, because it is no great strain on the intellect to make them.

The Persians who wrote these letters lodged with me, and we spent our time together. They considered me as a man from another world, and hid nothing from me. Certainly, men transplanted from so far away could no longer have had any secrets. They showed me most of their letters and I copied them; I even intercepted some which they would never have entrusted to me, because they were so mortifying to Persian self-esteem and jealousy.

My function, therefore, has been merely that of a translator; all I have taken the trouble to do is adapt the work to our own habits. I have relieved the reader of oriental turns of phrase as far as I have been able to do so, and preserved him from countless lofty expressions which would have bored him sublimely.[2]

But this is not all that I have done on his behalf. I have omitted the lengthy compliments which the Asians use as lavishly as we, and passed over an infinite number of those trivial details which cannot survive being brought into the light of day, and should live only between two friends.

If the majority of those who have published collections of letters had done the same they would have seen their works disappear.

Something which has often surprised me is the realization that these Persians knew as much as I did about the customs and way of life of our nation; they had grasped even the subtlest points, and noticed things which, I am sure, have escaped many a German who has travelled through France. I attribute this to the length of their stay here, apart from the fact that it is easier for an Asian to learn about the habits of Frenchmen in a year than for a Frenchman to learn about the habits of Asians in four, because the latter's readiness to talk about himself is equalled only by the reticence of the former.

The conventions allow any translator, and even the most un-civilized editor, to adorn the beginning of his translation or edition with a panegyric of the original, so as to bring out its usefulness, its merits, and its high quality. I have not done so, for reasons which will easily be guessed; one of the best of them is that it would be extremely tedious to have such a thing placed where there is enough tedium already, I mean in a preface.

Letter 1
Usbek to his friend Rustan, at Ispahan

We stayed only one day at Kum. We worshipped at the tomb of the virgin who gave birth to twelve prophets, we went on our way, and yesterday, the twenty-fifth day after our departure from Ispahan, we arrived at Tabriz.

Rica and I are perhaps the first Persians to have left our country for love of knowledge, to have abandoned the attractions of a quiet life in order to pursue the laborious search for wisdom.

The kingdom in which we were born is prosperous, but we did not think it right that our knowledge should be limited to its boundaries, and that we should see by the light of the East alone.

Tell me what people are saying about our departure. Do not flatter me; I don't expect many of them to approve. Send your letter to Erzerum, where I shall stay for a while.

Farewell, my dear Rustan; be assured that wherever I may be on earth, you have a faithful friend.

From Tabriz, the 15th of the moon of Saphar, 1711

Letter 2
Usbek to the First Black Eunuch, at his seraglio in Ispahan

You are the faithful guardian of the most beautiful women in Persia. I have entrusted to you the most valuable thing that I have in the world; your hands hold the keys of those fateful doors that are opened for me alone. As long as you are watching over this precious treasure of my heart, it remains at rest, in complete confidence. You keep guard both in the silence of the night and the tumult of day. Virtue, when it falters, has your untiring care to support it. If the women whom you watch over should want to depart from their duty, you would make them give up such a hope. You are the scourge of vice and the bastion of fidelity.

You are in charge of my wives, and you obey them. Blindly, you carry out their every desire, and, in the same way, make them carry out the laws of the harem. You glory in doing the most degrading services for them. It is with fear and respect that you submit to their lawful commands; you serve them as the slave of their slaves. But their power is transferred, and you are master like myself, whenever you fear some relaxation of the laws of chastity and modesty.

Always remember the nothingness from which I took you, when you were the lowest of my slaves, and I put you in this post and entrusted the delight of my heart to you. Humiliate yourself profoundly before the women who share my love, but at the same time make them aware of their own absolute dependence. Provide them with every pleasure which may be innocent; relieve them of their worries, fill their time with music, dancing, and sweet drinks, encourage them to meet frequently. If they wish to visit the country, you may take them, but see to it that any man who may appear before them is put to death.[1] Exhort them to be clean, since cleanliness symbolizes purity of soul. Speak to them sometimes of me. I look forward to seeing them again in the delightful place which they adorn.

Farewell.

From Tabriz, the 18th of the moon of Saphar, 1711

Letter 3
Zashi to Usbek, at Tabriz

We ordered the Chief Eunuch to take us out in the country; he will report to you that we came to no harm. When we had to cross the river and get out of our litters, we sat, as is the custom, in boxes:[1] two slaves carried us on their shoulders, and we avoided being seen by anyone.

How could I have remained, my dear Usbek, in your harem at

Ispahan, a place which constantly reminded me of past pleasures, and stimulated my desires with renewed violence every day? I wandered from room to room, searching for you all the time, and finding you nowhere; but everywhere I met with cruel memories of my former happiness. Once it was where, for the first time in my life, I lay with you in my arms; once it was where you decided that famous contest between your wives. Each of us claimed to be superior to the others in beauty. When we appeared before you we had used up every kind of ornament or embellishment that imagination could supply. You enjoyed looking at the miracles that our skill had produced, and you were surprised at the lengths to which we had gone in our eagerness to please you. But you soon made these borrowed attractions give way to more natural beauties, and destroyed all our handiwork. We had to strip off our ornaments, which now were getting in your way; we had to let you look at us in the simplicity of nature. I disregarded modesty, and thought only of the glory to be achieved. Happy Usbek, what delights were displayed before you! For a long time we saw you roam from enchantment to enchantment; for a long time, irresolute, your mind remained in doubt; every new attraction required a tribute from you; in an instant, all of us were covered in your kisses; your inquisitive eyes investigated our most secret places; at every moment you made us pose in a thousand different ways; new commands came all the time, and were constantly obeyed. I confess, Usbek, that an emotion keener than the desire to win made me want to please you. I could see that I was gradually becoming mistress of your heart. You came to me, you left me, you came back to me, and I succeeded in keeping you. The triumph was completely mine, for my rivals it was despair. We seemed to be alone on earth; nothing around us was worth bothering with. Would to God that my rivals had had the courage to stay and see all the different ways in which you showed your love for me! If they had witnessed my ecstasies, they would have seen the difference between my love and theirs; they would have seen that even though they may be able to compete with me in beauty, they cannot compete in feeling. . .

But where am I? Where has this empty story brought me? Not to be loved is a misfortune; but it is an insult to be loved no longer. You have left us, Usbek, to go wandering through the countries of barbarians. Do you really not care whether you are loved or not? Alas! you don't even know what it is that you have lost. I utter sighs, and they go unheard; my tears fall, but not for you to enjoy; the harem seems to breathe love, and you, bereft of feeling, leave it further and further behind. Ah! my dear Usbek, you should learn how to be happy.

From the seraglio of Fatme, the 21st of the moon of Muharram, 1711

Letter 4
Zephis to Usbek, at Erzerum

That black ogre has resolved to drive me to despair at last: come what may, he is determined to take my slave Zelid away from me, Zelid who serves me so faithfully, whose deft hands create beauty and grace wherever they go. That our separation should be painful is not enough for him: he wants it to be dishonourable as well. The brute refuses to regard the motives for my trust as innocent, and because I always send him outside the door and he gets bored, he boldly assumes that he has heard or seen things that I could not even imagine.[1] How miserable I am! My virtue and my retiring habits are powerless to preserve me from his fantastic suspicions; this mere slave carries his attacks on me right into your heart, and I have to defend myself there! But no, I have too much self-respect to descend to explanations. As warrant for my behaviour, all I need is yourself, your love, my own, and, since I cannot conceal it, my dear Usbek, my tears.

From the seraglio at Fatme, the 29th of the moon of Muharram, 1711

Letter 5
Rustan to Usbek, at Erzerum

At Ispahan you are the subject of every conversation; people talk of nothing but your departure. Some say it is because of frivolity of mind; others, because of some disappointment. Only your friends take your side, and they cannot persuade anyone. No one can understand how you could leave your wives, relatives, friends, and country, in order to travel in climates that nobody in Persia knows. Rica's mother is inconsolable; she asks you to give her back her son, whom, she says, you have kidnapped. For myself, my dear Usbek, my natural inclination is to approve of everything you do, but I cannot forgive your absence, and whatever reasons you may put forward I shall never be able to accept them wholeheartedly.

Farewell; love me always.

From Ispahan, the 28th of the first moon of Rabia, 1711

Letter 6
Usbek to his friend Nessir, at Ispahan

After a day's journey from Erivan we went out of Persia into the lands which are under Turkish control. Twelve days later we arrived at Erzerum, where we shall stay for three or four months.

I must admit, Nessir, that I felt a secret pain when I lost sight of Persia, and found myself among the faithless Osmanlis.[1] As I penetrated further into this profane land, I had the impression that I was becoming profane myself.

My country, my family, my friends came into my mind, my feelings became tender, a certain restiveness added to my emotion, and made me realize that I had undertaken too much for my own peace of mind.

45

But what troubles my heart above all is my wives: I cannot think of them without being eaten up with worry.

It is not, Nessir, that I love them. I find that my insensibility in that respect leaves me without desire. In the crowded seraglio in which I lived, I forestalled and destroyed love by love itself; but from my very lack of feeling has come a secret jealousy which is devouring me. I see a troop of women virtually left to themselves; I have only men of debased souls to answer for them. I could scarcely feel secure if my slaves were faithful. What will it be like if they are not? What dreadful news may reach me in the distant lands that I shall be travelling through! It is an evil for which my friends can provide no remedy: the seraglio is a place whose unhappy secrets they must ignore. For what could they do there? Would not impunity and concealment be a thousand times preferable to public chastisement? I commit all my woes to your heart, my dear Nessir; it is the only consolation left to me in my present state.

From Erzerum, the 10th of the second moon of Rajab, 1711

Letter 7
Fatme[1] to Usbek, at Erzerum

It is two months since you left, my dear Usbek, and in my present state of depression I still cannot believe it. I go hurrying through the whole seraglio, as if you were here: I have not yet realized my delusion. What can you expect a woman to do when she loves you; when she is used to holding you in her arms; whose only concern was to give you evidence of her affection for you: a free woman, by the accident of birth, but enslaved by the violence of her love?

When I married you, my eyes had not yet seen a man's face; you are still the only one whom I have been allowed to see,* for I do not count as men those horrible eunuchs, whose least imperfection is that they are not males. When I compare the beauty of your face

* Persian women are much more closely guarded than Turkish or Indian women.[2]

with the ugliness of theirs, I cannot help thinking myself happy. I cannot imagine anything more delightful than the wonderful beauty of your body. I swear, Usbek, even if I could leave this place, where I am imprisoned because my position requires it, even if I could escape from the guards around me, even if I were allowed to choose from all the men who live in this city, the capital of nations: Usbek, I swear, I should choose no one but you. There can be nobody on earth who deserves to be loved except you.

You must not think that your absence has made me neglect my beauty, since it is precious to you. Although no one is allowed to see me, although the ornaments I wear are wasted as far as your happiness is concerned, I still try to make a habit of being attractive. I never go to bed without using the most gorgeous scents. I remember those happy times when you used to come to my arms: a delightful illusion leads me on, showing me the image of what I love so dearly; my imagination loses itself in its desire, and deceives itself by its hopes. I sometimes think that you will get tired of the difficulties of your journey, and come back to us: the night passes in dreams which belong neither to sleep nor to wakefulness; I feel for you beside me, and it is as if you were eluding me; at last the fire devouring me itself dissipates the illusion and brings me back to myself. By then I am in such a state of excitement that. . . . You will not believe me, Usbek. It is impossible to live in this state: fire flows in my veins. Why can I not express what I feel so strongly! and why do I feel so strongly what I cannot express! At moments like these, Usbek, I would give the empire of the world for a single kiss from you. How wretched a woman is, having such violent desires, when she is deprived of the only man who can appease them; when, left to herself, with nothing to distract her, she must habitually spend her time in longing, in a frenzy of unsatisfied desire; when, so far from being contented, she has not even got the consolation of being necessary to someone else's contentment; a useless ornament in a seraglio, kept for the honour, not the happiness, of her husband!

You men are so cruel! It delights you that we have passions that we cannot satisfy. You treat us as if we had no feelings, and you would be extremely displeased if we hadn't; you think that our desires, having been repressed so long, will be aroused at the sight of you.

It is a difficult task to make someone love you; by tormenting our senses you achieve more quickly what you cannot expect to deserve on your merits alone.

Farewell, my dear Usbek, farewell. You can be certain that I live only to worship you; my soul is full of you; and your absence, far from making me forget you, would reinforce my love for you, if it were capable of becoming more violent.

From the seraglio at Ispahan, the 12th of the first moon of Rabia, 1711

Letter 8
Usbek to his friend Rustan, at Ispahan

Your letter has been delivered to me at Erzerum, which is where I am. I had fully expected my departure to cause some comment. It didn't worry me. Would you want me to consider what was best for my enemies, or for myself?

I appeared at court in my earliest youth. I can truthfully say that my heart did not become corrupt. I even undertook a great project: I dared to behave virtuously there. As soon as I had recognized vice for what it was, I kept away from it; but approached it again in order to expose it. I took truth to the steps of the throne. I spoke a language hitherto unknown there: I put flattery out of countenance and, at the same time, astonished both the flatterers and their idol.

But when I saw that my sincerity had made enemies, that I had aroused the ministers' jealousy, without gaining my sovereign's favour, that, in a corrupt court, I could only preserve myself by my own feeble virtue, I resolved to leave. I pretended to be very enthusiastic about my studies, and, by pretending, actually became so. I took no further part in public life, and retired to a country house. But even this course had its disadvantages. I still remained exposed to the malice of my enemies, and I had almost relinquished the means of protecting myself. Some secret information made me think seriously about my position. I decided to exile myself from my home country, and my withdrawal from court itself provided a plausible pretext. I went to the king, indicated that I wanted to instruct myself in Western knowledge, and implied that he might derive some benefit from my travels. I found favour in his eyes, departed, and deprived my enemies of their victim.[1]

This, Rustan, is the real reason for my journey. Let Ispahan talk; take my part only in front of those who are my friends. Leave my enemies to their evil-minded interpretations. I am fortunate that it is the only harm that they can do me.

People are talking about me at the moment. Perhaps I shall be forgotten all too easily, and my friends. . . . No, Rustan, I refuse to give in to such sad thoughts. I shall always be dear to them; I count on their loyalty, as I do on yours.

From Erzerum, the 20th of the second moon of Jomada, 1711

Letter 9
The First Eunuch[1] to Ibbi, at Erzerum

You accompany your former master on his travels; you cross provinces and kingdoms; anxieties can have no effect on you: you see new things at every moment, and everything around you is refreshing, making the time pass unnoticed.

It is not the same for me, who, shut inside this dreadful prison, am always surrounded by the same things and devoured by the same anxieties. Overcome by the weight of fifty years of trouble and worry, I lament my fate; during a long life I cannot say that I have had one day of serenity or a moment of calm.

When my first master formed the cruel plan of entrusting his wives to me, and had compelled me, by inducements backed up by innumerable threats, to be separated from myself for ever, I thought, weary as I was of being employed on the heaviest work, that I should be sacrificing my desires for the sake of my peace of mind and my career. Unhappy wretch that I was, with my preconceived ideas I could see only the advantages, not the deprivations. I anticipated that I should be freed from the onset of love by my powerlessness to satisfy it. But alas! the effects of my passions were eliminated, but not their cause; and far from finding relief, I found myself surrounded by scenes which continually aroused them. On entering the seraglio, everything made me yearn for what I had lost. I felt excited all the time. A thousand natural attractions revealed themselves to my eyes only, it seemed, in order to drive me to desperation. To crown my misfortune, I had a happy man permanently before my eyes. During that troubled time I never led a woman to my master's bed, I never undressed her, without returning to my room with fury in my heart and a terrible despair in my soul.

That is how I spent my wretched youth. I had no one but myself to confide in; laden with cares and mortifications, I had to accept them, and, faced with those same women whom I was tempted to gaze on so tenderly, my looks showed nothing but hostility. I was a lost man if they had guessed: what advantages could they not have taken?

I recall that one day, when I was putting a woman into the bath, I was so overcome that I lost my control entirely, and dared to put my hand in a place which I should have feared. I thought, as soon as I came to my senses, that that was the last of my days. I was, however, lucky enough to escape a dreadful death. But the beauty to whom I had revealed the secret of my weakness sold me her silence at a high price: I lost my authority completely, and she has since compelled me to overlook things which have exposed me to death a thousand times over.

Finally the fires of youth are past. I am old, and in that respect am in a state of tranquillity. I can look at women without emotion, and am paying them back for all their contempt, and all the torments that they have made me suffer. I never forget that I was born to command over them, and it is as if I become a man again on the occasions when I now give them orders. I hate them, now that I can face them with indifference, and my reason allows me to see all their weaknesses. Although I keep them for another man, the pleasure of making myself obeyed gives me a secret joy. When I deny them everything, it is as if I was doing it on my own behalf, and indirectly I always derive satisfaction from it. The seraglio for me is like a little empire, and my desire for power, the only emotion which remains to me, is to some extent satisfied. It pleases me to see that everything depends on me, and that I am needed constantly: I willingly endure being hated by all these women, which strengthens my position. Nor do they find me ungrateful: I always come between them and their most innocent amusements; I stand before them all the time like an immovable barrier. They make plans, and all at once I put a stop to them; my weapons are refusals; I bristle with scruples. Words like *duty, virtue, delicacy, modesty,* are always on my lips. I drive them to despair by talking endlessly about the weakness of their sex and their master's authority. Then I deplore the fact that I am obliged to be so strict, and it looks as if I am trying to make them understand that my only motives are deep devotion to them and concern for their welfare.

Not that I in turn do not have an infinite number of vexations, since these vindictive women spend every day trying to do better than I in creating irritation. Their counter-attacks can be terrible. Between us there is a sort of ebb and flow of authority and submission. They always ensure that the most humiliating tasks fall to me. They put on a unique air of contempt, and with no consideration for my age they make me get up ten times a night for the most trivial reasons. I am constantly overwhelmed with requests, commands, assignments, and caprices. It seems that they take it in relays to exercise me, and that their whims come in sequence. They often take pleasure in making me redouble my vigilance; they have false information brought to me; someone will come and tell me that a young man has appeared outside the walls, or that a noise has been heard, or that a letter is to be delivered. It all makes me worried, and they laugh at my worries; they are delighted to see me torment myself in this way. Another time they will keep me waiting outside their doors, tying me to it night and day. They are experts at simulating illness, or faintness, or alarm; they have no lack of pretexts to get me where they want me. On such occasions, blind obedience and unlimited indulgence are essential; a refusal, from the lips of a man like myself, would be unheard-of; and if I hesitated to obey, they would have the right to punish me. I would rather lose my life, my dear Ibbi, than descend to that humiliation.

Nor is that all. I am never certain of remaining in my master's favour for an instant. In his heart his wives are so many enemies of mine, whose only thought is to ruin me. They have their quarters of an hour when I go unheard, quarters of an hour when nothing is refused, when I am always in the wrong. The women I take to my master's bed are angry; do you think that anything will be done there on my behalf, or that my side will be the stronger? I have everything to fear from their tears, their sighs, their kisses, and even their own pleasure. They are in their place of triumph. Their beauty becomes a terror to me. Their present services instantly wipe out all my services in the past, and nothing can make me certain of a master who has lost control of himself.

On how many occasions have I gone to bed in favour, and got up in disgrace? On the day when I was so shamefully whipped all round the seraglio, what had I done? I left a woman in my master's arms. As soon as she saw that he was excited, her tears flowed in streams; she complained, and arranged things so that her complaints increased at the same rate as the love she was inspiring. How could I have defended myself at such a critical moment? I was lost when I least expected it. I fell victim to amorous negotiations and to a treaty based on sighs. These, my dear Ibbi, are the conditions under which I have always lived.

How fortunate you are! Your duties are limited entirely to Usbek himself. It is easy to please him, and to remain in his favour until the end of your days.

From the seraglio at Ispahan, the last day of the moon of Saphar, 1711

Letter 10
Mirza to his friend Usbek, at Erzerum

You alone could have compensated for Rica's absence, and nobody but Rica could console me for yours. We miss you, Usbek: you were the soul of our circle of friends. What violence it needs to break attachments formed by both heart and mind!

We argue here a great deal; our arguments are usually about moral questions. Yesterday the subject under discussion was whether men are made happy by pleasure, and the satisfaction of the senses, or by the practice of virtue. I have often heard you say that men were born to be virtuous, and that justice is a quality which is as proper to them as existence. Please explain to me what you mean.

I have asked our mullahs about it, but they drive me to desperation with their quotations from the Koran: for I am not consulting them as a true believer, but as a man, as a citizen, and as a father.

Farewell.

From Ispahan, the last day of the moon of Saphar, 1711

Letter 11[1]
Usbek to Mirza, at Ispahan

You abandon your own powers of reason in order to try out mine; you condescend to consult me; you believe me capable of instructing you. My dear Mirza, there is one thing that flatters me more than the good opinion which you have formed of me: it is your friendship, to which I owe it.

To comply with your request, it seemed to me that there was no need to use any very abstract arguments. With truths of a certain kind, it is not enough to make them appear convincing: one must also make them felt. Of such a kind are moral truths. Perhaps this fragment of history will make a deeper impression on you than philosophical subtleties.

There was in Arabia a small nation of people called Troglodytes, descended from those Troglodytes of former times who, if we are to believe the historians, were more like animals than men. Ours were not so deformed as that: they were not hairy like bears, they did not hiss, they had two eyes; but they were so wicked and ferocious that there were no principles of equity or justice among them.

They had a king of foreign origin, who, in an attempt to reform their natural wickedness, treated them with severity; but they conspired against him, killed him, and exterminated all the royal family.

The deed accomplished, they held a meeting to choose a government, and after many disagreements they elected ministers. But hardly had they elected them than they found them unbearable; and they massacred them too. Freed of this new restriction, the nation let itself be ruled only by its natural wildness. Each individual agreed that he would not obey anybody any more, but that each one would look after his own interests exclusively, without considering those of others.

This unanimous decision greatly appealed to each individual Troglodyte. They said: 'What business is it of mine to go and kill myself working for people who mean nothing to me? I shall think uniquely of myself; I shall be happy, what does it matter to me if the others are or not? I shall get all I need, and provided that I do, I shan't care if all the other Troglodytes are miserable.'

It was the month for sowing the crops. Everybody said: 'I shall plough only enough land to grow the wheat necessary to feed myself. I should have no use for a larger amount; I won't put myself out to no purpose.'

The soil of this small country was not all the same. There were arid, mountainous districts, and others on low ground which were irrigated by a number of streams. That year it was extremely dry, so that the fields which were high up failed completely, while those which could be watered were very fertile: so that almost all the mountain dwellers died of hunger, because of the harshness of the others, who refused to share the harvest with them.

Next year it was very rainy. The high ground was unusually fertile, and the low-lying regions were inundated. For a second time, half the population cried famine; but the poor wretches found that the others were as harsh as they had been themselves.

One of the leading citizens had a very beautiful wife. His neighbour fell in love with her and abducted her. This caused a great quarrel, and after a good deal of insults and fighting they agreed to abide by the decision of a Troglodyte who, while the Republic had lasted, had had a certain amount of influence. They went to him, wanting to present their arguments. 'What does it matter to me,' he said, 'if this woman belongs to you, or to you? I have my land to plough; I am certainly not going to spend my time patching up your disputes, and looking after your affairs while I neglect my own. Please leave me in peace, and don't trouble me any more with your quarrels.' With this he left them and went off to work on his fields. The abductor, who was the stronger, swore that he would sooner die than give the woman up, and the other man, overcome by the injustice of his neighbour and the judge's callousness, was going home in despair when he came across a young and beautiful woman returning from the fountain. He no longer had a wife; he found this woman attractive, and he found her a great deal more attractive when he learnt that she was the wife of the man whom he had wanted to have as judge, and who had been so unfeeling about his misfortune. He carried her off and took her to his house.

There was a man who possessed quite a fertile piece of land, which he diligently cultivated. Two of his neighbours joined forces, turned him out of his house, and took possession of his field. They made an alliance to defend each other against any possible usurper, and did in fact manage to give each other mutual protection for several months. But one of the pair, tired of having to share something that he could have to himself, killed the other, and became sole master of the field. His reign was short: two other Troglodytes came and attacked him. He found that he was too weak to defend himself, and was massacred.

A Troglodyte with almost nothing to wear saw some wool for sale. He asked the price. The merchant said to himself: 'Ordinarily I could expect to get only as much for my wool as I should need to buy two measures of wheat; but I shall sell it for four times as much, so as to have eight measures.' There was no alternative, and the price had to be paid. 'That's good,' said the merchant; 'now I shall have some wheat.'

'What did you say?' retorted his customer. 'Do you need wheat? I have some to sell. There is only one thing that may surprise you, and that is the price. You must know that wheat is extremely expensive, and there is a famine almost everywhere. But give me my money back, and I will give you one measure of wheat: for otherwise I shall refuse to let any go, even if you were to die of hunger.'

Meanwhile, a cruel disease was rife throughout the area. A skilled doctor arrived from a neighbouring country, and gave treatment so expertly that he cured everyone who went to him. When the epidemic was over he went round all his patients to ask for payment, but he met with nothing but refusals. He went back to his own country, and arrived exhausted with the strain of his long journey. But soon afterwards he heard that the same disease had struck again, and was now taking a heavier toll than ever of the ungrateful country. This time the Troglodytes went to him, instead of waiting for him to come to them. 'Away with you!' he said, 'for you are unjust. In your souls is a poison deadlier than that for which you want a cure. You do not deserve to have a place on earth, because you have no humanity, and the rules of equity are unknown to you. It seems to me that I should be offending against the gods, who are punishing you, if I were to oppose their rightful anger.'

From Erzerum, the 3rd of the second moon of Jomada, 1711

Letter 12
Usbek to the same, at Ispahan

You have seen, my dear Mirza, how the Troglodytes perished because of their wickedness, and fell victim to their own injustice. Of all the families that there had been, only two remained, and escaped the national misfortune. There had been two very extraordinary men in this country. They were humane; they understood what justice was; they loved virtue. Attached to each other as much by the integrity of their own hearts as by the corruption of the others, they saw the general desolation and felt nothing but pity: which was another bond between them. They worked with equal solicitude in the common interest; they had no disagreements except those which were due to their tender and affectionate friendship; and in the remotest part of the country, separated from their compatriots, who were unworthy to be with them, they led a calm and happy life. The earth seemed to produce of its own accord, cultivated by these virtuous hands.

They loved their wives, by whom they were tenderly cherished.

Their only concern was to bring up their children to be virtuous. They constantly described to them the distress of their fellow-countrymen, letting their wretchedness serve as an example to them. Above all they made them realize that the individual's self-interest is always to be found in the common interest; that wanting to cut oneself off from it is the same as wanting to ruin oneself; that virtue is not such as to cost us anything, and should not be considered as a wearisome exercise; and that justice to others is charity for ourselves.

Soon they had the reward of virtuous parents, which is to have children who resemble them. The younger generation which grew up before their eyes increased through happy marriages. As their numbers grew larger, they remained just as closely united, and virtue, so far from becoming weaker among the multitude, was on the contrary fortified by a greater number of examples.

Who could now describe the happiness of these Troglodytes? So just a race of men was bound to be cherished by the gods. As soon as they opened their eyes to know the gods, they learnt to fear them, and religion appeared, to soften any roughness of manner left over from nature.

They instituted festivals in the honour of the gods. The girls, adorned with flowers, and the youths celebrated them with dancing and the music of rustic harmonies. Then came feasting, and joy reigned equally with frugality. It was at these gatherings that the innocence of nature spoke. There the young people discovered how to give their hearts, and how to receive the gift; there virginal delicacy, blushing, made a confession obtained by surprise, but soon confirmed by the parents' consent; and there the affectionate mothers took pleasure in foreseeing a tender and faithful union from afar.

They would go to the temple to ask the favours of the gods: not the burdens of wealth and superfluity, for such wishes were unworthy of the happy Troglodytes; they were incapable of desiring them except for their fellow-countrymen. They had come to the altar only to ask for their fathers' health, unity among their brothers, their wives' affection, the love and obedience of their children. The young girls came with the tender sacrifice of their hearts, and asked no favour except to be able to make a Troglodyte happy.

In the evenings, as the herds came in from the fields and the tired oxen brought in the ploughs, they would gather together, and over a simple meal they would sing of the injustices of the first Troglodytes, their misfortunes, the rebirth of virtue with a new generation, and its happiness. They celebrated the greatness of the gods, the constancy with which they bestow their favours on those who pray to them, and the inevitability of their anger towards those who do not fear them. They described the delights of the pastoral life and the happiness of a situation that was always adorned by innocence. Soon they would abandon themselves to a sleep which was never interrupted by worry or anxiety.

Nature provided for their desires as abundantly as for their needs. In this happy land, cupidity was alien. They would give each other presents, and the giver always thought that the advantage was his. The Troglodyte nation regarded themselves as a single family; the herds were almost always mixed up together, and the only task that was usually neglected was that of sorting them out.

From Erzerum, the 6th of the second moon of Jomada, 1711

Letter 13
Usbek to the same

I shall never be able to tell you enough about the virtue of the Troglodytes. One of them said one day: 'My father will have to plough his field tomorrow; I shall get up two hours before him and, when he goes to his field, he will find it all ploughed.'

Another said to himself: 'I think that my sister has a liking for a young Troglodyte who is related to us. I must speak to my father and persuade him to arrange the marriage.'

Another was brought the news that thieves had stolen his herd of cattle. 'That makes me very angry,' he said, 'for there was a pure white heifer which I wanted to sacrifice to the gods.'

Another was heard to say: 'I must go to the temple to give thanks to the gods, because my brother, whom my father loves so much, and whom I am so fond of, has been restored to health.'

Or again: 'There is a field next to my father's, and the people who cultivate it are exposed every day to the heat of the sun. I must go and plant a couple of trees there, so that those poor people can go and rest sometimes in the shade.'

One day, when a number of Troglodytes were together, one of the older ones mentioned a young man whom he suspected of having committed a crime, and reproached him for it. 'We do not believe that he committed the crime,' said the younger Troglodytes, 'but if he did, may he be the last of his family to die!'

A Troglodyte was brought the news that strangers had looted his house and taken everything away with them. 'If they were not unjust,' he replied, 'it would be my wish that the gods should grant them the use of it for a longer time than I had.'

All this good fortune was not observed without envy. The neighbouring peoples met together and resolved, on an empty pretext, to make off with their herds. As soon as they knew of this decision the Troglodytes sent envoys to meet them and give them this message:

'What have the Troglodytes done to you? Have they taken away your wives, stolen your cattle, ravaged your country? No: we are just, and we fear the gods. What then do you want from us? Do you want wool to make yourselves clothes? Do you want milk for your herds,[1] or the fruit from our lands? Put down your weapons; come to us and we will give you all these things. But we swear, by whatever is most sacred, that if you enter our land with hostile intent, we shall regard you as unjust, and treat you like wild beasts.'

Their words were dismissed with contempt. These savage peoples, in arms, entered the country of the Troglodytes, whom they believed to be defended by their innocence alone.

But they were well prepared for defence. They had put their wives and children in the centre. They were appalled by the injustice of their enemies, and not by their numbers. A new kind of ardour possessed their hearts: one wanted to die for his father, another for his wife and children; one for his brothers, another for his friends; and all of them for the Troglodyte nation. As soon as one died, his place was taken by another, who, besides the common cause, had in addition an individual's death to avenge.

Such was the combat of injustice and virtue. These cowardly peoples, who wanted nothing but plunder, were not ashamed to run away, and yielded to the virtue of the Troglodytes while remaining unaffected by it.

From Erzerum, the 9th of the second moon of Jomada, 1711

Letter 14
Usbek to the same

Since the nation was daily increasing in numbers, the Troglodytes thought that it would be right to choose themselves a king. They agreed that the crown should be bestowed upon the justest among them, and their choice unanimously fell on an old man whose age, and years of virtue, made him venerable. He had not wanted to attend the assembly; he had retired to his house, his heart wrung with grief.

Deputies were sent to inform him that the choice had fallen on him. 'God forbid,' he said, 'that I should do such a wrong to the Troglodytes, and that it should be thought that no one among them is juster than I! You bring me the crown, and if you insist upon it absolutely I shall certainly have to take it. But be sure that I shall die of grief, having seen when I was born the Troglodytes in freedom, and seeing them subjects today.' As he spoke, tears began to stream down his face. 'Unhappy day!' he said, 'and why have I lived so long?' Then he cried in a stern voice: 'I see what it is quite well, oh Troglodytes! your virtue has begun to be a burden to you. In your present state, without a ruler, it is necessary for you to be virtuous despite yourselves. Otherwise you could not continue to exist, and you would fall into the misfortunes of your first ancestors. But this imposition seems too hard for you. You would prefer to be subject to a king, and obey his laws, which would be less rigid than your own customs. You know that you would then be able to satisfy your ambitions, accumulate wealth, and live idly in degrading luxury; that, provided you avoided falling into the worst crimes, you would have no need of virtue.' He paused a moment, and his tears fell faster than ever. 'And what is it that you expect of me? How could I command a Troglodyte to do something? Would you want him to perform a virtuous action because I tell him to, when he would have done it just the same without me, by natural inclination alone? Oh Troglodytes! I am at the end of my days, my blood is frozen in my veins, I shall soon see your blessed ancestors: why do you want me to grieve them, and to be obliged to tell them that I have left you under the rule of something other than virtue?'

From Erzerum, the 10th of the second moon of Jomada, 1711

Letter 15
The First Eunuch to Jahrum,[1] *one of the black eunuchs, at Erzerum*

I pray that Heaven may bring you back to this place and preserve you from every danger.

Although I am virtually unacquainted with the relationship that they call friendship, and have been entirely wrapped up in myself, you have made me feel that I still had a heart; and while I was as hard as bronze in my relations with all the slaves who were under my authority, it was with pleasure that I watched your growth as a child.

The time came when my master's choice fell on you. The voice of nature was far from having yet made itself heard when the blade of a knife separated you from nature. I shall not say whether I felt pity, or pleasure, on seeing that you had been raised to my level. I pacified your tears and cries. It seemed to me as if you had been born for a second time, leaving a state of slavery in which you would always have to obey and entering one in which you would issue commands. I took charge of your upbringing. The sternness which is inseparable from education prevented you for a long time from knowing that you were dear to me. Yet so you were, and I would say that I loved you as a father loves his son, if the names of father and son were appropriate to our condition.

You will be travelling through the lands of the Christians, who have never believed; it will be impossible for you to avoid contracting uncleanliness in many ways. How could the Prophet discern you among all those millions of his enemies? I should like my master, when he returns, to make a pilgrimage to Mecca: you would all be purified in the land of the angels.

From the seraglio at Ispahan, the 10th of the second moon of Jomada,

1711

Letter 16
Usbek to the Mullah Mohammed Ali,
Guardian of the Three Tombs, at Kum

Why do you live among the tombs, divine Mullah?[1] Living among the stars would suit you much better. No doubt you conceal yourself for fear of making the sun look dark. Whereas there are sun-spots on that heavenly body, in you there is no blemish; though you resemble it in covering yourself with clouds.

Your knowledge is an abyss deeper than the ocean; your mind is more piercing than Zufagar, Ali's sword,[2] which had two points; you know what happens in the nine choirs of the celestial powers; you read the Koran on the breast of our divine Prophet, and when you come to a difficult passage, an angel, on his orders, spreading his swift wings, descends from the throne to reveal its secrets to you.

Through you I can communicate intimately with the Seraphim: for are you not the thirteenth Imam,[3] the centre where Heaven touches the earth, and the junction between the Abyss and the Empyrean?

I am in the midst of a profane people. Permit me to purify myself with you; allow me to turn my face towards the sacred place in which you live; distinguish me from the wicked, as at the coming of dawn the white thread can be distinguished from the black; help me with your advice; take care of my soul; enrapture it with the spirit of the Prophets; nourish it with the knowledge of Paradise, and permit me to bring its afflictions to your feet.

Address your sacred letters to Erzerum, where I shall be staying for some months.

From Erzerum, the 11th of the second moon of Jomada, 1711

Letter 17
Usbek to the same

I am unable, divine Mullah, to calm my impatience; I cannot wait for the sublimities of your reply. I have doubts: they must be settled; I can feel my reason going astray: lead it back to its path. Source of light, give me illumination; annihilate, with a stroke of your divine pen, the difficulties that I am about to put to you; make me feel ashamed of myself and blush at the question that I am asking you.

Why is it that our Lawgiver deprives us of pig's meat, and of any meat that he calls *impure*? Why is it that he forbids us to touch a corpse, and that, in order to purify our souls, he commands us constantly to wash our bodies? It seems to me that things in themselves are neither pure nor impure. I cannot conceive of any inherent quality in objects which could make them so. Mud only seems dirty to us because it offends the sight, or some other sense; but in itself it is no more dirty than gold or diamonds. The idea of contracting uncleanliness by touching a corpse is due only to a certain natural repugnance that we have for doing so. If the bodies of those people who do not wash themselves did not offend either our sense of smell or our sight, how could anyone have imagined that they were impure?

It must be, then, divine Mullah, that the senses alone can judge whether things are pure or impure. But, since objects do not affect all men in the same way, since what produces a pleasant sensation in some men produces a feeling of disgust in others, it follows that the evidence of the senses cannot be used as a standard here; unless you say that everyone can decide the point as he sees fit, and distinguish, as far as he is concerned, between things that are pure and things that are not.

But, divine Mullah, would not this itself overthrow the distinctions established by our divine Prophet, and the fundamental points of the Law, which was written by the hands of angels?

From Erzerum, the 20th of the second moon of Jomada, 1711

Letter 18
Mohammed Ali, servant of the Prophets, to Usbek, at Erzerum

You keep on asking us questions that have been put to our holy Prophet a thousand times. Why not read the Traditions of the theologians? Why refuse to consult that pure source of all understanding? You would find all your doubts resolved.

Unhappy man, forever caught up in earthly things, you have never gazed on what is in Heaven, and revere the life of a Mullah without daring to take it up or imitate it!

Profane men, who never enter into the secrets of the eternal, the light of your mind is as the darkness of the abyss, and your arguments are as the dust thrown up by your feet when the sun is at its height, in the burning month of Shaaban.

So that your mind, even at its zenith, cannot reach the nadir of the lowliest imam's.* Your vain philosophy is like the flash that heralds storms and darkness; you are in the midst of the tempest, and wander at the behest of the winds.

It is very easy to answer your objection; it is only necessary to tell you what happened one day to our holy Prophet, when, tempted by the Christians and tested by the Jews, he confuted both equally.[1]

The Jew Abdullah ben Salem asked him why God had forbidden men to eat pig's meat. 'There is a good reason for it,' replied Mohammed; 'the animal is unclean, as I shall prove to you.' He drew

* This word is more commonly used by the Turks than by the Persians.

the shape of a man, in mud, on his hand; he threw it down and cried: 'Arise!' At once a man arose and said: 'I am Japhet, son of Noah.'

'Was your hair as white as that when you died?' asked the holy Prophet.

'No,' he replied, 'but when you aroused me I thought that the Day of Judgement had come, and I got such a fright that my hair turned white in an instant.'

'Well now,' said the Messenger of God, 'tell me all about Noah's Ark.' Japhet obeyed and gave an exact description of everything that had happened during the early months. After which he spoke as follows:

'We put all the animals' droppings on one side of the Ark, which made it lean over so much that we were mortally afraid, especially the women, who made a great fuss. Noah our father having gone to God for advice, he was commanded to take the elephant and put him so that he faced the side that was leaning over. The huge beast made so much filth that it produced a pig.'*

Do you now accept, Usbek, why we have abstained from pig's meat since that time, and regard it as an unclean animal?

But the pig stirred up the filth every day, and such a smell spread through the Ark that the pig itself could not refrain from sneezing; and a rat came out of its nose, and went round chewing at everything in its way. Noah found this so intolerable that he thought it right to consult God once more. God ordered him to hit the lion hard on the forehead: it sneezed as well, and out of its nose came a cat. Do you accept that these animals too are unclean? What do you think?

When therefore you cannot perceive the reason for the impurity of certain things, it is because you are ignorant of much else, and have no knowledge of what has come to pass amongst God, the angels, and men. You do not know the history of eternity. You have not read the books written in Heaven: what has been revealed to you is only a small part of the celestial library; and those who, like us, approach it more closely during this life, are still in shadows and darkness.

Farewell; Mohammed be in your heart.

From Kum, the last day of the moon of Shaaban, 1711

* This is a Muslim tradition.

Letter 19
Usbek to his friend Rustan, at Ispahan

We spent only eight days at Tokat; after thirty-five days' travel we arrived at Smyrna. Between Tokat and Smyrna there is not a single town worth mentioning. I was amazed to see the weakness of the Ottoman Empire. It is a diseased body, preserved not by gentle and moderate treatment, but by violent remedies which ceaselessly fatigue and undermine it.

The Pashas, who obtain their posts only by paying for them, are ruined by the time they take up their appointments, and despoil their provinces like a conquered country.[1] The militia is unruly, and subject only to its own caprices. The fortifications have been dismantled, the towns are deserted, the countryside laid waste, and agriculture and trade completely abandoned.

Impunity is the rule under this harsh government: the Christians, who cultivate the land, and the Jews, who raise taxes, suffer innumerable abuses of power.

Possession of land cannot be guaranteed, and consequently any eagerness to develop it is reduced; no title-deed or rights of possession will stand up before the capriciousness of the authorities.

These barbarians have paid so little attention to technical knowledge that they have even neglected the art of war. While the nations of Europe advance further every day, they remain as ignorant as they always were, and never think of taking over new European inventions until they have had them used against them thousands of times.

They have no naval experience, and no skill in manoeuvres. It is said that a handful of Christians, based on a rock,* make the Ottomans tremble with fear, and are a threat to their Empire.

They are incapable of carrying on trade, and it is almost with reluctance that they permit Europeans, who are always industrious and enterprising, to come and do it; they think they are doing a favour to these foreigners in allowing themselves to be enriched by them.

* This presumably means the Knights of Malta.[2]

In all the vast extent of land that I have crossed, the only town I have found which could be considered rich and powerful is Smyrna. It is the Europeans who have made it so, and it is through no fault of the Turks that this town does not resemble all the others.

That my dear Rustan, is a true description of this empire, which inside two hundred years will be the scene of the triumphs of some conqueror.

From Smyrna, the 2nd of the moon of Ramaddán, 1711

Letter 20
Usbek to Zashi, his wife, at the seraglio in Ispahan

You have offended me, Zashi, and the impulses that I feel in my heart are such that you should be afraid, except that the distance at which I am from you leaves you the time to make a change in your behaviour, and appease the violent jealousy by which I am afflicted.

I am told that you were found alone with Nadir, the white eunuch, who will pay with his life for his disloyalty and treachery. How can you have forgotten yourself so far as not to realize that you are prohibited to have a white eunuch in your room, so long as there are black ones to serve you? It is no use to say that eunuchs are not men, and that your virtue puts you above any ideas that you might get because of their incomplete resemblance to men. That is not enough for you, nor for me: not for you, in that you are doing something which the laws of the seraglio forbid; and not for me, in that you are destroying my honour by exposing yourself to the eyes of ... his eyes, did I say? perhaps to the attentions of a traitor who defiles you by his crimes, and even more by his regret and despair at being impotent.

Perhaps you will say that you have always been faithful to me. And how could you not have been? How could you have evaded the vigilance of the black eunuchs, who are so shocked at the life you lead? How could you have broken open the bolts and doors which keep you locked in? You give yourself credit for a virtue which is not free, and your impure desires may have removed, a thousand times over, any merit or value from the fidelity on which you pride yourself.

Suppose you are completely innocent of everything that I have a right to suspect; that the traitor did not touch you with his sacrilegious hands; that you refused to reveal to his gaze the delights that belong to his master; that you were covered by your clothes, leaving a flimsy barrier between him and you; that he, with a feeling of holy respect, himself lowered his eyes; that his boldness failed him and he trembled at the punishments in store for him. Even if it were all true, it is also true that you did something contrary to your duty. And if you transgressed it gratuitously, without satisfying your uncontrolled desires, what would you have done in order to satisfy them? What more would you do if you could get out of that holy place, which seems to you a harsh prison, while for your companions it is a welcome asylum against the onslaughts of vice, a sacred temple, where your sex loses its weakness and becomes invincible, despite all your natural disadvantages? What would you do if, left to yourself, you had nothing to defend you except your love for me, which has been gravely injured, and your duty, which you have betrayed so unworthily? How holy are the laws of the land in which you live, since they rescue you from being assaulted by loathsome slaves! You ought to be grateful for the restraints that I impose on you, since it is only because of them that you still deserve to live.

You cannot bear the Chief Eunuch, because he always observes how you behave, and gives you good advice. His ugliness, you say, is so great that you cannot look at him without repugnance; as if anything more handsome could be used for that kind of function. What upsets you is that, in place of him, you have not got the white eunuch who has dishonoured you.

And what is it that your chief slave-girl has done? She has told you that the familiarities you took with young Zelid were unseemly. That is the reason for your dislike.

I ought, Zashi, to be a strict judge; I am merely a husband trying to find you innocent. The love that I have for Roxana, my new wife, has left intact all the affection that I am bound to feel for you, who are no less beautiful. My love is divided between the two of you, and Roxana has no advantages except those that virtue may add to beauty.

From Smyrna, the 12th of the moon of Dulkaada, 1711

Letter 21
Usbek to the First White Eunuch

You should tremble as you open this letter; or rather you should have done, when you failed to prevent Nadir's treachery. You who are cold and apathetic with age, and cannot, without committing a criminal act, raise your eyes to the women whom I love and you must fear; you who are never allowed to commit the sacrilege of crossing the threshold of that terrible building which prevents anyone seeing them: you allow those for whose behaviour you are responsible to do what you have not the temerity to do, and can you not see the thunderbolt that is ready to fall on them and on yourself?

And what are you but mere tools, which I can break at will; who exist only insofar as you can obey; who are in the world only to live under my laws, or to die as soon as I command it; who breathe only as long as my happiness, my love, or even my jealousy, require your degraded selves; and who, finally, can have no other destiny but submission, whose soul can only be my will, whose only hope is that I should be happy?

I know that some of my wives are reluctant to submit to the stern laws of duty; that the continual presence of a black eunuch irritates them; that they are weary of seeing these dreadful creatures, whom they are given so as to make them turn back to their husband: this I know. But you, you who are an accomplice in this disorder, will be punished in such a manner as to bring terror to all who betray my trust.

I swear by all the prophets of Heaven, and by Ali, the greatest of all, that if you fail in your duty I shall take no more notice of your life than of the insects that I tread beneath my feet.

From Smyrna, the 12th of the moon of Dulkaada, 1711

Letter 22[1]
Jahrum to the First Eunuch

As Usbek goes further and further away from the seraglio he turns his head towards his sacred wives, sighs, and sheds tears; his sorrow is deepening, his suspicions are growing stronger. He wants to add to the number of their guardians. He is going to send me back with all the black slaves whom he has with him. He is no longer afraid on his own behalf: he fears for something that he cherishes a thousand times more dearly.

I shall, therefore, be living under your authority, and share your tasks. What a multitude of things, great God! are necessary to the happiness of one man!

Nature seems to have placed women in a state of dependence, and to have removed them from it again. Between the two sexes disorder arose, because their rights were reciprocal. But we form part of a new and harmonious scheme: between women and us we create hatred, and between women and men, love.

My expression will become strict. I shall look around with grimness in my eyes. Joy will depart from my lips. Externally I shall seem calm, but my mind will be uneasy. I shall not wait for the lines of old age to appear on my face before displaying the anxieties that go with it.

I should have liked to follow my master to the West; but my will belongs to him. He wants me to guard his wives, and I shall guard them faithfully. I know how to behave towards this sex, which, if not allowed to indulge its vanity, starts to grow arrogant, and which it is harder to humiliate than to destroy. I fall before you as you look on me.

From Smyrna, the 12th of the moon of Dulkaada, 1711

Letter 23
Usbek to his friend Ibben, at Smyrna

We arrived at Leghorn after a voyage of forty days. The town is new, and bears witness to the ability of the dukes of Tuscany, who have created, out of a village in the marshes, the most prosperous town in Italy.

The women here enjoy great freedom.[1] They are allowed to see men, through a kind of window called a *jealousy*; they can go out every day with a number of old women who accompany them; they have only one veil.* Their brothers-in-law, their uncles, their nephews can see them without their husbands ever protesting, or hardly ever.

It is a great sight, for a Muslim, to see a Christian town for the first time. I am not talking about the things which strike everyone straight away, such as the differences in architecture, or clothes, or way of life. Even in the slightest trivialities there is something curious, which I feel and cannot express.

We shall leave for Marseilles tomorrow; our stay there will be short. Rica and I plan to go immediately to Paris, which is the capital of the empire of Europe. Travellers always seek out the big cities, which are a sort of common homeland for every foreigner.

Farewell. Be assured that I shall always love you.

From Leghorn, the 12th of the moon of Saphar, 1711

* Persian women have four.

Letter 24
Rica to Ibben, at Smyrna

We have been in Paris for a month, and we have been in a continual whirl all the time. There is so much to be done before one can get lodgings, find the people to whom one has introductions, and obtain the necessities of life, all of which one needs simultaneously.

Paris is as big as Ispahan. The houses here are so high that you would swear that only astrologers would live in them. As you will realize, a town built in the air, with six or seven houses all on top of each other, is exceedingly full of people, and when everyone comes out into the street it makes a splendid muddle.

Perhaps you will not believe this, but during the month that I have been here I haven't yet seen anyone walk. No people in the world make their bodies work harder for them than Frenchmen: they run; they fly. The slow vehicles of Asia, the measured step of our camels, would give them apoplexy. As for me, who am not used to such a rush, and who often go on foot without changing my pace, I sometimes get as cross as a Christian: for, not to mention getting covered in mud from head to foot, I cannot forgive being regularly and systematically elbowed. A man coming up behind me turns me right round as he overtakes me; another, passing in the opposite direction, abruptly puts me back where the first one got me; and before I have gone a hundred yards I am in a worse state than if I had done ten leagues.

Do not expect me to be able to give you a thorough description of European ways and customs. I have only a superficial idea of them myself, and have had barely enough time to do anything except be astonished.

The King of France is the most powerful ruler in Europe. He has no goldmines like the King of Spain, his neighbour, but his riches are greater, because he extracts them from his subjects' vanity, which is more inexhaustible than mines. He has been known to undertake or sustain major wars with no other funds but what he gets from selling honorific titles, and by a miracle of human vanity, his troops are paid, his fortresses supplied, and his fleets equipped.

Moreover, this king is a great magician. He exerts authority even over the minds of his subjects; he makes them think what he wants. If there are only a million crowns in the exchequer, and he needs two million, all he has to do is persuade them that one crown is worth two, and they believe it. If he is involved in a difficult war without any money, all he has to do is to get it into their heads that a piece of paper will do for money, and they are immediately convinced of it. He even succeeds in making them believe that he can cure them of all sorts of diseases by touching them, such is the force and power that he has over their minds.[1]

You must not be amazed at what I tell you about this prince: there is another magician, stronger than he, who controls his mind as completely as he controls other people's. This magician is called the Pope. He will make the king believe that three are only one, or else that the bread one eats is not bread, or that the wine one drinks not wine, and a thousand other things of the same kind.[2]

And in order to keep him in training, so that he will not get out of the habit of believing, he gives him certain articles of belief as an exercise from time to time. Two years ago he sent him a long document called the *Constitution*,[3] and tried to make this king and his subjects believe everything in it, on pain of severe penalties. He succeeded with the king, who submitted at once, setting an example to his subjects. But some of them rebelled, and said that they refused to believe anything in the document. The instigators of this revolt, which has split the court, the whole kingdom, and every family, are women. The Constitution forbids them to read a book which all the Christians say was brought down to them from Heaven: it is really their Koran. The women, indignant at this insult to their sex, have started a whole movement against the Constitution. They have put the men, who in this case do not want to be privileged, on their side. You have to admit, all the same, that this Mufti argues perfectly reasonably; it must be, by the great prophet Ali! that he is acquainted with the principles of our Holy Law. For, since women are created

73

inferior to us, and our prophets say that they will not go to Paradise, why is it necessary for them to bother to read a book which is intended only to show the way to Paradise?[4]

I have heard things about the king that border on the miraculous, and I have no doubt that you will hesitate to believe them.

They say that while he was at war with his neighbours, who were all in league against him, he had an innumerable number of invisible enemies in his kingdom, surrounding him. They also say that he has searched for them for more than thirty years, and that, despite the indefatigable efforts of certain dervishes who are in his confidence, he has been unable to find a single one. They live with him; they are at his court, in his capital city, among his troops, in his lawcourts. Yet they say he will have the vexation of dying without being able to find them. It is as if they existed in general, and were nothing in particular: they are a class without any members. No doubt Heaven wants to punish this prince for not being sufficiently restrained towards his conquered enemies, since it gives him enemies who are invisible, and who are superior to him in their methods and in what they achieve.

I shall continue to write to you, and what I tell you will be far removed from the Persian character and way of doing things. The same earth carries us both; but the men in the country where I am living, and those in the country where you are, are men of very different sorts.

From Paris, the 4th of the second moon of Rabia, 1712

Letter 25
Usbek to Ibben, at Smyrna

I have received a letter from your nephew Rhedi. He tells me that he is leaving Smyrna with the intention of seeing Italy; that the only purpose of his visit is to educate himself and so to make himself worthier of you. You are happy to have a nephew who will one day be your consolation in old age.

Rica is writing you a long letter. He says that he has a great deal to tell you about this country. The liveliness of his mind is such that he readily understands everything. I myself, who think more slowly, am not in a position to tell you anything.

Our conversations about you are most affectionate. We cannot stop talking about the welcome you gave us at Smyrna, and the services that we owe to your friendship every day.

Generous Ibben, may you find friends everywhere who are as grateful and as faithful as we! May it not be long before I see you again, and find out once more how pleasantly the days go by when two friends are together! Farewell.

From Paris, the 4th of the second moon of Rabia, 1712

Letter 26
Usbek to Roxana, at the seraglio in Ispahan

Roxana, how fortunate you are to be in the sweet land of Persia, and not in these polluted climates, where modesty and virtue are unknown! How fortunate you are! In my seraglio you can live as though you were in the home of innocence, beyond the reach of all the crimes of mankind. It is a joy to you to find that you are in the happy position of not being able to fail in your duty. You have never been defiled by the lustful eyes of any man; your father-in-law even, in the informal atmosphere of holiday parties, has never seen the beauty of your lips; you have never neglected to conceal them by wearing a sacred veil. Fortunate Roxana! On your visits to the country you have always had eunuchs to walk in front of you and put to death any man who has had the audacity not to run away when he saw you. And what trouble I had myself, I to whom Heaven gave you to make me happy, before I became master of that treasure which you defended so steadfastly! What a disappointment it was, in the early days of our marriage, not to see you! And when I had seen you, what eagerness I felt! Yet you would not appease it; on the contrary, you made it worse by obstinately refusing me, out of modesty and fear.

You treated me in the same way as all the men from whom you had kept yourself constantly hidden. Do you remember the day when I lost you among your slaves, who treacherously prevented me from finding you? Do you remember that other day when, seeing that your tears were powerless, you appealed to your mother's authority in order to check the impetuousness of my love? Do you remember how, when everything else had failed, you found a last resource in your own courage? You took a dagger and threatened to destroy the husband who loved you, if he continued to demand something that meant more to you than he did. This struggle between love and virtue lasted two months. You carried the scruples of chastity too far: you did not surrender, even after you had been conquered; you defended your dying virginity at the very last extremity; you considered me as an enemy who had inflicted an outrage on you, not as a husband who had loved you. It was three months before you dared look at me without blushing; your embarrassment seemed to be reproaching me for taking advantage of you. I could not relax even when I was in possession of you: you deprived me, as far as you could, of your beauty and your grace, and I was intoxicated with the greatest privileges without having obtained the lesser.

If you had been brought up in this country, you would not have been so upset. The women here have lost all restraint. They leave their faces bare in the presence of men, as if they were asking to be made to yield; they look out for men, and see them in mosques, in parks, in their own houses; the custom of having eunuchs as servants is unknown. Instead of the dignified simplicity and pleasing delicacy of manner that is the rule among you, a crude immodesty prevails, which it is impossible to get used to.

If you were here, Roxana, you would certainly feel outraged by the dreadful ignominy into which your sex has fallen. You would flee from this hateful place, longing for the welcome seclusion which brings innocence, where you can be sure about yourself, where there are no dangers to fear, where, in a word, you can love me without the fear of ever losing the love that is due to me.

When you bring out the beauty of your complexion with the finest shades of colour, when you perfume your whole body with the most precious lotions, when you array yourself in your finest clothes, when you try to surpass your companions by the gracefulness of your dancing and the sweetness of your singing, and compete with them charmingly in a contest of beauty, tenderness and gaiety – I cannot imagine that you have any other purpose except to please me. And, when I see you shyly blush, when your eyes seek mine, when you win my heart by soft caressing words, I cannot, Roxana, doubt your love.

But what am I to think of these European women? Their skill in making up their faces, the jewels they bedeck themselves with, the trouble they take over their personal appearance, and the desire to be attractive that continually preoccupies them, simply detract from their virtue and are an affront to their husbands.

It is not, Roxana, that I believe that they carry their immorality as far as such conduct might imply, that they take corruption to such an extreme that it makes one shudder, and that they actually violate their marriage vows. There are very few women dissolute enough to go as far as that: they all have imprinted on their hearts a certain standard of virtue, which is given at birth, and which their upbringing may affect, but without destroying it. They may indeed fail to preserve the appearances that modesty requires, but when it comes to taking the final step, nature rebels. So that, when we shut you up so closely, when we guard you with so many slaves, and hold your desires back if they stray too far, it is not the final infidelity that we are afraid of; it is that we know that purity can never be too great, and that the slightest stain can spoil it.

I am sorry for you, Roxana. Your chastity, put to the test for such a long time, deserves a husband who would never leave you, and who could himself restrain the desires that your virtue alone can control.

From Paris, the 7th of the moon of Rajab, 1712

Letter 27
Usbek to Nessir, at Ispahan

We are now in Paris, the proud rival of the City of the Sun.*

When I left Smyrna, I entrusted my friend Ibben with the task of getting a crate to you which had some presents for you in it. You will receive this letter by the same means. Although I am five or six hundred leagues away from him, I can send him my news, and receive his, as easily as if he were at Ispahan and I were at Kum. I send my letters to Marseilles, whence ships depart all the time for Smyrna; from there he sends on those which are addressed to Persia by the Armenian caravans, which leave for Ispahan every day.

Rica is in perfect health: the strength of his constitution, his youth, and his natural cheerfulness allow him to rise above any tribulations.

But myself, I am not well; I am cast down in body and mind. I am giving in to thoughts which become more unhappy every day. My health, as it grows worse, takes me back to my country, and makes this one seem more alien.

But, my dear Nessir, I entreat you, see to it that my wives ignore the state that I am in. If they love me, I want to spare them any unhappiness, and if they do not, I do not want to make them more audacious.

If my eunuchs thought that I was in danger, if they could hope that any despicable indulgence on their part would go unpunished, they would soon stop being deaf to the cajoling voice of a sex which could make a stone listen to it, and move inanimate things.

Farewell, Nessir; it is a pleasure to give you evidence of my trust in you.

From Paris, the 5th of the moon of Shaaban, 1712

* Ispahan.

Letter 28
Rica to ★★★[1]

Yesterday I saw something rather odd, although in Paris it happens every day.

Towards the end of the afternoon, everyone assembles and goes to perform in a sort of show, called, so I have heard, a *play*. The main action is on a platform, called the *stage*. At each side you can see, in little compartments called *boxes*, men and women acting out scenes together, rather like those that we have in Persia. Here there may be a woman unhappy in love, who is expressing her amorous yearnings, while another, with greater vivacity, may be devouring her lover with her eyes, and he looks at her in the same way. Every emotion is displayed on the faces of these people, and conveyed with an eloquence which is all the more effective for being silent. Here the actresses are visible only down to the waist, and usually have a shawl, out of modesty, to cover their arms.[2] Down below there is a crowd of people standing up, who make fun of those who are performing above, and they in turn laugh at those below.

But those who exert themselves most are certain people who are chosen for this purpose at an early age, to endure fatigue. They are obliged to be everywhere: they go through places that nobody knows except themselves, and climb with surprising skill from tier to tier; they are up, they are down, and in every box; they dive, so to speak; they get lost, then reappear; often they go away from where one performance is going on in order to act in another. There are even some who, miraculously considering that they use crutches, can walk, and get about like the others.[3] Eventually everyone goes off to a room where they act a special sort of play: it begins with bows and continues with embraces. They say that however slightly one man knows another, he has the right to suffocate him. The place seems to breed affection.[4] Indeed, they say that the princesses who reign there are not very strict, and, except for two or three hours each day when they are rather fierce, they can be said to be approachable the rest of the time; their frenzies disappear easily.

It is much the same as I have said at another place also, called the Opera. The only difference is that they speak in one place and sing in the other. A friend of mine took me the other day to a dressing-room where one of the principal actresses was changing. We got to know each other so well that the next day I had this letter from her:[5]

Sir,

I am the unhappiest girl in the world; I have always been the most virtuous girl in the Opera. Seven or eight months ago I was in the room where we met yesterday. As I was dressing myself in the costume of a priestess of Diana, a young abbé came and found me there, and with no respect for my white dress, my veil and headband, he robbed me of my innocence. It was useless for me to tell him what a great sacrifice I had made for him: he started to laugh, and said that he had found that I was most unreligious. But now I am so fat that I dare not appear on stage any more, for you cannot imagine how sensitive I am where my honour is concerned, and I always maintain that, with a girl of good family, it is easier to make her lose her virtue than her sense of propriety. Since I am so sensitive, you will appreciate that the young abbé would never have succeeded if he had not promised to marry me. It was such a legitimate reason that it made me overlook the usual minor formalities, and begin where I should have ended up. But since his faithlessness has dishonoured me, I don't want to stay any longer at the Opera, where between you and me, I get hardly enough to live on; for now that I am older, and losing my attractiveness, my stipend, which has stayed the same, seems to be getting smaller every day. I found out from one of your servants that a good dancer is held in the highest esteem in your country, and that, if I were at Ispahan, I should make my fortune at once. If you saw fit to grant me your protection, and take me back to that country, you would have the credit of having helped a girl who would show, by her virtue and good behaviour, that she was not unworthy of your kindness.

Yours,

'.....'

From Paris, the 2nd of the moon of Shawall, 1712

Letter 29
Rica to Ibben, at Smyrna

The Pope is the chief of the Christians; he is an ancient idol, worshipped now from habit. Once he was formidable even to princes, for he would depose them as easily as our magnificent sultans depose the kings of Iremetia or Georgia. But nobody fears him any longer. He claims to be the successor of one of the earliest Christians, called Saint Peter, and it is certainly a rich succession, for his treasure is immense and he has a great country under his control.[1]

Bishops are men of the Law who are subordinate to him and have, under his authority, two very different functions. When they are assembled together, they compose articles of belief, like him; when they are on their own, virtually their only function is to dispense people from obedience to the Christian Law. For you must know that this religion is burdened with an infinity of very difficult observances; and so, considering that it is less easy to fulfil these duties than to have bishops who give dispensations, the latter course has been adopted as a matter of public utility. So that, if you do not want to fast during Ramadán, if you do not wish to submit to the formalities of marriage, if you want to break your vows, if you want to marry when the Christian Law forbids it, even at times if you want to go back on your sworn word, you go to a bishop or the Pope, who immediately gives a dispensation.

Bishops do not compose articles of belief on their own initiative. There is an infinite number of theologians, mostly dervishes, and they raise thousands of new questions about religion among themselves. They are left to argue for a long time, and the war goes on until a decision arrives to end it.

So that I can assure you that no kingdom has ever had as many civil wars as the kingdom of Christ.

Those who bring out some new proposition are immediately declared heretics. Each heresy has its name, which for those who are committed to it serves as a password. But nobody is a heretic against his will: all he has to do is to split the difference of opinion into two halves,[2] and provide a distinction for those who accuse him of heresy, and whatever the distinction may be, intelligible or not, it makes a man as white as snow, and he can have himself declared orthodox.

What I say applies to France and Germany; for I have heard that in Spain and Portugal there are certain dervishes who cannot see a joke, and who burn a man as they would straw. If anyone falls into the hands of such as they, it is lucky for him if he has always said his prayers with some little wooden beads in his hand, and has worn two pieces of cloth attached to two ribbons, and has sometimes visited a province called Galicia – otherwise the poor devil will find himself in a most awkward situation.[3] He could swear like a heathen that he is orthodox, but they could easily disagree with him about the meaning of the term, and burn him for being a heretic. It would be useless to draw distinctions: no distinctions! – he would be in ashes before it had even occurred to them to give him a hearing.

Other judges presume that the accused is innocent: these always presume him guilty. When in doubt, they opt for severity on principle, apparently because they believe that men are wicked. But in other respects they will hold them in such high esteem that they consider them incapable of lying, for they will accept evidence from sworn enemies of the accused, from women without morals, or from men who follow the most infamous profession. When passing sentence they pay their respects in a little speech, addressed to men who are clad in a smock of sulphurous yellow, and say that they are very sorry to see them so badly dressed, that they are lenient and detest bloodshed, and that they are in despair at having condemned them to death. But to console themselves they confiscate for their own benefit everything that the poor wretches possess.

Happy the land where the children of the prophets dwell! There such piteous sights are unknown.* The holy religion that the angels brought down is defended by its very truth; it does not need these violent methods in order to preserve itself.

From Paris, the 4th of the moon of Shawall, 1712

* The Persians are the most tolerant of all the Muslim nations.[4]

Letter 30
Rica to the same, at Smyrna

The inhabitants of Paris carry their curiosity almost to excess. When I arrived, they looked at me as though I had been sent from Heaven: old men and young, women and children, they all wanted to see me. If I went out, everyone stood at the windows; if I was in the Tuileries, I immediately became the centre of a circle; even the women surrounded me, like a rainbow composed of a thousand colours. If I was at a show, I would see a hundred lorgnettes focused on my face straight away. In a word, never was a man seen as much as I was. It made me smile sometimes, to hear people who had hardly ever been out of their rooms saying to each other: 'You've got to admit, he really does look Persian.' It was incredible: I found portraits of me everywhere; I saw multiples of myself in every shop and on every mantelpiece, so greatly did people fear that they had not had a good enough look at me.

To receive such honour as this is bound to become burdensome. I didn't believe myself to be so curious and unusual a person, and, although I have a very good opinion of myself, I would never have imagined that I was likely to create a disturbance in a great city where nobody knew me at all. This made me decide to give up Persian costume and dress like a European, to see if there was still anything remarkable about my countenance. The experiment made me realize what I was really worth. Free of all foreign adornments, I found myself assessed more exactly. I had reason to complain of my tailor, who, from one instant to the next, had made me lose the esteem and attention of the public; for all at once I fell into a terrible state of non-existence. Sometimes I would spend an hour in company without anyone looking at me, or giving me the opportunity to open my mouth. But, if someone happened to tell the company that I was Persian, I would immediately hear a buzz around me: 'Oh! oh! is he Persian? What a most extraordinary thing! How can one be Persian?'

From Paris, the 6th of the moon of Shawall, 1712

Letter 31
Rhedi to Usbek, at Paris

I am now in Venice, my dear Usbek. You can have seen every city in the world, and be surprised on arriving in Venice: it will always be amazing to see a town, with towers and mosques, rising out of the water, and to find countless people in a place where there should be nothing but fish.

But this city of infidels lacks the most precious treasure in the world, namely fresh water; it is impossible to perform a single ablution prescribed by the Law. The town is in abhorrence to our holy Prophet; aloft in Heaven, he never looks down on it without anger.

Apart from this, my dear Usbek, I should be delighted to live in a town where my mind is developing every day. I am learning about the secrets of commerce, the political interests of kings, and the forms of their government; I do not neglect even the superstitions of Europe. I am working at medicine, physics, and astronomy; I am studying the technical sciences; in brief, I am emerging from the clouds which covered my eyes in the land where I was born.

From Venice, the 16th of the moon of Shawall, 1712

Letter 32
Rica to ★★★

The other day I went to see an institution where about three hundred people are looked after, in conditions of some poverty. I had soon finished, for the church and the buildings are not worth looking at. The inmates of the institution were quite cheerful: a number of them were playing cards and other games unknown to me. As I was coming out, one of them came out too, and hearing me ask my way to the Marais, which is the most distant part of Paris, said: 'I'm going there, and I will take you; follow me.' He was a wonderful guide, getting me out of every difficulty, and skilfully preventing me from being hit by coaches and carriages. We were nearly there when I became curious. 'My good friend,' I said, 'will you not tell me who you are?'

'I am blind, sir,' he answered.

'What!' I said, 'blind! Then why didn't you ask the gentleman who was playing cards with you to show us the way?'

'He's blind too,' he replied. 'For four hundred years there have been three hundred blind men living in the building where you met me.[1] But I must leave you. Here is the street you asked for. I shall join this crowd; I am going into that church, where, believe me, I shall be more trouble to other people than they are to me.'

From Paris, the 17th of the moon of Shawall, 1712

Letter 33
Usbek to Rhedi, at Venice

Wine is so expensive in Paris, because of the taxes on it, that it seems as though an effort is being made to enforce the precepts of the divine Koran, which forbids us to drink it.

When I consider the terrible effects of this drink, I cannot but think that it is nature's most fearsome gift to men. If there is anything that has discredited the lives and reputations of our monarchs it is their intemperance, which is the deadliest source of their injustice and cruelty.

It is a reproach to mankind to say so, but, although the Law forbids our princes the use of wine, they drink it in such excess that it reduces them to a lower than human level; while on the other hand its use is permitted to Christian princes, and it is not obvious that they do any wrong because of it. The human mind is contradiction itself: dissolute and licentious, we furiously rebel against the rules; and the Law, designed to make us juster, often does nothing but make us guiltier.

But if I disapprove of the use of this drink which makes us lose our reason, I do not similarly condemn those by which it is enlivened. The wisdom of the orientals lies in the fact that they seek as diligently for remedies against unhappiness as for those against the most dangerous diseases. When a European suffers some misfortune, he has no resource but to read a philosopher called Seneca;[1] but Asians, showing more sense and a better knowledge of medicine, take drinks which can make a man cheerful and dispel the memory of his sorrows.[2]

Nothing is more depressing than consolations based on the necessity of evil, the uselessness of remedies, the inevitability of fate, the order of Providence, or the misery of the human condition. It is ridiculous to try to alleviate misfortune by observing that we are born to be miserable. It is much better to prevent the mind indulging in such reflections, and to treat men as emotional beings, instead of treating them as rational.

The soul, being united to the body, is constantly tyrannized by it. If the circulation is too sluggish, if the vital spirits have not been refined sufficiently, or if they are not in great enough quantities, we fall into apathy and dejection. But if we take the sort of drink that can alter our physical condition, our soul is again able to have sensations which exhilarate it, and it feels a secret pleasure in perceiving the mechanisms of the body recover, so to speak, their movement and life.

From Paris, the 25th of the moon of Dulkaada, 1713

Letter 34
Usbek to Ibben, at Smyrna

In Persia the women are more beautiful than they are in France, but the French women are prettier. It is difficult not to love the former, and not to be attracted to the latter; the former are more tender and retiring, the others more lively and gay.

The reason for the fine complexions found in Persia is the even tenor of women's life there. They do not gamble or keep late nights; they drink no wine and are hardly ever exposed to the open air. It must be confessed that the seraglio is more conducive to health than to pleasure; it is an equable life, without stimulus. Everything is based on subordination and duty. Even pleasures are taken seriously there, and joys are severely disciplined; they are hardly ever indulged in except as a means of indicating authority and subjection.

Even men in Persia do not have the same gaiety as the French: they lack that freedom of mind and that contented look that I find here among every class and in every station of life.

Things are far worse in Turkey, where you could find families in which, from father to son, nobody has laughed since the establishment of the monarchy.

This Asiatic seriousness comes from the little contact that they have with each other. They only see each other when social convention demands it. Friendship, that sweet union of hearts, which is what makes life so enjoyable here, is almost unknown to them. They withdraw to their houses, where they always find company waiting; so that each family is so to speak isolated.[1]

One day, when I was discussing the matter with a man from this country, he said to me: 'What shocks me most about your way of life is that you are obliged to live with slaves, whose hearts and minds are always influenced by their lowly condition. The virtuous impulses that we have naturally are in you weakened by these degraded beings, who from your childhood onwards corrupt them by their constant presence.

'After all, you must look at it without prejudice. What can you expect from an education given by a man for whom honour consists in guarding another man's wives, and who takes pride in the basest calling known to men; in whom even conscientiousness (which is his only virtue) is contemptible, because it is motivated by envy, jealousy, and despair; who longs to revenge himself on both sexes, being rejected by both, and allows himself to be dictated to by the stronger provided that he can cause distress to the weaker; who can distinguish himself in his profession only by his disfigurement, ugliness, and deformity, and is respected only because he is unworthy to be; who, finally, rivetted for ever to the door that he is tied to, harder than the bolts and hinges which hold it, boasts of having spent fifty years in his worthless post, where, entrusted with his master's jealousy, he has given full scope to his ignominy?'

From Paris, the 14th of the moon of Dulheggia, 1713

Letter 35
Usbek to Jemshid, his cousin, a dervish at the illustrious monastery of Tabriz

What, sublime dervish, are your views on the Christians? Do you believe that on the Day of Judgement they will be like the faithless Turks, who will be used as donkeys for the Jews,[1] to trot them quickly off down to Hell? I am well aware that they will not go to the dwelling-place of the prophets, and that the great prophet Ali did not come for them. But do you think, because they are not fortunate enough to have mosques in their country, that they are condemned to eternal torments, and that God will punish them for not having practised a religion that he did not reveal to them? Let me tell you this: I have often examined these Christians; I have interrogated them to see if they had any knowledge of the Lord Ali, who was the fairest of all men: I have found that they have never heard of him.

They do not resemble the infidels whom our holy prophets put to the edge of the sword, for refusing to believe in the miracles of Heaven. They are more like the unfortunates who lived in the darkness of idolatry before the divine light came and illuminated the face of our great Prophet.

Besides, if you examine their religion closely, you will find the rudiments, as it were, of our own dogmas. I have often marvelled at the secret ways of Providence, which seems to have wanted to prepare them in this way for general conversion. I have heard of a book by one of their theologians, entitled *Polygamy Triumphant*, which proves that Christians are commanded to practise polygamy. Their baptism is the image of our holy ablution, and the Christians are in error only about the efficacy that they attribute to this first ablution, which, they believe, suffices for all the others. Their priests and monks pray seven times a day like us. They hope to enjoy Paradise, where they will taste a thousand delights through the resurrection of the body. They have, like us, fixed days for fasting, and mortifications by which they hope to elicit the mercy of God. They worship the good angels and distrust the bad. They have a pious faith in the miracles which God performs by the agency of his servants. Like us, they realize that their merits are insufficient, and that they need a being to intercede on their behalf with God. I see Islam everywhere, though I cannot find Mohammed.[2] Whatever you do, truth will always emerge, shining through the darkness which surrounds it. A day will come when the Eternal will see only true believers on the earth; time, which consumes all things, will destroy error itself; all men will see with amazement that they are under the same flag; everything, even the Law, will be accomplished: the sacred books will be removed from earth, and carried away to celestial archives.

From Paris, the 20th of the moon of Dulheggia, 1713

Letter 36
Usbek to Rhedi, at Venice

Coffee is very popular in Paris; it is distributed in a large number of houses open to the public. In some of them people tell each other the news; in others they play chess. There is one where the coffee is prepared in such a way that it sharpens the wits of those who drink it; at any rate, there is nobody among them who, as he leaves, does not think that he is four times cleverer than when he went in.[1]

But what shocks me about these intellectuals is that they do not make themselves useful to their country, but fritter away their talents on puerilities. For instance, when I arrived in Paris I found them all heatedly arguing about the most trivial matter you could imagine. It concerned the reputation of an old Greek poet, whose place of birth, like the year of his death, has been unknown for two thousand years.[2] Both parties agreed that he was an excellent poet; the only question was the degree of merit that was to be ascribed to him. Everyone wanted to decide on his rating, but, among these distributors of reputations, some were more generous than others: hence the dispute. It was very bitter indeed; for both sides insulted each other with great conviction, and so rudely, and they made such acid witticisms, that I was surprised as much by the manner of their quarrel as by its subject-matter. If, I said to myself, anyone was foolish enough to go and attack the reputation of some worthy citizen in front of one of the defenders of this Greek poet, he would be reprimanded pretty sharply! and their zeal, which is so sensitive about dead men's reputations, would no doubt be roused to real fury in the defence of the living! But however that may be, I added, God preserved me from the hostility of the poet's enemies, since two thousand years in the tomb has not protected him from their implacable hatred! At present their blows fall on empty air: but what would it be like if their anger were to be aroused by the enemy's presence?

Those whom I have mentioned argue in the common tongue, and are to be distinguished from another kind of disputant, who uses a barbarous language which seems to increase the fury and obstinacy of the combatants.[3] In some parts of Paris you can see a dense black mob, as it were, of this class of person; they feed on distinctions; they live on unclear arguments and false conclusions. They might have been expected to die of hunger at this business, but it is profitable all the same. A whole nation, expelled from its country, was observed to cross the seas and settle in France, without anything to assist in providing the necessities of life except a redoubtable talent for debate.

Farewell.

From Paris, the last day of the moon of Dulheggia, 1713

Letter 37
Usbek to Ibben, at Smyrna

The King of France is old.[1] There is no case, anywhere in our history, of a king having reigned for such a long time. They say he possesses in a very high degree the talent of making himself obeyed: he governs his family, his court, and his country with equal ability. He has often been heard to say that of all the types of government in the world, he would most favour either that of the Turks, or that of our own august Sultan, such is his esteem for oriental policies.

I have studied his character, and found contradictions which I am unable to resolve. For instance, he has a minister who is only eighteen years old, and a mistress of eighty;[2] he is devoted to his religion, and cannot stand those who say that it should be observed strictly; although he avoids the bustle of towns, and is rarely seen in company, his one concern, from morning till night, is to get himself talked about. He adores trophies and victories, but he is as fearful of seeing a good general leading his troops as he would have cause to be if the same man were at the head of an enemy army. It has never, I believe, happened to anyone except him to be glutted with more wealth than any prince could hope for, and at the same time to be plunged in greater poverty than a private citizen could tolerate.

He likes to reward those who serve him, but he pays as generously for the attentions, or rather the indolence, of his courtiers, as for the campaigns laboriously carried on by his officers. He often prefers a man who unclothes him, or hands him his napkin when he sits down at table, to another who captures towns or wins battles for him. He does not believe that the grandeur of royalty should be restricted in the distribution of favours, and showers gifts on someone without examining whether he is a man of ability, in the belief that his choice will make him so; so that he has been known to give a small pension to a man who had fled two leagues, and an important post as governor to another who had fled four.

He is magnificent, especially as regards his buildings; there are more statues in his palace gardens than citizens in a large town. His corps of guards is as powerful as the Prince's before whom every throne topples over; his armies as numerous, his resources as great, and his finances as inexhaustible.

From Paris, the 7th of the moon of Muharram, 1713

Letter 38
Rica to Ibben, at Smyrna

It is a great problem for men to decide whether it is more advantageous to allow women their freedom, or to deprive them of it. It seems to me that there is a great deal to be said both for and against. If the Europeans say that it is ungenerous to make those we love unhappy, the Asians retort that it is ignoble for men to renounce the authority that nature gave them over women. If they are told that having a large number of women shut in will cause difficulties, they reply that ten women who obey cause less difficulty than one who does not. And if they in their turn argue that Europeans cannot be happy with women who are unfaithful to them, the answer is that this faithfulness, which they make so much of, does not prevent them feeling the indifference which always ensues when passion is satisfied; that our wives are too exclusively ours; that being so firmly in possession leaves us nothing to desire, or to fear; that a certain amount of fickleness is like salt, which adds flavour and prevents decay. A wiser man than I might perhaps be hard put to it to decide, for, if Asians are well advised to look for an appropriate way of allaying the anxiety they feel, Europeans are well advised also not to feel it.

After all, they say, even if we are unhappy as husbands, we can always find a way of redressing the balance as lovers. In order for there to be any justice in a man's complaint that his wife is unfaithful, there would have to be only three people on earth; they will always be on equal terms when there are four.

It is a different problem to decide whether women are subject to men by the law of nature. 'No,' a very chivalrous philosopher[1] said to me the other day, 'nature has laid down no such law. Our authority over women is absolutely tyrannical; they have allowed us to impose it only because they are more gentle than we are, and consequently more humane and reasonable. Their superiority in these respects, which would doubtless have given them the supremacy if we were reasonable beings, has caused them to lose it because we are not.

'However, if it is true that our power over women is mere tyranny, it is no less true that they have a natural power over us: that of beauty, which cannot be resisted. Our authority is not world-wide, but the power of beauty is universal. Why then should we be privileged? Because we are stronger? But that is completely unjust. We use all sorts of methods to reduce their courage. If our upbringing were similar, our strength would be also. Test them on the kinds of ability that their upbringing has not impaired, and we shall soon see if we are so superior.'

It must be admitted, although it runs counter to our way of thinking, that among the most civilized nations wives have always had authority over their husbands. It was decreed by law among the Egyptians in honour of Isis, and among the Babylonians in honour of Semiramis. It was said of the Romans that they commanded over every nation, but obeyed their wives. I will not say anything about the Sarmatians, who were completely subjugated by their women;[2] they were too barbaric to be used as an example.

As you see, my dear Ibben, I have got into the habits of this country, where they are fond of defending out-of-the-way opinions, and of treating everything paradoxically. The Prophet has decided the question, and defined the rights of each sex. Wives, he says, should honour their husbands; their husbands should honour them also, but have one degree of advantage over them.[3]

From Paris, the 26th of the second moon of Jomada, 1713

Letter 39
Hadji Ibbi★ to ben Joshua, a Jewish convert to Islam, at Smyrna

It seems to me, ben Joshua, that the birth of outstanding men is always preceded by extraordinary portents, as if nature were undergoing a sort of crisis, and as if the powers of Heaven could give birth only after great effort.

Nothing is more wonderful than the birth of Mohammed. God, who, by the decrees of his Providence, had decided from the beginning to send the mighty prophet down to men in order to put Satan into captivity, created, two thousand years before Adam, a source of light, which passing from saint to saint, from one ancestor of Mohammed to the next, finally came to him, as authentic testimony that he was descended from the patriarchs.

It was also because of the same prophet that God willed that no child should be conceived unless the woman had ceased to be impure, and the man had been subjected to circumcision.[1]

He came into the world circumcised, and joy was on his face from the moment of his birth; the earth shuddered thrice, as if she herself had borne a child; every idol bowed down before him; the thrones of kings were overturned; Lucifer was flung to the bottom of the sea, and only after swimming for forty days did he emerge from the abyss, and fled to the mountain of Kabkab,[2] where in a terrible voice he called upon the angels.

That night, God set a boundary between man and woman, that none could pass. The arts of magic and necromancy were powerless. A voice from Heaven was heard, which spoke these words: 'I have sent into the world my faithful friend.'

According to the testimony of Ibn Abbas,[3] the Arab historian, the generations of the birds, of the clouds, of the winds, and all the squadrons of angels, came together in order to bring up the child, and competed for the privilege among themselves. The twittering

★ 'Hadji' is applied to a man who has made a pilgrimage to Mecca.

birds said that it would be more convenient for them to care for him, since they were more easily able to collect fruit of various kinds from different places. The winds murmured and said: 'Rather is it for us to do it, because we can bring him the most fragrant odours from everywhere.'

'No, no,' said the clouds, 'no; he will be entrusted to our care, because we shall constantly convey to him the freshness of the waters.' Whereupon the angels were indignant, and cried: 'What then is left for us to do?' But a voice from the sky was heard, which ended every argument: 'He will not be removed from mortal hands, for blessed are the breasts that give him milk, blessed the hands that touch him, and the house in which he lives, and the bed in which he rests.'

After such remarkable testimony, my dear Joshua, it would need a heart of iron not to accept his holy Law. What more could Heaven do, to guarantee his sacred mission, without turning nature upside down and destroying the very men it wished to convince?

From Paris, the 20th of the moon of Rajab, 1713

Letter 40
Usbek to Ibben, at Smyrna

Whenever a great noble dies, everyone goes to a mosque to hear a funeral oration – a speech in his praise, from which it would be very awkward to decide just what the dead man's merit consisted in.

I should like to see funerals banned. There should be weeping at a man's birth, not at his death. What is the point of the ceremonies, with all their dreary paraphernalia, that are performed for a dying man in his last moments, or even of his family's tears and his friends' grief, except to underline the value of what he is about to lose?

Our blindness is so great that we do not know when to be sad and when to rejoice: virtually all our sorrows, and our joys, are false.

When I see that the Mogul goes every year, like a fool, to have himself weighed in a pair of scales,[1] when I see that his people rejoice

95

because their prince is of greater density, that is to say, less capable of governing them, I grieve, Ibben, at human irrationality.

From Paris, the 20th of the moon of Rajab, 1713

Letter 41
The First Black Eunuch to Usbek

Ismael, one of your black eunuchs, has just died, magnificent lord, and I cannot afford not to replace him. Since eunuchs are extremely scarce at the moment, I thought of using a black slave whom you have here in the country: but I have not yet succeeded in persuading him to allow himself to be initiated into this form of service. Since I can see that in fact it will be to his advantage, it was my intention, the other day, to use a little severity with him; and in collaboration with the superintendent of your gardens I ordered that despite his opposition he should be rendered capable of carrying out the services which are most in accordance with your heart's desires, and of living like myself in this awesome place, which he does not even dare to look at: but he began to scream as if he were going to be flayed, and struggled so much that he escaped from our hands and eluded the fateful operation. I have just learnt that he means to write to you to ask for mercy, maintaining that I conceived the plan only out of an insatiable desire to revenge myself for certain caustic jokes, which he says he made about me. Yet I swear, by the hundred thousand prophets, that I acted only out of concern for your service, which is the only thing I care for; I have eyes for nothing else. I prostrate myself at your feet.

From the seraglio of Fatme, the 7th of the moon of Muharram, 1713

Letter 42
Pharan to Usbek, his sovereign lord

If you were here, magnificent lord, I should appear before you all covered in white paper; but there would not be enough of it to contain all the wrongs which the First Black Eunuch, the wickedest of all men, has done me since you left.

He alleges that I made certain jokes about his unfortunate condition, and on this pretext he calls down never-ending vengeance on my head: he has influenced the cruel superintendent of your gardens against me, who since you left has heaped insurmountable labours on me, and I have nearly worn myself to death a thousand times, though my eagerness to serve you never slackened for a moment. How many times have I said to myself: 'I have a master who is kindness itself, but I am the wretchedest slave on the face of the earth!'

I confess, magnificent lord, that I did not believe that greater miseries lay in store for me: but that villainous eunuch attempted to excel himself in wickedness. Some days ago, acting on his own private authority, he assigned me to guard your sacred wives, that is to say, to suffer an operation which would be a thousand times crueller than death for me. Whoever has been, at birth, unhappy enough to receive such treatment at the hands of cruel parents may find solace in never having known anything different from his present condition; but if I were expelled from humanity, or deprived of humanity, I should die of grief, if not from the barbarous act itself.

I kiss your feet, sublime lord, in deepest humility. Make your decision such that the effects of your virtue, which is so widely respected, extend to me: and let it not be said that by your command there is another man on earth who is unhappy.

From the gardens of Fatme, the 7th of the moon of Muharram, 1713

Letter 43
Usbek to Pharan, in the gardens of Fatme

Let joy be in your heart, and recognize these sacred characters as mine: let them be kissed by the Chief Eunuch and the superintendent of my gardens. I forbid them to proceed against you in any way. Tell them to buy the eunuch that I need. Perform your duties as if I were always before your eyes; for let it be understood that, the greater my kindness, the more will you be punished if you abuse it.

From Paris, the 25th of the moon of Rajab, 1713

Letter 44
Usbek to Rhedi, at Venice

There are three estates in France: the Church, the nobles of the sword, and the nobles of the robe. Each has supreme contempt for the other two. For example, a man who ought to be despised because he is a fool is often despised only because he wears robes.

Even the humblest workers argue over the merits of the trade they have chosen; everyone believes himself to be above someone else of a different calling, proportionately to the idea he has formed of the superiority of his own.

Men are all, more or less, like that woman from the province of Erivan who, having received some favour from one of our monarchs, said time and again, in the blessings she gave him, that she hoped Heaven would make him Governor of Erivan.

I have read in a travel-book that a French vessel put in to the Guinea coast, and some of the crew wanted to land so as to buy some sheep. They were taken to the king, who was dispensing justice to his subjects beneath a tree. He was sitting on his throne, that is, on a log of wood, as proudly as if it were the throne of the Grand Mogul; he had three or four guards with wooden spears; a parasol, in the form of a canopy, protected him from the heat of the sun; his only adornments, like those of the queen, his wife, consisted of their black skin and a few rings. This prince, with a vanity which exceeded even his poverty, asked the strangers whether he was much spoken of in France. He thought that his name should be conveyed from pole to pole, and, unlike that conqueror of whom it has been said that he had put the whole world to silence,[1] this man believed that the whole universe should be talking about him.

When the Khan of Tartary has dined, a herald cries out that all the princes of the earth may go to dinner, if they wish; and this savage, who eats nothing but milk, has no house, and only lives through brigandage, considers all the kings in the world as his slaves, and insults them regularly twice a day.

From Paris, the 28th of the moon of Rajab, 1713

Letter 45
Rica to Usbek, at ★★★

Yesterday morning, while I was in bed, I heard a heavy banging on the door, and all at once it was opened, or battered down, by a man with whom I was moderately well acquainted; he seemed completely beside himself.

His clothes were considerably less than plain. His wig, which was all askew, had not even been combed. He had not had the time to have his black waistcoat sewn up, and had renounced for the day the sensible precautions which he usually took in order to disguise the dilapidated state of his outfit.

'Get up,' he said, 'I shall need you all day. I have hundreds of things to buy, and would be very glad to do it with you. First we must go to the Rue Saint-Honoré, to see a notary who has been commissioned to sell an estate worth fifty thousand pounds; I want him to give me first refusal. On my way here I stopped a moment in the Faubourg Saint–Germain, where I took a town house at a rent of two thousand crowns, and I hope to sign the contract today.'

As soon as I was dressed, or nearly dressed, my man hurried me downstairs. 'We must start,' he said, 'by buying a carriage, and get it fitted out.' In fact we bought not merely a carriage, but ten thousand pounds' worth of goods as well, in less than an hour. Everything went rapidly because my man never haggled or checked the bill; and he didn't pay out anything either.[1] I was reflecting on all this, and when I examined the man I found such an odd combination of rich and poor that I did not know what to think. But at last I broke my silence and, taking him on one side, I said: 'Tell me, who is going to pay for all this?'

'I am,' he said. 'Come up to my room, and I will show you immense treasure, riches that the greatest monarchs might envy. But you need not be envious, for I shall always share them with you.' I follow him; we climb to the fifth floor, and with a ladder we hoist ourselves up to a sixth, a gallery open to the four winds, and containing nothing but two or three dozen bowls full of a variety of liquids. 'I got up very early,' he said, 'and immediately did what I have done for twenty-five years, which is to go and inspect my experiments; I saw that the great day had come, which will make me richer than any man on earth. Do you see that crimson liquid? It now has all the qualities prescribed by the philosophers in order to achieve the transmutation of metals.[2] I extracted from it these grains that you see here. They are true gold in colour, though a little defective in weight. This secret, that Nicolas Flamel discovered, but that Raymond Lull and a million others were still looking for, has come down to me; and today I have had the good fortune to become an adept. May it be Heaven's will that I use all the treasure it has communicated to me only for its glory!'

I left, and went down, or rather flung myself down the staircase, overcome with anger, and left this man and all his wealth in his slum. Farewell, my dear Usbek. I shall come to see you tomorrow, and if you like we can come back to Paris together.

From Paris, the last day of the moon of Rajab, 1713

Letter 46
Usbek to Rhedi, at Venice

I observe that people here argue about religion interminably: but it appears that they are competing at the same time to see who can be the least devout.

Not only are they no better as Christians, they are not even better citizens, which is what affects me most: for, whatever religion one may have, obedience to the laws, love of mankind, and respect for one's parents are always the principal acts of religion.

For is it not the case that the chief concern of a religious man must be to please the Divinity who established the religion that he professes? But the surest way to achieve this is certainly to observe the rules of society, and the duties of humanity. For, whatever religion you may have, you must, immediately you suppose that there is a religion, suppose also that God loves mankind, since he founded a religion to make them happy; and if he loves mankind, you are certain to please him by loving them also; that is to say, in performing all the duties of charity and humanity towards them, and in not violating the laws under which they live.

In this way you are much more certain to please God than by carrying out some ceremony or other: for ritual has no degree of goodness in itself; it is only good conditionally, on the supposition that God ordained it. But this provides material for a great deal of discussion. It is easy to be mistaken, for it is necessary to choose the ceremonies of one religion out of two thousand.

A man made this prayer to God every day: 'Lord, I cannot understand anything of the continual disputes about you: I should like to serve you according to your will, but everyone whom I consult wants me to serve you according to his. When I want to pray to you, I do not know which language to speak to you in. Nor do I know what posture I should adopt. One man says I must pray standing up; another wants me to sit down; another insists that my body should be supported by my knees. That is not all: there are some who claim that I must wash in cold water every morning; others affirm that you will regard me with abhorrence if I do not have a small piece of my flesh cut off.[1] The other day, in a caravanserai, I happened to eat a rabbit. There were three men there who made me tremble: all three maintained that I had gravely offended you; the first,* because the animal was impure; the next,† because it had been strangled; and the last,‡ because it was not a fish. A brahmin passing by, whom I appealed to as judge, said: "They are wrong, since presumably you did not kill the animal yourself."

"'Yes I did," I said.

"'Ah! you have committed an abominable action, which God will never forgive," he said in a severe voice; "how do you know that the soul of your father had not passed into that creature?"[2]

'All these things, Lord, put me in the most terrible quandary. I cannot shake my head without being told that I risk offending you. Yet I should like to please you and use the life that I received from you in order to do so. I do not know if I am mistaken, but I believe that the best way to manage it is to live as a good citizen in the society into which you caused me to be born, and be a good father to the family which you have given me.'

From Paris, the 8th of the moon of Shaaban, 1713

Letter 47
Zashi to Usbek, at Paris

I have a great piece of news for you: Zephis and I are reconciled; the seraglio, which had been divided between us, is reunited. Only your presence is lacking here, where peace prevails: come to us, dear Usbek, come and let love reign triumphant.

I gave Zephis a great banquet, to which your mother, your wives, and your principal concubines were invited. Your aunts and a number

---

* A Jew.
† A Turk.
‡ An Armenian.[3]

of your cousins were also there; they had come on horseback, covered like a dark cloud in their veils and robes.

The next day we set out for the country, where we hoped to have greater freedom. We mounted our camels and four of us sat in each litter. Since the party had been arranged in haste, we did not have time to send messengers out to proclaim the *corrouk*,[1] but the Chief Eunuch, ingenious as ever, took another precaution: to the cloth which prevented us from being seen he added a curtain so thick that we were completely unable to see anyone.

When we had arrived at that river which has to be crossed, we each got into a box,[2] as is customary, and were taken on to the boat, for we were told that the river was full of people. A man who inquisitively came too near to where we were enclosed received a mortal blow, which deprived him for ever of the light of day; another man, found bathing naked on the bank, had the same fate, and your faithful eunuchs sacrificed this unlucky pair to your honour and to ours.

But you must hear the rest of our adventures. When we were in the middle of the river the wind started to blow so violently, and such a dreadful cloud covered the sky, that our sailors began to give up hope. Frightened by the danger, we almost all fainted. I can remember hearing the voices of our eunuchs raised in dispute, some saying that we should be warned of the peril we were in and released from confinement; but their chief continually maintained that he would sooner die than allow his master to be dishonoured in such a way, and that he would bury his dagger in the breast of any man who made such rash suggestions. One of my slaves, unclothed and beside herself, ran towards me to help me: but a black eunuch caught her roughly and made her go back to where she had come from. It was then that I fainted, and did not come to myself until the danger was over.

What troubles journeys cause for women! The only dangers that men are exposed to are those which threaten their lives; while we, at every moment, are in fear of losing our lives or our virtue. Farewell, my dear Usbek. I shall always adore you.

From the seraglio of Fatme, the 2nd of the moon of Ramadan, 1713

Letter 48
Usbek to Rhedi, at Venice

Those who enjoy learning are never idle. Although I have no important business to do, I am nonetheless continually occupied. I spend my life in inquiry. In the evening I write down what I have noticed, what I have seen or heard, during the day. Everything interests me, everything surprises me: I am like a child, whose organs are still delicate, so that even the most trivial things make an impression on them.

You may not believe it, but we are made welcome in every company and every sort of society. I think that I must owe a great deal to Rica's natural gaiety, which makes him want to see everyone, and everyone want to see him. Our foreign look no longer puts anyone off; we can even enjoy people's surprise when they find that we have some manners, for the French do not imagine that our climate can produce human beings. It must be admitted nonetheless that they are worth the trouble it takes to undeceive them.

I have spent a few days in a country house near Paris, with a man of some influence, who is delighted to have company. His wife is very nice, and combines a most decorous manner with the sort of gaiety that our Persian ladies always lack, because of their secluded life.

Being a foreigner, I had nothing better to do than to study the crowd of people who were ceaselessly arriving and provided me with something new all the time. I immediately noticed a man whose naturalness attracted me; I became attached to him, and he to me, so that we were always somewhere near each other.

One day, when there was a large circle of people talking, we were by ourselves, leaving the general conversation to itself. 'You may perhaps find,' I said, 'that I have more curiosity than politeness, but I beg you to allow me to ask you some questions, for I am getting tired of not understanding anything, and living among people whom I cannot fathom. I have been racking my brains for two days; each of these men has put me into agonies of perplexity a hundred times over, and I shall never make them out in a thousand years; for me they are as unknowable as the wives of our great king.'

'You have only to ask,' he replied, 'and I shall tell you all you wish to know; and the more readily since I believe you to be a man of discretion, who will not abuse a confidence.'

'Who is the man,' I said, 'who has talked such a lot about the meals he has given for high-ranking nobles, who is so familiar with your dukes, and speaks so often to your ministers, who are supposed to be so difficult to see? Obviously he must be a man of quality, but his expression is so vulgar that he scarcely does credit to people of quality, and besides, he seems to me not to have been properly brought up. I am a foreigner, but I should say in general terms that there is a certain politeness that is common to every nation, and in him I find it missing. Are your men of quality less well brought up than the others?'

'That man,' he replied with a laugh, 'is a tax-farmer.[1] In wealth he is as much superior to other people as he is inferior by birth. He would have the best table in Paris, if he could bring himself never to eat at it. He is extremely conceited and impolite, as you observe, but he excels by reason of his cook; nor is he ungrateful, for you have heard how he has been extolling him all day long.'

'And the big man dressed in black,' I said, 'whom that lady has had put next to her? Why does he have such gloomy clothes and such a bright complexion? He smiles charmingly as soon as he is spoken to; his costume is less extravagant than a woman's, but arranged with greater care.'

'That,' he replied, 'is a preacher, and, what is worse, a spiritual adviser.[2] As such, he knows more than husbands do. He knows a woman's weak point; and they know what his is too.'

'Really?' I said; 'he is always talking about something which he calls grace.'

'Not always,' he replied. 'In the ear of a pretty woman he is even readier to talk about her fall. He thunders in public, but in private he is as gentle as a lamb.'

'It seems to me,' I said, 'that he is much sought after, and treated with great consideration.'

'But of course he is sought after. He is a necessity. He is what makes a secluded life attractive; little bits of advice, thoughtful attentions, visits by appointment; he gets rid of a headache better than anyone in the world; he is splendid.'

'If I am not being a nuisance, tell me who that is opposite us, so badly dressed; who sometimes makes faces, and talks in a different style from other people; who lacks wit to talk with, but talks so as to seem witty?'

'That is a poet,' he said, 'the buffoon of the human race.[3] His kind of people say that they are born what they are, which is true, and it is what they will remain all their life, namely the most ridiculous of men, almost without exception. Consequently, they are shown no mercy; contempt is heaped upon them unstintingly. Starvation brought this one to the house, and he is well treated by the master and mistress, whose kindness never fails towards anyone. He wrote a wedding ode when they were married, which was the best thing he ever did in his life, for their marriage has turned out to be as happy as he predicted.

'You will not perhaps believe it,' he added, 'prejudiced as you are by oriental ideas, but there are some happy marriages among us, and some women whose virtue keeps them strictly guarded. The couple of whom we are speaking live in complete and undisturbed harmony with one another; they are beloved and respected by everyone. There is only one thing: their natural goodness makes them invite all sorts of people to their home, which means that they sometimes have bad company. Not that I am criticizing them. You have to take men as you find them, and when people are said to be good company, often the reason is simply that they have the more civilized kinds of vices; perhaps it is the same as with poisons, the subtlest of which are also the most dangerous.'

'And that old man,' I said in a low voice, 'who looks so bad-tempered? At first I took him for a foreigner, for apart from the fact that he is dressed differently from everyone else he criticizes everything that happens in France, and disapproves of your government.'

'He is an old army man,' he said, 'who makes all his listeners remember him by the length or time taken up by his exploits. He finds it intolerable that the French should have won battles at which he was not present, or that anyone should admire the handling of a siege if he was not there guarding the trenches. He believes that he is so essential to our history that it must have finished when he did; he thinks that some wounds which he suffered signify the dissolution of the monarchy; and, unlike those philosophers who say that we enjoy the present alone, and that the past is nothing, he on the contrary enjoys nothing but the past, and exists only in his campaigns; he breathes in times that have gone by, as heroes will live on in times yet to come.'

'But why did he give up the army?' I said.

'He didn't give it up,' he answered; 'it gave him up. He has been given a minor post and will spend the rest of his days recounting his adventures. The road to honour and glory is closed to him.'

'And why is that?' I asked.

'We have a maxim in France,' he replied, 'never to give high rank to officers who have spent their time patiently waiting in junior positions. We consider that they will have become narrow-minded by attention to detail, and that, because they are accustomed to little things, they will have become incapable of anything greater. We believe that if at the age of thirty a man does not possess the qualities required of a general, he will never possess them; that the man who lacks the vision to imagine a battlefield several leagues in extent in all its different aspects, and who lacks the presence of mind to use every advantage in victory and every resource in defeat, will never acquire these talents. It is for this reason that we have positions of pre-eminence for the sublimely great men to whom Heaven has granted the heart, as well as the ability, of a hero, and subordinate posts for those whose talents are subordinate too. Among them we include men who have grown old in unimportant wars; they will succeed, at best, only in what they have been doing all their lives; they should not be overburdened when they are beginning to weaken.'

A moment later curiosity again overtook me and I said: 'I promise not to ask any more questions, if you will allow me this one. Who is the large young man with the hair, who is not very bright, but extremely bumptious? Why is it that he talks louder than anyone else and is so pleased with himself for existing?'

'He is a Don Juan,' he replied. At these words some people came in, others went out, we stood up, someone came and talked to my companion, and I remained as ignorant as before. But a moment later, by some chance, the young man happened to be beside me, and turning towards me he said: 'It is a fine day, sir; would you care for a stroll in the garden?' I answered as civilly as I was able, and we went out together.

'I have come down to the country,' he said, 'so as to do a favour to the mistress of the house, with whom I am getting on rather well. I know that there is a certain lady in society who won't be very pleased, but what is one to do? I am friendly with the prettiest women in Paris, but I don't confine myself to one. They think me better than I am, for, between you and me, I am not a great performer.'[4]

'I presume, sir,' I said, 'that you have some post or function which prevents you being more attentive to them.'

'No, sir; the only function I have is to make husbands wild or fathers desperate. I enjoy frightening a woman who thinks she has me, by bringing her nearly to the point of losing me. There are a number of young men like me, who share out the whole of Paris between us in this way, so that the town takes an interest in every detail of our actions.'

'From what I can gather,' I said, 'you cause more talk than the bravest soldier, and have a wider reputation than a learned judge. If you were in Persia you would not enjoy all these privileges; you would find yourself better qualified to guard our wives-than to attract them.' The colour rose to my face, and I think that if I had said any more I should have been unable to prevent myself being rude to him.

What do you think of a country where such people are tolerated, and where a man who follows such a career is allowed to exist? where faithlessness, treachery, abduction, perfidy and injustice earn respect? where a man is esteemed for separating a daughter from her father, a wife from her husband, and for breaking up the most delightful and most sacred of attachments? Happy the children of Ali, who preserve their families from seduction and disgrace! Daylight is no purer than the fire which burns in our wives' hearts; our daughters never think without trembling of that day which must deprive them of the virtue that makes them similar to the angels and incorporeal powers.

Cherished land of my birth on which the sun looks first, you are not sullied by the horrible crimes which force that heavenly light to hide as soon as he appears in the blackness of the West!

From Paris, the 5th of the moon of Ramadan, 1713

Letter 49
Rica to Usbek, at ✱✱✱

The other day, as I was in my room, in came a dervish dressed in an extraordinary manner. His beard came down to the rope round his waist, his feet were bare, his costume was coarse and grey, with points on here and there. Altogether he looked so bizarre that my first idea was to send for a painter, to use him in a cartoon.

He started by making a long complimentary speech to me, in which he informed me that he was a man of merit, and, what was more, a Capuchin. 'I am told, sir,' he went on, 'that you will shortly be returning to the Persian court, where you hold a distinguished position. I have come to ask for your protection, and to request you to procure from the king some small place to live, near Kazvin, for two or three monks.'[1]

'Father,' I said, 'do you want to go to Persia, then?'

'I, sir?' he said. 'I haven't the slightest intention of doing so. I am the Provincial here, and I wouldn't swap jobs with any Capuchin on earth.'

'Then what the devil do you want from me?'

'The thing is,' he said, 'that if we had a hospice there, our brothers in Italy would send two or three of their monks there.'

'You must know them, presumably, these monks?' I said.

'No, sir, I do not.'

'Then, for goodness' sake, what does it matter to you whether they go to Persia? It's a fine plan, to send two Capuchins to breathe the air of Kazvin, and how useful it will be, both in Europe and Asia! To get royalty involved is absolutely essential: what a magnificent sort of colony it would be! Be off; you and your like are not suitable for transplanting, and you would be well advised to stay and creep about the place where you came up.'

From Paris, the 15th of the moon of Ramadan, 1713

Letter 50
Rica to ★★★

I have seen people in whom virtue was so natural that it was not even noticeable; they followed their duty without forcing themselves, performing it as if by instinct. Far from drawing attention to their unusual qualities by talking about them, it seemed as if the knowledge of these qualities had not penetrated to them. That is the sort of person I like, not these virtuous people who seem amazed by it, and who regard a good action as a remarkable phenomenon which must cause surprise when they tell of it.

If it is necessary for those to whom Heaven has given great talents to possess the virtue of modesty, what can one say of these insects who have the effrontery to display the kind of pride that would be dishonourable in the greatest of men?

Everywhere I see people who talk continually about themselves. Their conversation is a mirror which always shows their own conceited faces. They will talk to you about the tiniest events in their lives, which they expect to be magnified in your eyes by the interest that they themselves take in them. They have done everything, seen everything, said everything, thought of everything. They are a universal pattern, the subject of unending comparisons, an inexhaustible fount of examples. Oh, how empty is praise when it reflects back to its origin!

Some days ago a man of this character wore us down for two hours with himself, his merits and his talents; but as there is no such thing as perpetual motion in the world, he stopped talking. The conversation was therefore ours again, and we took it.

A man with a rather gloomy expression began by complaining of the boredom that prevails in conversation. 'Really! will we never have anything but those fools whose conversation is a self-portrait, and who relate everything to themselves?'

'You are right,' the prattler abruptly resumed, 'they should do as I do. I never boast. I am well off, of good family, I am not mean, my friends say that I am not without intelligence; but I never mention all this: if I have any good qualities, the one I esteem most highly is my modesty.'

I wondered at the fatuity of this man, and as he loudly continued I murmured: 'Happy is he who has enough vanity never to speak well of himself, who fears his listeners, and does not put his merits at risk from other people's pride!'

From Paris, the 20th of the moon of Ramadan, 1713

Letter 51
Nargum, Persian envoy to Muscovy, to Usbek, at Paris

I have been told, in a letter from Ispahan, that you have left Persia and are at present in Paris. Why do I have to receive your news from someone other than yourself?

I have been in this country for five years, on the orders of the King of Kings, and have carried through a number of important negotiations.

You will be aware that the Tsar is the only Christian ruler whose interests are at one with ours, since like us he is an enemy of Turkey.

His empire is larger than ours, for it is a thousand leagues from Moscow to the furthest outpost of his lands in the direction of China. He is absolute master of the lives and property of his subjects, all of whom are slaves except for four families.[1] The lieutenant of the prophets, the King of Kings, whose footstool is the sky, does not possess a more redoubtable power.

When you have seen how dreadful the climate is in Muscovy, you would never believe that to be exiled from it is a punishment, yet, whenever a great noble is disgraced, he is banished to Siberia.

Just as the Law of our Prophet forbids us to drink wine, the Muscovites are forbidden to drink it by a law made by their ruler.

They have a way of welcoming their guests which is very un-Persian. Whenever a stranger comes into the house the husband offers his wife to him, the stranger kisses her, and that is taken as an act of politeness to the husband.

Although fathers usually stipulate in their daughters' marriage contracts that the husband will not whip them, you would scarcely believe how much Muscovite women like to be beaten;* they cannot imagine that their husbands really love them unless they are properly beaten. For the husband to behave in any other way is a sign of unpardonable indifference. Here is a letter which one of them wrote recently to her mother.

My dear Mother,

I am the unhappiest woman in the world; I have done everything I can to make my husband love me, and I have never yet managed it. Yesterday I had hundreds of things to do in the house; I went out, and stayed out all day. I thought, when I came back, that he would beat me really hard, but he didn't say a single word. My sister is very differently treated; her husband beats her every day. If she so much as looks at another man he goes for her on the spot. They love each other deeply, and get on very well together.

That is why she is so proud of herself; but I won't give her the chance to look down on me for long. I am determined to make my husband love me at any cost. I will make him so furious that he will have to give me some sign of affection. I won't have it said that I do not get beaten and that I live in his house without any notice being taken of me. If he gives me the slightest touch I shall scream as loud as I can, so that people will think that he is actually beating me. If a neighbour came to my help I think I should strangle him. I beg you, dear Mother, please put it to my husband that it isn't right for him to treat me as he does. My father, who always does the right thing, did not behave like that, and I remember thinking when I was small that he sometimes loved you too much. I embrace you, dear Mother.

The Muscovites cannot leave their empire, even for the sake of travel. Consequently, separated from other nations by the law of the

* These customs have changed.³

112

land, they have kept their traditional customs all the more faithfully because they did not think that it was possible to have any others.

But the king who reigns at present wants to change everything. He has had terrible trouble with them over the question of their beards.[3] The clergy and the monks have fought just as fiercely to preserve their ignorance.

He is eager to encourage the growth of technical skills, and does all he can to enhance the reputation of his country in Europe and Asia, for it has been forgotten until now and is almost unknown except to itself.

Anxious, and constantly dissatisfied, he roams his vast territories, leaving evidence of his harsh nature everywhere.

Then he abandons them as if they could not contain him, and goes to Europe to search for other provinces and new domains.[4]

I embrace you, my dear Usbek. Send me news of yourself, I entreat you.

From Moscow, the 2nd of the moon of Shawall, 1713

Letter 52
Rica to Usbek, at ★★★

The other day, in company, I rather enjoyed myself. There were women of all ages there: one of eighty, one of sixty, and one of forty, who had a niece who was twenty or twenty-two. Some instinct made me go up to the youngest, and she whispered to me: 'What do you think of my aunt, wanting to have admirers at her age, and still trying to look pretty?'

'She is wrong,' I said, 'that sort of thing only suits you.'

A moment later I found myself next to the aunt, who said: 'What do you think of that woman, who is at least sixty years old, and spent over an hour making herself up today?'

'It's a waste of time,' I said, 'and nobody who is not as attractive as you should think of doing so.'

I went over to the unfortunate woman of sixty, and was feeling sorry for her when she whispered to me: 'Have you ever seen anything so absurd? Look at that woman, who is eighty years old, and wears flame-coloured ribbons. She wants to be youthful, and she has succeeded, for it verges on the childish.'

'Good Lord!' I said to myself, 'is it only other people whom we ever find ridiculous?' Then I thought: perhaps we are lucky to be able to console ourselves with other people's weaknesses. But I was in a mood to amuse myself, and said: 'We have ascended enough, let us now go down, starting with the old lady at the top. Ma'am, you and the lady I have just been talking to resemble each other so closely that you look like sisters, and I would guess that you must be about the same age.'

'Indeed, sir,' she said, 'when one of us dies, the other ought to feel thoroughly scared. I don't think there can be two days between us.' Having caught this decrepit woman, I went over to the one who was sixty years old. 'Ma'am, you must settle a bet I have made: I wagered that you and that lady,' and I pointed to the forty-year-old, 'are of the same age.'

'To be sure,' she said, 'I don't think there is six months' difference.'

So far so good; onwards. I descended further, and went across to the woman of forty. 'Be so good as to tell me, ma'am, if you are joking when you say that the young lady at the other table is your niece. You are as young as she, and her face is even a little past its best, which yours certainly isn't: those fresh colours which show in your complexion . . .'

'Let me explain,' she said, 'I am her aunt, but her mother was at least twenty-five years older than me; she and I had different mothers. I have heard my late sister say that her daughter and I were born the same year.'

'Just what I said, ma'am; I was right to be surprised.'

My dear Usbek, when women feel, as they lose their attractiveness, that their end is coming in advance, they would like to go backwards to youth again. How could they possibly not attempt to deceive other people? – they make every effort to deceive themselves, and to escape from the most distressing thought we can have.

From Paris, the 3rd of the moon of Shawall, 1713

Letter 53
Zelis to Usbek, at Paris

Never has there been so fierce, so passionate a love as that which Cosrou, a white eunuch, feels for my slave Zelid. He implores me to let him marry her, with such frenzy that I am unable to refuse – and why, indeed, should I object, since her mother does not, and Zelid herself seems satisfied with the idea of a marriage that is only a sham, and with the empty shadow that is offered her?

What does she think she will do with the poor wretch, who will show that he is a husband only in being jealous, who when he ceases to feel unmoved will be able to feel nothing but useless despair, who will always have the memory of what he once was, thus reminding her of what he is no longer; who, continually on the point of giving himself to her and never doing so, will be deceiving himself, and her, all the time, and will be constantly inflicting on her the full misery of his condition?

What! continually in the presence of phantoms and illusions? living in imagination alone? to be always close to pleasure, and never have it? lying unsatisfied in the poor man's arms, and instead of responding to his passion responding only to his regret?

How contemptuous one would feel towards such a man, who is capable only of guarding and never possessing! I look for the presence of love, but cannot find it.

I am talking freely to you because you like my natural candour, and prefer my lack of constraint and enjoyment of pleasure to the pretended delicacy of my companions. I have heard you say many many times that eunuchs experience pleasure with women, but of a sort unknown to us; that nature compensates for what it has lost, and has resources to make up for the disadvantages of their condition; that it is possible to stop being a man, but not to stop feeling, and that being in that state is like having a third sense, so that they simply exchange one pleasure for another, so to speak. If that were so, I think Zelid would be less to be pitied. It counts for something to live with people who are that much less unhappy.

Give me your orders on the matter, and let me know if you wish the marriage to take place in the seraglio. Farewell.

From the seraglio at Ispahan, the 5th of the moon of Shawall, 1713

Letter 54
Rica to Usbek, at ★★★

This morning I was in my room, which as you know is separated from the others only by a very thin partition, with gaps in it here and there, so that you can hear everything that is said in the next room. Someone was striding up and down and saying to another man: 'I don't know what the matter is, but nothing is going right for me. It is three days since I said anything which has done me credit. In every conversation I have been lost among the throng, without having the slightest attention paid to me, or being spoken to more than a couple of times. I had prepared some witty jokes, to add tone to what I was going to say: I was never given a chance to bring them out. I had a beautiful anecdote to tell, but while I was trying to work it in others kept avoiding it, as if they were doing it on purpose. For the last four days I have had some clever remarks getting older and older in my head, and I have been unable to make any use of them. If this goes on, I think I shall end up a fool: it seems to be my destiny; I can't escape. Yesterday I had hoped to shine with three or four old women who certainly did not overawe me, and I had some absolutely beautiful things to say. I spent more than a quarter of an hour working around to them, but they would never keep to the point. Like the three Greek fates they cut the thread of everything I said. If you ask my opinion, it needs a lot of effort to keep up a reputation for being witty. I don't know how you've managed it.'

'I have an idea,' replied the other. 'We must collaborate and be witty in partnership; we must join forces. Every day we shall tell each other what we are going to talk about. We shall give each other assistance, so that if someone comes and interrupts our ideas we'll bring the subject back ourselves; and if it won't come easily we'll drag it in willy-nilly. We will agree about where to show approval, where to smile, and where to laugh out loud. You'll see, we shall set the tone for every conversation, and people will admire our sharp wit and sparkling repartee. We shall provide mutual protection for ourselves by nodding or shaking our heads to each other. One day it will be your turn to shine, the next you will be my assistant. I shall go into a house and exclaim as I point you out: "I simply must tell you what an amusing answer this gentleman just gave to a man we met in the street," and turning to you I shall say: "He wasn't expecting it, he was quite taken aback." Or I shall recite some verses of mine and you will say: "I was there when he did them. It was at a supper-party, and he didn't have to think for a moment." Often we shall scoff at each other, you and I, and they will say: "Watch them attacking and defending themselves! They are showing each other no mercy: how will he get out of that one? – brilliant! what presence of mind! it's a genuine battle." But they won't say that we had a preliminary bout the night before. We shall have to get some of those books which are collections of jokes and epigrams intended for people who are not witty and want to make out that they are. Everything depends on having the right models. I want us to be able, inside six months, to hold a conversation an hour long with clever remarks all the way through. There is one thing that we must take care about, though: it is to see that they get plenty of support. Making a witty remark is not enough: it has to be publicized and distributed. Otherwise it's as good as lost. I can tell you that there is nothing more dispiriting than to see a well-turned remark that one has made going to its death in the ear of some fool of a listener. It is true that there is often a compensation, that we also say a lot of silly things which go *incognito*; it's the only consolation in such circumstances. That, my dear fellow, is the course that we must take. Do as I say, and I can promise you a seat in the French Academy inside six months – by which I mean that we shall not have to work for long, because you will then be able to retire: you will have become a witty man, whether you want to be or not. It has been observed in France that as soon as a man becomes a member of an institution he at once acquires what is called the *esprit de corps*;[1] it will be the same with you, and the only thing that I am afraid of in your case is that you will be too successful.'

From Paris, the 6th of the moon of Dulkaada, 1714

Letter 55
Rica to Ibben, at Smyrna

With the peoples of Europe, the first quarter of an hour of marriage settles every difficulty. The final surrender is invariably of the same date as the nuptial blessing; wives do not behave like our Persian women, who sometimes defend their territory for months on end. Nothing is so conclusive. If they do not lose anything, the reason is that they have nothing to lose. But what is so shameful is that the moment of their defeat is always known; and, without consulting the stars, one can forecast to the hour when their children will be born.

Frenchmen hardly ever talk about their wives: they are afraid to do so in front of people who may know them better than they.

Among them are some extremely unhappy men with whom nobody sympathizes: husbands who are jealous. There are men whom everybody detests: jealous husbands. There are those whom every man despises: again, jealous husbands.

Consequently, in no country are they so few in number as in France. The Frenchmen's equanimity is not based on the confidence he has in his wife, but, on the contrary, on the bad opinion he has of her. The prudent measures taken to protect women in Asia – veils to cover them up, prisons to keep them in, the watchfulness of the eunuchs – all seem to him more likely to sharpen the sex's wits than to defeat them. Married men here resign themselves with a good grace, and consider their wives' infidelities to be inevitably destined by the stars. A husband who wanted to have his wife all to himself would be looked upon as a disturber of the public pleasure, or as a madman who wanted to enjoy the sunshine to the exclusion of other men.

Here a husband who loves his wife is a man who has not enough merit to make another woman love him; who abuses the obligations imposed by law so as to compensate for his own lack of attraction; who exploits every advantage at his disposal to the prejudice of an entire society; who appropriates to his own use what was only given into his keeping, and does all that is in his power to destroy a tacit understanding which ensures the happiness of both sexes at once. To be known as the husband of a pretty woman, a title concealed so carefully in Asia, does not worry a man here. He feels in a position to give as good as he gets. A prince consoles himself for the loss of one stronghold by capturing another: while the Turks were getting Baghdad away from us, did not the Mogul's fortress of Candahar fall to us?[1]

A man who puts up generally with his wife's infidelities is not criticized; it is only individual cases that are dishonourable.

It is not that there are no virtuous women, and they can be said to be women of note; my guide always drew my attention to them; but they were all so ugly that one has to be a saint not to abhor virtue.

After what I have told you of the way of life in this country, you will easily imagine that the French do not exactly make a point of being faithful. They believe it is as ludicrous to swear eternal love to a woman as to assert that one will always be healthy, or always happy. When they promise to love a woman for ever, they assume on her side a promise to be always attractive; and if she breaks her word, they consider themselves no longer bound by theirs.

From Paris, the 7th of the moon of Dulkaada, 1714

Letter 56
Usbek to Ibben, at Smyrna

Gambling is very widespread in Europe. Being a gambler gives a man a position in society; it is a title which takes the place of birth, wealth, and probity. It promotes anyone who bears it into the best society without further examination, even though everyone knows that it is very often a mistake to believe such a thing. But people have agreed to be incorrigible.

Women are especially devoted to it. It is true that when they are young they hardly ever take it up except to help them satisfy a passion of which they are even more fond, but as they grow older their passion for gambling seems to rejuvenate itself, so that it fills the gap left by all the other passions.

Bent on ruining their husbands, they have, in order to succeed, methods to suit every age, from the tenderest youth to the most decrepit old age. Clothes and carriages begin the disruption, flirtation increases it, and gambling completes it. I have often watched nine or ten women, nine or ten centuries rather, placed round a table; I have watched their hopes, their fears, their joys, and above all their rage. You would have said that they would never have enough time to calm down, that their mood of despair would not pass away until they had done so themselves, and you would have been doubtful whether the people whom they were paying were their creditors or their heirs.

It would seem that our holy Prophet's main purpose must have been to deprive us of anything which disturbs our reason. He prohibited the use of wine, which is the burial-ground of reason, he specifically forbade games of chance, and when he was unable to remove the cause of a passion he reduced its power. Love with us does not produce either anxiety or frenzy. It is a subdued emotion, which leaves our soul in peace. Having a plurality of wives saves us from being ruled by them; it mitigates the violence of our desires.

From Paris, the 10th of the moon of Dulheggia, 1714

Letter 57
Usbek to Rhedi, at Venice

The libertines[1] here keep an infinite number of women, and the pious an innumerable number of dervishes. These dervishes make three vows, of obedience, poverty, and chastity. They say that the first one is observed best of all; as for the second, I can assure you that it is not; I leave the third to your imagination. But however rich these dervishes may be, they never cease to describe themselves as poor. Our glorious sultan would sooner give up his sublime and magnificent titles. They are right: for the fact that they are called poor prevents them from being so.

The doctors here, and a certain class of dervish called confessors, are either respected too much, or despised too much; though it is said that heirs find doctors more satisfactory than confessors.[2]

The other day I went to one of these dervishes' monasteries. One of them, with venerable white hair, received me with great politeness, and showed me all round the building. We went out into the garden and began to talk. 'Father,' I said, 'what is your position in your community?'

'Sir,' he replied, looking pleased at my question, 'I am a casuist.'

'A casuist?' I replied. 'I have not heard of that job in all the time that I have been in France.'

'What! don't you know what a casuist is? Well, listen, and the description that I shall give you will leave nothing to be desired. There are two sorts of sin: mortal, which debar the sinner from Paradise entirely, and venial, which do indeed offend God, but do not anger him to the point of preventing the sinner from attaining heavenly bliss. Now our whole business is to distinguish clearly between these two sorts of sin, for every Christian wants to go to Paradise, except for a few libertines, but there is nobody who does not want to go there as cheaply as possible. When you know which sins are mortal, you try to avoid committing them, and there you are. Some men do not aspire to the heights of perfection, and since they have no ambitions they don't mind who is in front; so they just manage to squeeze into Paradise. Provided that they get there, that is enough; they aim to do no more and no less. They don't so much go to Heaven as force their way in, and say to God: "Lord, I have strictly complied with the conditions. You cannot refuse to keep your promises; since I have done no more than you asked, I exonerate you from giving me more than you promised."

'So that we, sir, provide an essential service. But that is not all. Let me tell you something quite different. It is not the action that makes the crime, but whether the person committing it knows or not. If someone does something wrong while being able to believe that it is not wrong, he has a clear conscience, and since there is an infinite number of equivocal actions a casuist can give them the degree of goodness which they lack by declaring them good. Provided he can assert convincingly that there was no malicious intent, he can free them of it entirely. I am telling you the secrets of a trade in which I have spent my life, and explaining its finer points. There is a way of presenting everything, even things which seem the least promising.'[3]

'Father,' I said, 'that is all very well, but how do you manage about Heaven? If the Shah had a man at his court who behaved towards him as you do towards your God, putting distinctions between his commands and explaining to his subjects the different circumstances in which they had to carry them out or could transgress them, he would have him impaled on the spot.' I bowed to my dervish, and left without waiting for his reply.

From Paris, the 25th of the moon of Muharram, 1714

Letter 58
Rica to Rhedi, at Venice

Paris, my dear Rhedi, is a town of many trades. Here a man will obligingly come and, for a little money, present you with the secret of making gold.

Another will promise to let you sleep with aerial spirits, provided that you spend thirty years without seeing a woman.

You will also find soothsayers who are so proficient that they will tell you the whole of your life, provided that they have had a quarter of an hour's conversation with your servants.

There are clever women with whom virginity is a flower which perishes and is reborn once a day, and which, on being plucked for the hundredth time, gives more pain than on the first occasion.

There are others with the power to repair all the damage done by time, who know how to rescue a beautiful face on the brink of ruin, and even how to recall a woman from the pinnacle of old age and bring her down again to the tenderest years of her youth.

All these people live, or try to live, in a city which is the mother of invention. Its citizens never get their incomes through middlemen, for they consist only in intelligence and ingenuity; everyone has his own brand, which he puts to the best use he can.

He who would reckon up all the men of the Law who are in pursuit of the revenues from some mosque would sooner have counted the sands of the sea, or the slaves who serve our king.[1]

An infinite number of language teachers, and instructors in technical and academic subjects, give lessons on things they know nothing of, which is a very considerable talent, for it does not need much intelligence to reveal what you know, but an infinite amount is needed to teach something of which you are ignorant.

Sudden death is the only sort possible here: death could not exert its power in any other way, for at every corner you find people with remedies against every imaginable illness.

In all the shops there are invisible snares in which every customer gets caught. However, you can sometimes get away cheaply: a young shop-girl will spend a whole hour enticing a man to buy a packet of tooth-picks.

There is nobody who on leaving this city does not possess greater caution than when he arrived: by surrendering one's money to others one learns how to preserve it, which is the only advantage that foreigners derive from this city of enchantments.

From Paris, the 10th of the moon of Saphar, 1714

Letter 59
Rica to Usbek, at ★★★

The other day I was visiting a house where people of every sort had come to converse. I found that the conversation had been taken over by two old women, who had spent the whole morning trying in vain to make themselves look younger. 'You must admit,' said one of them, 'that men are very different nowadays from what we used to see in our youth. They used to be polished, agreeable, eager to please; but now I find them intolerably rude.'

'Everything has changed,' a man who seemed to be crippled by gout then said; 'things are not what they used to be. Forty years ago, everyone was fit and well, we walked, we were gay, all we asked was to laugh and dance. Nowadays, everyone is intolerably gloomy.'

A moment later the conversation turned to politics. 'Gad,' said an old nobleman, 'they don't know how to govern the country any more. Try and find a minister like Monsieur Colbert, these days. I knew him well, Monsieur Colbert, he was a friend of mine. He had my pension paid before anyone else. The finances were admirably organized. Everyone was well off; but today I am ruined.'

'Sir,' a cleric said next, 'the period to which you refer was the most wonderful of our invincible monarch's reign. Could there be anything more glorious than what he then did to destroy heresy?'

'And don't forget the abolition of duelling,' said a man who had not yet spoken, with a look of satisfaction.

'A judicious remark,' someone said in my ear. 'He is delighted at the prohibition. He obeys it so scrupulously that six months ago he was given a sound thrashing so as not to contravene it.'[1]

It seems to me, Usbek, that all our judgements are made with reference covertly to ourselves. I do not find it surprising that the negroes paint the devil sparkling white, and their gods black as coal, or that certain tribes have a Venus with her breasts hanging down to her thighs, or in brief that all the idolatrous peoples represent their gods with human faces, and endow them with all their own impulses. It has been well said that if triangles had a god, they would give him three sides.

My dear Usbek, when I see men creeping over an atom, I mean the earth, which is merely a point in the universe, and setting themselves up as direct models of Providence, I am unable to reconcile such extravagant pretensions with such tininess.

From Paris, the 14th of the moon of Saphar, 1714

Letter 60
Usbek to Ibben, at Smyrna

You ask if there are any Jews in France. You can be sure that wherever there is money, there are Jews as well. You ask me what they do here. Precisely the same as they do in Persia; nothing resembles a Jew in Asia so closely as a Jew in Europe.

Among the Christians as with us, they display that invincibly stubborn religious conviction which verges on folly. The Jewish religion is an aged tree-trunk which has covered the earth with the two branches that it has produced – Islam and Christianity; or rather, it is a mother who has given birth to two daughters, and they have inflicted a thousand wounds on her; for where religion is concerned, those most closely related are the greatest enemies. But despite the bad treatment she has had from them, she still prides herself on having brought them forth. Through them, she embraces the whole world; and similarly her venerable age embraces the whole of time.

The Jews, then, consider themselves to be the source of all sanctity and the origin of all religion. They consider us, on the contrary, as heretics who have made changes in the Law, or rather as rebel Jews.

If the changes had been made gradually, they believe that they would easily have been persuaded to accept them, but they happened suddenly and violently; they can fix the day and hour of both births, and are scandalized to find that our age can be determined; they hold fast to a religion which the world itself did not precede.

In Europe they have never enjoyed such freedom from disturbance as that which they now have. Among Christians there is beginning to be less of the spirit of intolerance that used to spur them on. It did no good to chase the Jews out of Spain, or, in France, to molest some Christians whose beliefs differed slightly from the king's.[1] It has been realized that zeal for the advancement of a religion is different from the attachment that one should have for it, and that in order to love and conform to one's religion it is not necessary to hate and persecute those who do not conform to it.

It is very desirable that the Muslims should take as sensible a view about the matter as the Christians; that we should make peace once and for all between Ali and Abu-bekr,[2] and leave it to God to decide between these holy prophets. I should like them to be honoured by acts of veneration and respect, not by meaningless acts of favouritism, and I should like men to try to earn their approval whatever place God has assigned to them, on his right hand or beneath the steps of his throne.

From Paris, the 18th of the moon of Saphar, 1714

Letter 61
Usbek to Rhedi, at Venice

The other day I visited a famous church called Notre-Dame. While I was admiring the magnificence of the building I happened to get into conversation with a clergyman who like me had been brought there by curiosity. The conversation fell upon the tranquillity of his calling. 'Most people,' he said, 'envy our pleasant life, and they are right. However, it has its disagreeable side. We are not so cut off from the outside world that we do not have to appear there on countless occasions, and we have a very difficult role to play. Worldly people are extraordinary. Whether we approve or condemn them, they find both equally unacceptable. If we try to reform them they consider us absurd, and if we give them our approval they regard us as unworthy of our position. Nothing is more humiliating than the thought of having shocked even unbelievers. We are therefore obliged to adopt an equivocal approach, and impress the libertines[1] not by the firmness of our attitude, but by leaving them uncertain of our reaction to what they say. It requires great ingenuity. This state of neutrality is difficult: people in the outside world take a chance on anything, and say whatever comes into their heads; according to how it is received, they follow it up or let it go, and succeed much better.

'That is not all. This happy, tranquil life, which everyone makes so much of, is lost to us in the outside world. As soon as we appear there, we have to argue. We have to undertake, for instance, the task of proving the usefulness of prayer to a man who does not believe in God, or the necessity of fasting to another who has spent his life denying the immortality of the soul. It is a laborious enterprise, and the humorists are not on our side. What is more, we suffer constantly from a certain desire to make other people share our views; it is part of our calling, so to speak. This is as ridiculous as it would be to see Europeans trying to turn the Africans' faces white, for the sake of human nature. We cause social disturbances and make ourselves suffer in order to spread religious beliefs which are not fundamental, and we resemble the Emperor of China who provoked his subjects to general rebellion by trying to compel them to cut their hair or their nails.[2]

'Even our zeal for making those for whom we are responsible perform the duties of our holy religion is often dangerous; we cannot be too circumspect about it. An emperor named Theodosius put the entire population of a village to the edge of the sword, even the women and children. When he later appeared at the entrance of a church, a bishop called Ambrose had the doors shut against him, for having committed murder and sacrilege, and in so doing he acted heroically.[3] When the emperor had done penance in the manner appropriate for such a crime and had been allowed to enter the church, he went to take a place among the priests. The same bishop made him leave, and in so doing he behaved like a fanatic.[4] It shows how carefully we should guard against zealotry. What did it matter, to the Church or to the state, whether the emperor had or had not a place among the priests?'

From Paris, the 1st of the first moon of Rabia, 1714

Letter 62
Zelis to Usbek, at Paris

Your daughter having reached her seventh year, I thought that it was time to bring her into the interior apartments of the seraglio, instead of waiting until she is ten years old to put her in the care of the black eunuchs. It is never too early to deprive a young girl of the freedom of childhood, and bring her up in sanctity between these sacred walls where chastity resides.

For I cannot share the opinion of those mothers who do not keep their daughters shut in until they are on the point of giving them a husband, and who by sentencing them to the seraglio rather than initiating them into it impose this way of life on them by violence, when they should have induced them to accept it by persuasion. Should we expect everything from the power of reason, and nothing from the easy ways of habit?

It is pointless to talk of the subordinate position that nature allocated to us. It is not sufficient to make us aware of it, we must also experience it in practice, so that we have some help at the critical moment when the passions begin to show themselves and encourage us to be independent.

If we were bound to you only by duty, we might sometimes neglect it; if we were motivated only by our feelings for you, stronger feelings might supplant them. But when law gives us to a man, it separates us from all the others, and makes us as remote from them as if we were a hundred thousand leagues away.

Nature, among the devices she employs for the benefit of men, did not confine herself to giving desires to them alone, but decreed that we too should have them, and should actively provide them with contentment. She made us feel the heat of passion so that their lives should be quiet. If they emerge from their state of indifference she provided us as a means for them to regain it, although we can never enjoy the good fortune that we ensure for them.

Do not however imagine, Usbek, that your present circumstances are happier than mine. Here I have enjoyed countless pleasures unknown to you. My imagination has been continually at work and made me realize their value; I have lived while you have merely repined.

Although you keep me imprisoned I am freer than you. Even if you were to pay twice as much attention to guarding me, I should simply take pleasure in your disquiet, and your suspicion, jealousy, and vexation are so many signs of your dependence. Continue, dear Usbek, and have me watched night and day. Do not trust even the usual precautions. Increase my happiness by guaranteeing your own, and remember that I fear nothing except your indifference.

From the seraglio at Ispahan, the 2nd of the first moon of Rabia, 1714

Letter 63
Rica to Usbek, at ★★★

I think you must want to spend your whole life in the country. Originally I was to be without you for two or three days, and now it is two weeks since I saw you. Of course, you are staying in a delightful house, the society there suits you, and you are able to discuss to your heart's content: that is all you need to make you oblivious of the rest of the universe.

As for me, I am leading more or less the sort of life you know. I move around in society and am trying to understand it. My mind is gradually losing whatever Asian habits it may still have, and is adjusting itself without difficulty to European ways. I am no longer so astonished to see five or six women in the same house as five or six men, and have come to the conclusion that it is not a bad idea.

I can tell you that I knew nothing about women until I came here. I have learnt more about them in a month than I should have done in thirty years inside a seraglio. With us everyone's character is uniformly the same, because they are forced. People do not seem what they are, but what they are obliged to be. Because of this enslavement of heart and mind, nothing is heard but the voice of fear, which has only one language, instead of nature, which expresses itself so diversely and appears in so many different forms. Dissimulation, which among us is so widely practised and essential an art, is unknown here. Everything is said, everything can be seen, and everything heard. The heart is exhibited as openly as the face. In conduct, in virtue, and even in vice, there is always something spontaneous to be perceived.

It is necessary, to please women, to have a kind of talent different from the one which pleases them even more. It consists in a certain spirit of humorous banter, which keeps them interested by seeming at every instant to promise something that can only be performed at over-long intervals. This humorous attitude, which is natural round a woman's dressing-table,[1] seems to have spread so far that it has influenced the character of the nation at large. They joke at the Council of State, they joke at the head of an army, they joke with an ambassador. The degree of ridicule attached to the professions depends on how seriously they take themselves. A doctor would no longer arouse ridicule if his clothes were less lugubrious, and if he killed his patients with a joke.

From Paris, the 10th of the first moon of Rabia, 1714

Letter 64
The Chief Black Eunuch to Usbek, at Paris

I am in a state of perplexity that is beyond my power to describe, magnificent lord. The seraglio is in appalling disorder and confusion. Your wives are at war with one another, your eunuchs on different sides. There is nothing to be heard but complaints, protests, and recriminations. My admonitions are ignored. It seems as if nothing is forbidden in this time of laxity, and my title has no meaning in the seraglio.

Each of your wives considers herself superior to the others because of her birth, her beauty, her intelligence, or your love; each of them flaunts some of these claims in order to have every kind of favour. Every moment I lose my habitual patience, which unhappily has dissatisfied all of them. My foresight, my indulgence even, which is such an uncommon, alien quality in the post that I hold, have been useless.

Do you wish me to disclose the cause, magnificent lord, of all this disorder? It lies entirely in your own heart, in your tender affection for your wives. If you did not restrain my hand, if instead of using admonitions you allowed me to punish, if, without letting yourself be softened by their complaints and their tears, you were to send them to weep in front of me, whom nothing softens, I would soon shape them to the yoke that they have to bear, and wear down their wilful and imperious temperament.

Having been carried off, at the age of fifteen, from the depths of Africa, my country, I was immediately sold to a master who had more than twenty wives or concubines. Having decided from my serious, taciturn air that I would be suitable for the seraglio, he ordered that my suitability should be definitely ensured, and had the operation performed on me. It was painful for a time, but beneficial later, since it gave me access to my masters' presence and gained me their confidence. I entered the seraglio, which for me was a new world. The Chief Eunuch, the sternest man I have seen in my life, ruled it with complete authority. Discord and quarrelling were never heard of. A deep silence prevailed everywhere. All the wives were sent to bed at the same time all the year round, and were woken up at the same time. They entered the bath each in turn, and left it at the slightest indication that we wished them to do so. For the rest of the time they were almost always shut in their rooms. One of his rules was to keep them absolutely clean, and he took an infinite amount of care over it. The slightest refusal to obey was mercilessly punished. 'I am a slave,' he would say, 'but I belong to a man who is your master as well as mine, and the power I use over you was given me by him. It is he who punishes you, not I; my hand is merely his instrument.' These women never went into my master's room unless they were summoned. They would receive this favour with delight, but were deprived of it without complaint. And finally I myself, the least important of the black eunuchs in this peaceful seraglio, was a thousand times more respected than I am in yours, where I command them all.

As soon as the great eunuch knew my character, his choice fell on me. He mentioned me to my master, saying that I would be capable of carrying out his ideas, and of taking over the post that he held. He was not put off by my extreme youth, believing that my assiduity would compensate for lack of experience. There is little more to tell; I had soon gained his confidence to such an extent that he no longer made any difficulty about letting me take charge of the keys to the awesome place that he had guarded for such a long time. It was under this great master that I learnt the difficult art of commanding, and trained myself in the principles of inflexible government. Under him I studied women's hearts. He taught me how to take advantage of their weaknesses and not to be imposed upon by their imperiousness. He would often enjoy watching me drive them to the furthest pitch of obedience; then he would gradually let them come back, and wanted me, for a time, to seem to give way myself. But he was at his best at moments when he found them on the brink of despair, full of entreaties and reproaches. He endured their tears without emotion, and would take pride in this kind of triumph. 'That,' he would say with satisfaction, 'is how to control women. It does not alarm me that there are a lot of them; I would look after all the wives of our great monarch in the same way. How can a man hope to capture their hearts, if his faithful eunuchs have not begun by subjugating their minds?'

He did not only possess firmness, but penetration as well. He could read their thoughts and their concealments. Their contrived gestures, their false expressions, hid nothing from him. He knew of their most secret actions and most private remarks. He would use them to spy on each other, and was pleased when he was able to reward even the most trivial information. Since they did not enter their husband's presence except when they were told in advance, he summoned which of them he wanted, drawing his master's attention to the one he had in mind. This mark of distinction was the reward for revealing some secret. He had persuaded his master that it was good for discipline if the choice was left to him, so that he would have greater authority. That was the method, magnificent lord, used to govern a seraglio which in my opinion was the best regulated in Persia.

Let me have a free hand. Allow me to make myself obeyed. A

week will re-established order in the midst of confusion. It is what your prestige requires and your security demands.

From your seraglio in Ispahan, the 9th of the first moon of Rabia, 1714

Letter 65
Usbek to his wives, at the seraglio in Ispahan

I am told that the seraglio is in disorder, full of quarrels and internal strife. Did I not urge you, when I left, to live together peacefully and in mutual understanding? You gave your promise: was it in order to catch me out?

It is you who would be caught if I decided to follow the Chief Eunuch's advice, and to employ my authority so as to make you behave in the manner that I recommended to you.

I am unable to use such violent methods until I have tried all the others, so do for your own sake what you have declined to do for mine.

The Chief Eunuch has good reason to complain, for he says that you have no respect for him. How can you reconcile such behaviour with the propriety that is suitable to your situation? Is it not he who in my absence is responsible for your virtuous behaviour? It is a holy treasure, of which he is the guardian. But the contempt which you exhibit towards him shows that those who are burdened with the duty of seeing that you abide by the laws of honour are themselves burdensome to you.

I urge you, then, to change your conduct, and behave in such a way that I shall be able to reject, another time, the suggestions which have been put to me, and which are prejudicial to your freedom and peace of mind.

For I would like you to forget that I am your master, and remember only that I am your husband.

From Paris, the 5th of the moon of Shaaban, 1714

Letter 66
Rica to ★★★

They are very keen on the pursuit of knowledge here, but I cannot say that they know a great deal. A man who doubts everything when speaking as a philosopher does not dare, as a theologian, to doubt anything; he is inconsistent, but always content with himself so long as the terms of reference have been agreed.[1]

The majority of Frenchmen have a mania for being clever, and the majority of those who want to be clever have a mania for writing books.

Yet no plan could be worse. Nature, in her wisdom, seems to have arranged it so that men's stupidities should be ephemeral, and books make them immortal. A fool ought to be content with having exasperated everyone around him, but he insists on tormenting future generations; he wants his foolishness to overcome the oblivion which he might have enjoyed like a tomb; he wants posterity to be informed that he existed, and to be aware for ever that he was a fool.

Of all writers, there are none whom I despise more than anthologists, who search on all sides for scraps out of other people's works, which they cram into their own like slabs of turf into a lawn.[2] They are no better than compositors arranging letters so that in combination they will form a book, for which they have done nothing but provide the use of their hands. I should like the originality of a book to be respected, and it seems to me that there is a kind of profanation in removing its component parts from their sanctuary and exposing them to contempt when they do not deserve it.

When a man has nothing new to say, why doesn't he keep quiet? Why do things have to be used twice over? 'But I want to put them in a new order.' 'What a clever thing to do! you come into my library, you move books from a high shelf to a low one, and from a low shelf to a high one: a fine piece of work that is!'

I am writing to you on this subject, ★★★, because I am irritated beyond endurance with a book that I have just given up; it is so thick that it looks as if it ought to contain everything that there is to know, but it has given me enormous trouble to read and failed to teach me anything.

From Paris, the 8th of the moon of Sha̧aban, 1714

Letter 67
Ibben to Usbek, at Paris

Three ships have put in here without bringing me news of you. Are you ill? or does it amuse you to make me anxious?

If you do not show me friendship in a country where you have no ties, what will it be like in the middle of Persia, surrounded by your family? But perhaps I am mistaken: you have the ability to make friends anywhere. The heart is a native of any country; how could someone with a fine nature prevent himself from forming friendships? I confess that I respect old alliances, but I do not object to making new ones wherever I am.

Whatever country I have been living in, I have behaved as if I were to spend my life there. I have felt the same enthusiasm for virtuous people, the same compassion, or rather tenderness, towards those in misfortune, the same esteem for those who have not been blinded by prosperity. That is my way, Usbek; wherever I find men, I shall choose myself friends.

Here there is a man of the Gabar[1] nation who, I think, has next to you the first place in my heart. He is the very soul of probity. For private reasons he was obliged to retire to this town, where he lives quietly on the proceeds of a respectable business, with a wife whom he loves. His life has been full of magnanimous actions, and although he wishes to live in obscurity he has greater heroism in his heart than the greatest of kings.

I have talked to him about you a thousand times. I show him all your letters, and have noticed that he enjoys them; I can already see that you have a friend who is unknown to you.

Here you will find his principal adventures. Despite his reluctance to write them down, he was unable as a friend to refuse them to me, and I confide them to you in the same way.

THE STORY OF APHERIDON AND ASTARTE[2]

'I was born among the Gabars, to a religion which is perhaps the most ancient in the world. I had the misfortune to be affected by love before acquiring the use of reason. Hardly was I six years old when I could not exist without my sister. My eyes were always fixed on her, and when she left me for a moment, she would find them filled with tears on her return. Each day my love increased with my age. My father, who was amazed by this powerful attraction, would willingly have married us to each other, following the ancient Gabar custom that was introduced by Cambyses,[3] but fear of the Muslims, to whose authority we are subject, prevents the members of our nation from considering these holy alliances, which are ordained rather than merely permitted by our religion, and in which the bond already formed by nature is so exactly mirrored.

'My father therefore, seeing that it would be dangerous to follow my, and his, inclinations, decided to extinguish our love, which he thought was newly born, but which was already at its height. He used a journey as an excuse to take me away with him, leaving my sister with one of his female relatives (for my mother had died two years earlier). I will not describe the despair we felt on being separated. I embraced my sister, who was in floods of tears, but I did not shed any myself, for grief had made me virtually insensible. We arrived at Tbilisi, where my father left me to be brought up by a relative and went back home.

'Some time later, I learnt that through the influence of a friend of his he had got my sister into the king's harem,[4] where she was in the service of a sultana. It would not have been a harder blow to me if I had been told that she was dead, for apart from the fact that I now had no hope of seeing her again, her entry into the harem meant that she had become a Muslim, and in accordance with the prejudices of her new religion she was now obliged to look on me with horror. Meanwhile, unable to remain in Tbilisi, weary with myself and with life, I had returned to Ispahan. My first words were bitter to my father. I reproached him for having sent his daughter to a place which it was possible to enter only by changing her religion. "You have brought down on your family," I told him, "the anger of God and of the sun who gives you light. What you have done is worse than if you had defiled the elements, since you have defiled your daughter's soul, which is no less pure. I shall die of grief and love; but may my death be the only punishment that God inflicts on you!" With these words I left, and spent the next two years of my life looking at the walls of the harem and watching the places where my sister might be, running the risk a thousand times a day of being massacred by the eunuchs who patrol around this fearful place.

'At last my father died. The sultana whose servant my sister was, seeing her beauty increasing every day, became jealous, and married her to a eunuch who passionately desired her. In this way my sister left the seraglio and together with her eunuch took a house in Ispahan. It was three months before I could talk to her, for the eunuch, who was jealous as any man could be, was always putting me off on various pretexts. At last I was admitted to his harem, and he made me talk to her through a screen. Even with the eyes of a lynx I should have been unable to make her out, she was so covered in clothes and veils, and I could recognize her only by the sound of her voice. What were my feelings on seeing that I was both so near and so remote from her! I contained myself, for I was being watched. As for her, it seemed to me that she shed a few tears. Her husband tried to make some feeble excuses, but I treated him as if he were the most despicable slave. He was completely at a loss when he saw me talking to my sister in a language which was unknown to him. It was ancient Persian, our sacred language.

'"So, sister!" I said, "is it true that you have given up the religion of your fathers? I know that when you entered the harem you had to declare yourself a Muslim, but tell me if your heart agreed like your lips to give up a religion by which I am enabled to love you? And for whom have you abandoned this religion which should be so dear to us? – for a wretch who is still disgraced by the chains he has worn, who, if he were a man at all, would be the most abject of them all."

'"Brother," she said, "the man of whom you speak is my husband.

I am bound to honour him, even though he seems unworthy to you, and I too would be the most abject of women if . . ."

'"Ah! sister," I said, "you are a Gabar. He is not your husband, and cannot be. If you have the faith of your fathers, you must regard him merely as a monstrosity."

'"Alas!" she said, "how distant that religion seems to me! I scarcely knew what it ordained before having to forget it. As you see, the language which I am speaking is no longer familiar to me, and I have the utmost difficulty in expressing myself; but you may be certain that the memory of our childhood still fills me with delight, and that since that time the only pleasures I have had have been illusory; that not a day has passed without my thinking of you, that you counted for more than you realize in my marriage, and that the only thing that made me decide to go through with it was the hope of seeing you again. But this day has cost me enough already: what is the price that still remains to be paid? I can see that you cannot control yourself, and my husband is trembling with rage and jealousy. I shall never see you again; I am doubtless speaking to you for the last time; if that were so, brother, my life will not be a long one." At these words she was overcome by her emotions, and realizing that she was in no state to keep up the conversation she went away, leaving me the most grief-stricken of men.

'Three or four days later I asked to see my sister. The brutish eunuch would have been glad to prevent me, but apart from the fact that a husband of that sort does not have the same authority over his wife as others do, he loved my sister so violently that he was unable to refuse her anything. I saw her in the same place again, with the same veils, and accompanied by two slaves, so that I resorted to our own language. "Sister," I asked, "how is it that I cannot see you without being placed in this dreadful situation? These walls that shut you in, with their bolts and bars, these infamous guards watching you, put me into a rage. How did you come to be deprived of the pleasures of being free, which your ancestors had? Your mother, who was so chaste, gave her husband no other guarantee of her virtue than her virtue itself. They lived in mutual trust and happiness together, and to them their simple way of life was more valuable by far than the false glitter which you seem to be enjoying amidst the luxury of this house. When you lost your religion, you lost your freedom, your happiness, and the precious gift of equality, which is the honour of your sex; but what is worse, you are not the wife, since you cannot be, but the slave of a slave who has been cut off from humanity."

"'Ah brother!" she said, "be more respectful to my husband, and to the religion that I have chosen, according to which I cannot listen to you or speak to you without committing a crime."

"'What, sister!" I said, beside myself, "do you believe that it is true then, this religion of yours?"

"'Ah!" she said, "how convenient it would be for me if it were not! I have sacrificed too much for its sake not to believe in it, and if my doubts . . ." At these words she fell silent.

"'Yes, sister? – your doubts, whatever they are, are well founded. What can you expect from a religion which makes you unhappy in this world and gives you no hope for the next? Remember that ours is the oldest religion in the world, that it has never ceased to flourish in Persia, and that it originated with the Persian empire, the beginnings of which are unknown; that it was only by chance that the religion of Mohammed was introduced, and that his sect established itself not by persuasion, but by conquest. If it were not for the weakness of our rightful princes, you would see the religion of the ancient magi still in force. If you go far back into the past, what you will hear everywhere is the voice of Magism, not of the Islamic sect, which several thousand years later was not even in its infancy."

"'But," she said, "even if my religion is younger than yours, it is at least purer, since it worships God alone, whereas you worship in addition the sun, the stars, fire and even the elements."

"'I can see that among the Muslims, sister, you have been taught to calumniate our sacred religion. We do not worship the stars or the elements, nor have our ancestors ever worshipped them; they never built temples to them, nor sacrificed to them; they simply revered them, in a religious manner, as being emanations and manifestations of the divinity. But in the name of God who gives us light, sister, take this book that I have brought for you. It is the book of our lawgiver Zoroaster. Read it without prejudice. Open your heart to the rays of light which will illumine you as you read. Remember your forefathers who honoured the sun for so many years in the holy city of Balkh, and finally remember me, whose hopes of peace, fortune and life depend entirely on your conversion." Transported with emotion, I departed, and left her on her own to make the most important decision in my life.

'I went back two days later. I said nothing, but waited silently for the verdict that meant life or death to me. "You are loved, brother," she said, "and the woman who loves you is a Gabar. It was a long struggle, but oh gods! what obstacles cannot be removed by love? How relieved I feel! I am no longer afraid of loving you too much. I can love you without restraint; even loving you to excess is legitimate. Ah! how exactly that matches my feelings! But although you have been able to break the chains that my mind has forged for itself, when will you break those which tie my hands? From now on I give myself to you. Show me how much you value the gift by your promptness in taking it. When I can embrace you for the first time, brother, I think I shall die in your arms." Nothing I say could properly express the joy that I felt at these words. I thought that I must be, and in fact became, from one instant to the next, the happiest of men. I saw everything I had ever wanted in twenty-five years of life on the point of being accomplished, and all the sorrows that had made life such a burden disappearing. But when I had become a little more accustomed to these delightful ideas, I realized that I was not so close to being happy as I had imagined at first, even though I had overcome the greatest obstacle that stood in my way. I had to circumvent the vigilance of her guards; I dared not confide the vital secret to anyone: I had nobody but my sister and she had nobody but me. If the attempt failed, I ran the risk of being impaled, but there was no punishment that seemed worse than failure. We agreed that she would send me a request for a clock that her father had left her, and that I would put a file inside, to cut through the shutters of a window over the street, and a knotted rope to climb down with; that I would not continue to see her, but go and wait every night beneath the window until she carried out her plan. I spent fifteen whole nights without seeing anyone, because she had not been able to find a suitable moment. At last, on the sixteenth night, I heard the sound of a file. Now and again there would be an interruption, and in the intervals I felt inexpressibly afraid. After an hour's work, I saw her tying the rope; she let herself go and slid down into my arms. I was no longer aware of danger, and remained motionless for a long time. I led her outside the town, where I had a horse ready, mounted her behind me, and so escaped, at a speed that may be imagined, from a place which could have been disastrous to us both.

'Before daybreak we arrived at the house of a Gabar, in a deserted spot to which he had retired, living frugally on what he produced by his own work. We thought it better not to stay with him, and on his advice we went into a thick forest, and settled ourselves in the hollow trunk of an old oak until the excitement caused by our escape had died down. Together we lived in this remote habitation, unseen by anyone, constantly repeating that we would love each other for ever and waiting until the opportunity came for a Gabar priest to perform the marriage ceremony prescribed by our holy books. "Sister," I would say to her, "how blessed our union is! We were united by nature, and our sacred laws will unite us again." At last a priest arrived and calmed the impatience we felt to be lovers. He performed all the marriage ceremonies in the peasant's house, blessed us and wished us a thousand times over all the vigour of Vishtaspa and the holiness of Aurvataspa.[5] Soon afterwards we left Persia, where we were not safe, and withdrew to Georgia. We lived there a year, our delight in each other increasing every day. But since my money was nearly gone and I was afraid of being poor, for my sister's sake rather than my own I left her to seek help from our family. Our farewells were the tenderest ever known. My journey, however, was not only futile but disastrous, for having discovered on the one hand that all our goods had been confiscated, and on the other that our relatives were almost powerless to help me, I brought back only just enough money for my journey. But what despair I felt on finding my sister gone! A few days before my return some Tartars had raided the town she was in, and finding her beautiful they took her and sold her to some Jews who were on their way to Turkey, leaving only a little girl to whom she had given birth a few months earlier. I set off after the Jews and caught up with them three leagues away. My tearful entreaties were in vain. They wanted thirty tomans,[6] and refused to take even a toman off the price. Having sought help from everyone, and begged for the protection of both Turkish and Christian priests, I approached an Armenian merchant. I sold him my daughter and myself as well for thirty-five tomans. I went to the Jews, gave them thirty tomans and took the remaining five to my sister, whom I had not yet seen. "You are at liberty, sister, and I can embrace you; here are five tomans that I have brought for you. I am sorry that they did not pay more for me."

"'What!" she said, "have you sold yourself?"

"'Yes," I said.

"'Ah! wretched man, what have you done? Was my misfortune not great enough already without being added to by your efforts? It consoled me to think that you were free; to think of you in slavery will bring me to the grave. Ah, brother, how cruelly you love! And my daughter; I do not see her?"

"'I sold her also," I said. We both broke down and wept, without having the strength to say anything to each other. Finally I went to find my master. My sister arrived almost at the same time as myself and threw herself at his feet. "What I ask is slavery," she said, "as others ask for freedom. Take me: you will sell me for more money than my husband." The dispute that then ensued brought tears to my master's eyes. "For shame!" she said, "did you think I could accept liberty at the expense of yours? Master, you see here an unhappy pair who will die if they are separated. I give myself to you, pay for me. Perhaps the money, and the work I shall do for you, may one day obtain a favour that I do not dare to request from you. It is in your interest not to separate us: let me assure you that his life depends on me." The Armenian was a kind man, and was touched by our misfortunes. "If you both work for me with loyalty and enthusiasm, I promise that in a year's time I will give you your freedom. I can see that neither of you deserves to be in such unhappy circumstances. If when you are free you have the good luck that you deserve, if fortune is kind to you, I am sure that you will compensate me for the loss that I shall incur." We both fell at his knees, and followed him on his travels. We comforted each other through the labours of our servitude, and I was delighted when I had been able to do the work alloted to my sister.

'The end of the year arrived, our master kept his word, and set us free. We returned to Tbilisi. There I found an old friend of my father's who had made a successful career in medicine in the town. He lent me some money, which I used to do some trade. Later some business affairs brought me to Smyrna, where I settled down. I have lived here for six years, and enjoy the sweetest and most loving relationship in the world. Harmony reigns in my family, and I would not change places with any king on earth. I have been lucky enough to find the Armenian merchant to whom I owe everything, and I have done some important services for him.'

From Smyrna, the 7th of the second moon of Jomada, 1714

Letter 68
Rica to Usbek, at ★★★

The other day I went to have dinner with a legal man, who had asked me several times to do so. Having discussed many things I said to him: 'It seems to me, sir, that your profession must be extremely difficult.'

'Not as difficult as you imagine,' he replied. 'Our manner of doing things means that it is simply a way of passing the time.'

'But surely, isn't your head always full of other people's business? Are you not continually preoccupied with things which are no concern of yours?'

'You are right to say that such things are not our concern, for we do not concern ourselves with them at all, and that in itself means that the profession is less tiring than you said.'

When I saw that he was so off hand about the matter, I went further and said: 'Sir, I have not seen your study.'

'I can well believe it, for I haven't got one. When I took this post, I needed some money to pay for it; I sold my library, and the book-seller who took it left me, out of a fantastic number of volumes, only my household accounts book. It is not that I regret losing them: we judges are not puffed up with empty learning. What point is there in having all those volumes of laws? Almost every case is hypothetical or is an exception to the general rule.'

'But perhaps, sir, the reason is that you make it an exception. For after all, why would every nation in the world have laws if they had no application? And how can you apply them if you do not know what they are?'

'If you knew the lawcourts,' the legal man replied, 'you would not speak as you do. We have living books, I mean barristers. They do the work for us and take the responsibility of instructing us.'

'And are they not sometimes also responsible for deceiving you?' I answered. 'It would be sensible, therefore, to prevent yourselves from falling into the traps they set. They have weapons with which to assail your sense of equity; it would be a good idea for you to be armed as well, in order to defend it, and not to go lightly dressed into the thick of a battle with people covered in armour all over.'

From Paris, the 13th of the moon of Shaaban, 1714

Letter 69
Usbek to Rhedi, at Venice

You would never have imagined that I had become more of a metaphysician than I was already, but such is the case, and you will be convinced of it when you have been subjected to this outburst of philosophizing from me.

The most sensible of the philosophers who have reflected on the nature of God have said that he is a being of supreme perfection, but have seriously misused this concept. They have enumerated all the perfections that man is capable of possessing or of imagining, and have applied them to the idea of divinity without realizing that these attributes are often incompatible, and cannot subsist in the same subject without invalidating each other.

The Western poets relate that there was a painter[1] who, having decided to do a portrait of the goddess of beauty, gathered together the most beautiful women in Greece, and selected the most attractive feature of each, which he combined together so as to make a likeness of the most beautiful goddess of all. If someone had thereupon deduced that she was blonde and dark, her eyes blue and black, and that she was both mild and imposing, he would have made a fool of himself.

God often lacks a perfection which could cause him to have a serious imperfection, but he is never limited except by himself; he is his own necessity. Thus although God is omnipotent, he cannot break his promises, or deceive mankind. Often, indeed, the lack of power is not in God but in things, which are relative; and that is the reason why he cannot alter the essences of things.

So that there is no cause to be surprised if some of our theologians have dared to deny that God has infinite foreknowledge, on the grounds that it is incompatible with his justice.

Despite the boldness of this idea, it is admirably adapted to metaphysical treatment. According to metaphysical principles it is not possible for God to foresee things which are determined by the decision of a free cause, because what has not yet happened does not exist, and in consequence cannot be known, since nothingness has no properties and cannot be perceived. God cannot make out an act of will which does not exist or, in a soul, see something which is not there, for until the soul has reached a decision the action by which it is determined is not in it.

The soul is the instrument of its own determination, but there are occasions when it is undecided to a sufficient extent for it not even to know which course to decide on. Often indeed it comes to a decision only in order to make use of its liberty, so that God cannot see the decision in advance, either in the actions of the soul or in the action exerted on it by objects.

In what way could God foresee things which are determined by the decision of a free cause? There are only two ways in which he could see them: by conjecture, which is inconsistent with infinite prescience; or else by seeing them as effects which are necessary, in that they inevitably follow from a cause which also produces them inevitably; and this is even more contradictory. For the presupposition would be that the soul is free, but it would not be so in fact, any more than a billiard-ball is free to move when struck by another one.

However, you must not think that I want to limit the extent of God's knowledge. Since he makes created beings act as he wishes, he knows everything that he wants to know. But although he can see everything, he does not always use his power. He usually allows created beings the possibility of taking action or not, so as to allow them the possibility of showing merit or demerit; at these times he renounces his right to influence and determine them. But when he wants to know something, he always knows it, because he has only to want it to come to pass as he sees it, and make created beings act in accordance with his will. It is in this manner that he selects, among all the things that are purely possible, the things that must happen, fixing the future decisions of a mind by his decrees, and depriving it of the power which he granted it of acting or not acting.

If I may use a comparison for something which transcends comparisons: suppose that a monarch does not know what his ambassador will do in some important matter. If he wants to know, he has only to order him to take a certain course, and he can be certain that what he intends will come to pass.

The Koran and the books of the Jews contradict the dogma of absolute prescience continually. In them God never appears to know the future decisions of minds, and this seems to have been the first truth that Moses revealed to mankind.

God puts Adam in the terrestrial paradise on condition that he will not eat a certain fruit, a requirement which would be absurd in a being who knew the future decisions of the soul; for after all, could such a being attach conditions to the favours he bestows without making them meaningless? It is as if someone who knew about the capture of Baghdad were to say to another person: 'I will give you a hundred tomans if Baghdad is not captured.' Would it not be a very bad joke?

My dear Rhedi, why so much philosophy? God is so high that we cannot even see his clouds. We know him properly through his precepts alone. He is measureless, spiritual, infinite. May his grandeur remind us of our weakness; always to be humble is to worship him always.[2]

From Paris, the last day of the moon of Shaaban, 1714

Letter 70
Zelis to Usbek, at Paris

Suleiman, your friend, is in despair over an insult that he has just suffered. For the past three months a young fool by the name of Suphis had been a suitor for the hand of his daughter. He seemed satisfied with the girl's looks from the reports and the description of her that he had been given by women who had seen her in childhood; the dowry had been agreed on, and everything had gone without incident. Yesterday, after the preliminary ceremonies, the daughter left the house on horseback, escorted by her eunuch and covered from head to foot by her clothes, as the custom is. But as soon as she arrived at the house of her husband-to-be he had the door shut against her, and swore that he would refuse to have her unless the dowry was increased. The families on both sides came in haste to put the matter right, and after many protests Suleiman agreed to make a small present to his son-in-law. The marriage rites were performed and the girl was taken to the marriage-bed not without violence; but an hour later, the young fool got up in a rage, slashed her face in several places, asserting that she was not a virgin, and sent her back to her father. This outrage has shaken him as deeply as anyone could be. There are some who maintain that the girl is innocent.[1] It is dreadful for fathers to be exposed to such insults. If my daughter were treated in such a way, I think it would make me die of grief.

Farewell.

From the seraglio of Fatme, the 9th of the first moon of Jomada, 1714

Letter 71
Usbek to Zelis

I feel all the more sorry for Suleiman since there is no way of putting the damage right, and his son-in-law has not done anything prohibited by law. I find it very harsh that this law should make a family's honour depend on the caprices of an idiot. It is pointless to say that there are infallible methods of ascertaining the truth in such matters: that is a long-standing fallacy which has now been exposed, and our doctors' arguments against the reliability of these methods are irrefutable. Even the Christians regard them as chimerical, although they are clearly expounded in their holy books, and according to their ancient legislator[1] every girl's innocence or guilt depended on them.

It is good to hear of the care that you are taking over the upbringing of your own daughter. God grant that her husband may find her as fair and pure as Fatima, that she may have ten eunuchs to guard her, that she may be the honour and the adornment of the seraglio which she is destined to enter, that over her head there may be nothing but ceilings of gold and nothing but sumptuous carpets under her feet! And as my final wish, may my eyes see her in all her glory!

From Paris, the 5th of the moon of Shawall, 1714

Letter 72
Rica to Usbek, at ★★★

I was in company the other day and saw a man who was extremely satisfied with himself. In a quarter of an hour he had decided three questions of ethics, four problems of history, and five scientific matters. Never have I seen such a universal decisioneer; his mind was never troubled by the slightest doubt. We turned from intellectual questions to current affairs; he decided about current affairs. Wanting to catch him out, I said to myself: 'I must put myself in a strong position. I shall take refuge in my country.' I mentioned Persia to him, but I had hardly uttered four words when he contradicted me twice over, on the authority of books by Messrs Tavernier and Chardin.[1] 'Good Lord!' I said to myself, 'what sort of a man is this? In a moment he'll know the streets of Ispahan better than I do!' My mind was soon made up: I fell silent and let him talk; and he is still deciding.

From Paris, the 8th of the moon of Dulkaada, 1715

Letter 73
Rica to ★★★

I have been told about a kind of tribunal called the French Academy. It is the least respected court of law in the world, for they say that as soon as it gives a decision the people quashes its verdict, and subjects it to laws that it is obliged to follow.[1]

Some time ago now, in order to assert its authority, it made a compilation of its judgements: this child, with so many fathers, was approaching old age when it was born, and although it was legitimate, a bastard which had already appeared almost smothered it at birth.

The members of the tribunal have no work to do except to chat endlessly: eulogy appears of its own accord, so it seems, in their eternal gossip, and as soon as they are initiated into its mysteries they are seized by a mania for panegyrics,[2] which never leaves them.

This body has forty heads, all full of images, metaphors, and antitheses. All these mouths hardly utter anything except exclamations. Its ears want to hear harmonious cadences all the time. As for its eyes, there is nothing to be said; it seems to be equipped for speaking, but not for seeing. Its feet are unsteady, since time, which is its bugbear, unsettles it at every moment, and destroys everything that it has done. People used to say once that its hands were grasping, but I shall say nothing about that, leaving it to be decided by those who know better than I.[3]

These oddities, ★★★, are unknown to us in Persia. Our minds have no inclination for such bizarre and extraordinary institutions; we always want to be natural in our simple customs and spontaneous manners.

From Paris, the 27th of the moon of Dulheggia, 1715

Letter 74
Usbek to Rica, at ★★★

Some days ago a man I know said to me: 'I promised to introduce you to the best houses in Paris; I am now taking you to see a great lord who is one of the best men in the kingdom at keeping up his position.'

'What do you mean, sir? Is he more polite, or more affable than other men?'

'No,' he said.

'Aha! I have it. He makes anyone who goes near him constantly aware of his superiority to them; if it's like that, I don't need to see him; I concede everything, and accept my sentence.'

But I had to set off just the same, and I saw such a haughty little man, he took a pinch of snuff so arrogantly, he blew his nose so remorselessly, he spat with such a phlegmatic air, he patted his dogs in a manner which was so offensive to mankind, that my wonder and admiration never flagged. 'Goodness!' I said to myself, 'if when I was at the Persian court I had kept up my position like that, it would have been a very foolish position!' We should have had to be very ill-natured, Rica, to go and inflict hundreds of petty insults on people who came to see us daily to show us their goodwill. They knew quite well that we were above them, and, if they had not, the benefits we provided would have made it clear to them each day. We did not need to do anything to make ourselves respected, so we did everything we could to be agreeable. We made ourselves available to the least important members of society. Surrounded by magnificence, which always hardens the heart, they found that we were sympathetic, and saw that it was only our feelings that were above them; we would descend to the level of their needs. But when it was necessary to maintain the dignity of the king at public ceremonies, when it was necessary to make foreigners treat the nation with respect, when finally it was necessary, in situations of danger, to put heart into the soldiers, we ascended a hundred times further than we had descended. Our faces resumed their expression of pride, and it was sometimes felt that we had kept up our position rather well.

From Paris, the 10th of the moon of Saphar, 1715

Letter 75
Usbek to Rhedi, at Venice

I must admit to you that I have not observed among Christians the same lively faith in their religion that is to be found among Muslims. It is a long way with them from professing their religion to belief in it, from belief to being convinced, and from being convinced to practising it. Religion does not so much provide an opportunity for regeneration as for controversy, in which everyone takes part. Courtiers, soldiers, women even, rise up in opposition to the clergy and ask for things to be proved, when they have resolved not to believe them. It is not that they have made up their minds rationally, and have taken the trouble to examine the truth or falsity of the religion that they are rejecting; they are rebels who, having felt the weight of their yoke, have shaken themselves free before becoming acquainted with it. Consequently, they are no more steadfast in their incredulity than in their faith, but live in an ebb and flow of belief which carries them ceaselessly from one to the other. One of them said to me one day: 'I believe in the immortality of the soul periodically. My opinions depend entirely on my physical condition. According to whether I have greater or less vitality, or my digestion is functioning well or badly, or the atmosphere I breathe is thick or thin, or the food I eat is light or heavy, I am a Spinozist, a Socinian or a Catholic, unbelieving or devout. When the doctor is at my bedside, my confessor has the advantage. I know how to prevent religion from disturbing me when I am well, but I allow it to console me when I am ill: when I have no hope left in that respect, along comes religion and wins me over by its promises; I am quite willing to surrender myself to it so as to die with hope on my side.'

A long time ago the Christian kings freed all the serfs in their states because, they said, Christianity makes all men equal. It is true that this act of religion was extremely useful to them: it was a means of diminishing the power of the nobles, by removing the lower classes from their control. Subsequently they made conquests in countries where they realized that it was advantageous to have slaves. They gave permission for them to be bought and sold, forgetting the religious principle which had affected them so deeply. Shall I tell you what I think? – what is true at one time is false at another. Why do we not do the same as the Christians? It is very naïve of us to refuse to found colonies and make conquests in a favourable climate, when we could easily do so,★ because the water is not pure enough there for us to wash according to the precepts of the holy Koran.[1]

I give thanks to Almighty God, whose envoy is the great prophet Ali, that I belong to a religion which has priority over all human interests and is as pure as Heaven, whence it is descended.

From Paris, the 13th of the moon of Saphar, 1715

Letter 76
Usbek to his friend Ibben, at Smyrna

In Europe the law treats suicides with the utmost ferocity. They are put to death for a second time, so to speak; their bodies are dragged in disgrace through the streets and branded, to denote infamy, and their goods are confiscated.

★ The Muslims do not bother to capture Venice, because they would not be able to find any water there for their rites of purification.

It seems to me, Ibben, that these laws are very unjust. When I am overcome by anguish, poverty, or humiliation, why must I be prevented from putting an end to my troubles, and harshly deprived of the remedy which lies in my power?

Why am I required to work for a society from which I consent to be excluded, and to submit against my will to a convention which was made without my participation? Society is based on mutual advantage, but when I find it onerous what is to prevent me renouncing it? Life was given to me as a favour, so I may abandon it when it is one no longer; when the cause disappears, the effect should disappear also.

Would the king want me to be subject to him when I derive no advantages from being a subject? Can my fellow-citizens be so unfair as to drive me to despair for their convenience? Is God to be different from every other benefactor, and is it his will that I should be condemned to accept favours which make me wretched?

I am obliged to obey the law so long as I continue to live under its authority, but when I no longer do so does it still apply to me?

But, it will be said, you are disturbing the providential order. God united your soul to your body, and you are separating them; you are therefore going against his intentions, and resisting him.

What does that imply? Am I disturbing the order of Providence when I modify the arrangement of matter and turn a sphere into a cube, when it had been given its spherical shape by the first laws of motion, that is to say the laws of creation and conservation? Of course not: I am merely exercising a right which I have been given; and in this sense I could disrupt the whole of nature at will, and it would be impossible to say that I am opposing Providence.

When my soul is separated from my body, will the universe be less orderly or less well arranged? Do you believe that the new synthesis will be less perfect, or less dependent on general laws, or that the world will have lost anything by it? that the works of God will be any the less great, or rather less immense? When my body has been turned into a grain of wheat, or a worm, or a piece of turf, do you think that these products of nature are less worthy of her? or that when my soul has been purged of every terrestrial ingredient it will be less exalted?

All such ideas, my dear Ibben, originate in our pride alone. We do not realize our littleness, and in spite of everything we want to count for something in the universe, play a part, be a person of importance. We imagine that the annihilation of a being as perfect as ourselves would detract from nature as a whole, and we cannot conceive that one man more or less in the world, and indeed the whole of mankind, a hundred million heads like ours, are only a minute, intangible speck, which God perceives simply because of the immensity of his knowledge.

From Paris, the 15th of the moon of Saphar, 1715

Letter 77[1]
Ibben to Usbek, at Paris

My dear Usbek, it seems to me that for a true Muslim misfortune is less a punishment than a threat. Those days which encourage us to expiate our wrongs are precious indeed; it is our periods of prosperity that need to be curtailed. What is the point of all this impatience, except to demonstrate that we want to be happy independently of him who gives all felicity, being felicity itself?

If something is composed of two elements,[2] and the necessity for preserving the union between them is more indicative of obedience to the orders of the Creator, then it is possible for it to have been made into a religious law; if this necessity for preserving their union is a surer guarantee of men's actions, then it is possible for it to have been made into a civil law.

From Smyrna, the last day of the moon of Saphar, 1715

Letter 78
Rica to Usbek, at ★★★

I enclose a copy of a letter[1] which was sent here by a Frenchman who is in Spain, and which I think you will enjoy reading.

I have been travelling through Spain and Portugal for six months, living with two peoples who hold every other nation in contempt; the French alone have the honour of being hated by them.

The outstanding feature of both nations is their solemnity. It manifests itself in two principal ways: wearing spectacles and having a moustache.

Spectacles demonstrate conclusively that their owner is a man of consummate learning, so deeply buried in study that it has weakened his eyesight; any nose which they adorn, or encumber, undeniably qualifies as the nose of a scholar.

As for moustaches, they are respected on their own account, independently of the circumstances, though sometimes they can be of the greatest value to the king's service and to national honour, as was well shown by a famous Portuguese general★ in the Indies;[2] for, finding himself in need of money, he cut off one side of his moustache and sent it to the citizens of Goa as a pledge, with a request for twenty thousand pounds. The loan was granted at once, and later he honourably redeemed his pledge.

It will readily be imagined that nations as serious and phlegmatic as these are likely to have their pride, and so they do. It is usually based on two factors of the utmost importance: those who live in continental Spain and Portugal have a great feeling of inner superiority if they are what they call 'old Christians,' which means not descended from people whom the Inquisition had persuaded to take up Christianity in recent centuries;[3] and those who live in the Indies are no less pleased with themselves when they reflect that they possess the supreme merit of being, as they call it, 'men of white flesh.' No queen in the Ottoman emperor's harem ever took such pride in her beauty as the oldest and ugliest ruffian does in the dingy olive whiteness of his complexion, sitting with his arms crossed in his doorway in a Mexican town. A man

★ Juan de Castro

of such importance, a creature so perfect, would not go to work for all the treasure in the world, and could never bring himself to compromise the honour and dignity of his skin by degrading menial toil.

For it must be realized that in Spain, when a man has some talent, as for instance when in addition to the qualities I have just mentioned he is the proprietor of a large sword, or has learnt from his father the art of twanging away at an out-of-tune guitar, he does no more work. His honour is connected with the repose of his limbs. A man who sits down for ten hours a day receives precisely half as much respect again as another man who sits for five only,⁴ because it is on chairs that nobility is acquired.

But although these invincible enemies of work put on a show of philosophical serenity, it does not extend down to their hearts, for they are permanently in love. No one on earth is more willing to die of love-sickness under their mistresses' windows, and a Spaniard who is not suffering from a cold cannot expect to be regarded as a true lover.

They are devout first and foremost, and secondly jealous. They would never expose their wives to the attentions of a crippled soldier or a decrepit functionary, but they will shut them up with an ardent young monk who lowers his eyes, or a sturdy Franciscan who raises them.

They allow their wives to appear in public with their breasts uncovered, but refuse to allow their heels to be seen, so that they will not be taken unawares by the feet.

People say everywhere that the rigours of love are cruel, but they are even more so for Spaniards. The women do cure their sufferings, but it is only to replace them with another kind, and they are often left with a prolonged and distressing memory of a vanished passion.

They are polite in minor ways which in France would seem out of place. For example, an officer never beats one of his men without asking his permission, and the Inquisition never burns a Jew without making an apology.

Those Spaniards who do not get burnt seem to be so attached to the Inquisition that it would be churlish to take it away from them. All I should like is that another should be established, not against heretics, but against those who encourage heresy, by attributing the same efficacity to trivial monkish practices as to the seven sacraments, by idolizing anything that they revere, and by being so devout that they are scarcely Christian.

You can find intelligence and sense among the Spaniards, but do not look for it in their books. If you saw one of their libraries, with romances on one side and scholastic philosophy on the other, you would say that its parts had been created, and put together to form a whole, by some secret enemy of human reason.

The only good book that they have produced is one which reveals the absurdity of all the others.[5]

They have made enormous discoveries in the New World, and do not yet know their own continent. There are bridges across their rivers which have not yet been discovered, and nations* as yet unknown to them in their mountains.[6]

They say that the sun rises and sets in their territory, but it must be added that on its way it sees nothing but derelict countryside and empty wastes.

I should not be sorry, Usbek, to see a letter written to Madrid by a Spaniard travelling in France; I am sure that he would be able to avenge his country. What immense scope there would be for a thoughtful and cool-headed man! I imagine him beginning his description of Paris like this:

'Here they have a building to put madmen in; you will at once conclude that it is the largest in the town, but no, the remedy is completely inadequate for the disease. Presumably the French, who are much criticized by their neighbours, put a few madmen inside a building so as to give the impression that the ones outside are sane.'

So much for my Spaniard. Farewell, Usbek.

From Paris, the 17th of the moon of Saphar, 1715

Letter 79
The Chief Black Eunuch to Usbek, at Paris

Yesterday some Armenians brought a young Circassian slave to the seraglio, wanting to sell her. I took her into the secret apartments, undressed her, and examined her critically. The more I examined her, the more attractions I found; with virginal modesty she seemed to want to conceal them from my sight. I could see what it cost her to obey: she reddened at finding herself naked even in front of me,

* The Batuecas.

who am exempt from any passion which might be alarming to chaste women, am indifferent to the power of their sex, and, being an agent of modesty, can be completely free in my actions while having nothing but chastity in my eyes, and inspiring nothing but innocence.

As soon as I had judged her worthy of you I lowered my eyes, put a scarlet gown around her and a golden ring on her finger, and prostrated myself at her feet; I worshipped her as the queen of your heart. I paid the Armenians and hid her from all eyes. Happy Usbek! you possess more beauties than there are in all the palaces of the Orient. What a pleasure it will be for you to find the most ravishing things in Persia on your return, and to see beauty reborn in your seraglio while time and habit combine to destroy it!

From the seraglio of Fatme, the 1st of the first moon of Rabia, 1715

Letter 80
Usbek to Rhedi, at Venice

During my stay in Europe, my dear Rhedi, I have seen many sorts of government. It is different from Asia, where the rules of politics are the same everywhere.

I have often tried to decide which government was most in conformity with reason.[1] I have come to think that the most perfect is the one which attains its purpose with the least trouble, so that the one which controls men in the manner best adapted to their inclinations and desires is the most perfect.

If a nation is as obedient under a mild government as when the government is strict, the first alternative is preferable, because it is more in conformity with reason and because harshness is an extraneous factor.

You may be certain, my dear Rhedi, that however cruel the penalties are in a state, they do not make people more obedient to the law. In countries where punishments are moderate, they are as much feared as where they are despotic and terrible.

Whether the government acts with moderation or with cruelty, there are always different degrees of punishment; major or minor penalties are applied to major or minor crimes. The imagination adjusts itself automatically to the customs of the country that one is in. A week's imprisonment, or a small fine, impress the mind of a European who has been brought up in a humane country as greatly as the loss of an arm would intimidate an Asian. Each of them attaches a certain degree of fear to a certain degree of punishment, but interprets it in his own way: despair at incurring disgrace will overwhelm a Frenchman sentenced to a penalty that would not make a Turk lose a quarter of an hour's sleep.

Furthermore, I do not see that public order, justice, and equity are better preserved in Turkey, or Persia, or under the Mogul, than in the republics of Holland, Venice, or even England.[2] I do not see that fewer crimes are committed there, or that men are more law-abiding because they are intimidated by the magnitude of the penalties.

I notice on the contrary a source of injustice and persecution at the centre of these states.

I even find that the prince, who is the law itself, is less in control than anywhere else.

I see that at such times of severe repression there are always tumultuous disturbances, where no one is in command, and that once the authority of violence is disregarded no one has any authority to re-impose it; that the certainty of being punished strengthens and extends disorder; that in these states there is never a minor rebellion, nothing between protest and insurrection; that there is no longer any necessity for important events to depend on important causes: instead, the slightest incident produces a major revolution, which is often as little foreseen by its agents as by its victims.

When Osman, the Turkish emperor,[3] was deposed, none of the men who performed the deed had any intention of carrying it out; they were simply petitioners asking for some cause of complaint to be put right. A voice which was never identified came by chance from the crowd, the name of Mustapha was uttered, and suddenly Mustapha was emperor.

From Paris, the 2nd of the first moon of Rabia, 1715

Letter 81
Nargum, the Persian envoy to Muscovy, to Usbek, at Paris

Of all the nations in the world, my dear Usbek, there is none which has surpassed the Tartars[1] in the glory or the magnitude of its conquests. This nation truly dominates the universe; all the others seem fit only to be its servants. It both creates and destroys empires; in every period of history it has proved its power across the earth, in every age it has been the scourge of nations.

The Tartars have conquered China twice, and still have it under their control.[2]

They are dominant in the vast lands which form the Mogul Empire.[3]

As masters of Persia, they hold the sceptre of Cyrus and Vishtaspa;[4] they have subjugated Muscovy; under the name of Turks,[5] they have made enormous conquests in Europe, Asia, and Africa, and they dominate these three parts of the world. To refer to more remote times, it is from among them also that came some of the nations which overthrew the Roman Empire.[6]

What are the conquests of Alexander in comparison with those of Genghis Khan?

This victorious nation lacked nothing, except historians to celebrate the memory of its miraculous achievements. How many of its immortal deeds lie buried in oblivion, how many nations whose origins are now unknown were founded by it! A warlike nation, solely concerned with its present glory and certain of conquering at any time, it did not think of making itself known to the future by the memory of its conquests in the past.

From Moscow, the 4th of the first moon of Rabia, 1715

Letter 82
Rica to Ibben, at Smyrna

Although the French are great talkers, among them are to be found dervishes of a taciturn kind called Carthusians. They are said to cut out their tongues on entering the monastery,[1] and everyone would be very pleased if all the other dervishes were to remove everything which, because of their profession, is no further use to them.

While I am on the subject of taciturn people, I should mention another much more peculiar kind. Their talent is the extraordinary one of knowing how to talk without saying anything. They can keep a conversation going for two hours, while making it impossible to tell what they mean, copy them, or remember a word that they have said.

This sort of person is worshipped by women, but not to the same extent as others on whom nature has bestowed the agreeable talent of smiling at the appropriate moment, that is to say all the time, and who favour anything a woman says with joyful approbation.

For them, the height of wit is to see hidden meanings in everything, and find a thousand clever little implications in the most ordinary remarks.

I have come across others who have done well to bring inanimate things into the conversation, by making their embroidered suit, their blond wig, their snuff-box, stick and gloves speak on their behalf. It helps when they can start to make themselves heard from the street, by driving up noisily in their carriages and banging loudly with the door-knocker: this introduction augurs well for the remarks that are to follow; after such a fine beginning we can put up with all the subsequent idiocies, which have the good fortune to arrive later.

You can take my word for it that these little talents, of which no account would be taken at home, are extremely useful here, for anyone who is fortunate enough to possess them, and that a sensible man cuts a poor figure by comparison.

From Paris, the 6th of the second moon of Rabia, 1715

Letter 83[1]
Usbek to Rhedi, at Venice

If there is a God, my dear Rhedi, he must necessarily be just; for if he were not, he would be the worst and most imperfect being of all.

Justice is a relation of suitability, which actually exists between two things. This relationship is always the same, by whatever being it is perceived, whether by God, or by an angel, or finally by a man.

It is true that men do not see these relationships all the time. Often, indeed, when they do see them, they turn away from them, and what they see best is always their self-interest. Justice raises its voice, but has difficulty in making itself heard amongst the tumult of the passions.

Men are capable of unjust actions because it is in their interest to do them, and they prefer their own satisfaction to that of others. They always act with reference to themselves – no one is gratuitously wicked; there must be a determinant reason, and this reason is always a reason of self-interest.

But it is not possible that God should ever do anything unjust. Once it is assumed that he perceives what is just, he must necessarily act in accordance with it, for since he has no need of anything, and is sufficient to himself, he would be the wickedest of all beings if he were wicked without self-interest.

Consequently, even if there were no God, we should nonetheless still love justice, that is to say, make an effort to resemble this being of whom we have so exalted a conception, and who if he existed would be just necessarily. Even if we were to be free of the constraints of religion, we ought not to be free of those imposed by equity.

It is this, Rhedi, which has led me to think that justice is eternal, and does not depend on human conventions. Even if it were to depend on them, this truth would be a terrible one, and we should have to conceal it from ourselves.

We are surrounded by men who are stronger than we are. They can do us harm in a thousand different ways, and threequarters of the time they can do it with impunity. What peace of mind it is for us to know that all these men have in their hearts an inner principle which is on our side, and protects us from any action that they might undertake against us!

But for that, we should be perpetually afraid. We should walk about among men as if they were wild lions, and we should never be sure for a moment of our possessions, our happiness, or our lives.

All these reflections make me indignant with theologians who represent God as a being who exercises his power tyrannically, making him behave in a way in which we should not want to behave ourselves for fear of offending him; they attribute to him all the imperfections that he punishes in us, and contradictorily represent him sometimes as an evil being, sometimes as a being who hates evil and punishes it.[2]

When a man takes stock of himself, how satisfying it is for him to conclude that he has justice in his heart! – it may be an austere pleasure, but it is bound to cause him delight, as he realizes that his state is as far above those without justice as he is above tigers and bears. Truly, Rhedi, if I were sure that I could put into practice, constantly and unfailingly, that equity which I can visualize, I should consider myself supreme among men.

From Paris, the 1st of the first moon of Jomada, 1715

Letter 84

Rica to ★★★

Yesterday I went to the Hôtel des Invalides.[1] If I were a king, to have founded this establishment would make me as happy as if I had won three battles. Throughout, it shows the hand of a great monarch; I think it must be more worthy of respect than any other place on earth.

What a spectacle it is to see together in this one spot all these martyrs to their country, drawing breath only in order to defend it, and, with the same feelings as before, though without their former strength, complaining of nothing except their powerlessness to sacrifice themselves for it again!

What could be more admirable than to see these enfeebled warriors observing discipline in their place of retirement, as strictly as if they were forced to do so by the presence of an enemy, seeking a last satisfaction in this imitation of war, and dividing their hearts and minds between the duties of religion and those of military skill!

I should like the names of soldiers who die for their country to be preserved in churches, and inscribed in registers which would become as it were the foundation of glory and nobility.

From Paris, the 15th of the first moon of Jomada, 1715

Letter 85
Usbek to Mirza, at Ispahan

Once, as you know, Mirza, some of Shah Suleiman's[1] ministers made a plan to force all the Armenians in Persia either to leave the kingdom or to become Muslims, in the belief that our empire would be contaminated as long as infidels remained within it.

It would have put an end to the greatness of Persia if blind religious piety had had its way on this occasion.

Nobody knows why the plan came to nothing. Neither those who made the proposal, nor those who rejected it, foresaw the consequences; it was chance that took over the functions of reason and good government, and saved the empire from a danger greater than if it had been defeated in battle and suffered the loss of two towns.

To have proscribed the Armenians would have meant wiping out in a single day all the businessmen and almost all the skilled workers in the kingdom. I am sure that the great Shah Abbas[2] would sooner have had his two arms cut off than to have signed such a decree, and that in sending his most highly-skilled subjects away to the Mogul and other Indian kings he would have felt as if he were presenting them with half his territory.

The persecutions that our Muslim zealots have inflicted on the Gabars have forced large numbers of them to emigrate to India, causing Persia to lose a nation which was dedicated to agriculture:

they were the only people capable of doing the work necessary to overcome the sterility of our soil.

All that the zealots needed to do was to strike a second blow and wreck our industry, thus ensuring that the empire fell of its own accord, and with it, by an inevitable consequence, that same religion whose growth it was intended to encourage so vigorously.

Assuming that we should reason without prejudice, Mirza, I think that it is just as well for there to be several religions in a state.

It is noticeable that the adherents of a tolerated minority religion normally make themselves more useful to their country than the adherents of the dominant religion, because they are disqualified from high office and can distinguish themselves only by having money and possessions; they are therefore likely to work in order to acquire these things, and will undertake the most ungrateful social functions.

Furthermore, since in every religion there are precepts which are useful to society, it is as well that they should be obeyed with enthusiasm, and what is more likely to encourage this enthusiasm than a multiplicity of religions?

They are rivals who forgive each other nothing. This emulation influences even private individuals: everyone is on his guard, afraid of doing something which would dishonour his side, and expose it to the pitiless contempt and criticism of the other side.

That is why it has always been observed that the introduction of a new sect into a society was the surest method of remedying all the defects of the old one.

It is no use to say that it is not in the king's interest to allow more than one religion in the state. Even if every religion in the world gathered together there it would not do him any harm, since every single one of them commands obedience and preaches respect for authority.

I admit that the history books are full of religious wars; but it should be carefully noted that these wars are not produced by the fact that there is more than one religion, but by the spirit of intolerance, urging on the one which believed itself to be dominant.

It is this proselytizing spirit that the Jews acquired from the

Egyptians, and which from them passed like a nation-wide epidemic to the Muslims and the Christians.

It is in sum a spirit of dizzy madness, the spread of which can only be regarded as the total eclipse of human reason.

For after all, even if there were no inhumanity in doing violence to other people's consciences, even if it produced none of the bad effects which flow from it in thousands, one would have to be out of one's mind to think of the idea. Someone who tries to make me change my religion does so only, I presume, because he would not change his own, even if attempts were made to compel him; so that he finds it strange that I will not do something that he would not do himself, perhaps not even to be ruler of the world.

From Paris, the 25th of the first moon of Jomada, 1715

Letter 86
Rica to ★★★

Here it seems as if families are left to govern themselves. Husbands have only a vestige of authority over their wives; it is the same with fathers and children, or masters and slaves. The law intervenes in every dispute between them, and you can be sure that it is always against the jealous husband, the bad-tempered father, or the awkward master.

The other day I went to see the place where justice is administered. Before you get there you have to run the gauntlet of an infinite number of pretty shop-girls,[1] calling to you in deceptive voices. This initial scene is pleasant enough, but it becomes dismal when you go into the main rooms, where the only people you see are dressed in a manner that is even more gloomy than their faces. Finally, you enter the sanctum where all the family secrets are revealed, and the most private acts are brought into the open.

It is here that a girl modestly comes and explains the torments of protecting her virginity too long, her struggles, and her painful efforts to resist; so unassuming is she about her victory that she threatens soon to be defeated, and in order that her father may no longer remain ignorant of her needs she makes them clear to the entire public. Then a woman comes shamelessly in to describe the outrages she has done to her husband as a reason for being separated from him.

With equal delicacy another comes to say that she is tired of bearing the title of wife without enjoying her rights. She reveals the mysteries hidden in the darkness of marriage, and demands to be handed over for examination by the greatest experts, so that a verdict from them will restore to her all the rights of virginity. There are even those who dare to issue a challenge to their husbands, and ask for the encounter to take place in public,[2] although it is so difficult before witnesses; it is a trial which is as humiliating for the wife who is successful as for the husband who fails.

An infinite number of girls who have been ravished or seduced make men seem much worse than they are. The court reverberates with love; all you hear of is enraged fathers, deceived daughters, faithless lovers and dissatisfied husbands.

According to a law which is followed there, any child born in wedlock is to be considered as the husband's; even if he has good reason not to believe it, the law believes it for him, and spares him any inquiries or scruples.

In this court decisions go by majority vote, but it is said that experience has shown that it would be better to follow the minority opinion. Which is natural enough, for there are very few good minds, and everyone agrees that there is an infinite number of bad ones.

From Paris, the 1st of the second moon of Jomada, 1715

Letter 87
Rica to ★★★

Man is said to be a sociable animal: from this point of view, it seems to me that a Frenchman is more human than other men, human in the highest degree, for he seems to have been made uniquely for society.

Moreover, I have noticed people here who are not merely sociable, but are in themselves an entire society. They multiply in every corner; in a single moment they inhabit every district in a town; a hundred men of this kind make a bigger crowd than a population of two thousand. They would be able, in the eyes of foreigners, to compensate for the ravages of plague or famine. Whether a body can be in more than one place simultaneously is debated in the universities: they can prove what philosophers argue about.

They are always in a hurry, because they have important business to do, which is to ask everyone they see where they are going and where they have come from.

It would be impossible to stop them thinking that the proper thing to do is to visit the public one by one every day – without counting the mass visits they make in places of common resort: a short cut of this kind counts for nothing in their rules of procedure.

Front doors suffer more from the way they bang the knocker than from winds and storms. If you were to examine the visitors' books in porters' lodges you would find their names misspelt in a thousand different ways each day, in Swiss handwriting.[1] They spend their lives at funerals, on visits of condolence, or offering their congratulations on a marriage. Whenever the king confers a favour on one of his subjects, it costs them the price of a carriage across town so as to express their delight. At last, worn out, they go home to rest, in order to resume their tiring duties next day.

The other day one of them died of fatigue, and the following epitaph was put on his tomb:

Here rests a man who never rested before. He attended 530 funerals. He rejoiced at the birth of 2,680 children. The royal pensions on which he congratulated his friends, in different terms each time, amount to £300,000; the distance he covered along the pavement to 9,600 furlongs, and the distance he covered in the country, to thirty-six. His conversation was entertaining: he had a supply of 365 stories ready for use; since his youth he had also possessed 118 aphorisms taken from the ancients, which he used on special occasions. He finally died in his sixtieth year. Traveller, I say no more: for how could I ever finish the description of what he did and what he saw?

From Paris, the 3rd of the second moon of Jomada, 1715

Letter 88
Usbek to Rhedi, at Venice

In Paris, liberty and equality prevail: neither birth, nor virtue, nor even success in war, however outstanding, can save a man from being lost in the crowd. Social jealousy is unknown. They say that the leader of Parisian society is the man who has the best horses to his carriage.

A great lord is a man who sees the king, speaks to ministers, and has ancestors, debts, and government pensions. If, in addition, he can conceal the fact that he has nothing to do by looking busy, or by pretending to be fond of the pleasures of life, he thinks himself the most fortunate of men.

In Persia, a man becomes a great lord only if the monarch gives him some share in the government;[1] here, there are men who are great because of their birth, but they are without influence. Kings, like skilful craftsmen, always use the simplest devices to carry out their tasks.

Influence at court is the great French god. Its high priest is the chief minister, and many are the victims that he sacrifices to it. Its acolytes are not arrayed in white; sometimes priests and sometimes victims, they dedicate themselves, together with the whole nation, to their idol.

From Paris, the 9th of the second moon of Jomada, 1715

Letter 89
Usbek to Ibben, at Smyrna

The desire for fame and glory is no different in kind from the instinct for self-conservation which every creature possesses. We seem to be adding to what we are when we are able to impose ourselves on the memory of others; we acquire a new life, which becomes as precious to us as the one we receive from Heaven.

But, just as not all men are equally attached to life, they are also unequally influenced by glory. It is a noble emotion which, certainly, is always enshrined in their hearts, but their mentality and upbringing modify it in countless ways.

These differences which are found between individuals are even more noticeable between one nation and another.

It can be stated as a principle that, in each country, the desire for glory increases in proportion to the liberty of the subject, and diminishes similarly; glory is never coupled with servitude.

A man of sense said to me the other day: 'In France, in many respects, there is greater freedom than in Persia, and so there is a greater love of glory. This fortunate peculiarity makes a Frenchman, willingly and with pleasure, do things that your Sultan can only get out of his subjects by ceaseless exhortation with rewards and punishments.

'Consequently, with us, the sovereign jealously guards the honour of his lowliest subjects, and in order to protect it he has lawcourts¹ which are regarded with respect; they are a sacred national treasure, which is unique in that the sovereign does not control it. He could not do so without damaging his own interests, for if the sovereign should do wrong to the honour of a subject, he will immediately leave the king's court, employment and service, and retire to his home.

'The difference between French troops and your own is that the latter consist of slaves, who are naturally cowardly, and can overcome the fear of death only by the fear of being punished, which causes a new kind of terror in their souls and virtually stupefies them; whereas ours gladly face the enemy's attacks, banishing their fear by a satisfaction which is superior to it.

'But it seems that the sanctuary of honour, reputation, and virtue is to be found in republics, and the lands where men can speak of "my country". In Rome, Athens, and Sparta, honour alone was the reward for the greatest of services. A wreath of oak-leaves or laurel, a statue or public congratulations was an immense reward for winning a battle or capturing a town.

'In these cities, a man who had accomplished some great feat was sufficiently rewarded by the accomplishment itself. He could not meet any of his fellow-citizens without feeling the pleasure of having done something for him; he could calculate the extent of his services by the number of his countrymen. Everybody is ·capable of doing good to one man, but it is god-like to contribute to the happiness of an entire society.

'Now this noble feeling of emulation must surely be completely dead in the hearts of your Persians, since for them official positions and honours depend merely on the monarch's whim. Reputation and virtue are there considered unreal unless they are accompanied by royal favour, which brings them to life, and kills them too. A man whose reputation stands high with the public can never be sure that he will not be dishonoured tomorrow. Today he is the general of an army; the monarch is perhaps about to make him the royal cook, leaving him no hope of winning praise except by means of a good stew.'

From Paris, the 15th of the second moon of Jomada, 1715

Letter 90
Usbek to the same, at Smyrna

From this passion for glory that the French nation has in general, there has developed, in the minds of individuals, a certain something called the *point of honour*.[1] Properly speaking it characterizes every profession, but it is more noticeable among military people, where it is found in the highest degree. I should find it very difficult to make you appreciate what it consists in, for we have really no conception of what it is.

The French, especially the nobles, used in the past to observe scarcely any laws except those of this code of honour, which governed the conduct of their entire life. Its laws were so strict that it was impossible for a man not merely not to break them, but even to neglect the most trivial of their conditions.

When it was a matter of settling disputes, they had virtually one method only of deciding, by means of duelling, which eliminated every difficulty. But the trouble was that the decision involved other parties besides those immediately concerned.

If a man knew one of the parties, however slightly, he was forced into the quarrel, and had to suffer the consequences personally, as if he himself had had cause for anger. He invariably felt honoured by being chosen and by receiving such a flattering sign of favour; and a man who would have been reluctant to give someone else five pounds in order to save him from the gallows, him and his whole family as well, would make no bones about going to risk his life for him a thousand times over.

This method of deciding was not very well thought out, since from the fact that a man was stronger or more adroit than another it did not follow that his arguments were any better.

Consequently, kings have prohibited it on pain of severe penalties,[2] but in vain; honour, which always insists on being obeyed, becomes mutinous, and refuses to accept any law.

The French, therefore, are in a state of violent tension, for these same laws of honour oblige a man to avenge himself when he has been insulted; but conversely, the judge will condemn him to the most rigorous punishment when he takes his revenge. If he follows the laws of honour he dies on the scaffold, and if he follows those of justice he is banished for ever from the society of men: he cannot avoid the cruel dilemma of either dying, or being unworthy to live.

From Paris, the 18th of the second moon of Jomada, 1715

Letter 91
Usbek to Rustan, at Ispahan

There has appeared here a personage got up as a Persian ambassador,[1] who has insolently played a trick on the two greatest kings in the world. To the sovereign of the French people he brings gifts that our own monarch would not bestow on a king of Imeretia or Georgia;

by his disgraceful meanness he has tarnished the majesty of both empires.

He has made himself the laughing-stock of a nation which claims to be the most civilized in Europe, and has made people say in the West that the King of Kings rules only over barbarians.

He has received honours which he seems to be trying to have refused to him; and as if the French court cared more about the greatness of Persia than he does, it has treated him with dignity in front of a nation which despises him.

Say nothing of this at Ispahan; spare the unfortunate man's life. I do not want our ministers to punish him for their own carelessness in making such an unworthy choice.

From Paris, the last day of the second moon of Jomada, 1715

Letter 92
Usbek to Rhedi, at Venice

The monarch who has reigned for so long is no more.* He made many people talk in the course of his life; at his death all men were silent. In his last moments he was steadfast and courageous, and seemed to be yielding to destiny alone. Such was the death of the great Shah Abbas, who had filled the whole earth with his name.

You must not think that this great event has given rise to nothing but moral reflections here. Everyone has been thinking of his own interests, trying to get some advantage out of the change. The king is a great-grandson of the deceased monarch, and is only five years old, so a prince, his uncle, has been declared regent.

The late king had made a will limiting the authority of the regent, but he is an intelligent man and went to the Parlement, where after making clear all the rights due to his birth he had the provisions of the will set aside;[1] the dead king, in an effort to outlive himself, seemed to have claimed the right to go on ruling after his death.

The Parlements are like a ruin which can be trodden underfoot,

* He died on 1 September 1715.

but can still summon up the idea of a temple famous in some former religion. Almost the only function they still have is to dispense justice, and their authority always remains precarious unless some unexpected combination of events occurs to revive their life and strength. These great institutions have suffered the fate of human things: they have yielded to time, which destroys everything, to moral corruption, which weakens everything, and to the supremacy of the central authority, by which everything has been laid low.[2]

But the regent, wishing to render himself acceptable to the people, at once gave the impression of respecting this symbol of public freedom, and as if he had intended to raise from the earth both the temple and its idol, he wanted the Parlements to be regarded as a bastion of the monarchy and the basis of all lawful authority.

From Paris, the 4th of the moon of Rajab, 1715

Letter 93
Usbek to his brother, a santon[1] at the
monastery of Kazvin

I humble myself before you, holy santon, and prostrate myself; to me the ground beneath your feet is as it were the apple of my eye. Your sanctity is so great that the heart of our holy Prophet seems to reside in you; your austerities amaze Heaven itself; the angels look down from the heights of glory, saying: 'Why does he remain on earth, since his spirit is with us, in flight around the throne which stands on the clouds?'

And how could I not honour you, I who have been taught by our theologians that a dervish, even if he is an infidel, always has the mark of holiness which makes all true believers respect him, and that God, choosing souls purer than the rest for himself, in every corner of the earth, has removed them from the impious world, so that their mortifications and fervent prayers should turn away his wrath, suspended over all the nations which defy him?

The Christians say the most astonishing things about their first santons, thousands of whom took refuge in the atrocious deserts of the Thebaid, and whose chiefs were Paul, Anthony, and Pacomius. If what they say is true, their lives were as full of marvels as those of our most sacred imams. Sometimes they spent ten whole years without seeing a single person; but they lived with demons night and day. They were constantly tormented by evil spirits; they found them in bed, they found them at table; there was no escape. If all this is true, venerable santon, it must be admitted that nobody has ever lived in worse company.

Sensible Christians regard all these stories as having a perfectly natural allegorical meaning,[2] which may be of use in making us aware of the unhappiness of the human condition. It is in vain that we look for tranquillity in desert places, temptation will still be with us; our passions, symbolized by demons, will not leave us. These monsters in our hearts, these delusions of our minds, empty ghosts of error and mendacity, still appear before us in order to lead us astray, and attack us even amid fasting and penance; that is, even at our points of strength.

As for myself, venerable santon, I know that the messenger of God put Satan in chains, and hurled him into the abyss; he has purified the world, that was once in Satan's power, and made it fit for the angels and the prophets to dwell in.

From Paris, the 9th of the moon of Shaaban, 1715

Letter 94
Usbek to Rhedi, at Venice

Every discussion of international law that I have ever heard has begun with a careful investigation into the origin of society, which seems to me absurd. If men did not form societies, if they separated and fled from each other, then we should have to inquire the reason for it, and try to find out why they lived apart from each other: but they are all associated with each other at birth; a son is born in his father's home, and stays there: there you have society, and the cause of society.

International law is better known in Europe than in Asia, yet it can be said that royal passions, the submissiveness of their subjects, and sycophantic writers have corrupted all its principles.

In its present state, this branch of law is a science which explains to kings how far they can violate justice without damaging their own interests.[1] What a dreadful idea, Rhedi, to systematize injustice in order to harden their consciences, and turn it into sets of rules, laying down principles and deducing what follows from them!

The unlimited power of our sultans, which is governed only by itself, does not produce such monstrosities as this degradation of the intellect, which, though justice is unyielding, tries to make it pliable.

You would almost think, Rhedi, that there were two entirely different types of justice: one, regulating the affairs of private individuals, rules civil law; the other, regulating the differences that arise between nations, tyrannizes over international law; as if international law itself were not a kind of civil law, not indeed the law of a particular country, but of the world.

I will tell you my views on the subject in another letter.

From Paris, the 1st of the moon of Dulheggia, 1716

Letter 95
Usbek to the same

As between citizens, judges have to administer justice; as between nations, each nation has to administer it itself. In the second of these processes of justice the principles employed cannot be different from those which apply in the first.

Between nations it is seldom necessary to have a third party to act as judge, because the matters in dispute are almost always clear and easy to settle. The interests of two nations are usually so distinct that in order to make a just decision it is only necessary to love justice; it is difficult to be prejudiced in one's own cause.

It is not the same with the differences which arise between private individuals. Since they live in society, their interests are so entangled and confused, they come in so many different categories, that it is necessary for a third party to elucidate matters which each side, in its cupidity, tries to conceal.

There are only two cases in which war is just: first, in order to resist the aggression of an enemy, and second, in order to help an ally who has been attacked.

There would be no justice in making war on account of the private disputes of the monarch, except where the case was so serious as to warrant the death of the monarch or nation which was at fault. Thus a sovereign cannot make war because he is refused an honour due to him, or because his ambassadors have not been treated properly, or for other such reasons, any more than a private individual can kill someone who refuses to give him precedence.[1] The reason is that since a declaration of war should be an act of justice, which always requires the punishment to be appropriate to the crime, it is necessary to find out whether the enemy on whom war is declared deserves to be put to death. For to make war on someone is to want to inflict the death-penalty on him.

In international law war is the severest act of justice, since it can result in the destruction of a society.

To take reprisals is a penalty one degree less serious; a law which the courts have been unable to ignore is that the punishment must be measured by the crime.

A third act of justice is to deprive a sovereign of the advantages that we can bestow on him; still adjusting the punishment to the offence.

The fourth act of justice, which ought to be the commonest, is to withdraw from an alliance with a nation against which there are grounds for complaint. This penalty corresponds to banishment, which the courts brought into use so as to expel convicted criminals from society. Thus a monarch whose alliance we renounce is expelled from our society and ceases to be one of its members.

There is no greater insult to a sovereign than to renounce his alliance, and no way of doing him greater honour than to become his ally. Among men there is no greater cause for pride, and nothing more useful, than to have others permanently devoted to our protection.

But for the alliance to remain binding on us it must be just. Thus an alliance between two nations which was made in order to do harm to a third is not legitimate, and can be broken without committing any crime.

Indeed, it is not suitable for the honour and dignity of the monarch to ally himself to a tyrant. It is said that an Egyptian monarch sent a warning to the King of Samos about his cruelty and tyranny, and summoned him to mend his ways; as he failed to do so, he sent word that he was renouncing his friendship and his alliance.[2]

Conquest in itself confers no rights. If the population survives, conquest provides an assurance that peace will be maintained and that amends will be made for the wrong that had been committed; and if the population is destroyed, or scattered, it is a monument to tyranny.

Men regard peace-treaties with such veneration that they might almost be the voice of nature claiming its rights. They are all in accordance with law if their provisions permit both nations to continue in existence; if not, the one which is threatened with extinction may try, since it is deprived of its natural defence by a treaty of peace, to defend itself in war.

For nature, which has established the different degrees of power and weakness among men, has also often made the weak equal to the powerful through the strength of their despair.[3]

This, Rhedi, is what I call international law; this is the law of nations, or rather of reason.

From Paris, the 4th of the moon of Dulheggia, 1716

Letter 96
The First Eunuch to Usbek, at Paris

A large number of yellow-skinned women from the kingdom of Bijapur have arrived here. I have bought one of them for your brother the governor of Mazandaran, who sent me a month ago his revered orders with a hundred tomans.

I am a connoisseur of women, the more so because they cannot catch me off my guard. With me, the impulses of the emotions do not distract the eye.

I have never seen beauty so regular and perfect. The brilliance of her eyes brings her face to life, and enhances the quality of a complexion which could eclipse all the splendours of Circassia.

The chief eunuch of an Ispahan merchant was bidding for her against me, but she disdainfully avoided his eyes and seemed to be trying to catch mine, as if she wanted to say that a mere merchant was unworthy of her, and that she was destined for a more illustrious husband.

I confess that I feel a secret inner joy when I think of the beauty of this lovely young woman. I can imagine her appearing in your brother's seraglio: it gives me pleasure to foresee how taken aback his wives will be, some of them majestic in their affliction, and others mute but more distressed; the malicious satisfaction of those who have nothing left to hope for, and the stimulus given to the ambitions of those whose hopes still remain.

From one end of the kingdom to the other, I am going to cause a revolution throughout a whole seraglio. What passions I shall instigate! what fears and sorrows are in store!

And yet, despite this internal commotion, the exterior will be no less calm; great upheavals will be hidden deep inside the heart; chagrin will be absorbed and joy repressed; obedience will be just as punctilious, the rules just as inflexible; that meekness which will still have to be displayed will emerge from the very depths of despair.

We have observed that the more women we have to supervise, the less trouble they give. A greater need to be attractive, more difficulty in forming alliances, a larger number of examples of obedience: it all helps to keep them in servitude. They are all constantly spying on each other's behaviour; they might almost be collaborating with us so as to reduce their independence; they do some of our work for us, and open our eyes when we close them. Not only this, but they continually urge on their master against their rivals, failing to perceive the similarity between themselves and those who are punished.

But all this, magnificent lord, all this is as nothing, without the master's presence. What can we do with our empty shadow of authority, which can never be transferred completely? We represent only a half of yourself, and even that poorly; the only way for us to treat your wives is with odious strictness. You, on the other hand, temper fear with hope, and are more completely dominant when you make love than when you threaten.

Return here, therefore, magnificent lord, return and display your authority throughout the seraglio. Come back so as to soothe these desperate passions, to remove any pretext for disobedience, to pacify discontented love, and make an act of love out of duty itself; come back, finally, so as to relieve your faithful eunuchs of a burden which is growing heavier every day.

From the seraglio at Ispahan, the 8th of the moon of Dulheggia, 1716

Letter 97
Usbek to Hosain, a dervish of the mountain of Jahrum[1]

Oh wise dervish, whose inquisitive mind is so rich in knowledge, attend to what I have to say.

There are scientists here who have not, it is true, attained the peaks of Eastern wisdom; they have not been transported to the throne of light, nor heard the ineffable words resounding from angelic choirs, nor felt the fearful onset of divine ecstasy; but, left to themselves, bereft of these wonders of Heaven, they silently follow the path of human reason.

You would not believe how far this method has led them. They have put order into chaos, and explained by simple mechanics the organization of God's architecture. The creator of nature gave movement to matter: that is all that was needed to produce the prodigious variety of phenomena that we can observe in the universe.

It is for ordinary legislators to suggest laws for the regulation of human societies, laws which are as changeable as the minds of the men who invented them or the nations which obey them; but these others tell us only of general laws, immutable and eternal, which are observed without any exceptions, with infinite regularity, immediacy, and orderliness, in the immensity of space.

And what, oh man of God, do you think these laws consist in? You will perhaps imagine that having been allowed into the councils of the Eternal you are about to be lost in amazement at the greatness of these mysteries; you abandon in advance any hope of understanding, and expect to do nothing but admire.

But you will soon change your ideas. These laws do not dazzle the eye with misleading brilliance. Their simplicity caused them to be underestimated for a long time, and it is only after much reflection that their fertility and scope have been realized.

The first is that all bodies tend to travel in a straight line, unless they meet an obstacle which makes them change their course; and the second, which is simply a corollary of the first, is that all bodies moving in a circle around a centre tend to move away from it, because the further they are from it the more their course approximates to a straight line.[2]

There, sublime dervish, you have the key to nature; and from these fertile principles consequences without limit can be drawn.

The knowledge of five or six truths has filled natural science with miracles, and has allowed it to perform almost as many prodigious and wonderful feats as are to be found in all the stories of our holy prophets.

For after all, I am convinced that any of our theologians would have been at a loss if he had been told to weigh in a balance all the air which surrounds the earth, or to measure the total annual rainfall over its surface; and would have had to think for a moment or two before being able to say how many leagues sound travels in an hour, how long it takes for a ray of light to arrive here from the sun, how many yards it is from here to Saturn, or which sort of curve should be used in designing a ship so as to make it sail as well as possible.

If some man of God had phrased the works of these scientists in elevated and magnificent expressions, if he had added bold metaphors and mysterious allegories, he might perhaps have produced a fine work, which would have come second only to the holy Koran.

However, since I must say what I think, I don't really approve of ornate style. In our Koran there is a large number of trivialities, which

I shall always regard as such, although they are improved by the force and vividness of the writing. It might seem at first sight as if a book written under inspiration should contain the ideas of God conveyed in human language. In our Koran, on the other hand, you often find the language of God and the ideas of men, as if, by a remarkable act of caprice, God had dictated the words, while mankind provided the thoughts.

You will perhaps say that I am speaking too freely of the holiest thing we possess, and you will think that it is a result of the independence of life in this country. No; thanks be to Heaven, my mind has not corrupted my heart, and Ali will be my prophet as long as I live.

From Paris, the 10th of the moon of Shaaban, 1716

Letter 98
Usbek to Ibben, at Smyrna

In no other country in the world is fortune so inconstant as it is here. Every ten years there are upheavals which plunge rich men into destitution and swiftly raise the poor, as if on wings, to the heights of opulence. The former is bewildered by his poverty, and the latter by his wealth. The man who has just become rich is amazed at the wisdom of Providence, and the poor man at the blind inevitability of fate.

Those who collect taxes swim in a sea of treasure; among them, it is hard to find a Tantalus. They begin their career, however, in complete penury. They are treated like mud as long as they remain poor; when they are rich, they receive a certain amount of respect; accordingly they do everything in their power to be respected.

At the moment they are in a dreadful situation. A commission of inquiry has been set up, called the Chamber of Justice because it is going to seize all their money. They can neither elude suspicion nor conceal what they possess, for they are obliged to declare it in detail, on pain of death; so that they have to tread an extremely narrow path, I mean between their money and their life. To add to their misfortunes there is a minister, well known for his wit, who favours them with his jokes, and treats all the commission's deliberations humorously.[1] It is not every day that you find ministers who are prepared to make the public laugh, and he is to be congratulated on having tried it.

The profession of lackey deserves more respect in France than elsewhere, for it is a nursery of noble lords: it fills up the gaps left by other classes. Its members replace great men who have come to grief, legal officials who have been ruined, gentlemen killed in the paroxysms of war; and when they cannot take their places themselves, they restore great families by means of their daughters, who are a sort of manure for fertilizing land which is both high and dry.

I find, Ibben, that Providence is to be admired for the manner in which it shares out wealth: if it had been granted only to good people, it would not have been possible to differentiate clearly enough between it and virtue, and its worthlessness would not have been fully appreciated. But when you consider which people have accumulated the largest amounts of it, you come at last, through despising rich men, to despise riches.

From Paris, the 26th of the moon of Muharram, 1717

Letter 99
Rica to Rhedi, at Venice

I find that in France the capriciousness of fashion is amazing.[1] They have forgotten how they were dressed this summer; still less do they know how they will be dressed this winter. But the hardest thing of all to believe is how much it costs for a husband to keep his wife in fashion.

What use would it be to give you an exact description of their clothes and their accessories? A new fashion would come along and destroy all my work, together with that of their tailors, and before you had received my letter everything would have changed.

A woman who leaves Paris to spend six months in the country comes back looking as antiquated as if she had been away for thirty years. A son will fail to recognize a portrait of his mother because the dress in which she had been painted seems so alien to him; he will imagine that it is a picture of some Red Indian squaw, or that the artist decided to paint some fantasy of his own.

Sometimes women's hair styles gradually go up and up, until a revolution suddenly brings them down again. There was a time when because of their enormous height a woman's face was in the middle of her body. At another time her feet occupied the same position; her heels were pedestals supporting them in mid-air. It is almost beyond belief, but architects have often been obliged to make doorways higher, lower or wider according as women's fashions required such alterations, and the conventions of their profession have been subordinated to caprice. Sometimes you see a prodigious number of beauty-spots on a woman's face, and they all disappear the next day. Once women had waists and teeth; nowadays such things are out of the question. With this changing nation, whatever the humorists say, the daughters are different from their mothers.

It is the same with manners and modes of behaviour as with fashion: the French change their ways according to the age of their king. The monarch might even manage to make the nation serious if he were to attempt it. The sovereign imposes his attitudes on the court, the court on the town, and the town on the provinces; his mind is the pattern which determines the shape of all the others.

From Paris, the 8th of the moon of Saphar, 1717

Letter 100
Rica to the same

I was telling you the other day how extraordinarily capricious the French are about fashion. Yet it is incredible how obsessed they are with it; they relate everything to it: it is the standard by which they judge everything that happens in other countries; they always think that anything foreign is absurd. I admit that I find it hard to see how this infatuation with their clothes fits in with the inconstant way in which they alter them every day.

When I say that they look down on anything foreign, I am referring only to trivial things, for in matters of importance they seem to distrust themselves to the point of self-abasement. They cheerfully admit that other nations are wiser, provided you agree that they are better dressed; they are quite ready to be governed by the laws of a rival nation, provided that French wig-makers have jurisdiction over the shape of foreigners' wigs. They think that there is nothing finer than to see their chefs' recipes holding sway from the Pole to the Equator, and their hairdressers' creations conveyed to every dressing-table in Europe.

With all these noble advantages why should they care that they get their common sense from elsewhere, or that they have taken from their neighbours everything relating to political and civil government?

Who would think that the oldest and most powerful kingdom in Europe has been governed for more than ten centuries by laws which were not made for it?[1] If the French had been conquered it would not be hard to understand, but it is they who have been the conquerors.

They have abandoned their ancient laws, made by their first kings at national general assemblies, and the odd thing is that the Roman laws, which they adopted instead, were in part made and in part drafted by emperors who were contemporary with their own legislators.[2]

And in order to make their acquisitions complete, and to get all their good ideas from elsewhere,[3] they have taken over all the papal decrees, and used them to produce another section of their laws, and another form of servitude.

It is true that recently some of the statutes of their towns and provinces have been written down; but they are almost all taken from Roman law.

This mass of law that has been adopted, and so to speak naturalized, is so great as to overwhelm both justice and judges. But the volumes of law are as nothing in comparison to the terrible army of annotators, commentators, and compilers, a class of people whose lack of sense makes them as weak in the head as they are powerful because of their vast numbers.

This is not all: these foreign laws have brought with them procedural formalities which, carried too far, are a disgrace to human reason. It would not be easy to decide whether rules of procedure were more pernicious when they appeared in jurisprudence or when they installed themselves in medicine, whether they have done more damage in legal robes or beneath a doctor's wide hat, and whether in the one case they have ruined a larger number of people than they have killed in the other.

From Paris, the 12th of the moon of Saphar, 1717

Letter 101
Usbek to ✶✶✶

The Constitution is still being talked about here.[1] The other day I went into someone's house where the first thing I saw was a large man with a bright red face, saying in a loud voice: 'I have issued my pastoral letter, and I am not going to reply to everything you say; but just read the letter, and you will see that it resolves all your doubts. I had to work like a horse at it,' he said, mopping his brow. 'I put everything I knew into it, and I had to read a large number of Latin writers.'

'I can well believe it,' said a man who was there, 'for it is a fine work, and I would be ready to bet that the Jesuit who comes to see you so often couldn't have done a better one.'

'Well then, read it,' the other resumed, 'and you will be better informed about these matters in a quarter of an hour than if I had talked to you about them all day.' In this way he avoided being drawn into discussion or putting his self-satisfaction at risk. But under pressure he was forced to come out of his defences, and began, in a theological manner, to say a lot of silly things, with the assistance of a dervish who delivered them to him with great respect. When two men who were present denied some principle of his, he would immediately say: 'It is certainly so, we have judged it to be so; and we are infallible judges.'

'And how,' I said at this point, 'can you be infallible?'

'Can't you see,' he replied, 'that we are enlightened by the Holy Spirit?'

'That is just as well,' I answered, 'for from the way in which you have been talking all today, I perceive that you are in great need of being enlightened.'

From Paris, the 18th of the first moon of Rabia, 1717

Letter 102
Usbek to Ibben, at Smyrna

The most powerful states in Europe are those of the German Emperor and the kings of France, Spain and England. Italy and much of Germany are split up into an infinite number of little states whose princes, properly speaking, are the martyrs of the monarchical system. Our glorious sultans have more wives than some of them have subjects. The Italian princes, who are less united, are more to be pitied: their states lie open like caravanserais, and they are obliged to take in anyone who comes along; so they have to attach themselves to great rulers, bestowing fear rather than friendship on them.

Most European governments are monarchies; at least that is what they are called, for I do not know that there have ever been such things. At any rate, it would have been difficult for them to have existed for long in a pure form. Monarchy is a state of tension, which always degenerates into despotism or republicanism. Power can never be divided equally between prince and people: it is too difficult to keep the balance. The power must necessarily decrease on one side and increase on the other, but usually the ruler is at an advantage, being in control of the armed forces.

Thus the power of European kings is very great, and they can be said to have as much of it as they want; but they do not use it to the same extent as our sultans, first, because they do not want to go against their peoples' customs and religious beliefs, and second, because it is not in their interest to carry it so far.

There is nothing which does more to bring our rulers down to the level of their subjects than the immense power they have over them; there is nothing which makes them more vulnerable to the changes and caprices of fortune.

Their habit of having anyone who displeases them executed, at a wave of the hand, destroys the proper relationship between crime and punishment, which is as it were the soul of a state, and the harmony of empires; and the scrupulousness with which the Christian rulers preserve this relationship gives them an infinite advantage over our sultans.

A Persian, who through imprudence or bad luck has brought upon himself his sovereign's displeasure, is sure to die; the slightest fault, or the slightest caprice, can make it inevitable. But if he had made an attempt on his sovereign's life or had tried to betray his fortresses to the enemy, he could not have lost more than his life: so that he runs no greater risk in the latter case than in the former.

Consequently, if he is even slightly out of favour, seeing that death is certain and that there is no worse alternative, he is naturally inclined to subvert the state and conspire against the sovereign; it is his only resource.

It is different for the great European nobles, who when in disgrace have nothing to lose except their sovereign's favour and goodwill. They retire from court, and their only concern is to enjoy a quiet life and the benefits due to their rank. Since they are hardly ever put to death except for the crime of high treason, it is a crime which they are afraid to commit, out of consideration for what they have to lose and the little they stand to gain; which is why there are not many rebellions, and not many sovereigns who die by violence.

If our princes, with their unbounded authority, did not take so many precautions to preserve their lives, they would not survive for a day; and if they did not finance an innumerable number of troops, to tyrannize the rest of their subjects, their empire would not continue to exist for a month.

It is only four or five hundred years ago that a king of France[1] began to have guards, contrary to the custom of the period, in order to protect himself against some assassins that a minor Asian king had sent to kill him; until then kings had lived quietly in the midst of their subjects, like fathers among their children.

The kings of France, far from being able of their own accord, like our sultans, to take the life of one of their subjects, carry with them forgiveness for every crime, wherever they go. It is sufficient, in order that a man should cease to be unfit to live, for him to have the good fortune to have seen the face of his royal sovereign.² These monarchs are like the sun, which brings warmth and life everywhere.

From Paris, the 8th of the second moon of Rabia, 1717

Letter 103
Usbek to the same

Continuing the theme of my last letter, here, more or less, is what an intelligent European was saying to me the other day:

'Asian kings could have taken no worse course than to hide themselves as they do. They intend to inspire greater respect, but they inspire respect for royalty, not for the king, and fix their subjects' minds on a particular throne, not on a particular person.

'This invisible ruling power always remains identical for the people. Even if a dozen kings, whom they know only by name, were to slaughter each other in turn, they would not be aware of any difference: it would be as if they had been governed by a succession of phantoms.

'If the detestable murderer of our great King Henri IV¹ had carried out his crime on some Indian king, he would have been in control of the royal seal, and of a vast treasure accumulated, so it would have seemed, for his benefit, and he would calmly have taken over the reins of empire, without a single person thinking to protest on behalf of his king, or the royal family and children.

'People are surprised that there is scarcely ever any change in the methods of government used by oriental sovereigns: what other reason can there be except that their methods are tyrannical and atrocious?

'Changes can only be made by the sovereign or the people. But in these countries the king has no desire to make them, because, with power as extensive as his, he has everything that it is possible to have: if he changed anything, it could only be to his prejudice.

'As for the subjects, if one of them wants to put some resolution into effect he is unable to do anything to the State; he would have to get on equal terms, all at once, with a formidable power which is never divided. He lacks time as well as means. But he has only to go to the source of this power, and all he needs is a single arm and a single moment.

'As the murderer ascends the throne, the monarch descends, to fall and die at his feet.

'In Europe a disaffected subject makes plans to obtain secret information, go over to the enemy, capture some stronghold, or start some empty movement of protest among the people. In Asia such a man goes straight to the ruler, to startle, strike, and throw him down. He wipes out the very idea of him; from one moment to the next, he is slave and master, usurper and legitimate.

'Alas for the king who has but one head! His power seems to be wholly concentrated there only in order to show anyone with ambition where he can find it all in one place.'

From Paris, the 17th of the second moon of Rabia, 1717

Letter 104
Usbek to the same

Not all the nations of Europe are equally submissive to their rulers. The English, for example, with their restive disposition, hardly give their king the time to assert his authority. Meekness and compliance are the virtues on which they pride themselves least. They say the most extraordinary things on the subject. According to them, there is only one thing which can form a bond between men, and that is gratitude: husband and wife, father and daughter, are united only by their love for each other or the benefits they confer on each other; and these different motives for gratitude lie at the origin of every kingdom and every society.[1]

But if a ruler, so far from keeping his subjects happy, wants to tyrannize or destroy them, the basis of obedience is lost; nothing unites them, nothing attaches them to him; and they go back to their natural liberty. They maintain that unlimited authority can never be legitimate, because it can never have had a legitimate origin. For, they say, we cannot give someone else greater power over us than we have ourselves; ·we do not have limitless power over ourselves – for instance, we may not take our lives; therefore nobody, they conclude, has such a power.

The crime of high treason, according to them, is simply a crime committed by a weaker party against a stronger by disobeying, whatever form this disobedience takes. Thus the English people, finding themselves the stronger party in a conflict with one of their kings,[2] declared that it was a crime of high treason for a prince to make war on his subjects. They have therefore good reasons for saying that the precept in their Koran, to be subject to the powers that be,[3] is not very difficult to follow, since it is impossible for them not to follow it; and the more so because they are not required to submit to whoever is the most virtuous, but to the strongest.

The English say that one of their kings, having defeated and taken prisoner a prince who was a rival for his crown, wanted to reproach him for his disloyalty and treachery. 'It is only a moment ago,' said the unfortunate prince, 'that it was decided which of us is the traitor.'[4]

A usurper will declare that anyone who has not persecuted the country like him is a rebel; and in the belief that there is no law where he cannot see a judge, he causes the caprices of chance and fortune to be venerated as if they were the decrees of Heaven.

From Paris, the 20th of the second moon of Rabia, 1717

Letter 105
Rhedi to Usbek, at Paris

You wrote at some length, in one of your letters, about the development of the arts, science and technology in the West. You will think me a barbarian, but I do not know whether the utility that we derive from them compensates mankind for the abuse that is constantly made of them.

I have heard it said that the invention of explosives alone had deprived every nation in Europe of its freedom. Kings, unable any longer to entrust the protection of fortified towns to the townspeople, since they would have surrendered at the first cannonball, had a pretext for maintaining large numbers of regular troops, which they used subsequently to oppress their subjects.

You are aware that since the invention of gunpowder no fort is impregnable: which means, Usbek, that there is no asylum on earth against injustice and violence.

I am always afraid that they will eventually succeed in discovering some secret which will provide a quicker way of making men die, and exterminate whole countries and nations.

You have read the historians; you should look at them carefully. Almost every kingdom was established only because the arts and sciences were unknown, and destroyed only because they were cultivated to excess. We have an example familiar to us in the ancient Persian empire.

I have not been in Europe long, but I have heard intelligent people speak of the damage done by chemistry.[1] It seems to be a fourth scourge of mankind, which harms and destroys men piecemeal, but continually, while war, plague and famine destroy them wholesale, but at intervals.

In what way has the invention of the compass, and the discovery of so many peoples, been useful, except in that they have conveyed to us not so much their wealth, but their diseases?[2] Gold and silver had been accepted, by general agreement, as a means of paying for all goods and as a guarantee of their value, for the reason that these metals are rare and unfit for any other use: why then was it necessary for them to become commoner, and, in order to indicate the value of merchandise, for there to be two or three signs instead of one? It was simply more cumbersome.

But this invention was absolutely pernicious in another respect to the countries which were discovered. Whole nations were destroyed, and men who escaped death were reduced to such abject slavery that we Muslims shudder to think of it.

Happy is the ignorance of the children of Mohammed! It is a quality which, by its attractive ingenuousness, so dear to our holy Prophet, always reminds me of the simplicity characteristic of olden times, and the serenity which reigned in the hearts of our first fathers!

From Venice, the 5th of the moon of Ramadan, 1717

Letter 106
Usbek to Rhedi, at Venice

Either you do not believe in what you are saying, or else what you do is better than what you say. You leave your country in order to educate yourself, and you despise every type of education; in order to become cultivated, you go to a country where the arts are encouraged, and you consider them pernicious.

May I say, Rhedi, that I am more in agreement with you than you are yourself?

Have you ever thought about the state of barbarism and misery into which we should be plunged if knowledge and culture were to be lost – there is no need to imagine it, you could see for yourself: there are still tribes in the world among whom a reasonably well-educated ape could live and be respected; he would be on roughly the same level as the others; his ideas would not be considered peculiar, or his character strange; he would get by like anyone else, and indeed would stand out because of his gentle nature.

You say that founders of empires have almost all been ignorant of the arts of mankind. I will not deny that there have been barbarian races which, like rushing torrents, have managed to spread across the earth and overrun the best-organized kingdoms with their armies; but you must not forget that they have either learnt technical and artistic skills, or else have made the conquered peoples cultivate them; otherwise, their power would have vanished like the sound of thunder and storms.

You say that you are afraid of the discovery of some method of destruction that is crueller than those which are used now. No; if such a fateful invention came to be discovered, it would soon be banned by international law; by the unanimous consent-of every country the discovery would be buried. It is not in the interest of rulers to make conquests by such means: they ought to look for subjects, not territory.

You protest at the invention of gunpowder and shells; you find it surprising that there are no longer any impregnable strongholds; that is to say, you find it surprising that wars are over more quickly today than they used to be in the past.

You must have noticed in reading history that since the invention of gunpowder battles are much less bloody than they were, because there is hardly any hand-to-hand fighting.

And even if a particular instance were found in which some human skill was harmful, should it be rejected on that account? Do you think, Rhedi, that the religion brought down from Heaven by our holy Prophet is pernicious because one day it will be used to confound the faithless Christians?

You believe that knowledge and culture make nations soft, and therefore cause empires to fall, and you refer to the destruction of the ancient Persian empire as being due to its effeteness; but this example is far from being conclusive, since the Greeks, who conquered the Persians so many times, and subjugated them, cultivated the arts much more assiduously than they did.

When people say that the arts of civilization make men effeminate, they cannot at any rate be referring to the men who practise them; for they are never idle, and of all the vices idleness is the one which does most to diminish a man's courage.

The question therefore concerns only those who benefit from their skills. But since in a developed country those who enjoy the products of one skill are obliged to practise another if they are not to be reduced to poverty and disgrace, it follows that idleness and effeminacy are incompatible with the arts of civilization.

Paris, which is perhaps the most sensuous town in the world, is where pleasures are most subtly cultivated, but it is perhaps also the place where one leads the hardest life. For one man to live in luxury, a hundred others must work without respite. A woman gets it into her head that she must wear a particular outfit on some occasion, and at once it becomes impossible for fifty craftsmen to get any sleep or have leisure to eat and drink; she gives her commands and is obeyed more promptly than our monarch, since self-interest is the greatest monarch on earth.

This enthusiasm for work, this passion for getting rich, is transmitted from class to class, from workmen up to great nobles. Nobody likes to be poorer than somebody whom he recently saw just below him. In Paris you can see a man with enough to live on till Judgement Day working all the time, and running the risk of shortening his life, in order, he says, to get enough to live on.

This attitude is spreading through the nation: the scene is one of universal industry and ingenuity. Where then is the effeminate nation which you talk about so much?

Let us assume, Rhedi, that there was a kingdom in which no skills were allowed except those essential to agriculture, which in themselves are very numerous, and that all those serving only to produce fancy goods and luxuries were banned. I maintain that this state would be one of the most wretched on earth.

Even if the inhabitants had enough resolution to do without all the things that their requirements call for, the population would decrease all the time, and the nation would become so weak that any other power, however small, would be able to conquer it.

It would be easy for me to go into great detail and show you that the incomes of private individuals would be reduced almost to nothing, and that the same thing would therefore happen to the prince's. Economic relationships between citizens would virtually cease; there would be an end of the mutual exchange of money and progressive transference of earnings which derives from the dependence of one trade on others. Each individual citizen would live on his land, taking from it exactly what he needed, and no more, so as not to die of hunger.[1] But since in some cases that would correspond to less than a twentieth of the national income, the number of inhabitants would necessarily decrease in the same ratio, and only a twentieth would remain.

It is important to remember how much income can be earned by professional skill. Capital provides its owner with an annual income amounting to a twentieth of its value, but with a pound's worth of paints an artist can produce a picture which will earn him fifty. The same can be said of jewellers, wool and silk workers, and every type of craftsman.

From all this, Rhedi, it must be concluded that, for a king to remain powerful, his subjects must live luxuriously. He must take as much care to provide them with every sort of superfluity as to provide them with the necessities of life.

From Paris, the 14th of the moon of Shawall, 1717

Letter 107
Rica to Ibben, at Smyrna

I have seen the young monarch. His life is precious indeed to his subjects; it is no less so to the whole of Europe, because of the great disturbances that his death might bring.[1]

But kings are like gods, and as long as they are alive we must believe them immortal. His expression is majestic but delightful; the excellence of his upbringing seems to be allied to a propitious character, and already betokens a great prince.

They say that it is impossible to tell the character of Western kings until they have been subjected to two great ordeals, their mistress and their confessor.[2] It will not be long before we see both of them hard at work to seize control of the king's mind; it will be a mighty struggle. For under a young prince, these two powers are always rivals, though they are reconciled and join forces under an old one.

Under a young prince, the dervish has a hard time maintaining his position; the king's strength is his weakness, while his adversary's triumphs come from his strength and his weakness as well.

When I arrived in France, I found the late king completely ruled by women, although at his age I think he needed them less than any other king on earth. One day I heard a woman saying: 'Something must be done for this young colonel. I know what he is capable of. I will speak to the minister about it.' Another said: 'It is surprising that this young abbé should have been forgotten. He must be given a diocese. He is a man of good birth, and I can vouch for his morals.' You must not, however, imagine that the women who made these remarks were favourites of the prince: they might not have spoken to him more than twice in their lives, though that is easy enough with European princes. The thing is that, for every man who has any post at court, in Paris, or in the country, there is a woman through whose hands pass all the favours and sometimes the injustices that he does. These women are all in touch with one another, and compose a sort of commonwealth whose members are always busy giving each other mutual help and support.[3]

It is like another state within the state, and a man who watches the actions of ministers, officials, or prelates at court, in Paris or in the country, without knowing the women who rule them, is like a man who can see a machine in action but does not know what makes it work.

Would you say, Ibben, that a woman sets out to become mistress of a minister in order to sleep with him? – what an idea! It is so as to present half a dozen requests to him every morning; and the natural goodness of women is shown by their eagerness to do good deeds for countless unhappy men who provide them with ten thousand pounds a year.

In Persia we complain that the kingdom is governed by two or three women. It is much worse in France, where women in general govern, not only taking over the authority wholesale, but even dividing it up piecemeal among themselves.

From Paris, the last day of the moon of Shawall, 1717

Letter 108
Usbek to ★★★

Here there is a sort of book[1] which is unknown to us in Persia, but seems to me to be very much in fashion: literary journals. They make being lazy seem an achievement: it is delightful to be able to get through thirty volumes in a quarter of an hour.

In most books, the reader is already at his last gasp before the author has finished the conventional flattering dedications and acknowledgements, and half-dead by the time he gets on to the subject, which has been submerged in an ocean of words. One author wants to immortalize himself by a duodecimo, another by a quarto, while another, aiming higher, aspires to a full folio volume; so he has to extend his subject proportionately, which he does without mercy, taking no account of the hapless reader and his struggles, as he wears himself out trying to abbreviate the material that the author took such trouble to amplify.

I don't know, ★★★, what merit there is in producing such works. I could easily do the same, if I wanted to ruin my health and the publisher.

The great mistake made by reviewers is that they write only about new books, as if the truth could ever be new. It seems to me that until a man has read all the old books he has no reason to prefer new ones instead.

But having made it a rule only to discuss works which are still hot from the oven, they also make it a rule to be extremely boring. They would never take it upon themselves to criticize the books which they report on, even if they have strong reasons for doing so; and indeed, what man would be so bold as to want to make ten or twelve enemies every month?

The majority of authors are like poets, and will put up with a good thrashing without complaint;[2] but although where their shoulders are concerned they are not sensitive, they are about their writings, so much so that they cannot bear the slightest criticism. One must there-

fore take the utmost care not to attack them in such a tender spot, as
the reviewers know well. So they do just the opposite, and begin by
praising the choice of subject, which is their first inanity, and then go
on to praise the author, which is compulsory; for they are up against
men who still have plenty of breath left, and are quite ready to
defend their honour and annihilate, with a stroke of the pen, the rash
reviewer.

From Paris, the 5th of the moon of Dulkaada, 1718

Letter 109
Rica to ★★★

The University of Paris is the eldest daughter of the kings of France,
and very much so, for she is more than nine hundred years old;[1]
so she is somewhat dreamy at times.

I have been told that some time ago she had a great controversy
with some scholars concerning the letter Q,★ which the university
wanted to be pronounced like a K. The dispute became so violent
that some of the participants had their property confiscated. The
Parlement had to step in so as to put an end to the quarrel, and in a
solemn decree it granted every subject of the King of France
permission to pronounce the letter as he saw fit. A fine sight, to see
the two most important institutions in Europe occupied in deciding
the fate of a letter of the alphabet!

It would appear, my dear ★★★, that the greatest men find their
minds becoming stunted when they are assembled together, and that
with more wise men there is also less wisdom. Great institutions are
always so attached to minute detail and empty formalities that the
main business gets left to the end. I have heard that a king of Aragon†
once called the representatives of Aragon and Catalonia to a meeting
of the States General, and the first sessions were spent in deciding
which language would be used for the discussions. It was a heated

★ He is referring to the Ramus affair.[2]
† This happened in 1610.[3]

argument, and the States General seemed perpetually on the point of breaking up, until an expedient was devised, which was the question should be in Catalan and the reply in Aragonese.

From Paris, the 25th of the moon of Dulheggia, 1718

Letter 110
Rica to ★★★

The part a pretty woman has to play is much more serious than people think. Nothing is of greater gravity than the morning's events at her dressing-table, amidst her servants: an army commander would not devote more attention to positioning his right wing or his reserve troops than she to the placing of a beauty-spot which could fail, though she hopes and anticipates that it will be successful.

What anguish of mind she undergoes, what concentration she needs, in order to keep reconciling the interests of rival lovers, to seem neutral to both while yielding to each, and to ensure that all the causes of complaint she gives them are brought to her for arbitration!

What a business it is to ensure that one party follows another, successively reborn, and ward off all the accidents which might interfere with them!

Apart from all this, the hardest struggle is not to be amused, but to appear to be. You can bore women as much as you like and they will forgive you, provided everyone else thinks they have enjoyed themselves.

A few days ago I was at a supper in the country, given by some women. On the way, they kept saying: 'At any rate we must have some good jokes and enjoy ourselves properly.'

We turned out to be rather badly assorted, and somewhat serious in consequence. 'You must admit,' said one of the women, 'that we are greatly enjoying ourselves: none of the parties in Paris today is as gay as ours.' I was getting more and more bored when a woman remonstrated and said: 'Really! we are in a good mood, aren't we?'

'Yes,' I answered with a yawn, 'I think I'm going to die of

laughter.' But gloom still had the ascendancy, despite what anybody said; as for me, I felt myself borne down by yawn after yawn towards a deathly slumber which ended any pleasure.

From Paris, the 11th of the moon of Muharram, 1718

Letter 111[1]
Usbek to ★★★

The late king ruled for such a long time that the end of his reign has made people forget how it began. Nowadays the fashion is to take an interest only in the events that occurred during his minority, and nobody reads anything except memoirs from that period.[2]

The following is a speech delivered at a council of war by one of the generals on the side of the city of Paris, and I confess that I cannot understand much of it.

'Gentlemen: Although our troops have been repulsed and have suffered some losses, I believe that we shall easily make up for this setback. I have six verses of a song all ready for publication, which, I am certain, will restore the balance completely. I have picked on some very clear voices, which, emerging from the depths of some very powerful chests, will stir up popular feeling in the most marvellous way. The words are to a tune which, up to now, has had a very special effect.

'If that is not enough, we shall have a print made of Mazarin on the gallows.

'Fortunately for us, he cannot speak French well; he misuses it so badly that his situation is bound to deteriorate. We make sure to tell the public about the absurd tone in which he pronounces his words.[3] A few days ago we convicted him of such a dreadful mistake of grammar that it became the subject of farces that were performed at every street corner.

'I hope that before a week is up the public will be using the name Mazarin as a general word to mean any animal used for carrying loads or pulling vehicles.[4]

'Since our defeat, our music has assailed him so vigorously on the subject of original sin that, in order to prevent himself losing half his followers, he has been compelled to dismiss all his pages.[5]

'So cheer up, take fresh heart, and let me assure you that we shall shout and hiss him back across the Alps.'

From Paris, the 4th of the moon of Shaaban, 1718

Letter 112
Rhedi to Usbek, at Paris

During my stay in Europe I am reading ancient and modern history. I compare each period with others, and I enjoy watching them pass in front of me, so to speak. Above all I am concentrating on the great changes which have made every age so different from every other, and the earth so unlike what it had been.

Perhaps you have not noticed something which continually surprises me. Why is it that the world is so thinly populated in comparison with former times?[1] How is it that nature has managed to lose the prodigious fertility that she had originally? Could she be already in old age, and failing from lack of strength?

I have stayed in Italy for more than a year, and have seen only the remnants of the old Italy that was once so famous. Although everyone lives in the towns, they are quite empty and unpopulated: they seem to subsist only so as to mark the sites of the powerful cities about which historians have written so much.

There are those who claim that the city of Rome alone used to contain more people than there are today in a large kingdom. There were Roman citizens who had ten or even twenty thousand slaves, not counting those who worked on their country estates; and since there were reckoned to be four or five hundred thousand citizens, the imagination protests if we calculate the number of inhabitants.

There were powerful kingdoms in Sicily once, with large populations, which have since disappeared: there is nothing worth noting on the island now except volcanoes.

Greece is so desolate that it does not contain a hundredth of its former inhabitants.

In Spain, once so full of people, there is nothing to be seen today but deserted countryside; and France is as nothing in comparison with ancient Gaul as it was described by Caesar.

The northern countries are very depleted, and their peoples are far from being obliged to split up, as they once had to, and send out colonies and whole nations, like swarms of bees, to look for other places to live in.

Poland and the Turkish territories in Europe have hardly any population left.

It is impossible to find in America a fiftieth of the number of men who once formed the great empires there.

Asia is hardly in a better condition. In Asia Minor, which used to contain such powerful kingdoms and such a fantastic number of great cities, only about two or three remain. On the Asian mainland, the part of it under Turkish control is no longer inhabited; and as for what is under our own king's control, if you compare it to its previous flourishing state, you will see that it has only a small fraction of the inhabitants who lived there in countless numbers at the time of Xerxes and Darius.

As regards the smaller states which surround these great empires, they are really deserted: this is true of the kingdoms of Imeretia, Circassia, and Guria.[2] Their sovereigns, on their enormous lands, scarcely have fifty thousand subjects.

Egypt has lost as much as the other countries.

In a word, as I scan the earth, all I find is ruins; I seem to see it recovering from the ravages of plague and famine.

Africa has always been so little known that one cannot speak about it so exactly as about the other parts of the world, but, to leave everything out of account except the Mediterranean coastline, which has always been known, it is obvious that it has declined a very long way from what it used to be under the Carthaginians and the Romans. Today its princes are so weak that they are the most insignificant of the world's powers.

After making as exact a calculation as is possible with this sort of subject, I have come to the conclusion that there is scarcely a tenth of the number of men on earth that there was in former times.[3] The startling thing is that the world is constantly becoming less populous, and, if this continues, in ten centuries it will be nothing more than a desert.

This, Usbek, is the most terrible catastrophe which has ever happened to the world. But it has scarcely been noticed, because it has occurred gradually, in the course of a great many centuries; and that indicates that there is some internal defect, some secret, hidden poison, some wasting disease, which is attacking human nature.

From Venice, the 10th of the moon of Rajab, 1718

Letter 113
Usbek to Rhedi, at Venice

The world, my dear Rhedi, is not immune to decay; nor are the heavens themselves. Astronomers act as eye-witnesses of the alterations that occur in them, which are the natural consequences of universal motion. The earth, like the other planets, obeys the laws of motion; it is subject to a perpetual inner conflict between its constituent elements. Sea and land seem to be eternally at war, and at every moment new combinations emerge.

The human race, living in an environment which is so liable to change, is in just as uncertain a condition. There are a hundred thousand factors which may be operative and are capable of destroying it, and even more so, therefore, of increasing or decreasing its numbers.

I shall pass over those partial disasters, so common in history, which have destroyed whole towns or kingdoms: there have been all-embracing disasters which have frequently brought the human race within a hairbreadth of destruction.

The history books are full of universal plagues which have taken it in turns to lay waste the universe. We are told of one, among others, which was so violent that it even scorched the roots of plants, and spread through the whole of the known world, as far as the empire of

Cathay.¹ If the disintegration had gone one degree further, it might perhaps, in a single day, have destroyed humanity entirely.

It is only two hundred years since the most shameful of all diseases² made its effects felt in Europe, Asia, and Africa. It had the most terrible consequences in a very short time; it would have been all over for mankind if it had continued to progress at the same furious rate. Stricken with ills at birth, unable to bear the burden of their social responsibilities, men would have perished miserably.

What might not have happened if the infection had been slightly more potent? It would no doubt have become so, if we had not had the good fortune to find the powerful remedy that has been discovered. Perhaps, in attacking the reproductive organs, the disease would have attacked reproduction itself.

But why say that the destruction of the human race might have occurred? Did it not actually happen? And was mankind not reduced to a single family by the Flood?

Some philosophers assert that there are two different creations, one of things and one of man. They cannot understand how matter and created things can be only six thousand years old, how the works of God could have been postponed for all eternity, so that God made use of his creative power only yesterday. Was it because he was unable to, or because he did not want to? But if he was unable to at one time, then he must have been unable to at another. It must have been, therefore, because he did not want to; but since there can be no before and after in God, he must have wanted something always, from the beginning, if we accept that he wanted it once.

*Yet all the historians speak of one first father. They show us human nature at its birth. Is it not natural to think that Adam was rescued from a universal misfortune, like Noah from the Flood, and that such events have occurred frequently on earth since the creation of the universe?

But destruction does not always happen violently; we can see that in several regions of the earth the provision of nourishment for mankind is being exhausted. How do we know that there are not generic

---

* In earlier editions, before this paragraph came the following:

'We must not, then, calculate the age of the world; the number of grains of sand in the sea is no more than an instant in comparison.'

causes of exhaustion, gradual and imperceptible, applying to the whole world?

I am glad to have been able to go into general considerations before replying more particularly to your letter on the decrease of population over the last seventeen or eighteen hundred years. I shall show you in a further letter that, independently of physical causes, there **are** moral ones which have produced this effect.

From Paris, the 8th of the moon of Shaaban, 1718

Letter 114
Usbek to the same

You want to know the reason why the earth is less thickly populated than in the past. If you consider the matter carefully, you will see that the great difference lies in the way customs have changed.

Since the Christian and Muslim religions divided the Roman world between them, things have altered considerably. The masters of the world had a religion much more favourable to the propagation of the species than these two are.

With them, polygamy was forbidden, which was a great advantage over the Muslim religion, while divorce was allowed, and this was another advantage, just as important, over Christianity.

There is nothing which I find more inconsistent than the plurality of wives which is permitted by the holy Koran, together with the order to satisfy them, which is given in the same book.

'Look to your wives,' says the Prophet, 'because to them you are as necessary as their clothes, and they are as necessary to you as your clothes.' This is a precept which would make the life of a true Muslim very laborious. If a man had four wives as laid down by the Law, and not more than the same number of concubines and slaves, would he not be crushed by all those clothes?

'Your wives are your ploughlands,' says the Prophet furthermore, 'therefore go to your ploughlands; do good to your souls, and you will find the good one day.'

It seems to me that a Muslim is like an athlete doomed to compete without respite, who is soon weakened and overcome by his initial efforts, and languishes on the very field of victory, lying buried, so to speak, beneath his own triumphs.

Nature always acts slowly, and with economy, as it were. She never operates violently; even when producing she demands restraint; she always moves regularly and temperately; if she is hurried, she soon becomes sluggish, using all her remaining strength for self-preservation, and completely losing her productive abilities and powers of generation.

It is to this state of debility that we are always reduced by the large number of wives we have, which is more likely to wear us out than to satisfy us. It is very common with us to see a man with a vast seraglio and a minute number of children. In most cases the children themselves are weak and unhealthy, having been affected by their father's lethargy.

Nor is that all. The women, forced into compulsory obedience, need men in order to guard them, who can only be eunuchs; religion, jealousy, and reason itself will not allow any others to go near them. There have to be large numbers of these guardians, both to preserve internal tranquillity amidst the continual wars that go on between the wives, and to prevent any attacks from outside. Consequently, a man with ten wives, or concubines, will find that ten eunuchs is not too many to guard them. But what a loss for society there is in this multitude of men who are dead from birth! What a decline in population must result!

The slave girls in the seraglio, who, together with the eunuchs, look after this great number of women, almost always grow old there in a miserable state of virginity.

They cannot get married as long as they remain there, and their mistresses, once they are used to them, hardly ever get rid of them.

This is how the pleasures of one man monopolize so many citizens of both sexes, so that they are dead as far as the State is concerned, and useless for the propagation of the species.

Constantinople and Ispahan are the capitals of the two greatest empires in the world: everything should be directed towards them, and people make their way there from all sides, attracted for innumerable reasons. Yet they are perishing of their own accord, and would soon be destroyed if their sovereigns did not bring in whole nations, almost once a century, in order to repopulate them. I shall conclude this subject in another letter.

From Paris, the 13th of the moon of Shaaban, 1718

Letter 115
Usbek to the same

The Romans had no fewer slaves than we, in fact they had more, but they made better use of them.

Far from using force to prevent them from increasing in numbers, they encouraged them to do so by every means in their power. They associated them with each other as much as possible, in a kind of marriage;[1] by this means they supplied their houses with servants, of both sexes and of all ages, and the state with innumerable subjects.

These children, who in the long run made their master rich, were born in countless numbers around him; he alone was responsible for their nourishment and upbringing. The fathers, free of this burden, followed their natural inclinations alone, and got more children with no fear of having too large a family.

I have said that, with us, all the slaves are engaged in guarding our women, and in nothing else. As regards the State they are in a permanent state of inertia, so that industrial and agricultural activity is necessarily restricted to a few free men, a few heads of families, and even they devote as little time to it as possible.

It was not the same with the Romans. The republic used its slave population to incalculable advantage. Each slave was given an allowance,[2] which he had on the conditions imposed by his master: he used it to work with, taking up whatever his own abilities suggested. One would go in for banking, another for shipping, one became a retailer, another applied himself to some technical trade, or farmed out lands and improved them; but there was no one who failed to do everything he could to make a profit from his allowance, which both made him comfortable while he remained a slave, and assured him of freedom in the future: this made for a hard-working population and stimulated industrial and technical skills.

These slaves, who had become rich by hard work and application, were made freemen and became citizens. The republic constantly renewed itself, allowing new families in as the old ones were destroyed.

In the following letters I shall perhaps take the opportunity to prove to you that the more men there are in a state, the more trade flourishes; the two things are interdependent and provide mutual stimulus.

If this is so, how great an increase there was bound to be in this huge number of slaves, always working hard! Industriousness and affluence produced them, and they in turn produced affluence and industriousness.

From Paris, the 16th of the moon of Shaaban, 1718

Letter 116
Usbek to the same

Up to now we have been speaking of Muslim countries, and attempting to find out why they are less populated than when they were under Roman domination: let us now examine what has produced this effect with the Christians.

Divorce, which had been allowed by the pagan religion, was forbidden to the Christians. This change, which at first seemed so unimportant, gradually had terrible consequences, in a way that is almost unbelievable.

Not only did it take all the pleasure out of marriage, but it also discouraged its purpose. The intention was to strengthen the bonds of marriage, but they were weakened; and instead of uniting two hearts, as had been planned, they were separated forever.

On an act so freely undertaken, in which emotion should play so large a part, were imposed constraint, necessity, and the inevitability of fate itself. No account was taken of distaste, personal whims, and temperamental incompatibility; an effort was made to control the human heart, that is to say, the most variable and inconstant thing in nature; people were coupled together irrevocably and hopelessly, a mutual burden, almost always ill-assorted: it was like those tyrants who had living men tied to dead bodies.

Nothing had made a greater contribution to mutual attachment than the possibility of divorce. A husband and wife were inclined to put up with domestic troubles patiently, because they knew that it was in their power to bring them to an end, and often they had this power at their disposal all their lives without using it, for the unique reason that they were free to do so.

It is not the same with the Christians; their present troubles make them despair of the future. Faced with the disagreeable aspects of marriage, all they can see is that they will persist, and forever, so to speak. This is a cause of dislike, quarrelling, and contempt, and posterity is to that extent the loser. After scarcely three years of marriage, its main purpose is neglected, and thirty years are then spent frigidly together;[1] separations take place in private which are as complete as if they were public, and perhaps more damaging. Both sides live for themselves, permanently, and it is all to the disadvantage of future generations. Soon, tired of having a wife in perpetuity, the man will resort to prostitutes, a shameful and anti-social kind of union which cannot fulfil the purpose of marriage, and at best reproduces its pleasures alone.

If one of the two persons bound together in this way is unable to accomplish nature's purposes and propagate the species, either for reasons of character or because of age, he or she incapacitates the other as well, and both become equally useless.

We must not therefore be surprised to find that among Christians such a large number of marriages provides such a small number of citizens. Divorce has been abolished; unsuitable marriages can no longer be readjusted; wives no longer, as with the Romans, pass through the hands of several husbands in succession, who make the best possible use of them on the way.

I would go so far as to say that if a republic such as that of Sparta, where the citizens were always encumbered with odd and ingenious laws, and where there was only one family, which was the republic itself, had decided that husbands would change their wives every year, it would have produced countless numbers of citizens.

It is not easy to explain clearly the reasons which led the Christians to abolish divorce. With every nation in the world marriage is a sort of contract which can have any sort of conditions attached to it, and the only ones which should have been excluded are those which might have weakened its purpose. But the Christians do not regard it from this point of view, and consequently have difficulty in saying what it is. They do not define it as consisting in sensual pleasure, which they seem, on the contrary, to want to banish from it as far as possible, as I have already told you; instead it is an image, a symbol, and something mysterious which I cannot understand.

From Paris, the 19th of the moon of Shaaban, 1718

Letter 117
Usbek to the same

The prohibition of divorce is not the only cause of depopulation in Christian countries; another, no less important, is the great number of eunuchs among them.

I refer to the priests and dervishes, of both sexes, who make a vow of perpetual chastity. This, for the Christians, is virtue in its purest form; I cannot understand it, not knowing what sort of virtue it is that produces nothing.

I find that their theologians are manifestly inconsistent to say that marriage is sacred, and that celibacy, its opposite, is even more sacred; not to mention that, where fundamental principles and dogmas are concerned, the good and the best are always the same.

The number of people who commit themselves to celibacy is incredible. There was a time when a father would impose this fate on children still in the cradle. Nowadays they themselves take their vows at the age of fourteen,[1] which amounts to much the same thing.

This career of chastity has annihilated more men than plagues or the most savage wars. In every monastic institution is an everlasting family to which no children are born, and which maintains itself at the expense of all other families. Their houses stand open all the time like so many abysses, for future generations to be engulfed in.

Such a policy is very different from that of the Romans, who laid down laws[2] penalizing those who, infringing the laws of marriage, wanted to enjoy a freedom which was of so little use to the public.

I am referring here only to Catholic countries. In the Protestant religion, everyone has the right to have children. Priests and dervishes are not allowed, and if, while this religion, which went back to early Christianity in every respect, was being established, its founders had not constantly been accused of carnality, there can be no doubt that, having extended the use of marriage to everyone, they would not have gone on to make it even less restrictive, and completely removed the barrier which separates the Nazarene and Mohammed in this respect.

But however that may be, it is certain that their religion gives the Protestants an infinite advantage over the Catholics.

I will go so far as to say that with Europe in its present state the Catholic religion cannot possibly last another five hundred years.

Before the power of Spain was reduced, the Catholics were much stronger than the Protestants. The latter have gradually got onto an equal footing. The Protestants will become richer and more powerful, and the Catholics weaker.

Protestant countries ought to be, and are in reality, more populous than Catholic ones. It follows, first, that revenue from taxes is higher, because it increases proportionately to the number of taxpayers; second, that the land is better cultivated; third, that business is in a more flourishing state, because there are more people with their fortunes to make, and because, although their needs are greater, there are also more resources. When the number of people is only enough for the cultivation of the land, trade inevitably collapses, and when there are only enough for the maintenance of trade, agriculture is inevitably ruined; which means that both decay together, since a man cannot engage in one except at the expense of the other.

As for the Catholic countries, not only has agriculture been abandoned, but industriousness itself is harmful: it consists only in learning five or six words of a dead language.[3] As soon as a man has equipped himself in this way, he no longer needs to trouble about his career; in a monastery, he can have a quiet life which he would have sweated and laboured to achieve in the outside world.

This is not all. The dervishes have almost all the wealth of the nation in their hands.[4] They form a society of misers, constantly acquiring and never giving back; they accumulate income all the time so as to build up capital. All this wealth becomes paralysed; it no longer circulates, and there is no more commercial, cultural or industrial activity.

There is not a single Protestant ruler who does not raise more taxes from his people than the Pope from his subjects; yet the latter are poor, while the former live in opulence. With them, commerce brings everything to life, while with the others monasticism carries death with it everywhere.

From Paris, the 26th of the moon of Shaaban, 1718

Letter 118
Usbek to the same

There is nothing more to be said about Asia and Europe; let us go on to Africa. We can discuss scarcely any of it except the coastal regions, the interior being unknown.

The Barbary coasts, where the Muslim religion prevails, are not as populous as they were in Roman times, for the reasons I have mentioned already. As for the Guinea coast, it must have been terribly depleted over the two hundred years during which the petty kings, or village chiefs, have been selling their subjects to European rulers, for transportation to their American colonies.

The odd thing is that America, where new inhabitants arrive every year, is desolate itself, and fails to profit from Africa's continual losses. The slaves, having been transported to another climate, perish there in thousands; and working in the mines, which employ natives as well as imported labour all the time, destroys them inexorably, because of the dangerous exhalations which are given off there, and the necessity of always using mercury.[1]

Nothing is more absurd than to cause the death of countless thousands of men so as to get gold and silver out of the depths of the earth. These metals are absolutely useless in themselves, and are identical with wealth only because they have been chosen to be the sign of it.

From Paris, the last day of the moon of Shaaban, 1718

Letter 119
Usbek to the same

A nation's birthrate sometimes depends on the most trivial circumstances imaginable, so that often a change of attitude is all that is required for it to become much more populous than before.

The Jews, who have constantly been exterminated and are constantly rising again, have found a remedy for this continual loss and destruction simply by their hopes, which are cherished by every family, of seeing a powerful king born among them to be lord of the earth.[1]

The ancient kings of Persia had so many thousands of subjects only because one of the doctrines of the religion of the magi said that the best ways for men to please God were to beget a child, to plough a field, and to plant a tree.[2]

If China[3] has such a fantastic number of people inside its boundaries, the reason is simply a particular way of thinking; for children regard their fathers as gods, venerating them as such during their lifetime, and honouring them after death by sacrifices in which their souls, so they believe, having been annihilated in the T'ien,[4] take on new life; and the tendency is for everyone to increase his family, since it is so submissive in this life and necessary in the next.

The Muslim countries, on the other hand, are becoming emptier all the time, because of a belief which, holy though it is, nevertheless has the most pernicious results when it is deeply rooted in men's minds.

We consider that we are travellers who should always be thinking of our other homeland; to us there seems to be something unjustifiable about doing useful, durable work, or making efforts to ensure security for our children, or planning for when our short and ephemeral life is over. We are calm about the present, unworried by the future, and do not take the trouble to keep our public buildings in good repair, or to clear waste ground, or to work at land which is capable of being cultivated: we live in a state of general apathy, leaving everything to be done by Providence.

Among the Europeans, an attitude of vanity has given rise to the unfair law of primogeniture, which is so unfavourable to the pro-creation of children, since it fixes the father's attention on one child alone, and stops him from attending to the others; it compels him, in order to ensure that the fortune of one of them is on a firm footing, to be reluctant to make provision for more than one; finally, it destroys equality between citizens, on which their prosperity entirely depends.

From Paris, the 4th of the moon of Ramadán, 1718

Letter 120
Usbek to the same

Countries inhabited by savages are usually thinly populated, because of their universal opposition to agriculture and work.

This unfortunate aversion is so strong that when they call down curses on an enemy their one desire is that he should be reduced to ploughing a field; they believe that the only pursuits which are noble and deserve their attention are hunting and fishing.

But, since there are often years when hunting and fishing provide very little, they are frequently ravaged by famine, not to mention that no country is sufficiently abundant in game and fish to provide food for a large nation, because animals always avoid places which are too thickly populated.

Besides, native villages with two or three hundred inhabitants, being unattached to each other and with interests as distinct as those of two separate empires, cannot maintain themselves; they are without the resources available to large states, where all the parts are inter-related and mutually beneficial.

Among savages there is another custom which is no less harmful than the first: it is the women's cruel habit of having abortions, so that pregnancy will not make them unattractive to their husbands.[1]

Here, there are terrifying laws against this offence; they are not far from being ferocious.[2] Any unmarried girl who has not made an official declaration of pregnancy is punished by death, if the infant dies; neither modesty nor shame, nor even an accident can excuse her.

From Paris, the 9th of the moon of Ramadán, 1718

Letter 121
Usbek to the same

Colonies usually have the effect of weakening the mother-country without adding to the population of the country in which they are established.

Men ought to stay where they are. There are illnesses which come from changing a good climate for a bad one, and others which are due simply to the change of climate itself.

The atmosphere is loaded, as plants are, with particles from the soil of each country. It affects us to such an extent that our metabolism becomes fixed. When we are transported to another country we fall ill. The fluids in our bodies are used to a particular density, the solids to a particular arrangement, and both to a certain degree of motion, so that they are no longer able to tolerate anything else, and resist any readjustment.[1]

When a country is unpopulated, the assumption must be that there is some particular defect in the nature of the terrain or of the climate; consequently, when men are removed from a favourable atmosphere and sent to such a country, the effect is precisely opposite to what was intended.

The Romans knew this by experience. They banished all their criminals to Sardinia; they also made Jews live there.[2] Then they had to find some consolation for being bereaved of them, which was greatly facilitated by their contempt for these poor wretches.

Shah Abbas the Great, wanting to deprive the Turks of any means of maintaining large armies on the frontier, moved almost all the Armenians out of their country, and sent more than twenty thousand families to the province of Gilan, where they almost all perished in a very short time.[3]

In no case has the importation of communities into Constantinople ever succeeded.[4]

The fantastic number of negroes of which we have spoken has failed to replenish America.

Since the destruction of the Jews under Hadrian, Palestine is uninhabited.

It must therefore be accepted that destruction on a large scale is almost irreparable. A nation which suffers losses beyond a certain point remains in the state to which it has been reduced; and if by chance it should recover, it needs hundreds of years to do so.

Furthermore, if in its weakened state the most trivial of the circumstances that I have mentioned should also be present, it not only fails to re-establish itself, but continues to diminish, and is liable to be annihilated.

The effects of the expulsion of the Moors from Spain[5] are as perceptible now as on the day after it occurred. Far from the gap having been filled, it is growing larger all the time.

Since the devastation of America, the Spaniards, who have replaced its former inhabitants, have been unable to repopulate it; on the contrary, by a fatality which ought rather to be described as divine justice, the destroyers are themselves being destroyed, and are disappearing daily.

Rulers should not therefore think of populating large countries by colonization. I will not deny that they sometimes succeed. Some climates are so favourable that the species always multiplies there, as is testified by the islands* which have been populated by invalids who were abandoned by various ships and recovered their health there.[6]

* The author is perhaps referring to Reunion Island.

But even if the colonies were to succeed, they would merely divide the national power, instead of increasing it; unless they were very small in extent, such as those sent to garrison some fortress for reasons of trade.

The Carthaginians, like the Spaniards, had discovered America, or at least some large islands with which they did an enormous amount of trade. But when it was realized that the number of the inhabitants was decreasing, the republic wisely forbade its subjects to sail or do trade there. I will go so far as to say that instead of transferring Spaniards to the Indies, the Indians and half-castes should be sent back to Spain. The kingdom should have all its scattered inhabitants brought back, and if it were to keep only half of its great colonies Spain would become the most formidable power in Europe.

An empire can be compared to a tree with branches which, if they spread too far, take all the sap from the trunk, and do nothing but provide shade.

Nothing is better calculated to cure monarchs of their passion for making conquests in remote places than the example of the Portuguese and the Spaniards.

These two nations, having conquered immense kingdoms with unbelievable rapidity, and more startled by their victory than the conquered races by their defeat, had to think of a way of preserving them; and each took a different course.

The Spaniards, giving up any hope of ensuring the loyalty of the conquered nations, chose to exterminate them, and to send out a loyal population from Spain; never has a wicked plan been more punctiliously carried out. A people as numerous as the whole population of Europe was seen to disappear from the earth at the arrival of these barbarians, whose only thought, in conquering the Indies, seems to have been to reveal to mankind the ultimate limits of cruelty.

By this piece of barbarism they kept the country under their domination. You can judge from this example how fatal it is to make conquests, since they have results such as these: for after all, this atrocious solution was the only one available. How could they have ensured the continued obedience of so many millions of men? How could they have carried on a civil war so far away? What would have happened to them if they had given the American tribes enough time to recover from their surprise at the arrival of these new gods and from their fear of their thunderbolts?

As for the Portuguese, they took exactly the opposite course, and did not use any cruelty. Consequently they were soon expelled from all the countries that they had discovered. The Dutch encouraged the natives to rebel, and profited from having done so.

What king would envy the fate of such conquerors? Who would have wanted these conquests, on these conditions? Some were expelled straight away, others created desert wastes and turned their own country into a desert also.

The destiny of heroes is to come to grief conquering lands which they abruptly lose, or subjugating nations which they are obliged to destroy themselves, like the madman who ruined himself buying statues to throw into the sea and mirrors which he immediately broke.[7]

From Paris, the 18th of the moon of Ramadán, 1718

Letter 122
Usbek to the same

Gentle methods of government have a wonderful effect on the propagation of the species. Evidence for this comes constantly from all the republics, especially Switzerland and Holland, which are the worst countries in Europe if the nature of their terrain is considered, and which are nonetheless the most populous.

Nothing encourages immigration more than freedom, together with prosperity, which always accompanies it: the former is desirable in itself, and our needs take us to countries where the latter is to be found. The species multiplies in a land where affluence provides enough for children to live on without reducing the quantity available for their parents.

Equality between citizens, which usually produces an equal

distribution of wealth, itself conveys life and prosperity throughout the nation, diffusing them everywhere.

It is not the same with countries subjected to arbitrary power. The king, the courtiers, and a few private individuals possess all the wealth, while all the others languish in the depths of poverty.

If a man is in difficulties and aware that any children he has will be poorer than he is, he will not get married; or if he does marry, he will be afraid of having too many children, who might finally ruin him, and go down to a lower social class themselves.

I agree that the countryman or peasant, once married, will breed in any case, whether he is rich or poor. This consideration does not affect him; he can always leave one inheritance to his children, which is his mattock, and there is nothing to prevent him blindly following his natural instincts.

But what use to the state is this quantity of children wasting away in destitution? They almost all die as they are born; they never prosper; they are weak and debilitated, and die individually for thousands of reasons, while they are carried off in the mass by the frequent epidemics that poverty and malnutrition always produce. Those who escape attain the age, but not the strength of manhood, and remain feeble for the rest of their lives.

Men are like plants, which never grow well unless they are properly cultivated; in nations stricken by poverty the species suffers, and sometimes even degenerates.

France provides an excellent example of all this. During the recent wars all the sons of families, afraid of being enrolled in the militia,[1] were obliged to get married, while they were too young and without money at all.

This large number of marriages produced a lot of children whom the French are still looking for, and who have disappeared because of poverty, famine, and disease.

And if, in a climate as favourable as this, in a kingdom as well administered as France, such things are to be observed, what is it like in other states?

From Paris, the 23rd of the moon of Ramadán, 1718

Letter 123
Usbek to the Mullah Mohammed Ali, Guardian of the Three Tombs, at Kum

What use is it for our imams to fast, and for our mullahs to wear hairshirts? The hand of God has twice smitten the children of the Law: the sun has grown dark, and seems to illumine their defeat alone: their armies assemble and are scattered like dust.

The Ottoman empire has been shaken by the two severest blows it has ever suffered. A Christian mufti is supporting it, but with difficulty.[1] The grand vizir of Germany is the scourge of God, sent to chastise the disciples of Omar: everywhere he brings the wrath of Heaven, angered by their rebelliousness and infidelity. Your soul is that of our holy imams, and you weep night and day for the children of the Prophet, led astray by the abominable Omar: at the sight of their distress your bowels are moved to pity: you desire not their destruction but their conversion: you wish to see them united beneath the banner of Ali[2] by the tears of the saints, not dispersed into mountains and deserts by fear of the infidel.

From Paris, the 1st of the moon of Shawall, 1718

Letter 124
Usbek to Rhedi, at Venice

What motive can there be for the immense generosity which kings display towards their courtiers? Do they want to win their allegiance? – they are already as devoted as they can be. And furthermore, if they can buy the devotion of some of their subjects, by the same token they must lose an infinite number of others by making them poor.

When I think of the position that sovereigns are in, continually surrounded by greedy and insatiable men, I can do nothing but pity them; and I pity them even more when they lack the strength to resist requests, which are always a burden to those who are not asking for anything.

Whenever I hear about their generosity or about favours and pensions granted by them, I cannot help indulging in lengthy reflections; ideas come crowding into my mind, and I imagine myself hearing a decree proclaimed:[1]

'Our royal magnificence having been harassed without respite by certain of our subjects asking us, with untiring courage, for pensions, we have finally yielded to the multitude of requests which they have presented, and to which the Crown has always given its most careful attention. They have asked us to consider that they have never failed, since our accession to the throne, to be present when we were getting up; that we have always been able to observe them as we passed, as motionless as milestones; and that they have climbed as high as they could, on the tallest shoulders, so as to see our Serene Majesty. We have moreover received a number of requests from certain members of the fair sex, who have entreated us to bear in mind that they are notoriously difficult to maintain; some indeed, of great antiquity, have shakily begged us to consider that they used to adorn the courts of our royal predecessors, and that while their generals made the state formidable by their military feats, these ladies made the court no less celebrated by their intrigues. In consequence of which, wishing to treat all our suppliants generously, and grant all their pleas, we have decreed as follows:

'"That every agricultural labourer having five children is to reduce their daily allowance of bread by one-fifth. Heads of households are exhorted to be as precise as possible in reducing each child's share.

'"It is expressly forbidden to anyone who is occupied in cultivating land which he has inherited, or who has leased it for farming, to make any repairs of whatever sort.

'"It is decreed that all persons engaged in low menial employment, who have never been present while our Majesty gets up, shall henceforward cease to buy clothes for themselves, their wives, and their children, more than once in every four years; besides which they are most strictly forbidden the little celebrations which they have been accustomed to have in their homes on the principal annual holidays.

"'And insofar as we are advised that the majority of the citizens of our loyal towns devote themselves entirely to making provision for the dowries of their daughters, who have distinguished themselves in the eyes of the State solely by their dull and tiresome propriety, they are commanded to defer their marriages until, having reached the age-limit prescribed by law, marriage becomes compulsory.[2] Our legal officers are forbidden to provide for the education of their children.'"

From Paris, the 1st of the moon of Shawall, 1718

Letter 125
Rica to ★★★

In no religion is it an easy matter to describe the pleasures destined for those who have led virtuous lives. It is easy to terrify the wicked by threatening them with a long succession of punishments, but with the virtuous nobody knows what promises to make. It seems that the nature of pleasures is to be of short duration; the mind has difficulty in imagining anything different.

I have read descriptions of Paradise which would make any sensible person stop wanting to go there: according to some, the spirits of the blessed spend all their time playing the flute; others sentence them to walk about for ever; others again claim that while up there they dream about their mistresses down here, considering that a hundred million years is not too long for them to lose their taste for being love-sick.

In this connection I remember a story I heard from a man who had been to the Mogul empire; it shows that Indian priests are just as uninspired as the others in their ideas about the pleasures of Paradise.

A woman who had recently lost her husband paid a ceremonial visit to the governor of the town to ask permission to burn herself; but since in the countries under Muslim control everything possible is done to abolish this cruel custom,[1] he refused point-blank.

When she saw that her pleas had no effect she flew into a furious temper. 'Look how awkward they make things for you! They won't even let a poor woman burn herself when she wants to! Have you ever seen anything like it? My mother and my aunts and my sisters burnt themselves, and when I come and ask this wretched governor for permission, he gets cross and starts shouting as if he'd gone mad!'

A young bonze[2] happened by chance to be there. 'Is it you, faithless man,' the governor said to him, 'who gave this woman the idea of doing this insane deed?'

'No,' he said, 'I have never spoken to her; but if she were to take my advice she would perform the sacrifice. Her action will be pleasing to the god Brahma, and she will be well rewarded, for in the next world she will be reunited with her husband, and will begin a second marriage with him.'

'What did you say?' said the woman in surprise. 'Reunited with my husband? Oh! I shan't burn myself then. He was jealous and bad-tempered, and in any case so old that unless the god Brahma has improved him in certain respects he certainly has no need of me. Burn myself for him? I wouldn't burn the tip of my finger to get him out of the depths of Hell. There were two old bonzes who had led me astray, knowing what our relations were, and they took good care not to tell me everything: but if the god Brahma has nothing more than that to offer me, it is the kind of bliss that I can do without. Your Excellency, I shall become a Muslim. And as for you,' she said, turning to the bonze, 'you can go and tell my husband, if you like, that I am in the best of health.'

From Paris, the 2nd of the moon of Shawall, 1718

Letter 126
Rica to Usbek, at ★★★

I expect you here tomorrow, but in the meantime I am sending you your letters from Ispahan. Mine say that the ambassador of the Grand Mogul has been ordered to leave the kingdom. They also say that the prince, the king's uncle, who is in charge of his education, has been arrested; that he has been taken to a castle where he is very closely guarded, and that he has been stripped of all his honours.[1] The fate of this prince moves me, and I feel sorry for him.

I must admit, Usbek, that I have never seen anyone in tears without being affected. My feelings of humanity are aroused by those who are unhappy, as if only they were men, and even with great lords, for whom I find myself feeling little sympathy in their greatness, I feel more kindly disposed towards them as soon as they fall.

In prosperity, after all, what good to them is our useless affection? It makes us seem too near to being their equals. They much prefer to be respected, which requires nothing in return. But when they have lost their eminence, our pity can remind them of it.

I find something very sincere, and very great as well, in the words of a king[2] who, on the point of falling into his enemy's hands, saw his courtiers weeping around him and said: 'From your tears, I realize that I am still your king.'

From Paris, the 3rd of the moon of Shawall, 1718

Letter 127
Rica to Ibben, at Smyrna

You have heard about the famous King of Sweden countless times. He was besieging a town in a kingdom called Norway, and while he was inspecting the earthworks, accompanied only by a fortifications expert, he received a wound in the head and died from it. His Prime Minister was immediately arrested; the States General have met and sentenced him to be executed.[1]

The accusation against him was very serious: it was that he had slandered the nation, making it lose the king's confidence[2] – a crime which in my opinion deserves the death penalty a thousand times over.

For after all, if it is wrong to give the humblest subject a bad reputation with his king, how can I describe the denigration of an entire nation, causing it to lose the goodwill of the man whom Providence has chosen to ensure its happiness?

I could wish that men spoke to kings as the angels speak to our holy Prophet.

You know that at the solemn festivals when the King of Kings comes down from the loftiest of the world's thrones to mingle with his slaves, I used to impose on myself a strict rule to curb my rebellious tongue; I have never been known to let drop a single word which might have been unwelcome to the humblest of his people. When I have been obliged to abandon sobriety, I have not abandoned decent behaviour, and when our faithfulness has been tested in this way I have risked my life, but never my integrity.

I do not know why it is that there is scarcely ever a king so badly-intentioned that his minister is not even more so. If a king does some bad deed it is almost always at someone else's instigation, so that the ambition of princes is never as dangerous as the ignoble souls of their advisers. But can you understand why it is that a man who has had a ministry only since yesterday, and perhaps will have lost it tomorrow, can become, from one moment to the next, an enemy to himself, to his family, to his country, and to all the generations which will ever be born from the people who, because of him, are going to suffer oppression?

A prince has emotions, and the minister inflames them; that is the principle which controls his policies. That is his only purpose, and he has no wish to know of any other. Courtiers seduce the king by flattery; the minister flatters him in a more dangerous manner, by the advice he gives, the plans he suggests, and the precepts he puts forward.

From Paris, the 25th of the moon of Saphar, 1719

Letter 128
Rica to Usbek, at ★★★

The other day, as I was on the Pont-Neuf with a friend of mine, he met someone he knew, who, he told me, was a mathematician; and so it certainly appeared, for he was deep in meditation, and my friend had to spend some time tugging at his sleeve and shaking him in order to bring him back to himself, so preoccupied was he with the properties of a curve which had been torturing him for perhaps a week or more. They greeted each other very politely and exchanged news about the world of learning. Their conversation brought them to the entrance of a coffee-house and I went in with them.

I noticed that everyone greeted our mathematician warmly, and that the waiters paid more attention to him than to two musketeers sitting in a corner. As for him, it was clear that he was in a place that he liked, for his face relaxed a little, and he began to laugh as if he didn't know the first thing about mathematics.

At the same time his regular mind was gauging everything that was said in the course of conversation. He resembled the man walking in the garden who, with his sword, cut off the heads of all the flowers which stood higher than the rest.[1] He was a martyr to his own exactitude, and was pained by anything that stood out, in the same way that people with delicate eyesight are pained by too strong a light. Nothing was indifferent to him, provided that it was true. As a result, his conversation was odd. That day he had returned from the country with a man who had seen a superb mansion with magnificent gardens, and he himself had seen nothing but a building sixty feet long and thirty-five feet wide, and a grove of rectangular shape, ten acres in extent; he would very much have liked the rules of perspective to have been followed in such a way that the avenues approaching the house appeared to be of constant width, and he would have been able to provide an infallible method for achieving this. He seemed very pleased about a sundial which he had deciphered, of a most curious design, and he became very indignant with a scholar sitting by me, who unfortunately asked him if the sundial indicated ancient Babylonian time.[2] A newsmonger mentioned the bombardment of the fortress of Fontarabia,[3] and he immediately gave us the properties of the trajectory described by the shells; he was delighted at knowing this, and quite willing to remain in ignorance of the outcome. A man complained that the previous winter he had been ruined by floods. 'I am very pleased to hear it,' said the mathematician, 'I see that I was not mistaken in my observations, and that there was at least two inches more rainfall than the year before.'

A moment later he left, and we followed. Since he was walking rather fast, and did not look where he was going, another man came into direct contact with him. The collision was violent, and they each recoiled from the blow in direct proportion to their speed and mass.[4] When they had recovered a little from the shock, the other man, holding his head, said to the mathematician, 'I am delighted that you bumped into me, for I have a great piece of news to tell you: I have just given my Horace to the public.'

'What?' said the mathematician, 'the public has had him for two thousand years.'

'You misunderstand,' the other replied; 'it is a translation of the ancient poet that I have just published. I have spent twenty years doing translations.'

'What, sir!' said the mathematician, 'haven't you had a thought for twenty years? Do you speak for others while they think for you?'

'Sir,' said the learned man, 'do you not agree that I have done the public a great service by giving it the chance to read good authors as a matter of course?'

'That is not quite what I mean; I have as much respect as anyone for the supreme geniuses that you have disfigured. But you will never resemble them, for if you go on translating all the time nobody will ever translate you. Translations are like copper coins, which are worth the same amount as a gold piece, and indeed are more useful for the majority, but they are always of poor quality and never ring true.

'What you say you want is to make the famous men of the past live again among us, and I admit that you give them a body, but you cannot give them life; the spirit which might animate them will always be lacking.

'Why don't you devote yourself instead to the quest for all the great truths which simple calculations enable us to discover every day?' After which little piece of advice they parted, I should think, extremely displeased with each other.

From Paris, the last day of the second moon of Rabia, 1719

Letter 129
Usbek to Rhedi, at Venice

Most legislators have been men of limited abilities who have become leaders by chance, and have taken scarcely anything into account except their own whims and prejudices. They seem not even to have been aware of the grandeur and dignity of their task: they have passed the time making puerile regulations, which, it is true, have satisfied those without much intelligence, but have discredited them with men of sense.[1]

They have buried themselves in useless detail and descended to particular cases: this indicates lack of vision, which means seeing things partially and never taking a comprehensive view.

Some of them have affected not to use the common language but another one, which is absurd for someone making laws. How can they be observed if they are unknown?

They have often abolished unnecessarily the laws that they found in force, and this has meant throwing their countries into the confusion which is inseparable from change.

It is true that by an oddity that is due rather to human nature than to the human mind, it is sometimes necessary to change certain laws. But this situation is uncommon, and when it occurs they should be amended only in fear and trembling. There should be so much solemnity about it, and so many precautions should be taken, that the people should naturally conclude that laws are deeply sacred, since so many formalities are required in order to repeal them.

Legislators have often made their laws too ingenious, applying logical notions rather than natural equity. Subsequently these laws have turned out to be too harsh; and it is then thought right, in equity, to depart from them; but such a remedy does further harm. Whatever the laws may be, they must always be followed, and should be regarded as the public conscience, with which the individual's conscience should always be in conformity.

It must, however, be admitted that some legislators have taken care to do something that shows much wisdom: they have given fathers a large measure of authority over their children. Nothing gives greater relief to the judicial authorities, nothing does more to keep young people out of the courts, and nothing, finally, is more conducive to tranquillity throughout the state, since good citizens are always produced more by custom than by law. Of all forms of power, it is the one that is misused least; it is the holiest kind of judicial authority; it is the only one which does not depend on conventions established by society, and indeed precedes them.

It is noticeable that in countries where fathers are given wider powers to punish and reward, families are better run. Fathers resemble the creator of the universe, who, although he could lead men by love, also binds them to him by the motives of hope and fear.

I must not finish this letter without giving you an example of the strangeness of the French mind. They are said to have preserved an infinite number of things from Roman law that are useless, or worse, and they have failed to preserve the power of fathers, which it affirmed to be the first legitimate type of authority.

> From Paris, the 4th of the second moon of Jomada, 1719

Letter 130
Rica to ★★★

I am going to devote this letter to a certain race known as newsmongers,[1] who meet in a magnificent garden, where they have nothing to do but are always busy. They are entirely useless to the state, and what they have been saying for fifty years has had as much effect as if they had kept silent for the same length of time. Yet they believe themselves to be important, since they discuss lofty policies and deal in mighty interests of state.

The basis of their conversations is a petty and absurd inquisitiveness. No cabinet secrets are so well kept that they do not claim to have discovered them. They cannot accept the idea that anything is unknown to them; they know how many wives our august sultan has and how many children he fathers each year; they spend nothing on espionage, but they are informed of the measures he takes to humiliate the Turkish and the Mogul emperors.

They have scarcely finished with the present before plunging into the future. They go to meet Providence and give it advance notice of everything that mankind is to do. They will lead a general along step by step, and, having praised him for thousands of stupid actions that he did not do, they supply him with thousands more that he will not do either.

They make armies fly through the air like flocks of cranes, and fortified walls fall down like cards. They have bridges over every river, secret passes across every mountain, vast depôts in the burning desert; all they lack is sense.

A man who lodges with me received the following letter from a newsmonger, which I kept, since I found it interesting, and here it is.

Sir:

I am seldom mistaken in my conjectures about current affairs. On 1 January 1711 I forecast that the Emperor Joseph would die within the year. It is true that since he was in excellent health I thought that I would be laughed at if I expressed myself absolutely clearly, and as a result I used terms which were slightly enigmatic; but anyone who knew how to use his reason understood me very well. On 17 April of the same year he died of smallpox.

As soon as war was declared between the emperor and the Turks[2] I went and searched for my colleagues all through the Tuileries, and having assembled them near the pond I predicted that Belgrade would be besieged and that it would be captured. I had the good fortune to see my predictions fulfilled. It is true that about halfway through the siege I bet a hundred pounds that it would be taken on 18 August,* and it was not taken until the day after: how could such a certainty fail?

When I heard that the Spanish fleet was landing on Sardinia, I concluded that it would conquer the island; I said so, and it turned out to be true. Elated by this success, I went on to say that the victorious fleet would make a landing at Finale, so as to conquer the duchy of Milan. Finding that this idea met with some resistance, I was determined to do something glorious in its support; I bet fifty pounds, and lost again, because that devil Alberoni paid no attention to the treaties anᵈ

* 1717.

sent his fleet to Sicily, thus deceiving two great statesmen at once, the Duke of Savoy and myself.

All this, sir, has upset me so much that I have decided to stick to making forecasts, but never to bet. In the old days gambling was unknown in the Tuileries, and the late Count de L. would scarcely permit it; but now that a crowd of young men about town has intruded on us we no longer know where we are. We can hardly open our mouths to give the latest news without one of them offering to bet against us.

The other day, as I was getting out my papers and adjusting my glasses on my nose, one of these young popinjays said, catching me just between my first word and my second: 'A hundred pounds it isn't so!' I pretended not to pay any attention to this outburst, and resumed, saying in a louder voice: 'Marshal ***, having been informed that . . .'

'It's not true,' he said. 'Your news is always fantastic; that's all nonsense.' I should be most grateful, sir, if you would be so kind as to lend me fifty pounds, for these bets have put me in a very difficult position. I am enclosing copies of two letters that I wrote to the minister.

I am, yours, etc.

LETTERS FROM A NEWSMONGER TO THE MINISTER

My Lord,

I am the most zealous subject that the king has ever had. It was I who made a friend of mine carry out a plan I had devised, for a book proving that Louis the Great was the greatest of all the kings who deserve to be called great. I have been working for a long time on another book which will do our nation even more honour, if your noble lordship would be willing to grant me a permit to publish it. My intention is to prove that since the beginning of the monarchy the French have never been defeated, and that whatever the historians have hitherto written about our being worsted is sheer fabrication. I find myself obliged to correct them on many occasions, and I flatter myself that I am especially distinguished for my critical abilities.

I am, My Lord, yours, etc.

My Lord,

Since we have lost the Count de L., we beg you graciously to permit us to elect a president. Disorder is creeping into our assemblies, and affairs of state are not discussed as seriously as before. Our younger members behave with complete lack of respect for their elders, and are undisciplined among themselves; it is a real council of Rehoboam, in which the young impose on the old.[3] It is no use our telling them that we were in peaceful possession of the Tuileries twenty years before they came into the world; I think they will eventually force us to go away, and that if we are obliged to leave here, where we have so often paid homage to the ghosts of French heroes, we shall have to go and hold our meetings in the King's Gardens or some more remote spot.

I am, etc.

From Paris, the 7th of the second moon of Jomada, 1719

Letter 131
Rhedi to Rica, at Paris

One of the things which has aroused my curiosity since my arrival in Europe is the origin and history of republics. As you know, most Asians have no idea that this type of government exists; their imaginations have not stretched far enough to make them realize that there can be any other sort on earth except despotism.

The first governments of which we have any knowledge were monarchies: it was only by chance, and through the passage of hundreds of years, that republics came into being.

After Greece was devastated by flooding, new inhabitants came to repopulate it. Almost all its settlements came from the neighbouring Asian countries and Egypt; since these countries were ruled by kings, the people who came from them were ruled in the same way. But the tyranny of these princes became too oppressive, their authority was thrown off, and upon the ruins of all these kingdoms arose the republics which made Greece, the one civilized country among barbarians, so successful.

Love of freedom and hatred of kings preserved Greek independence for a long time, and extended republican government to distant parts. The Greek cities found allies in Asia Minor, and established settlements there which were as free as themselves; they used them as ramparts against anything the Persian kings might attempt. Not only this, but Greece peopled Italy, Spain, and perhaps Gaul also. It is known that Hesperia, the ideal country that was so famous among the ancients, was originally Greece, which its neighbours regarded as an abode of bliss.[1] The Greeks, failing to find this happy land in their own country, went to look for it in Italy; the people of Italy went to Spain, and those of Spain to Betica or Portugal; so that all these countries bore the name of Hesperia among the ancients. These Greek settlements brought with them a spirit of freedom which they had acquired in their own delightful country. Thus, in those remote times, there are hardly any monarchies to be found in Italy, Spain or Gaul. You will see shortly that the races of Germany and the North were no less free; if any traces of royalty have been found among them it is because chiefs of armies or republics have been taken for kings.

All this was in Europe; as for Asia and Africa, they have always been crushed under despotism, if you except the few towns of Asia Minor which we have mentioned, and the city of Carthage in Africa.

The world was divided between two powerful republics, Rome and Carthage. Nothing is better known than the beginnings of the Roman republic, and nothing less known than the origin of Carthage. We are totally ignorant of the succession of African princes after Dido, and of the way in which they lost their power. The enormous extension of the Roman republic would have been very beneficial for everyone, if there had not been an unjust distinction between Roman citizens and the subject peoples; if the provincial governors had been given less authority; if the august laws against their tyranny had been observed; and if, in order to stifle these laws, the governors had not used the very treasure that they had amassed by their injustice.[2]

Caesar oppressed the Roman republic, and subjected it to arbitrary power.

For a long time Europe languished under violent, militaristic government, and Roman moderation was changed into cruelty and oppression.

Meanwhile an infinite number of unknown tribes came out of the north and spread like torrents through the Roman provinces; finding it as easy to make conquests as to live by brigandage, they dismembered the Empire and founded kingdoms. These tribes were free; and they limited the authority of their king so strictly that in reality he was only a chief or a general. Consequently, these kingdoms, although established by force, never felt the conqueror's yoke. When Asian tribes such as the Turks or the Tartars made conquests, subordinated as they were to the control of a single person, their only thought was to provide him with more subjects, and to give him the authority of violence by force of arms; but the northern tribes were free in their own lands, and when they seized the Roman provinces they did not give great authority to their chiefs. Some of these tribes, such as the Vandals in Africa and the Goths in Spain, even deposed their kings, whenever they were dissatisfied with them, and in other tribes the ruler's authority was restricted in a thousand different ways. A large number of lords shared it with him; wars could not be undertaken without their consent; plunder was divided between the chief and the soldiers; there was no tax for the ruler's benefit; laws were made at tribal assemblies. Such were the fundamental principles of all the states which developed out of the ruins of the Roman Empire.[3]

From Venice, the 20th of the moon of Rajab, 1719

Letter 132
Rica to ★★★

Five or six months ago I went into a coffee house where I noticed a gentleman who was quite well dressed and whose remarks were attracting attention. He was talking about the pleasures of life in Paris, and complaining that his circumstances obliged him to lead a dull existence in the country. 'I get eight hundred a year from my estates,' he said, 'and I should count myself happy to have only a quarter of that amount in cash and letters of credit that I could take anywhere. It is no good putting pressure on my tenants and overwhelming them with legal costs, it only makes them more insolvent;

I have never succeeded in getting fifty pounds together at once. If I owed a thousand pounds all my estates would be confiscated, and I'd be in the poorhouse.'[1]

I left without having taken much notice of what he had said, but yesterday, being in that part of town, I went to the same place and saw a serious-looking man, with a pale, elongated face; he was surrounded by half a dozen people who were all talking, and seemed downcast and full of his own thoughts until he suddenly broke into the conversation and said, raising his voice, 'Yes, gentlemen, I am ruined. I no longer have enough to live on, for what I now have in my house is ten thousand pounds in bank notes and a hundred thousand silver crowns. I am in a terrible situation; I thought I was rich, and now I shall be in the poorhouse. If only I had a small estate to retire to, I could be sure of having something to live on; but I haven't a spadeful of land to call my own.'

I chanced to look in another direction and saw another man, who was making faces like a man possessed. 'You can't trust anyone these days,' he cried. 'The villain! I thought he was a friend of mine, and lent him all my money: and he paid it back![2] The wickedness of it! He can do what he likes now, but he's lost my respect for ever!'

Just nearby was a man very badly dressed, who, raising his eyes up to Heaven, said: 'God bless government policies! May I live to see shares going up to two thousand, and all the lackeys of Paris richer than their masters!' Out of curiosity I asked who he was. 'He is an extremely poor man,' I was told, 'and he has a correspondingly poor sort of job: he is a genealogist. He is hoping that his trade will become profitable if fortunes continue to be made, and that all those who have just got rich will need him to ennoble their names, clean up their ancestry, and decorate their coaches. He thinks that he is going to create as many nobles as he would like, and he is trembling with joy to see how many more clients are coming to him.'

Finally I saw a pale and wizened old man come in, whom I recognized as a newsmonger before he had sat down. He was not one of the sort whose optimism triumphs over every setback, and who are always forecasting victories and prizes; he was the opposite, one of the quaking sort, whose news is always bad. 'Things are going very badly on the Spanish front,' he said; 'we have no cavalry on the frontier, and there is reason to fear that Prince Pio,[3] whose cavalry force is large, will make the whole of Languedoc pay a levy.'

Facing me was a rather down-at-heel intellectual who was full of contempt for the newsmonger: the more the one raised his voice, the more the other raised his eyebrows. I went up to him, and he whispered in my ear: 'You see that fool who has been telling us for the last hour how frightened he is about Languedoc? Well, yesterday evening I saw a sunspot which, if it gets any bigger, could paralyse the whole universe;[4] and I haven't said a single word.'

From Paris, the 17th of the moon of Ramadán, 1719

Letter 133
Rica to ★★★

The other day I went to a monastery to look at a large library; it is in the safekeeping, so to speak, of the dervishes, but they are obliged to let anyone in at certain times.[1]

As I entered I saw a man solemnly walking up and down amidst an innumerable number of volumes surrounding him on every side. I went up to him and asked him to tell me what was in some books which, I could see, were in better bindings than the others. 'Sir,' he said, 'this is foreign territory to me; I don't know anyone here. Many people ask me questions such as yours, but it will be obvious to you that I can't go and read all these books in order to satisfy their curiosity. I have a librarian who will give you satisfaction. He spends night and day deciphering everything you see here; he is good for nothing, and is a great burden to us, since he does no work for the monastery. But I hear the bell ringing for our meal. Those who, like myself, are placed at the head of a community, should be the first to arrive for every exercise.'

With these words the monk pushed me outside, shut the door, and vanished from my sight as if he had wings.

From Paris, the 21st of the moon of Ramadán, 1719

Letter 134
Rica to the same

The next day I went back to the library, and found a man there who was completely different from the one I had seen first. He was un-affected, with a witty, intelligent expression, and friendly manners.[1] As soon as I had revealed my curiosity he took it upon himself to satisfy it, and because I was a foreigner to instruct me also.

'Father,' I said, 'what are those large volumes which take up all this side of the library?'

'Those,' he said, 'are books which explain the scriptures.'

'What a lot of them there are!' I replied; 'the scriptures must have been very obscure before, and as clear as daylight now. Do any doubts remain? Can there be any controversial points?'

'Any?' he answered. 'Can there be any? Good Lord! There are almost as many as there are lines.'

'Really?' I said. 'And what have all these writers been doing, then?'

'These writers,' he replied, 'did not consult scripture so as to find out what we must believe, but to find what they believed them-selves. They did not think of it as a book containing doctrines which they ought to accept, but as a work which might give authority to their own ideas. That is the reason why they have corrupted every aspect of its meaning and inflicted torture on every passage. Scripture is a country where men of every sect make raids, as if in order to pillage it; it is a battleground where hostile nations meet frequently in combat, attacking and skirmishing in numerous ways.

'Just by them you can see the ascetical treatises or books of piety; then books on morality, which are much more useful; and on theology, which are doubly incomprehensible, both because of their subject and their way of discussing it; and the works of the mystics, that is, devout persons of an emotional disposition.'

'Ah! Just a moment, father,' I said, 'don't go so fast; tell me about these mystics.'

'Piety, sir,' he said, 'in those of an emotional disposition, heats the blood. The blood gives off a vapour which rises to the brain, heating it also, and so causing ecstasies and trances. This condition is devoutness in delirium; it often develops, or rather degenerates, into quietism[2] – as you know, a quietist is a man of unsound mind, no less, a pious libertine.

'Here you see the casuists, who bring the secrets of the night out into the light of day; who, in imagination, create every monstrosity that the demon of love can produce, put them together, compare them, and think about them endlessly; and it is lucky for them if their emotions do not get involved, or even become the accomplices of all these perversions, so openly described and so nakedly portrayed.[3]

'You will see, sir, that I think freely, and tell you all my thoughts. I am candid by nature, especially with you who, being a foreigner, want to know about things, and know about them as they are. If I wanted to I would express nothing but wonder and admiration as I talked to you about all this. I should constantly be saying: "This is inspired, that commands our respect, here is something marvellous." And this could have only one result: I would either deceive you, or lose your good opinion.'

We went no further, since the dervish had to attend to some business, which interrupted our conversation until the next day.

From Paris, the 23rd of the moon of Ramadán, 1719

Letter 135
Rica to the same

I went back at the time we had arranged, and my guide took me to exactly the place where we had parted. 'Here,' he said, 'are the grammarians, editors and commentators.'

'Father,' I asked, 'is it not the case that all these people can manage without any commonsense?'

'Yes,' he said, 'they can, and it doesn't even show; their works are none the worse for it, which is very convenient for them.'

'True enough,' I said; 'I know many a philosopher who would do well to apply himself to that sort of scholarship.'

'Here are the orators,' he went on, 'who have the gift of persuasion independently of argument, and the mathematicians, who oblige a man to be persuaded against his will, and override him tyrannically.

'These are books on metaphysics, which discuss vast matters, where you come up against the infinite everywhere; and on physics, which treat the mighty structure of the universe as if it were no more marvellous than the simplest machine used by our artisans; books on medicine, monuments to natural weakness and curative power, which make the reader shiver when they describe the mildest disease, because they portray the presence of death so vividly, but give complete confidence when describing the effectiveness of their remedies, as if we had become immortal.

'Just nearby are books on anatomy, which do not so much contain descriptions of the parts of the body as the outlandish names which they have been given; a thing that cures neither the patient's disease nor the doctor's ignorance.

'Here is alchemy,[1] which sometimes inhabits the poorhouse and sometimes the madhouse, since both places are equally suitable for it.

'These books are on our knowledge, or rather ignorance, of the occult.[2] Of such a kind are those containing different sorts of black magic; an abomination in most people's opinion, and pitiful in mine. Of this kind too are books on judicial astrology.'

'What did you say, father? Books on judicial astrology!' I retorted hotly. 'But they are the books that we value most of all in Persia: they govern everything we do in life, and control our decisions in everything we undertake. Astrologers are really our spiritual directors, and more, for they play a part in the government of the State.'

'If that is so,' he said, 'you are under an authority much harsher than the rule of reason. This is the strangest of all forms of dominion; I feel very sorry for a family, and even more for a nation, which allows itself to be so completely dominated by the planets.'

'We use astrology,' I replied, 'as you do mathematics. Every nation has its own principles by which it regulates its policies. All our astrologers together never did anything so stupid in Persia as one single mathematician of yours did here. Can't you see that the fortuitous conjunctions of the stars are as sure a guide as the fine arguments of your systematic planners?[3] If you took a vote on it in France and Persia, astrology would have good cause to congratulate itself. You would see your calculators utterly humiliated; the conclusion to be inferred would be overwhelmingly to their disadvantage.'

Our argument was interrupted and we had to part.

From Paris, the 26th of the moon of Ramadán, 1719

Letter 136
Rica to the same

At our next meeting my learned friend led me into a private room. 'Here are the books on modern history,' he said. 'First you will see the historians of the church and the papacy, books which I read for edification, and which often have exactly the opposite effect on me.

'Over there are the authors who have written about the decline of the mighty Roman Empire, which sprang up out of the ruins of so many monarchies, and on whose fall so many new ones sprang up also. An infinite number of barbarian peoples, as little known as the lands they inhabited, appeared suddenly, inundated and pillaged it, tore it to pieces and founded all the kingdoms that now compose Europe. These peoples were not truly barbarous, since they were free, but they have become so now that most of them have submitted to dictatorship, and lost the sweetness of freedom, which is in such close concord with reason, humanity and nature.[1]

'You see here the historians of the German Empire, only a shadow of the first empire,[2] but which must be the only power on earth, I believe, which has not been weakened by division, and the only one again, I believe, which grows stronger in proportion to its losses, and though it is slow to profit from victory, becomes unconquerable through its defeats.

'Here are the historians of France, where royal power is at first to be seen in the process of formation; dying twice, being reborn twice more; later, going into decline for several centuries, but gradually recovering its strength, making gains on every side and reaching the peak of its development;³ like rivers which on their way diminish in size or disappear underground, then emerge again and, swollen by the rivers which flow into them, sweep away rapidly everything which lies in their path.

'There you can see the Spanish nation appearing from a few mountains, the Muslim princes subdued by a process as slow as their own conquests had been rapid, numerous kingdoms united in one vast monarchy, which came to be almost unique, until it was crushed under its own greatness and its unreal prosperity,⁴ lost its strength, and even its reputation, and kept nothing but pride in its former power.

'Here are the historians of England, where you see freedom constantly arising from the flames of discord and sedition, and the sovereign perched unsteadily on an unshakable throne; a restive nation, wise even in fury, mistress of the seas (a thing without precedent), and combining trade with empire.⁵

'Just by them are the historians of that other queen of the seas, the republic of Holland, so widely respected in Europe and so formidable in Asia, where its merchants often see kings prostrated before them.

'The historians of Italy will show you a nation which was once the mistress of the world, and is now a slave to all the others, its princes divided and weak, the only attribute of sovereignty that they possess being an empty show of policy-making.

'These are the historians of the republics: of Switzerland, the image of freedom; of Venice, whose only resources consist in using them sparingly; and of Genoa, whose magnificence resides in its buildings alone.⁶

'These are the historians of the North, and, among others, Poland, which makes such bad use of its freedom and its right to elect its kings that it seems to be trying to console the adjoining nations, which have lost both one and the other.'⁷

At this we parted until the next day.

From Paris, the 2nd of the moon of Shawall, 1719

Letter 137
Rica to the same

The next day he took me into another room. 'These are the poets,' he told me; 'that is to say, writers whose business it is to put obstacles in the way of commonsense, and dress up reason in frills, just as women were once buried in jewels and ornaments. They will be known to you; they are not uncommon in the East, where the sun is stronger and seems to heat up even men's imaginations.[1]

'Here are the epic poems.'

'Oh! and what is an epic poem?'

'To be honest,' he said, 'I really don't know. The experts say that only two have ever been written, and that others which bear the name are not epics at all; and I know nothing about that either. They say furthermore that it is impossible to write any new ones, which is even more surprising.

'Here are the dramatic poets, who in my opinion are supreme among their kind; they are the masters of our emotions. There are two sorts: the writers of comedy, who arouse such enjoyable feelings in us, and the tragedians, who agitate and disturb us with such violence.

'Here are the lyric poets, whom I despise as much as I esteem the others, and who use their art to create melodious extravaganzas.

'We come next to the writers of idylls and eclogues, who are popular even in court society, because they produce an image of a certain kind of tranquillity which is lacking at court, and which they convey by their descriptions of the life led by shepherds.[2]

'Of all the authors we have seen, here are the most dangerous: those who write cutting epigrams, delicate little arrows which make deep wounds inaccessible to remedies.

'Here you see the romances.[3] Their authors are poets of a sort; with them the language both of the heart and the head is equally exaggerated; they spend their lives trying to achieve naturalness and constantly failing to find it; their heroes are as remote from nature as flying dragons and hippocentaurs.'

'I have seen some of your romances,' I said, 'and if you saw ours you would be even more shocked. They are just as unnatural; moreover, the customs of our country make things very awkward for them. It needs ten years of passion before a lover can even see the face of his beloved, yet the writer is compelled to take his readers through these tedious preliminaries. Since it is impossible to diversify the incidents of the story, he resorts to a device which is worse than the defect which it is supposed to remedy, and uses miracles. I am sure that you would not approve of an army being conjured out of the ground by a sorceress, or of another, a hundred thousand strong, being destroyed single-handed by the hero. However, that is what our novels are like. The frequent repetition of these insipid adventures is boring, and the nonsensical miracles are repellent.'

From Paris, the 6th of the moon of Shawall, 1719

Letter 138
Rica to Ibben, at Smyrna

Ministers here replace and cancel each other out like the seasons: in three years I have seen financial policy changed four times.[1] In Persia and Turkey taxes are raised by the same methods today as when these kingdoms were founded, which is far from being the case here. It is true that we are not as clever about it as the Westerners are. We believe that the difference between administering the incomes of a king and of a private individual is no more than the difference between counting a hundred thousand tomans and counting a hundred; but here things are a great deal more esoteric and expert. Great geniuses have to work night and day, bringing forth new projects incessantly, with great labour, listening to the opinions of an infinity of people who do their work for them without being asked,[2] and retiring to live in the depths of an office which is inaccessible to the aristocracy and sacred to the common people; they have to have their heads continuously full of important secrets, miraculous schemes, and novel policies, and, plunged in meditation, be bereft not only of the use of speech but sometimes even of good manners.

As soon as the late king's eyes were closed, thought was given to setting up a new form of administration. Things were felt to be bad, but nobody knew how to make them better. The unlimited authority of previous ministers had had bad results; an effort was made to share it out. To this end, six or seven councils were created,[3] and of all governments they were perhaps the one which has ruled France with the most sense; their duration was short, like the benefits they produced.

France, on the death of the late king, was a body which had succumbed to a multitude of ills. N***, scalpel in hand, removed the excess flesh and applied some local remedies on the outside, but an internal fault still remained to be cured. A foreigner arrived and undertook to treat it.[4] After administering many drastic medicines he thought that he had got the country back into shape, but all he had done was swell it up.

Everyone who was rich six months ago is now in poverty, and those who had no bread then are gorged with riches. Never have the two extremes been so close. The foreigner has turned the state about like a tailor with a second-hand coat; he has turned it inside out and put the top to the bottom. Fortunes have been made so unexpectedly that even those who made them can't believe it; God does not create men from nothing with greater speed. The number of valets there are who are being served by their comrades, and tomorrow, perhaps, by their masters!

The effects of all this are often extraordinary. Footmen who made their fortunes under the last reign nowadays boast of their lineage. Towards others like them who have just left their livery behind in a certain street[5] they behave with as much disdain as they themselves experienced six months ago; they cry at the top of their voices: 'The nobility is ruined! the State is in chaos! the classes are in confusion! Everywhere you look there are nobodies getting to the top!' I can promise you that the nobodies will get their own back with a vengeance on those who come after them, and that in thirty years' time these aristocrats will have plenty to say for themselves.

From Paris, the 1st of the moon of Dulkaada, 1720

Letter 139
Rica to the same

Here is a wonderful example of conjugal affection, and not in a woman merely, but in a queen. The Queen of Sweden,[1] wishing at all costs to bestow the crown on the prince, her husband, sent the States General, in order to eliminate every difficulty, a declaration saying that she would renounce the regency if he were to be elected.

Sixty-odd years ago another queen, whose name was Christina, abdicated in order to devote herself entirely to philosophy.[2] I do not known which of these two examples is the more remarkable.

Although I like a man to stay firmly where he has been placed by nature, and cannot approve of the weakness of those who find themselves inferior to their position and abandon it, which is a kind of desertion, I am nevertheless impressed by the greatness of soul shown by these two queens, and to see that the mind of the one, and the emotions of the other, are superior to their destiny. Christina concentrated on knowledge at a time when others only wanted enjoyment, and the other wanted to enjoy the crown only so as to place her whole happiness in the hands of her illustrious husband.

From Paris, the 27th of the moon of Muharram, 1720

Letter 140
Rica to Usbek, at ★★★

The Parlement of Paris has just been banished to a little town called Pontoise. The Council sent it, for registration or approval, a declaration which dishonours it, and it registered this declaration in a manner which dishonours the Council.[1]

Some other Parlements in the kingdom are threatened with similar treatment.

These institutions invariably meet with odium: they come into the presence of their king only in order to convey unhappy truths to him, and while a crowd of courtiers are continually making out how happy his people is under his government, the Parlements come and contradict the flatterers, bringing to the foot of the throne the tears and lamentations with which they have been charged.

Truth, my dear Usbek, is a heavy load to bring to princes! They must surely realize that those who decide to do such a thing are compelled to, and that they would never take it upon themselves to carry out an action which is so unwelcome and distressing for those who do it, if they were not forced to by their duty, their respect, and indeed their love.

From Paris, the 21st of the first moon of Jomada, 1720

Letter 141
Rica to the same

I shall be coming to see you at the end of the week. How pleasantly the days will pass in your company!

I was introduced a few days ago to a lady of the court who wished to see my foreign countenance. I found her beautiful, worthy of being looked on by our monarch, and of holding a high rank in the sacred dwelling-place of his affections.

She asked me thousands of questions about the ways of Persian men and the life of Persian women. It became clear to me that life in a seraglio was not to her taste; she found it objectionable that one man should be shared among ten or twelve women. She was unable to contemplate the happiness of the one without envy and the state of the others without pity. Since she is fond of reading, especially poetry and novels, she said that she would like me to tell her about ours, and what I said increased her curiosity. She asked me to have a translation made for her of some part of the books I have brought with me. I did so, and a few days later sent her a Persian tale. You may perhaps enjoy reading it in a new guise.

In the time of Sheik Ali Khan[1] there lived in Persia a woman by the name of Zulema. She knew the whole of the holy Koran by heart; no dervish understood the traditions of the holy prophets better than she; nothing the Arab theologians had said was so sublime that she was unable to understand every aspect of its meaning, and with all this knowledge she combined the sort of humorous attitude which made it almost impossible to guess, when she was talking to someone, whether she wanted to entertain them or instruct them.

One day when she was with her companions in a room in the seraglio, one of them asked her what she thought of life after death, and if she accepted that ancient theological tradition of ours, that Paradise is only for men.[2]

'That is the common view,' she said; 'nothing has been neglected in order to degrade our sex. There is even a nation spread throughout Persia, called the Jews, which maintains on the authority of its holy books that we have no soul.

'Such insulting opinions as these are due solely to the pride of men, who want to preserve their superiority after their lifetime, not realizing that on the great day every creature will appear as nothing in the sight of God, with no distinctions between them except those which are due to virtue.

'God will not set limits to his rewards, and just as men who have lived well, and used their power over us well, will go to a Paradise full of ravishing celestial beauties, of such a kind that if a mortal man were to see them he would take his life at once in his eagerness to enjoy them, so too will virtuous women go to a place of delight, where they will be intoxicated by floods of ecstasy with god-like men who will be subject to them. Each woman will have a seraglio to keep them in, and eunuchs, even more faithful than ours, to guard them.

'I have read in an Arab book,' she went on, 'that there was a man called Ibrahim who was jealous to an intolerable degree. He had twelve extremely beautiful wives whom he treated very harshly. He no longer trusted his eunuchs or the walls of his seraglio, but kept them locked up almost all the time, in their rooms, without letting them see or talk to each other, for even innocent friendship made him jealous. Everything he did bore the trace of his natural brutality; he never uttered a kind word, and every least command of his added to the rigours of their captivity.

'One day when he had assembled them all in a room in his seraglio, one of them, braver than the others, reproached him for his unpleasant nature.

'"When a man tries so hard to find ways of making himself feared," she said, "he always finds ways of making himself hated first. We are so wretched that we cannot not want something different. Others in my place would wish that you would die; I wish only to die myself, and since that is the only way in which I can hope to be separated from you, I shall still find such a separation pleasant."

'These words, which should have made him take pity, put him into such a furious rage that he seized his dagger and plunged it into her breast. "My dear companions," she said with her dying breath, "if Heaven has mercy on my virtue, you will be revenged." As she spoke she left this life of misery to go to the sojourn of delight where women who have lived well have their happiness perpetually renewed.

'The first thing she saw was an attractive meadow, its greenness enhanced by patterns of flowers in the freshest colours. A stream, its water purer than crystal, twisted and turned innumerable times on its way across. Next she went into an enchanting wood where the silence was broken only by the sweetness of birdsong. Then some magnificent gardens appeared; they were adorned with all nature's simplicity and splendour. Finally she found a superb palace made ready for her, full of celestial men intended for her pleasures.

'Two of them immediately appeared in order to undress her. Others took her to a bath, and perfumed her with the most delicious essences. Then she was given clothes infinitely richer than her own, after which she was taken to a room where she found a fire burning aromatic wood and a table covered with the most exquisite dishes. Everything seemed to contribute to her sensuous delight; on one side she heard music which grew more divine as it grew more impassioned; elsewhere she saw only dances performed by the god-like men whose unique concern was to please her. But all these pleasures were intended only to lead her gradually to greater ones. She was taken to her room, and after she had been undressed once more she was carried to a sumptuous bed, where two men of entrancing beauty took her in their arms. It was then that she was intoxicated with delight, and that her ecstasies surpassed even her desires. "I am beside myself," she told them; "I should believe myself to be dying, if I were not certain of being immortal. It is too much, leave me; I am overwhelmed by excess of pleasure. Ah, you have allowed my senses to grow a little calmer; I am beginning to breathe again and coming back to myself. Why is it that the torches have been taken away? Why am I unable still to gaze on your divine beauty? Why can I not see . . .? but why see? You are renewing my previous ecstasies. Oh gods! how lovely this darkness is! Am I then to be immortal, and immortal with you? I shall be . . . no, I beg for mercy; for it is obvious that you are not the sort to ask for it yourselves."

'After repeating her commands several times she was obeyed, but only when she really wanted to be. She lay back drowsily and went to sleep in their arms. A few moments' sleep removed her tiredness; she felt two kisses which abruptly aroused her and made her open her eyes. "I am worried," she told them, "I am afraid that you no longer love me." She was reluctant to remain in doubt for long, and so she received from them all the assurances that she could desire. "I was mistaken," she cried, "forgive me, forgive me, I am sure of you. You do not say anything, but your proofs are better than anything that you could say; yes, yes, I admit, never has anyone been loved so much. But what is this? Are you both claiming the honour of convincing me? Ah! if you quarrel, if you try to outdo each other, as well as have the pleasure of defeating me, I am lost. Both of you will be the victors, I alone shall be vanquished, but I shall sell you the victory dearly."

'All this was interrupted only by daylight. Her devoted and charming servants came to her room and got the two young men out of bed, to be taken away by two old men to where they were kept for her pleasures. Then she rose and appeared to her adoring court, first looking lovely in simple informal dress, and later covered in the most gorgeous jewels. The night had made her more beautiful; it had put life into her complexion and made her beauty more eloquent. All day long there was nothing but dances, music, parties, games, walks, and it was observed that Anaïs disappeared from time to time, and sped towards her two young heroes. After a few precious moments together she would return to the company she had left, looking more serene each time. Eventually, towards evening, she was not to be found at all. She went and shut herself in the seraglio, where, she said, she wanted to make the acquaintance of the immortal captives who were to live with her forever. She therefore visited the remotest and pleasantest rooms of the building, and counted fifty slaves of miraculous beauty; she roamed all night from room to room, everywhere receiving acts of homage which were always different and always the same.

'Such was the way in which the immortal Anaïs passed her life, enjoying herself sometimes in a whirl of pleasures and sometimes on her own, being admired by a brilliant company or loved by a passionate lover. Often she would leave an enchanted palace to enter a country grove; flowers seemed to spring up beneath her feet, and amusements thronged around her.

'She had been in this happy abode for more than a week, and in her constant rapture she had not spent a moment in reflection. She had enjoyed her happiness without being conscious of it, or having any of those moments of tranquillity in which the soul takes stock of itself, as it were, and examines itself while the emotions are silent.

'The blessed have such keen pleasures that they seldom enjoy this freedom of mind. Consequently, being utterly absorbed in the present, they entirely lose their memories of the past, and no longer care about anything they knew or loved in their former life.

'But Anaïs, who had the mind of a true philosopher, had spent almost all her life in meditation; she had carried her reflections much further than might have been expected from a woman left on her own. This had been the only advantage of the rigorous seclusion that her husband had imposed on her.

'It was because of this strength of mind that she had disregarded both fear, which had overawed her companions, and death, which was to be the end of her troubles and the beginning of her happiness.

'Thus she gradually ceased to be intoxicated with pleasure, and shut herself up alone in an apartment in her palace. She surrendered herself to the most delightful thoughts about her former existence and her present happiness; she could not avoid feeling sorry for her unhappy companions; we sympathize about ordeals that we have shared. Anaïs did not confine herself merely to compassion; her feelings for these unfortunate women went deeper than that, and she felt disposed to help them.

'She ordered one of the young men around her to take on the appearance of her husband, go down to his seraglio, take charge, and drive him out; and to stay there in his place until she recalled him.

'Her orders were promptly carried out. Flying through the air he arrived outside the seraglio; Ibrahim was away. He knocks; all the doors are opened; the eunuchs fall at his feet. He goes swiftly to the apartments where Ibrahim's wives are shut in. On his way, having made himself invisible, he had stolen the keys from their jealous husband's pocket. He enters, and they are immediately surprised by his polite and gentle manner; soon afterwards he surprises them a great deal more by his ardour and the speed of his operations. They all had their share of the general astonishment, and they would have taken it for a dream if it had not been so real.

'While these unprecedented scenes were going on in the seraglio, Ibrahim was banging on the door calling his name, storming and shouting. After meeting with many difficulties he got in, plunging the eunuchs into the greatest confusion. Striding forward he fell back as if the ground had given way beneath his feet on seeing the false Ibrahim, his exact copy, taking all the liberties of a master. He called for help, tried to make the eunuchs help him kill the impostor, but was not obeyed. His only resource was a poor one: it was to appeal to the judgement of his wives. In one hour the false Ibrahim had seduced all his judges. The other was driven out and dragged outside the seraglio in disgrace, and would have been killed a thousand times over if his rival had not ordered that his life was to be spared. Finally, the new Ibrahim, victor on the field of battle, showed time and again that he had deserved to be chosen by the wives, and distinguished himself by unheard-of achievements. "You are not like Ibrahim," said the wives.

'"Don't say that; say rather that the impostor is not like me," the triumphant Ibrahim replied; "what does a man have to do in order to be your husband, if what I do is not enough?"

"'Ah! we do not want to doubt your word," said the wives. "If you are not Ibrahim, it is enough for us that you fully deserve to be. You are more of an Ibrahim in one day than he has been in the course of ten years."

"'Do you promise me then," he replied, "that you will testify in my favour against the impostor?"

"'Have no doubt," they said with one voice; "we swear to be eternally faithful to you. We have been deceived only too long. The villain did not suspect that we were virtuous, but only that we were weak. We can see clearly that other men are not like him; it is you, no doubt, that they resemble. If you only knew how much you make us loathe him!"

"'Ah! I shall often provide you with new reasons for loathing him," the false Ibrahim replied; "you do not yet know all the wrongs that he has done you."

"'We can judge how unjust he has been by the extent of your vengeance," they answered.

"'You are right," said the man from Heaven. "I have made his retribution fit the crime; I am delighted that you are happy with my way of punishing him."

"'But if the impostor comes back," said the wives, "what shall we do?"

"'It would be difficult, I think," he answered, "to deceive you. It is scarcely possible to keep up the position I hold towards you by pretending; and besides, I shall send him so far away that you will never hear him mentioned again. Then I shall myself take the responsibility for keeping you happy. I shall not be jealous; I shall be able to rely on you without placing any restrictions on you. I am sufficiently convinced of my abilities to believe that you will be faithful to me: if you are not virtuous on my behalf, could you be virtuous for anyone?" The conversation between him and the wives went on for a long time. They were more struck by the difference between the two Ibrahims than by the resemblance between them, and did not even think of asking for an explanation of all these marvels. Eventually they were disturbed once more by the husband returning, in desperation. He found the whole household full of joy, and his wives were more incredulous than ever. It was no place for a jealous man; he went off in a fury, to be followed a moment later by the false Ibrahim, who seized him, carried him through the air, and left him two thousand leagues away.

'Heavens! how miserable the wives felt while their beloved Ibrahim was away! Their eunuchs had already resumed their natural severity; the whole house was in tears; the wives would sometimes imagine that everything that had happened was only a dream; they would all look at each other and recall the smallest details of their strange adventures. At last the celestial Ibrahim came back, more attractive than ever, and it became apparent to them that his journey had not been too wearisome. The new master's behaviour was so different from the old one's that it surprised the whole neighbourhood. He dismissed all the eunuchs and threw his house open to everyone; he did not allow his women even to wear veils. It was more than a little unusual to see them at parties, in the company of men and as free as they were. Ibrahim rightly considered that the local customs did not apply to citizens like him. Meanwhile he spared himself no expense. With immense prodigality he used up the wealth of the jealous husband, who, returning three years later from the distant land to which he had been transported, found nothing left but his wives and thirty-six children.'

From Paris, the 26th of the first moon of Jomada, 1720

Letter 142
Rica to Usbek, at ★★★

I received this letter from a learned man yesterday; you will find it interesting.

Sir,

Six months ago I inherited a legacy from a very rich uncle, who left me about thirty thousand pounds and a beautifully furnished house. It is good to be well off when one knows how to use money properly. I have no ambitions or taste for pleasure; I confine myself almost exclusively to my study, where I pursue a life of research; there you will find that I am an enthusiastic student of the remote and venerable past.

When my uncle passed away, I should very much have liked to bury him according to the ceremonies observed by the ancient Greeks and Romans, but at the time I did not possess any antique lachrymatories, urns, or lamps.

But since then I have provided myself with these precious rarities. A few days ago I sold my silver dinner-service to buy an earthenware lamp which had been used by one of the Stoic philosophers. I have got rid of all the mirrors with which my uncle had covered almost every wall of his rooms, in order to have a small looking-glass, slightly cracked, which was once in Virgil's possession. It enchants me to see my face reflected in it instead of the swan of Mantua's. This is not all: I have spent a hundred golden sovereigns on five or six copper coins in a currency which was in use two thousand years ago. As far as I know, every bit of furniture I have now in my house was made before the Dark Ages. I have a small study filled with the most precious and expensive manuscripts. Although it ruins my eyesight to read them, I prefer to use them instead of the printed versions, which are not so correct, and which are in everybody's possession. Although I hardly ever go out, I have nonetheless an extreme desire to know all the ancient roads which existed in Roman times. There is one near me[1] made by a proconsul of Gaul about twelve hundred years ago, and when I go to my country house I never fail to go along it, although it is very inconvenient, and takes me more than a league out of my way. But what makes me furious is that they have put wooden posts at intervals along it, to show how far away the neighbouring towns are. I am appalled to see these miserable signposts in place of the milliary columns which were there once. I fully intend to have them restored by my heirs, and I shall require them to spend the necessary amount in my will. If, sir, you have a Persian manuscript, I should be obliged to you for letting me have it. I will pay whatever you want for it, and give you into the bargain some works of my own composition, so that you will see that I am far from being a useless member of the intellectual world. You will notice among others a dissertation in which I show that the wreaths once used in triumphal processions were made of oak-leaves, not of laurel; you will be impressed by another in which I prove, by learned conjectures based on the most reliable Greek writers, that Cambyses was wounded in the left leg, not in the right; and by another in which I demonstrate that a narrow forehead was a mark of beauty much sought after by the Romans. I shall also send you a quarto volume consisting of an explanation of a line from the sixth book of Virgil's *Aeneid*. You will not receive all this for a few days; for the moment I shall content myself with sending you this fragment from an ancient Greek mythologist, which has not appeared before, and which I found covered in dust in a library. I must leave you in order to see to an important matter that I have to deal with; it concerns the restitution of a fine passage from Pliny the Elder, which was extraordinarily distorted by fifth-century copyists.

I remain, yours, etc.

FRAGMENT FROM AN ANCIENT MYTHOLOGIST

In an island near the Orcades a child was born,[2] whose father was Aeolus, god of the winds, and whose mother was a Caledonian nymph. He is said to have learnt all by himself to count on his fingers, and, at four years of age, to have been able to distinguish between the different metals so exactly that when his mother tried to give him a ring made of brass, instead of gold, he realized that it was a trick and threw the ring on the ground.

As soon as he was fully grown his father taught him the secret of catching the wind in balloons, which he then sold to travellers. However, since his wares were not greatly appreciated in his own country, he left, and began to lead a wandering life in the company of the blind god of chance.[3]

In his travels he learnt that in Betica everything shone with gold, which made him hurry to get there. He was made very unwelcome by Saturn,[4] who was then on the throne, but once the god had departed from the earth he had an idea, and went out to every street-corner, where he continually shouted in a hoarse voice: 'Citizens of Betica, you think yourselves rich, because you have silver and gold. Your delusion is pitiable. Take my advice: leave the land of worthless metal and enter the realms of imagination, and I promise you such riches that you will be astonished.' He immediately opened a large number of the balloons he had brought and distributed his wares[5] to anyone who wanted them.

The next day, he went back to the same street-corners and shouted: 'Citizens of Betica, do you want to be rich? Imagine to yourselves that I am very rich, and that you are too. Every morning, make yourselves believe that your wealth has doubled during the night. Then get up, and if you owe anyone anything, go and pay them the money that you have imagined, and tell them that it is their turn to start imagining.'

He reappeared some days later, and spoke as follows: 'Citizens of Betica, it is obvious that your imaginations are not as powerful as they were at first. Let yourselves be guided by mine. Every morning I shall hang up a notice-board in front of you, which will be the basis of your riches; it will bear only four words,[6] but they will be extremely significant, for they will control your wives' dowries, your children's inheritances, and the number of servants you have. But as for you,' he said to the nearest members of his company, 'as for you, my beloved children (I can call you that, since you have received a second birth from me), my notice-board will determine the magnificence of your carriages, the sumptuousness of your banquets, the number of mistresses you have, and the amount of their official allowances.'

Some days later he arrived on the corner out of breath, and cried in a fury of rage: 'Citizens of Betica, I advised you to use your imaginations, and I find that you have not done so: well, now I command you to.'[7] Thereupon he left abruptly, but second thoughts called him back. 'I am told that some of you are behaving atrociously and holding on to your gold and silver.[8] It is not so bad about the silver, but as for the gold ... as for the gold ... Oh! it makes me so indignant that ... I swear, by my sacred balloons, that if you fail to bring it back to me I will punish you severely.' Then he added in a most persuasive manner: 'Do you think that I am asking you for these miserable metals in order to keep them? It is a sign of my sincerity that a few days ago, when you brought them to me, I immediately gave you back half.'[9]

The next day, he was seen from afar, and came sidling up saying in a soft, ingratiating voice: 'Citizens of Betica, I am told that you keep some of your treasure abroad. I beg of you, let me have it; you will be doing me a favour, and I shall be eternally grateful to you.'

The son of Aeolus was addressing an audience which did not feel much like laughing, but they could not stop themselves, which made him turn away in great embarrassment. But he took courage once more and risked another little plea: 'I know that you possess precious jewels; in the name of Jupiter, get rid of them; nothing impoverishes you more than that sort of thing; get rid of them, I tell you. If you cannot manage it by yourselves, I will give you some excellent business advisers. Wealth will flow in abundance among you if you do as I advise. Truly, I promise you the purest air that my balloons contain.'

Eventually he got on a platform and said, putting on a tone of confidence: 'Citizens of Betica, I have compared your present happy state with the condition in which I found you when I arrived here. I see that you are the richest nation on earth; but to make your fortune complete, allow me to take away half of what you possess.'[10] With these words, flying lightly away, the son of Aeolus disappeared, and left his audience in indescribable consternation. This made him come back the next day and speak as follows: 'I noticed yesterday that what I said was extremely unpopular with you. Well, forget that I said anything. It is true that half is too much; all we have to do is to take other measures to achieve what I set out to do. Let us put all our riches together in the same place, which we can do easily, for they do not take up much room.' And immediately three-quarters of them vanished.[11]

From Paris, the 9th of the moon of Shaaban, 1720

Letter 143
Rica to Nathaniel Levi, a Jewish doctor, at Leghorn

You ask me what I think about the effectiveness of amulets and the powers of talismans.[1] Why consult me? You are a Jew, and I am a Muslim, which means that we are both very credulous.

I always have on me over two thousand passages from the holy Koran; tied round my arm I have a little packet containing the names of more than two hundred dervishes; the names of Ali, Fatima, and all the saints are concealed in over twenty places in my clothes.

At the same time, I am not against those who deny the powers which we attribute to particular words: it is much harder for us to answer their arguments than for them to refute our evidence.

I carry about all these hallowed bits of frippery because it has long been my habit to do so, and so as to conform to a universal practice. I believe that, even if their power is no greater than that of the rings and other ornaments which people wear, neither is it any less. But you place your trust completely in a few mystic letters, and without this safeguard you would be in a state of continual dread.

What unhappy beings men are! They constantly waver between false hopes and silly fears, and instead of relying on reason they create monsters to frighten themselves with, and phantoms which lead them astray.

What consequences can be produced, do you think, by arranging certain letters in a certain order? and what consequences can be prevented, do you think, by altering the arrangement? What connection do they have with the winds, that they can bring calm to storms, or with gunpowder, that they can nullify its force, or with what doctors call the *peccant humour* or the *morbific cause* of disease, that they can cure it?

The extraordinary thing is that people who do their reason violence, in order to establish that occult powers have a relationship with some event, have to work just as hard in order to prevent themselves from seeing the real cause.

You will tell me that a battle was won by certain magic spells, and I will tell you that you must be blind not to find causes, in the geography of the terrain, in the number of soldiers, or their morale, and in the degree of experience possessed by their officers, which are sufficient to produce this effect, while you refuse to admit even that it has a cause.

I will concede for a moment that there are magic spells, provided that you too concede to me for a moment that there are none; which is not impossible. Your concession does not prevent two armies from fighting: would you then believe that, if they do, neither can be victorious?

Do you think that their fate will remain uncertain, until the appearance of an invisible power by which it will be decided? that all their blows will be wasted, all their cunning useless, and all their courage unavailing?

Do you think that the presence of death, which on these occasions is manifest in a thousand ways, could not produce panic among the soldiers, a form of terror which you have such difficulty in explaining? Do you believe that in an army of a hundred thousand men it is impossible for there to be a single coward? Do you think that his faint-heartedness could not cause another man to lose heart? that the second, deserting a third, could not soon cause him to abandon a fourth? That is all that is necessary for a whole army at once to give up hope of victory, and the more numerous it is the more easily will it give up.

Everyone knows and everyone feels that men, like all creatures which strive for their own preservation, love life passionately: we know it as a general principle, and we wonder why, on one particular occasion, they are afraid to lose it.

Although the sacred books of every nation are full of these panic or supernatural terrors,[2] I can think of nothing more unjustified, because, in order to be sure that an effect is supernatural, when it might have been due to a hundred thousand natural causes, it would be necessary to examine beforehand whether any one of these causes was operative, which is impossible.

I will say nothing more, Nathaniel: it seems to me that the subject does not deserve such serious treatment.

From Paris, the 20th of the moon of Shaaban, 1720

P.S. As I was finishing this, I heard the shouts of a street-vendor selling a 'Letter from a Doctor in the Country to a Doctor in Paris' (for here every piece of nonsense gets printed and published, and bought). I thought that it was worth sending to you, since it is connected with our subject. It contains many things which I do not understand, but you, being a doctor, should be able to understand your colleagues' professional jargon.

LETTER FROM A DOCTOR IN THE COUNTRY
TO A DOCTOR IN PARIS

In our town there was a sick man who had had no sleep for thirty-five days. His doctor prescribed opium, but he could not make his mind up to take it, and even with the glass in his hand he was as irresolute as ever. At last he said to the doctor: 'Doctor, take mercy on me just till tomorrow: I know a man who does not practise medicine, but has in his house an innumerable number of remedies for insomnia. Let me send for him, and if I don't go to sleep tonight, I promise to come back to you.' Having got rid of the doctor, the patient had the curtains drawn and said to a little servant boy: 'Here, off you go to Mr Anis,³ and tell him to come and have a word with me.' Mr Anis arrives. 'Mr Anis, I am dying; I cannot sleep; would you have by any chance in your shop a *K. of the G.*,⁴ or some work of piety written by a R.F. of the S.J.⁵ that you have been unable to sell? for often the medicines which have been kept longest are the best.'

'Sir,' says the bookseller, 'I have Father Caussin's *Sacred Court*, in six volumes, at your service. I will send it round and I hope it will do you good. If you want the works of the Reverend Father Rodriguez, the Spanish Jesuit, you must certainly have them.⁶ But take my advice, and stick to Father Caussin: I hope that one sentence from Father Caussin, with God's help, will have as much effect on you as a whole page of the *K. of the G.*' With which Mr Anis hurries off to his shop to find the remedy. The *Sacred Court* arrives; the dust is shaken off; the patient's son, a young schoolboy, begins to read; he was the first to feel its effects: by the second page, his pronunciation was already slurred, and everyone present felt tired; a moment later they were all snoring, except the patient, who, having held out for a long time, finally dropped off.

The doctor arrives early in the morning. 'Well! Did he take my opium, then?' No one answers: the wife, the daughter, and the little boy, in transports of joy, all point to Father Caussin. He asks what it is, they say: 'Long live Father Caussin! we must send him to the book-binder's. Who could have known? who would have believed it? it's a miracle. Come on doctor, come and look at Father Caussin;

this is the book that put my father to sleep.' And so they explained how it had all happened.[7]

The doctor was a clever man, well versed in the mysteries of the Kabbala and the powers of magic spells and spirits. The incident impressed him, and after some thought he decided to change his practice completely. 'That was a most curious phenomenon,' he said. 'I have my experiment; I must take it further. Why should the mind not transmit the qualities it has itself to the works it produces? It happens every day. At any rate, it's certainly worth a try. I am tired of apothecaries: their syrups, their linctuses, and all Galen's drugs, ruin the patients and their health. I must change my methods; let us try the powers of the mind.' Following this principle, he drew up a new sort of pharmacopoeia, as you will see from the following description of the chief remedies that he used:

Laxative infusion

Take three leaves from Aristotle's logic, in Greek; two leaves from one of the most stringent treatises of scholastic theology, as, for example, that of the subtle Duns Scotus; four from Paracelsus; one from Avicenna; six from Averrhoes; three from Porphyry; the same from Plotinus; the same from Iamblichus. Make an infusion of the whole for twenty-four hours. To be taken four times daily.

A stronger laxative

Take ten D . . . of the C . . . concerning the B . . . and the C . . . of the I . . .;[8] soak them in a double boiler; dilute one drop of the harsh and pungent liquid which will be produced in a glass of ordinary water. The entire mixture to be taken by mouth, with confidence.

Emetic

Take six official speeches, a dozen funeral orations, at choice, taking care however not to use any by M. de N . . .; a set of new operas; fifty romances; thirty new articles. Place the whole in a long-necked flask; leave to simmer for two days; then infuse over a low heat. And if all that is not sufficient,

Another, more powerful

Take a sheet of marbled paper which has been used as a cover for a set of poems for the F . . . G . . . ;[9] infuse for a period of three minutes; heat up one teaspoonful of the infusion. To be taken orally.

Very simple remedy for asthma

Read out the complete works of the Reverend Father Maimbourg,[10] formerly of the Society of Jesus, taking care not to stop reading until the end of every sentence, and you will feel your ability to breathe gradually coming back; there will be no need to repeat the remedy.

To prevent itch, blepharitis, ringworm and farcy in horses

Take three Aristotelian categories, two metaphysical modes, a theological distinction, six lines from Chapelain,[11] a sentence from the letters of the Abbé de Saint-Cyran;[12] write the whole on a piece of paper, fold, and tie with a ribbon. To be carried round the neck.

[13]*A miraculous chemical reaction, being a process of violent fermentation with fire, flame and smoke*

Mix an infusion of Quesnel with an infusion of Lallement;[14] it will ferment with great force, impetus, and noise, the acids and alkaline salts reacting violently and combining with each other; fiery vapours will be given off. Place the fermented liquor in an alembic: you will extract nothing from it, and find nothing except a death's head.

Lenitive[15]

Take two leaves from the soothing Molina; six pages from the aperient Escobar; one leaf from the emollient Vasquez; infuse in four pints of ordinary water. When half the water has been taken up, sieve and squeeze out; and in the liquid thus produced dissolve four leaves of the demulcent Bauny and the abstergent Tamburini. For use as an enema.

For chlorosis, commonly known as green sickness, or love-sickness[16]

Take four illustrations from Aretino; two leaves from the Reverend Tomás Sanchez, *On Marriage*. Infuse in five pints of ordinary water. For use as an aperient mixture.

Such were the medicines which our doctor brought into use, with results that can be imagined. He was reluctant, he said, in order not to ruin his patients, to use remedies that were rare and almost unobtainable, such as, for example, a dedicatory epistle which had never made anyone yawn, a preface which was too short, a pastoral letter written by the bishop himself, or a work by a Jansenist which had been criticized by another Jansenist or admired by a Jesuit. He said that that kind of remedy served only to encourage charlatanry, for which he had an insurmountable aversion.

Letter 144[1]
Usbek to Rica

A few days ago, in a country house where I was staying, I met two learned men who are very well known here. Their character seemed extraordinary to me. The first one's conversation, correctly described, could be reduced to this: 'What I have said is true, because I said it.' The second one's conversation was about something else: 'What I did not say is not true, because I didn't say it.'

I rather liked the first one, for if a man is opinionated it doesn't matter at all to me; but if he is arrogant it matters a great deal. The first is defending his own ideas: they belong to him; the second is attacking other men's ideas, and they belong to everybody.

Oh! my dear Rica, what a disadvantage vanity is to those who have a stronger share of it than is naturally necessary for self-preservation! Such men wish to get themselves admired by dint of being disagreeable. They try to be superior, and they are not even equal.

Modest men, come forward, that I may embrace you! It is you

who make life agreeable and charming. You believe that you have nothing, and I tell you that you have everything. You think that you are not humiliating anyone, although you humiliate everyone. And when I compare you, in my own mind, with the overbearing men whom I see all round me, I hurl them down from their platforms, and put them at your feet.

From Paris, the 22nd of the moon of Shaaban, 1720

Letter 145
Usbek to ★★★

An intelligent man is usually difficult when he goes into society. Few men meet with his approval; he is bored with the large number of people whom he chooses to describe as bad company. Inevitably they become aware, to some extent, of his disapproval, and he has made so many enemies.

Certain of making himself liked when he wants to, he often neglects to do so.

He is inclined to criticize, because he notices more than other people, and is more sensitive.

He almost always wastes his money, because his intelligence suggests a larger number of ways of doing so.

He fails in what he undertakes because he takes great risks. His vision reaches a long way, so that he sees things which are at too great a distance.

Not to mention that in the first stages of planning he is less impressed by the difficulties, which are inherent in the thing itself, than by their solutions, which are his, and come from his own resources.

He neglects small details, although the success of almost every major project depends on them.

The ordinary man, on the contrary, tries to take advantage of everything: he is well aware that he cannot afford to risk anything by being negligent.

General approval most commonly goes to the ordinary man. People are delighted to give him something and to take it away from the other one. While envy pounces on the latter, and nothing is forgiven him, every allowance is made for the former: vanity is on his side.

But if the man of intelligence has so many disadvantages, how shall I describe the hard life of a learned scientist?

Whenever I think about this I am reminded of a letter from one of them to a friend of his. Here it is:[1]

Sir,

I am a man who spends every night looking through a telescope thirty feet long at the mighty bodies in motion above our heads; and when I need relaxation I take my little microscopes and observe an animalcule or mite.

I am not rich, and have only one room; I do not even dare light a fire, because I keep my thermometer there and the extra heat would make it rise. Last winter I nearly died of cold, and although my thermometer, at its lowest point, warned me that my hands were about to go numb, I did not disturb my arrangements. I have the consolation of being exactly informed of the slightest changes of temperature throughout last year.

I see very few people, and I know none of the people whom I see. But there is one man in Stockholm, one in Leipzig, and one in London, whom I have never seen, and doubtless never will see, and with them I correspond so regularly that I write to them unfailingly by every post.

But although I do not know anybody in the district I have such a bad reputation that I shall eventually be obliged to leave it. Five years ago, I was violently insulted by a woman who is a neighbour of mine, for having dissected a dog which, she alleged, belonged to her. A butcher's wife who was there joined in. And while the first covered me with insults the other hurled stones at me, and at Dr . . . as well, who was with me, and who received a terrible blow on the frontal occipital bone, which seriously affected the seat of his reason.

Since that time, whenever some dog gets lost at the end of the street, it is immediately decided that it has gone through my hands. A good lady who had lost a little dog which, she said, she loved more than her children, came and fainted away in my room the other day; and failing to find it she had a writ issued against me. It seems that I shall never be delivered from these malicious and importunate females whose yelping voices are constantly deafening me with the funeral orations of every automaton[2] that has died during the last ten years.

Yours, etc.

All learned men used to be accused of magic. It does not surprise me. Everybody must have said to himself: 'It would be impossible for natural ability to go farther than it does in me, yet a certain scientist has the advantage of me: there must be devilry in it somewhere.'[3]

Now that this sort of accusation has fallen into disrepute, another line is taken, and a learned man can scarcely avoid the accusation of being irreligious or heretical.[4] It is no use his being absolved by the public; the wound has been made, and will never heal up completely; it will always remain a weak spot.

Thirty years later, an opponent will come along saying meekly: 'God forbid that I should say that what you are accused of is true; but you were obliged to defend yourself.' In this way even the proof of his innocence is turned against him.

If he writes history, and has some nobility of mind and integrity of feeling, he will be persecuted in a thousand different ways.[5] The authorities will be asked to proceed against him, on account of an event that occurred a thousand years ago; and he will be expected to keep his pen captive if he is not to sell himself.

This, however, is better for him than to share the ignominy of those[6] who surrender their good faith for a meagre pension; who, if their falsifications are taken one by one, get less than a farthing apiece for them; who distort the constitution of the Empire, minimize the rights of one power, exaggerate those of another, are generous with kings and extortionate with their subjects, resuscitate obsolete claims, encourage the passions which are currently in favour and the vices which are on the throne; who mislead posterity, and the more shamefully in that it has no means of destroying their testimony.[7]

But it is not enough for an author to have to endure all these indignities, not enough for him to have lived in a state of constant anxiety over the fate of his book. It comes out at last, the book that has cost him so much; and it gets him involved in controversy on every side. How can he avoid it? He has his opinion, he upholds it in his book, and he is not to know that someone else two hundred leagues away has said just the opposite. But there it is, and war is declared.

It might not matter if he could win some respect, but no: he is esteemed, at best, only by those who have taken up the same speciality as he. A philosopher is supremely disdainful of a man whose head is full of facts; and is considered a visionary, in his turn, by the man who has a good memory.

As for those who proclaim that they are ignorant and proud of it, what they would like is to see the whole of mankind forgotten as completely as they will be themselves.

A man who lacks some talent makes up for it by despising it, and so removes this obstacle lying between himself and personal merit; this is how he gets on the same level as the man whose work he finds redoubtable.

Finally, to an equivocal reputation must be added the denial of pleasure and the loss of health.

From Paris, the 26th of the moon of Shaaban, 1720

Letter 146
Usbek to Rhedi, at Venice

For a long time it has been said that good faith is the soul of ministerial greatness.

For a private individual, a position of obscurity can be advantageous: he loses his reputation only with a few people, and is safe from the gaze of others; but a minister who offends against probity has as many witnesses, and as many judges, as there are people under his government.

I would go so far as to say that the greatest harm that a minister who lacks probity can do is not to serve his king badly or to ruin the country, but something else which, in my opinion, is a thousand times more dangerous: it is to set a bad example.

You know that I spent a long time travelling in India. There I saw a nation which was noble by nature perverted in a moment, from the humblest citizen up to the highest in the land, by the bad example given by a minister.[1] There I saw a whole people, among whom magnanimity, probity, frankness and good faith have always been taken for natural qualities, suddenly changing into the most worthless of nations; I saw the disease spreading until it affected even the healthiest parts of the organism; the most virtuous men committing shameful deeds and violating the first principles of justice, on the empty pretext that they had been victims of a similar violation.

They appealed to detestable laws in justification of the most disgraceful actions, and described injustice and treachery as necessity.

I saw contractual honour dismissed, the most sacred conventions annihilated, every law of the family overthrown. I saw debtors full of avarice, proud and insolent in their poverty, worthless instruments of the ferocity of the law and the harshness of the time, pretending to pay their debts, not doing so, but stabbing their benefactors instead.

More shamefully still, I saw others buying notes for almost nothing, or rather picking up oak-leaves from the ground[2] and putting them in the place of the subsistence of widows and orphans.

I saw an insatiable lust for money suddenly springing up in every heart. I saw the instantaneous development of a hateful conspiracy to get rich, not by honourable work and unstinting endeavour, but by ruining the king, the state and other citizens.

In these unhappy times I saw a respectable man who never went to bed without saying: 'I have ruined one family today, I shall ruin another tomorrow.'

Another would say: 'Together with a man in black who carries a writing-case in his hand and a sharp pointed piece of iron behind his ear,[3] I am going to strike down everyone to whom I have any obligation.'

'I see that my affairs are improving,' said another. 'It is true that a few days ago, when I went to make a certain payment, I left a whole family in tears, scattered the dowries of two respectable girls, and deprived a small boy of his education; the father will perish of grief, the mother is dying of sorrow: but I did no more than the law allowed.'

Can there be any crime greater than that of a government minister who corrupts the morals of an entire nation, debases the noblest souls, sullies the prestige of high office, blots out virtue itself, and involves the highest nobility[4] in this universal degradation?

What will posterity say, when it is made to feel ashamed at its forefathers' disgrace? What will the new generation say, when it compares the iron which its ancestors had to the gold possessed by its immediate forebears? I am sure that nobles will remove from their genealogies a dishonourable and unworthy degree of nobility, and leave the present generation in the appalling state of nothingness to which it has committed itself.

From Paris, the 11th of the moon of Ramadán, 1720

Letter 147
The Chief Eunuch to Usbek, at Paris

Things have come to such a pass that it is no longer to be endured. Your wives have come to think that your departure meant complete impunity for them. What is happening here is dreadful; I myself tremble at the brutal account that I am about to give you.

Zelis, a few days ago, on her way to the mosque, dropped her veil and was seen by the people with her face almost uncovered.

I found Zashi in bed with one of her slaves, which is so strictly forbidden by the laws of the seraglio.

By a remarkable coincidence I intercepted a letter which I enclose; I have never been able to discover to whom it was addressed.

Yesterday evening a youth was found in the garden of the seraglio, and he escaped over the wall.

To all this must be added whatever has not come to my knowledge, for you have certainly been betrayed. I await your orders: and until I am happy enough to receive them my situation will be critical. But if you do not give me entire discretion with these women, I cannot answer for any of them, and I shall have equally bad news to send you every day.

From the seraglio at Ispahan, the 1st of the moon of Rajab, 1717[1]

Letter 148
Usbek to the First Eunuch, at the seraglio in Ispahan

This letter gives you unlimited powers over the entire seraglio. Your commands have as much authority as my own. Let fear and terror be your companions; go with all speed to punish and chastise in room after room; everyone must live in dread, everyone must weep before you. Interrogate the whole seraglio, beginning with the slaves. Do not spare the women whom I love; each of them must undergo this terrible investigation. Expose the darkest secrets, purify this place of infamy, and bring back virtue from its exile. For from this moment I hold you responsible for the slightest fault that is committed. I suspect that the letter which you intercepted was addressed to Zelis: examine this matter with the eyes of a lynx.

From ***, the 11th of the moon of Dulheggia, 1718

Letter 149
Narsit to Usbek, at Paris

The Chief Eunuch has just died, magnificent lord. Since I am the oldest of your slaves, I have taken his place until you have made known on whom your choice has fallen.

Two days after his death, I was brought one of your letters, addressed to him. I took good care not to open it; I have wrapped it up with the greatest respect, and have put it away until you tell me of your sacred decisions.

Yesterday a slave came to me in the middle of the night to say that he had found a young man in the seraglio. I got up, examined the matter, and found that it was a vision.

I kiss your feet, sublime lord, and beg you to count on my zeal, experience, and age.

From the seraglio at Ispahan, the 5th of the first moon of Jomada, 1718

Letter 150
Usbek to Narsit, at the seraglio in Ispahan

Wretched creature that you are, you hold in your hands letters containing urgent and ruthless orders from me. The slightest delay may drive me to despair, and you, on an empty pretext, remain idle.

What is happening is dreadful, perhaps as many as half of my slaves deserve death. I am sending you the letter that the First Eunuch sent to tell me about it before he died. If you had opened the packet addressed to him you would have found the most savage commands. Read them therefore, these commands, and you will perish if you do not carry them out.

From ***, the 25th of the moon of Shawall, 1718

Letter 151
Solim to Usbek, at Paris

If I were to remain silent any longer, I should be as culpable as all the criminals in your seraglio.

I was in the confidence of the Grand Eunuch, who was the most faithful of your slaves. When he realized that he was on the point of death, he called me to him, and spoke to me as follows: 'I am dying; but my only regret on ceasing to live is that, as I look at my master's wives for the last time, I find them guilty. May Heaven preserve him from all the misfortunes that I foresee! When I am dead, may my ghost come with threats to remind these treacherous women of their duty, and intimidate them still! Here are the keys of this place of dread; go and take them to the oldest black slave. But if, after my death, his vigilance should fail, see to it that you warn my master.' As he finished speaking, he died in my arms.

I know that he wrote to you, some time before his death, about the behaviour of your wives: in the seraglio is a letter which would have brought terror with it if it had been opened. The one which you wrote later has been intercepted three leagues away from here. I cannot tell why, but everything seems to turn out badly.

At the same time your wives have abandoned all restraint. Since the Grand Eunuch died, it seems as if they are allowed to do anything. Only Roxana has remained dutiful and continues to behave with decorum. Their conduct is becoming more corrupt every day. The stern and steadfast expression of virtue which used to be seen on their faces no longer prevails. There is a new atmosphere of gaiety everywhere here, which in my view is a sure sign of some new-found contentment. In the most trivial matters I notice liberties being taken which were formerly unknown. Even among your slaves, I am surprised to see a certain slackness in the performance of their duty and in their obedience to rules; they no longer have the enthusiastic keenness to serve you which seemed to pervade the whole seraglio.

Your wives have been in the country for a week, at one of your remotest houses. The slave who is responsible for it is said to have been bribed, and, the day before they arrived, to have hidden two men in a stone alcove in the wall of the main room, so that they could get out when we retired for the night. The old eunuch who is at present in charge of us is an imbecile who can be made to believe anything.

I am filled with an angry desire to avenge all this perfidy, and if Heaven so willed it, for the good of your service, that you were to consider me capable of taking control, I promise you that even if your wives are not virtuous, at least they will not betray you.

From the seraglio at Ispahan, the 6th of the first moon of Rabia, 1719

Letter 152
Narsit to Usbek, at Paris

Roxana and Zelis wished to go to the country, and I thought it would be wrong to prevent them. Happy Usbek! your wives are faithful, your slaves are vigilant; the place where I command seems to be a shelter chosen by virtue. You may be sure that nothing happens here that would be offensive to your eyes.

A misfortune has occurred which is causing me much concern. Some Armenian merchants who have recently arrived in Ispahan had brought a letter of yours for me. I sent a slave to fetch it, he was robbed on his way back, and the letter is lost. For this reason, write to me quickly, since I presume that in the new situation here you must have important orders to send me.

From the seraglio of Fatme, the 6th of the first moon of Rabia, 1719

Letter 153
Usbek to Solim, at the seraglio in Ispahan

I am putting the sword into your hands; I am entrusting to you the dearest thing I now have in the world, my vengeance. When you start on your new duties, leave pity and tenderness behind. I am writing to my wives to tell them to obey you blindly; in their guilty confusion at all their crimes they will fall to the ground beneath your gaze. I must rely on you to restore my happiness and peace of mind. Make my seraglio what it was when I left it; but begin by expiation: exterminate the criminals, and strike dread into those who contemplated becoming so. There is nothing that you cannot hope to receive from your master for such an outstanding service. It depends on you alone whether you rise higher even than your present status, and earn greater rewards than you have ever desired.

From Paris, the 4th of the moon of Shaaban, 1719

Letter 154
Usbek to his wives, at the seraglio in Ispahan

May this letter be like a thunderbolt amidst lightning and storms! Solim is the Chief Eunuch, not in order to guard you but to punish you. The whole seraglio will kneel before him. He is to judge your past actions, and in the future he will keep you under such harsh restrictions that you will regret your freedom if you do not regret your virtue.

From Paris, the 4th of the moon of Shaaban, 1719

Letter 155
Usbek to Nessir, at Ispahan

Happy is the man who knows the value of a quiet and tranquil life, whose heart remains in peace amidst his family, a stranger to every land but the one in which he was born!

I am living in a barbarous region, in the presence of everything that I find oppressive, and absent from everything I care about. I am prey to sombre melancholy and fall into dreadful despair; I seem not to exist any more, and I become aware of myself again only when lurking jealousy flares up in my heart and there breeds alarm, suspicion, hatred and regret.

You know me, Nessir; my feelings have always been as well-known to you as your own. You would pity me if you saw the wretched state I am in. Sometimes I spend six whole months waiting for news from the seraglio. I count every moment as it passes, and my impatience always draws it out, but when the man I have so long waited for is shortly to arrive, my emotions suddenly change. My hand trembles as it opens the fateful letter, the anxiety which tormented me seems to be the happiest state I could possibly be in, and I am afraid that I will be deprived of it by a blow which I would find worse than a thousand deaths.

However strong my reasons were for leaving my country, and although I owe my life to my departure, I can no longer, Nessir, remain in this appalling exile. Would I not die in any case, falling victim to my woes? I have urged Rica thousands of times to leave this foreign land, but he resists all my suggestions. He keeps me here on countless pretexts; he seems to have forgotten his country, or rather he seems to have forgotten me, such is his indifference to my unhappiness.

Miserable wretch that I am, I say that I want to see my country again, and there perhaps I shall be even more wretched! For what will I do there? I will be giving myself up to my enemies. Not only that, but I shall go to the seraglio, and shall have to ask for a report on the disastrous period while I was away; and if I find any of them guilty, what will become of me? If the mere idea of it appals me when I am so far away, what will it be like when I am present and it is more vivid? What will it be like to have to see and hear things that I cannot imagine without shuddering? What will it be like, finally, if I have to pronounce verdicts which will be a permanent record of my shame and despair?

I shall be surrounded by walls more horrible for me than for the women they enclose. My suspicion will remain intact; their ardour will do nothing to rid me of it. In my bed, in their arms, all I shall enjoy will be anxiety; at moments when it is incongruous to speculate, jealousy will make me do so. Contemptible rejects of the human race, degraded slaves whose hearts are closed for ever to any feeling of love, you would no longer bewail your fate if you knew the misery of mine.

From Paris, the 4th of the moon of Shaaban, 1719

Letter 156
Roxana to Usbek, at Paris

Horror, darkness, and dread rule the seraglio; it is filled with terrible lamentation; it is subject at every moment to the unchecked rage of a tiger. He has tortured two white eunuchs, whose only confessions have been confessions of innocence; he has sold some of our slaves and obliged us to change our remaining servants among ourselves. Zashi and Zelis have been humiliated by the treatment they have received in their rooms in the darkness of night: he was not afraid to commit the sacrilege of striking them with his own vile hands. He keeps each of us shut up in her apartment, and although we are alone there he makes us wear veils. We are no longer allowed to speak to each other; it would be a crime to write; the only freedom we are allowed is to weep.

A squad of new eunuchs has been brought into the seraglio, and they besiege us night and day; our sleep is constantly being interrupted by their suspicions, real or imaginary. My consolation is that all this will not last for long, and that these miseries will end with my life. It will not be a long one, cruel Usbek; I shall not give you the time to put a stop to all these outrages.

From the seraglio at Ispahan, the 2nd of the moon of Muharram,
1720

Letter 157[1]
Zashi to Usbek, at Paris

Oh gods,! a savage has outraged me even by the way in which he has chastised me! He inflicted on me that punishment which begins by making propriety take fright, that punishment which involves the deepest humiliation, that punishment which reduces us to infancy, as it were.

My soul, at first, was annihilated by shame, but I came back to myself, and was beginning to express my indignation when my screams rang out through my apartment; I was heard pleading for mercy from the most degraded of all men, and appealing to his pity as his ruthlessness increased.

Since that time his arrogant and slavish soul has gained an ascendancy over mine. I am crushed by his presence, his looks, his words, and every kind of misfortune. When I am alone, I have at least the consolation of tears, but when he appears before me I am seized by fury, and finding it powerless I relapse into despair.

The tiger dares to tell me that you are the instigator of all this savagery. He would like to extirpate my love, and defile even the emotions in my heart. When he utters the name of the man I love I am unable to protest; I can only die.

I have endured your absence, and preserved my love, by the strength of that very love. Nights, days, and moments have all been for you. My love itself made me proud, and yours made the seraglio respect me. But now . . . No, I can no longer endure the humiliation which has overtaken me. If I am innocent, come back and love me. Come back for me to die at your feet if I am guilty.

From the seraglio at Ispahan, the 2nd of the moon of Muharram,
1720

Letter 158
Zelis[1] to Usbek, at Paris

You are a thousand leagues away from me, and you judge me guilty; a thousand leagues away, and you punish me.

If a brutal eunuch raises his disgusting hand to me, he does so on your orders. It is by the tyrant that the outrage is committed, not by the man who carries out his tyranny.

You can intensify your harsh treatment as you please. My heart has been at peace since it has no longer been able to love you. Your soul has lost its nobility, and you are becoming cruel. You may be sure that you are unhappy.

Farewell.

From the seraglio at Ispahan, the 2nd of the moon of Muharram,
1720

Letter 159
Solim to Usbek, at Paris

I am grieved for myself, magnificent lord, and I grieve for you. Never has a loyal servant fallen into the terrible despair which I am in. Here is the account of your miseries and mine; as I write of them I can only shudder.

I swear by all the prophets of Heaven that since you entrusted your wives to me I have watched over them night and day; my solicitude has been maintained without a moment's interruption. I began my term of office with punishments, and discontinued them without relaxing my natural strictness.

But what am I saying? Why boast of my fidelity when it has been useless to you? Forget all my past services, consider me as a traitor, and punish me for all the crimes that I have failed to prevent.

Roxana, the proud Roxana, oh gods! who is to be trusted henceforward? You suspected Zelis, and were entirely sure of Roxana. But her stern virtue was a cruel trick, a veil which covered treachery. I caught her in the arms of a young man who, as soon as he saw that he was discovered, attacked me. He stabbed me twice with his dagger. The eunuchs came running at the noise and surrounded him; he defended himself for a long time and wounded several of them. He even wanted to get back into the bedroom, so as to die, he said, before Roxana's eyes. But finally he yielded to numbers and fell at our feet.

I do not know whether, sublime lord, I shall wait for your rigorous commands. You placed your vengeance in my hands, and I must not let it be delayed.

From the seraglio at Ispahan, the 8th of the first moon of Rabia,
1720

Letter 160
Solim to Usbek, at Paris

I have taken my decision. Your troubles will disappear; I am going to punish.

Already I feel a secret joy. My soul and yours will be pacified. We shall exterminate crime, and innocence will be appalled.

You women whose only destiny is seemingly to ignore all your sensations, and to be indignant even at your desires, eternal victims of shame and propriety, why cannot I bring you crowding into this unhappy seraglio, and see your stupor at all the blood I am about to shed here!

From the seraglio at Ispahan, the 8th of the first moon of Rabia,

1720

Letter 161
Roxana to Usbek, at Paris

Yes, I deceived you. I suborned your eunuchs, outwitted your jealousy, and managed to turn your terrible seraglio into a place of delightful pleasures.

I am going to die; poison will flow through my veins. What is there for me to do here, since the only man who kept me alive breathes no more? I am dying, but my spirit will depart properly escorted: I have just despatched in advance the sacrilegious guards who shed the most precious blood on earth.

How could you have thought me credulous enough to imagine that I was in the world only in order to worship your caprices? that while you allowed yourself everything, you had the right to thwart all my desires? No: I may have lived in servitude, but I have always been free. I have amended your laws according to the laws of nature, and my mind has always remained independent.

You should even be grateful to me for the sacrifice that I made on your account, for having demeaned myself so far as to seem faithful to you, for having had the cowardice to guard in my heart something that I ought to have revealed to the whole earth, and finally for having profaned the name of virtue by permitting it to be applied to my acceptance of your whims.

You were surprised not to find me carried away by the ecstasy of love;[1] if you had known me properly you would have found in me all the violence of hate.

But you had for a long time the benefit of thinking that a heart like mine was subject to you. We were both happy: you thought that I had been deceived, while I was deceiving you.

Such language is new to you, no doubt. Is it possible that after having overwhelmed you with grief I could force you to admire my courage? But it is all over, the poison is destroying me. I am losing my strength, the pen is falling from my hands, I can feel even my hatred growing weaker; I am dying.

From the seraglio at Ispahan, the 8th of the first moon of Rabia,
1720

SOME REFLECTIONS ON
THE PERSIAN LETTERS[1]

Nothing pleased the public more, in the *Persian Letters*, than to find unexpectedly a sort of novel. Its beginning, development, and ending are apparent; the different characters are placed in a chain which links them together. As their stay in Europe goes on, the customs of this part of the world come to seem, in their minds, less wonderful, less surprising; also, they react more or less strongly to the surprise and wonder of it in accordance with the difference in their characters. At the same time, disorder increases in the Eastern seraglio, in proportion to the length of Usbek's absence; that is to say, as passions become more uncontrolled and love declines.

Besides, it is usual for this type of novel to be successful, because the writers are giving a description of their present state themselves, which communicates emotion more effectively than any narrative could do. This is the reason for the success of some attractive works which have appeared since the *Persian Letters*.[2]

Finally, in ordinary novels, digressions are permissible only when they themselves form a new story. Serious discussion has to be excluded; none of the characters having been introduced for purposes of discussion, it would be contrary to the nature and intention of the work. But in using the letter form, in which neither the choice of characters, nor the subjects discussed, have to fit in with any preconceived intentions or plans, the author has taken advantage of the fact that he can include philosophy, politics, and moral discourse with the novel, and can connect everything together with a secret chain which remains, as it were, invisible.

The *Persian Letters* had from the start such an enormous sale that publishers did everything in their power to get a sequel. They went about pulling the sleeves of everyone they met. 'Sir,' they would say, 'do some Persian Letters for me, I beg you.'

But what I have just said is enough to show that these letters are not capable of having any sequel, and even less of being continued with letters from another hand, however skilfully composed they might be.[3]

There are some passages which many people have found too audacious; but I would request them to take note of the nature of the work. The Persians who have such an important part to play in it suddenly found themselves transplanted to Europe, that is, to another universe. At a certain point they necessarily had to be shown as full of ignorance and prejudice. My only concern was to reveal the origin and development of their ideas. Their first thoughts were bound to be strange: the only thing to do, it seemed, was to attribute to them the kind of strangeness which is compatible with intelligence. The only thing that had to be described was their reaction whenever something appeared to them to be extraordinary. Far from having any intention of implicating our religion, I did not even suspect myself of imprudence. The passages in question are related in each case to feelings of surprise and astonishment, not to any idea of scrutiny, still less of criticism. When they spoke of our religion, these Persians could not appear more knowledgeable than when speaking of our customs and behaviour. And if they sometimes find our dogmas odd, the oddity is always characterized by their total ignorance of the way in which these dogmas are linked with our other truths.

It is out of love for these great truths that I make this justification, quite apart from my respect for humanity, which it was certainly never my intention to strike in its tenderest spot. The reader is therefore asked not to cease for a moment to consider the passages to which I refer as being due to feelings of surprise, in men who were bound to feel it, or as being epigrammatic remarks made by men who were not really in a position to make them. He is also asked to bear in mind that the whole effect was due to the perpetual contrast between the reality of things and the odd, naïve, or strange way in which they were perceived. Certainly the nature and intention of the *Persian Letters* are so manifest that they will deceive only those who wish to deceive themselves.[4]

APPENDIX: LETTERS AND FRAGMENTS
NOT PUBLISHED BY MONTESQUIEU

A number of complete or fragmentary Persian Letters have been found since the eighteenth century. This Appendix contains those which are more or less complete in themselves. The majority were discovered by Barckhausen; no. 15 was discovered by M. L. Desgraves in 1950, while nos. 17 to 20 were republished with some other fragments and variants by Mme E. Carayol in the *Revue d'histoire littéraire de la France* of 1965. I have followed Vernière's edition as regards the selection and arrangement of nos. 1 to 16.

(1)

Persian Letters. When this work appeared, people did not regard it as a serious work; and it was not serious. Two or three rash remarks were pardoned in appreciation of a complete openness of conscience which, while critical of everything, was never ill-intentioned. Each reader could testify to it himself: the only thing he remembered was that he had been entertained. People could be angry in those days just as they can today; but they knew better in those days when it was necessary to be angry.

(2)

Apologia for the *Persian Letters.* The passages in the *Persian Letters* which have been alleged to be contrary to religion cannot really be held against the work.

These passages are never associated with any idea of scrutiny, but with the idea of strangeness; never with any idea of criticism, but with the idea of something extraordinary.

It was a Persian who was speaking; everything he saw and everthing he heard was bound to make a deep impression on him.

This being so, when he speaks about religion he cannot appear to be better informed about it than about other matters, such as the nation's customs and way of life, which he does not see as being either good or bad, but as being incredible.

Just as he finds our customs strange, there are times when he finds something curious about certain aspects of our dogmas, because he is ignorant of them; and he explains them badly because he knows nothing about the way in which they are associated, or about the chain which links them together.

It is true that it was somewhat indiscreet to have mentioned these matters, since we can never be as sure of what others may think as of what we think ourselves.

(3)[1]

It was remarkable to see the delight shown by all the Troglodytes, while their prince wept bitterly. When he appeared before them the next day, his face revealed no trace either of sadness or joy. He seemed concerned only with the business of governing. But the secret sorrow which was consuming him inwardly soon sent him to his grave; so died the greatest king ever to have ruled over men.

He was mourned for forty days; everyone felt as if he had lost his father; everyone said: 'What hope is there for us Troglodytes now? We have lost you, beloved king! You believed yourself unfit to rule us: Heaven has shown that we were unfit to obey you. But we swear, by your holy shade, that since you would not govern us by your laws, we shall be guided by your example.'

Another king had to be elected, and the extraordinary thing was that, out of all the dead king's relatives, none laid claim to the crown. The wisest and justest member of the whole family was chosen.

Towards the end of his reign some of the Troglodytes thought that it was necessary to institute trade and commerce among them. A national assembly was called and the decision to do so was taken.

The king spoke as follows: 'You decreed that I should take the crown, and you considered me sufficiently virtuous to govern you. Heaven is my witness that since that moment the only object of my concern has been to make the Troglodytes happy. It is my glory that no Troglodyte has done anything disgraceful to spoil my reign. Do you now want to have wealth rather than your virtue?'

'Sir,' said one of them, 'we are happy; we have an excellent foundation to build on. May I say that it will be you alone who decides whether wealth is or is not to be harmful to your people? If they see that you would rather have wealth than virtue, they will soon fall into the same habit; in this matter your attitude will determine theirs. If you raise a man to an important post, or bring him into your confidence, merely because he is rich, you may be sure that you have struck a mortal blow at his virtue, and that you will imperceptibly create as many unscrupulous people as there are men who have noticed this lamentable mark of discrimination. The foundation of your people's virtue, sir, as you know, is their education. Change this education, and those who are not bold enough to be criminals will soon be ashamed of being virtuous.

'There are two things that we have to do: to make both meanness and extravagance equally shameful. Everyone must be accountable to the State for the administration of his property, and the man who ignobly demeans himself, by denying himself a reasonable standard of living, must be judged as severely as the man who squanders his children's patrimony. Each citizen must spend his own wealth as equitably as if it belonged to someone else.'

'Troglodytes,' said the king, 'you are about to acquire the use of riches; but I declare to you that if you are not virtuous you will be one of the unhappiest nations on earth. As things are at present, all that is required of me is to be juster than you: it is the sign of my royal authority, and no other that I could find would be more illustrious. If you seek to distinguish yourselves only by riches, which in themselves are nothing, I shall certainly have to distinguish myself by the same means, so as not to remain in what you would consider to be a contemptible state of poverty. At present it is within myself that I find all my riches; but then you would have to wear yourselves out to make me rich, and would not benefit from the wealth which you valued so highly: it would all go into my treasury. Oh Troglodytes! there could be a noble bond between us: if you are virtuous so shall I be; if I am virtuous, so will you be.'

$(4)^2$

They have finally published a decree which condemns the Foreigner to the asylum and all the French to the poorhouse! Shares and bank-notes have lost half their value. At a stroke of the pen, French subjects have been deprived of thirty times a hundred million francs – that is to say, of a sum which scarcely exists in the whole world, and which would be enough to buy all the assets owned by the kingdom of Persia. The entire country is in tears. This unhappy kingdom is engulfed in darkness and grief: it resembles a town which has been taken by assault, or devastated by fire. In the midst of all this unhappiness, only the Foreigner seems satisfied with himself, and is still talking of continuing with his disastrous System. Here I am living in the Land of Despair: my eyes see nothing but misfortune descending on the Infidels. A wind has got up and is blowing away their riches; their empty affluence is disappearing like a mirage.

I have heard this very moment that the decree of which I spoke has just been revoked. You must not think that this change is anything extraordinary; here, one policy drives away others like clouds driving away clouds. The decree has been rescinded; but not the damage it has caused. The Ministry will never recover from the admission which it has just made to the people.

From Paris, the 21st of the first moon of Rabia, 1720

(5)

You tell me that our great king's only concern is to make his justice secure against violation, to remove the common people from the tyranny of the great, and to make the great respected by the common people. Eternal glory be to so noble a prince: may Heaven grant that his power is limited only by his justice!

(6)

You ask me to define the Regency. It is a series of policy failures and inconsistent ideas; witty remarks got up to look like theories; a shapeless mixture of weakness and authority; all the heavy-handedness, but not the seriousness, of a ministry; a style of government which is always too harsh or too mild – encouragement for the disobedient, together with disappointment for those with rightful aspirations; deplorable inconstancy, even where abandoning bad policies is concerned; a Council which sometimes diminishes and sometimes multiplies itself, which appears and disappears from the public view in a manner either subdued or ostentatious, and which has as many changes among its members as among the aims they set themselves.

(7)

There is a kind of turban[3] which causes half the idiocies performed in France. A candidate who means to have this hat, at any price, imagines that it will cover up all the unscrupulous actions he has done in order to obtain it.

Almost any king would consider himself honoured to have it. Almost any scoundrel can aspire to it. Beneath its scarlet shade the classes of society are all indistinguishable; it haughtily allies itself to all of them.

(8)

I remember that when we arrived in France, Hadji Ibbi regarded the King with contempt when he was told that he had no wives, no eunuchs, and no seraglio; that nobody fled as he went by; that, when he was in the capital, most people scarcely made any difference between his carriage and that of a private citizen.

(9)[4]

The Chief Eunuch to Janum, at . . .

I pray that Heaven may bring you back to this place and preserve you from every danger.

Marked out as you are for a post in this seraglio, which is under my authority, one day you may perhaps reach the post I hold; that is what you must aim at.

Accordingly you must soon start thinking how to train yourself and attract your master's attention. Keep a strict expression on your face; look around you with grimness in your eyes; say little. Laughter must depart from your lips: melancholy suits our condition. Be outwardly calm, but from time to time disclose the apprehension in your mind. Do not wait until the lines of old age appear on your face before you display the anxieties that go with it.

It would be useless to constrain yourself to be weakly indulgent. We are all hated by women, hated to the point of fury. Do you believe that their implacable rage is due to the severity with which we treat them? Ah! they would forgive us our behaviour if they were able to forgive us our misfortune.

Do not make a point of being too meticulously honest. There is a degree of scrupulousness which is not really appropriate except for free men. Our condition does not leave us the power to be virtuous. Friendship, loyalty, promises, and respect for virtue are victims which we are constantly having to sacrifice. We are obliged to struggle ceaselessly to preserve our lives and avoid the punishments that are poised over our heads, and every method is legitimate; for wretches like us deception, fraud, and artifice are virtues.

If you ever reach the highest position your principal aim must be to achieve control over the seraglio. The more absolute your power, the more ways you will have for destroying subversive plots and the wives' passion for revenge. You must begin by breaking their spirit, and bury all their emotions in awe and fear. There is no surer way to succeed in this than by stimulating your master's jealousy. You must confide in him, from time to time, over small matters. Draw his attention to anything at all suspicious; later, make him remember it by adding some new details. Occasionally leave him to himself, letting him remain in a state of uncertainty for a while. Then go to see him; he will be delighted to have you there as a mediator between the claims of his love and his jealousy, and he will ask for your opinion. You may be lenient or severe; but either way you will have gained a protectress or humiliated an enemy.

It is not that you can make allegations about a criminal liaison just as you please: there are certain crimes of which women subjugated by close supervision cannot plausibly be accused. But you must leave these suspicions to be supplied by the resources which a man's love and desperation provide when his over-heated imagination catches at everything it encounters. Do not be afraid of saying too much; you can deceive with audacity. During all my long years of power, the things I have heard, and even seen, are unbelievable. My eyes have witnessed everything fury can devise, and everything that the demon of love can produce.

If you see that your master is a man liable to submit to the yoke of love, and that his feelings are becoming centred on one of his wives, be slightly less severe than usual as far as she is concerned; but bear down more heavily on her rivals, in an effort to please him both by your leniency and by your strictness.

But if you see that he is a man inconstant in his loves, and behaves in kingly fashion towards the beautiful women he owns; that he loves them, then leaves them, then takes them back; that in the morning he destroys the hopes he had aroused the night before; that having made his choice he becomes capricious; that having become capricious he loses interest – then, you will be in the most favourable situation possible. You will be master of all his wives; treat them as if they were continually in disgrace, and do not be afraid of their influence with him, since it will vanish as soon as they acquire it.

It is up to you, therefore, to help him be inconstant. Sometimes it happens that a beautiful woman triumphs, and preserves the love of the most changeable of men: however often he escapes, she always brings him back. Such constant reconciliations threaten to turn into a permanent attachment. You have to break this new tie at any cost. Open up the seraglio; bring in quantities of new rivals; create distractions everywhere; ensure that the proud and triumphant wife is lost in the crowd, and reduced to go on fighting for a prize that the others no longer had the power to defend.

These tactics will almost always succeed. This is the way to wear out his heart, so that he will be unable to feel anything. The attraction of women will disappear; all their beauty, which is invisible to the whole of the universe, will be invisible to his eyes as well. In competition with each other, his wives will try out their most formidable weapons on him, but in vain: they will be useless as objects of love, and he will remain attached to them through jealousy alone.

I have concealed nothing from you, as you see. Although I am virtually unacquainted with the relationship that they call friendship, and have been entirely wrapped up in myself, you have made me feel that I still had a heart; and while I was as hard as bronze in my relations with all the slaves who were under my authority, it was with pleasure that I watched you grow up through childhood.

I took charge of your upbringing. My severity, for severity is inseparable from education, prevented you for a long time from knowing that you were dear to me. Yet so you were, and I would say that I loved you as a father loves his son, if the names of father and son were not more calculated to bring back a dreadful memory to both of us than to suggest to us the satisfaction of emotional ties.

(10)[5]

Rica to Usbek

Here is a letter which has fallen into my possession:

My dear cousin,

Two men have left me one after the other. I laid siege to the one whose name you know; but he was like a rock. I am full of indignation at these daily insults to my feelings.

What did I not do in order to secure him? I was a hundred times more gracious than I usually am. 'Heavens above!' I said to myself, 'having had so many nice things said to me once by men, can I really be paying them back so generously, and to so little effect!'

You, my dear cousin, are two years younger, and much more attractive, than I am. But I beseech you not to abandon me in my decision to give up worldly pursuits. You have been the confidante of so many secrets; so many others have been entrusted to me! For more than thirty years our friendship has survived all the little quarrels that necessarily arise in a relationship when there are different intrigues going on and more than one interest at stake.

Although, as I have often told you, I used to be so fond of our young men about town, I cannot bear them any more. They are so pleased with themselves, and so critical of us; they put such a high price on their foolish faces. . . . Dear cousin, preserve me from their contempt.

I am beginning to acquire a taste for the company of religious people, to such an extent that they are my only consolation. I have not yet broken with worldly society sufficiently to give them confidence in me; but as I withdraw from it they come a little nearer to me. My new way of life is so restful, after all the noise and bustle, and the falseness, of society!

Dear cousin, I am going to abandon myself to them entirely. I shall explain to them the nature of my heart, which preserves every impression that anyone makes on it; it is not within my power to eliminate all my emotions: it is merely a question of regulating them.

There is one fundamental principle of a life of piety, and that is the complete suppression of all external ornaments. For, between ourselves, although they are always much more innocent when one is about to give them up than when one is beginning to wear them, they still indicate a certain wish to appear attractive in society, which pious people detest. They want us to appear before them without concealing the damage done by time, so as to show how much we despise it. As for you and me, dear cousin, it seems that we can still reveal ourselves just as we are. I have told you a hundred times how delightful you look when you appear quite unadorned, and that it shows great skill not to use your skills at all.

I hope that this letter may touch your heart and encourage you to make a decision which I have made only after having fought against it for a long time.

Farewell.

Piety, a sign of strength in some characters, is in others a sign of weakness. It is never without significance: for if on the one hand it is attractive in those who are virtuous, it completes the degradation of those who are not.

From Paris, the 25th of the moon of Rabia, 1717

(11)

Usbek to Zelis

You have applied to a judge for a separation. What an example to give your daughter! What a subject for gossip for everyone in the seraglio! You injure me far less by showing how little you love me than by showing how little you respect yourself.

Do you think that being virtuous is less of an ordeal for your companions than for you? that their life is less arduous than yours? Of course not; but the struggles they go through are concealed, the pain they suffer, when they have to fight too hard for victory, remains secret, and their virtue, even when they are oppressed by it, is shown by their decorous demeanour and expressions of calm.

I have no doubt that you are suffering all the frustrations of continence. I count on the vigilance of my eunuchs. They respected your age: they thought that you would be in control of your emotions. But now, knowing how powerful those emotions are, they will certainly redouble their efforts to support you. They will treat you as if you were still threatened by the dangers of youth, and will reimpose the discipline of your upbringing, which you have so completely ignored.

You must therefore abandon your ideas, and realize that the only recourse for you is my love and your penitence: for I am not the man to allow a woman I love to lie in another man's arms, even if I were to be regarded as the most barbarous of all men . . .

I shall say no more: you are aware of my feelings, and you know my meaning.

From ***, the 1st of the moon of Dulheggia, 1718

(12)

Rica to Usbek, in the country

While you are staying in the country, I am surrounded by the tumult of Paris. Yesterday I was with a lot of other people; a young man was talking a great deal, and, having seen him several times already, I knew that the extreme impertinence of his manner was matched by the fatuity of his conversation. On this occasion he was applying his mind to the task of destroying the reputations of some fifteen or twenty people. He paused a moment, which gave me time to say: 'It would appear, sir, that you don't know anyone else around here.'

'Why do you say that?' he asked.

'I thought so because you have stopped blackening anyone's character,' I answered.

'It's very good of you to get so worked up about it,' he said. 'I bet you don't know any of the people I have mentioned.'

'And I don't know any victims of highway robbery either,' I said, 'but I am still sorry that people get robbed. I know nothing of the people you have just been talking about, but one thing that is very much to their credit is that they are not here.'

My directness was not unfavourably received by others who were there, but it did not make him any the wiser. He began to expound the crudest sort of atheism, and then said, looking straight at me: 'I am sure this gentleman will not approve of my remarks.'

'On the contrary,' I replied. 'What you are saying concerns God alone. There is no great harm in it. The supreme being, who can perceive an insect like you only because he is immense, will certainly be able to punish you, so that I feel nothing but pity for you. But just now it made me indignant to see you causing distress to so many families.'

It seems to me a good thing, Usbek, for there to be men who, even if they are despicable, are out of the ordinary. The most virtuous of men could not make us love virtue as much as they do. There are some calumnies which incite me to love, and some blasphemies which raise me towards God as though I could hear hymns being sung.

$$(13)^6$$

Hadji Ibbi to the dervish Jemshid, at the mountain of Jahrum
Happy Jemshid! the Law of the holy Koran was not bestowed on you in vain: you can find hidden precepts in the least words of this divine book. It seems to grow as you consult it. You multiply opportunities for us to be obedient and continually add to the commandments of him who found us weak when he looked for us to be faithful.

Allow me to give you my views.

Where religion is concerned, the more trivial the issue, the more violent the dispute becomes. It gains strength from the insignificance of its subject. The fire lacks fuel, but flares up just the same.

You are aware of the slender reasons for our disputes about Ali and Abu-bekr. If these great men's followers had not displayed greater eagerness to defend their opinions than the great men themselves had displayed on their account, the Muslim religion would have been at peace; the Earth would not have disturbed Heaven, nor Heaven disturbed Earth. The acrimony was increased above all by the expressions of hostility which, out of fanaticism, were inserted into the two liturgies. Now as soon as either side reaches the point of being offended, even though these expressions are so general that they cannot reflect on any one person, natural equity and religious piety nonetheless require that they be removed, it being contrary to both that anyone should be the object of insults which he finds offensive, while it is also contrary to good sense that they should be expressed in the form of prayers.

From Paris, the last day of the moon of Shaaban, 1720

(14)

My desire to inform myself about the customs of this country makes me be as sociable as I can, and I am constantly trying to increase my knowledge. I have discovered a wonderful method of doing this – it is to listen; for a Frenchman likes talking. He enjoys telling everyone about his ancestry, his personal merit, his carriage, his servants, his property, and his success with women. He is delighted to find someone patient. He would be sorry for you to be ignorant of the story of his life, with all the incidental details. Lend him your ears, and you will have a friend. If he succeeds in making you laugh, he will be infinitely indebted to you. His gratitude will be everlasting if you can remember that he has an income of two hundred thousand aspers[7] a year, a pack of hunting dogs, and twenty slaves. You must be convinced above all that his profession is superior to anyone else's. If you can add that he excels in it, you will have the key to his heart.

(15)

Western books shed hardly any light on ancient history. There is a gap at the beginning of time, and everyone has agreed to cover it over. Even the ruins have disappeared, yet the reconstruction has to be done.

When history is missing, it is replaced by fables; it is like a poor country where virtually worthless coins have to be included in the currency. Poets are treated as serious writers, and inside their own territories they are paid as much attention as the most penetrating historians.

This history is not about men, but about gods. These gods are transformed into heroes with the development of civilization; the children of the heroes are mere men, because children are seen from a shorter distance away than their fathers; and thus the period of myth comes to an end and historical times begin.

In modern times indescribable chaos has surrounded the origins of the gods. Mythologists have behaved like two different sects, as divergent in their views as in the spirit behind them. Some, of a more literal turn of mind, distinguish between each individual deity, without being discouraged by their numbers. Others, more subtly, are always trying to simplify, and confuse one deity with another.

Poets belonged to the first group, philosophers to the second. But there was nothing very philosophical about undertaking the laborious task of making something coherent out of superstitions, and classifying material which had been constantly jumbled up by poetic divagations, pictorial fantasy, priestly greed and the prodigious inventiveness of the superstitious mind. But this was not the only point at issue in this interminable lawsuit. Some had a simpler approach and tried to take everything at face-value; others were more sophisticated, took everything figuratively, and related it all to morality and natural science.

The philosophers objected, wanting to cut down the prodigious number of divinities, which included even the names of abstract essences; but what difference was there, if any, between those who considered that everything in nature was animate, and those theollogians who said that all of nature was divine?

Usbek

(16)

They say that in Persia the rebel Mir-Vais[8] is making remarkable progress, and that everywhere the people are on his side.

Our princes up till now have exercised their power with so little restraint, they have imposed on human nature to such a degree, that it does not surprise me that God has allowed their subjects to become impatient and shake off the excessive weight of their authority. Subjects are in a deplorable position; they have hardly any legitimate methods of defending themselves against oppression, and when they are right in substance they find themselves technically in the wrong.

Take the history of any civil disturbance, at random. It is a thousand to one that the prince or his minister was the cause of it. The people are naturally fearful, and with reason; so far are they from having any thoughts of a direct attack on the great power of authority that they are hard put to it even to decide to protest.

In Persia we are so firmly convinced of this principle that we constantly put it into practice: when disputes arise in a province the courts will always come down on the side of the people, against the representatives of the prince.

Authority of a despotic nature should never, in fact, be delegated. Arbitrary commands should not be carried out in an arbitrary manner, and it is in the interest of an unjust prince that the man responsible for carrying out his decrees, even when they are completely tyrannical, should observe the strictest rules of justice in the manner of carrying them out.

Under a dictatorship, one is on the people's side and against the governor or government official. It is quite the opposite in a monarchy.

(17)⁹

Usbek to Ibben, at Smyrna

I am so distrustful of Christians that I always keep on my guard when I am with them.

I know things about them which make me have a very bad opinion of them: even those who appear to be men of absolute integrity have certain practices which make them suspect to me.

What do you think of men who need to make themselves respectable again once a week, and who have the effrontery to go and say to God: 'Lord, let's forget the past; for fifty years I have been misleading you regularly each week, but let's try again this time and make a fresh start'?

The children of Ali go on a pilgrimage to Mecca once in their life-times: they make a gift, once in their lives, of one-tenth of all they own, but they do not constantly strain divine mercy by new crimes and new acts of expiation. They are concerned about their former debts, their obligations towards God are never discharged; they are afraid of contracting new ones, and of overstepping the limit and reaching the point where paternal goodness is exhausted.

(18)

Usbek to ***

I don't know how it came about, but one day a Turk fell in with a cannibal. 'It is very cruel of you,' said the Muslim, 'to eat your prisoners of war.'

'What do you do with yours?' the cannibal replied.

'We kill them; but when they are dead we don't eat them.'

Is it really worth it, for such a minor detail, to distinguish ourselves from the savages? We see barbarity in habits which are virtually without significance, and fail to see it when every rule of humanity is violated and every feeling of pity ignored.

From Paris, the 10th of the moon of Shaaban, 1715

(19)[10]

Hadji Ibbi to Jemshid, a dervish of the mountain of Jahrum

How can I describe to you, Jemshid, the way in which my heart was torn during the terrible crossing that I had to make from Smyrna to Marseilles? – twice in forty days I was unable to make a single prayer. The more the wind affected the boat, the less fit I was to speak to God. While I was more and more in need of mercy, it became less and less possible to ask for it. 'What use was my pilgrimage to Mecca,' I said to myself, 'if on this boat I have to live and perhaps even die an infidel, and if whatever position I adopt I am never unmoved, and nonetheless never in a proper condition to pray?'

At times, watching the weather, I was pleased to see that it was becoming calmer, but having examined myself carefully I realized that I was still in motion, and fortunately felt a certain scruple in my heart which prevented me from profaning the holy name that I wanted to praise. 'How long,' I said, 'will my religious zeal be unavailing? Why is it that, although my heart is pure, I am unable to carry out what the Law commands? Will I never be worthy again, back on the immovable earth, which rests upon the Camel, to prostrate myself before God and confer with the angels?' When you pray, happy Jemshid, you have the mountain of Jahrum beneath your feet, which is where the Prophet first turns his eyes when he looks towards the earth.

The Law of the holy Koran was not bestowed on you in vain: you can find hidden precepts in the least word of this divine book. It seems to grow as you consult it. You multiply opportunities for us to be obedient; you do not confine yourself to a few rigid precepts but, with equal strictness, follow the advice of him who could have compelled us to do everything he advises, and who found us weak when he looked for us to be faithful.

From Paris, the 25th of the moon of Rajab, 1713

(20)

Usbek to ★★★

The earliest heroes did good deeds, protected travellers, rid the earth of monsters, and undertook useful work: such were Hercules and Theseus.

Subsequently they were merely courageous, like Achilles, Ajax, and Diomedes: after that, they were great conquerors, like Philip and Alexander.

Finally they became lovers, like the heroes in romances.

At present I don't know what they do. They are merely subject to the caprices of Fortune. An empire is exploited in the same way as a farmer exploits his land, in order to get as much as possible out of it. If there is a war, it is carried out as an assignment, with the sole purpose of obtaining territories to provide subsidies; what used to be called 'glory', 'the laurels of war', 'trophies', 'triumphs', 'crowns of victory', is nowadays ready money.

From Paris, the 3rd of Rabia, 1717

NOTES

THE most important modern editions of the *Lettres persanes* are those by Barckhausen (1897 and 1913), Carcassonne (1929), Adam (1954), and Vernière (1960). The first two used Montesquieu's notebooks, dating from 1754, and discovered by Barckhausen, as the basis of their editions, while the last two preferred the text of the edition of 1758, thus avoiding the often timid or prudent revisions made by Montesquieu in the notebooks. I have worked from the latter editions. This affects the numbering of the letters, since L. 145, included in the main text by Adam and Vernière, was put into an appendix by Barckhausen. There are of course many variant readings to be found in the four principal early editions (two in 1721, 1754, 1758) and the notebooks; in the following notes variants are mentioned only if they add something substantial or are relevant for the understanding of the text. The notes otherwise draw heavily on the work of the modern editors; where appropriate, explanatory suggestions are credited to them. I have also used other editions and translations, notably that by Ozell, first published in 1722.

The notes refer frequently to some important sources or predecessors of Montesquieu: Chardin and Tavernier, for information about the East (see the note to L. 72), and Jean-Paul Marana, whose lengthy work in letter form, published in the 1680s and 1690s and known as *L'Espion Turc* (The Turkish Spy), purported to be the secret correspondence of a Turkish agent in France. It was the most obvious model for the form of the *Persian Letters* and discusses many of the same subjects as Montesquieu.

The calendar used in the *Persian Letters* needs some explanation. It was disentangled by Shackleton (see the article listed on p. 35), and turns out to be a somewhat rough and ready affair. In reality, the Muslim months follow the lunar months, and so do not have a fixed number of days; consequently, the Gregorian (solar) year gradually moves forward with respect to the Muslim calendar. Montesquieu took no account of this point (he refers to the month of Shaaban in L. 18 as if it were always hot); he also, after hesitating with the year

1712, makes the Muslim year begin in Dulkaada (in European style) instead of Muharram. What he did in principle was simply to give the Gregorian months Muslim names, as follows:

January	– Dulkaada	July	– Jomada (1)
February	– Dulheggia	August	– Jomada (2)
March	– Muharram	September	– Rajab
April	– Saphar	October	– Shaaban
May	– Rabia (1)	November	– Ramadán
June	– Rabia (2)	December	– Shawall

The reader may notice occasional irregularities such as the omission to specify the first or second month of Rabia and Jomada. Montesquieu sometimes arranges the letters from Persia to France according to the date of their receipt, on the assumption that the journey would have taken five to six months; e.g. Zelis's Letter 70, dated the 9th day of the first month of Jomada, is placed after Usbek's Letter 69, dated the last day of Shaaban.

In transliterating Islamic proper names I have used forms which may appear over-simplified or archaic (e.g. Mohammed, Ramadán), but they seem to suit the rather elementary brand of exoticism employed by Montesquieu. Another device, the use of oriental terms such as 'dervish', 'mufti' or 'men of the Law' to denote Western types (monk, Pope, ecclesiastics), will presumably cause the reader no difficulty.

In translating sums of money, I have normally rendered the *livre* or *franc* (the basic unit) as 'shilling', the *écu* (three *livres*) as 'crown', and the *louis* (24 *livres*) as 'pound', making adjustments as appropriate. The English values are intended to represent those of the eighteenth century, not of modern times.

Finally it should be pointed out that the notes found in the main text, marked with an asterisk or dagger, are Montesquieu's own, as given in the 1758 edition (except with L. 143 – see note 7 to this letter).

MONTESQUIEU'S PREFACE

1. This is traditionally supposed to be a reference to Montesquieu's wife.

2. 'Bored him sublimely' translates '*l'auraient ennuyé jusque dans les nues*', literally, 'would have bored him even in the clouds', an ironic reference to the combination of boredom and sublimity which Montesquieu dislikes in the 'oriental' style. This reading, found in almost all editions in the eighteenth century and followed by Barckhausen and Carcassonne, is rejected by Adam and Vernière for no good reason. They prefer the reading '*l'auraient envoyé jusque dans les nues*' ('would have sent him up to the clouds'), which lacks point and has no particular authority.

LETTER 2

1. Usbek means what he says – cf. L. 47.

LETTER 3

1. These boxes ('*boîtes*') appear to have been something like a sedan-chair; the information comes from Chardin.

LETTER 4

1. Chardin states that the Lesbianism here denied by Zephis was common in Asia.

LETTER 6

1. Usbek refers to the Turks as 'faithless' because they belong to the Sunnite branch of the Muslim religion, while the Persians are Shiites; see note 2 to L. 60.

LETTER 7

1. The name Fatme is also used in the address from which several

letters from Usbek's wives are sent. It is not clear whether this has any significance but I would guess that it has not.

2. Montesquieu's note is based on Chardin, who says that Persians are more lustful than other Eastern peoples.

LETTER 8

1. It was claimed by P. Barrière in the *Revue d'histoire littéraire de la France* for 1951 that Usbek's life was based on Montesquieu's own. Both shared a taste for study, but the threats to Usbek's life (referred to again in L. 155) are, it is to be hoped, without any basis in reality.

LETTER 9

1. This eunuch is presumably black, although Montesquieu does not say so. The Chief (or 'First') Black Eunuch is a more important character in the book than his white counterpart; white eunuchs were employed for duties outside the women's apartments.

LETTER 11

1. The famous series of letters on the Troglodytes also includes one not published by Montesquieu; see Appendix, p. 286. The name of Troglodytes was given in antiquity to a tribe, mentioned by Herodotus, about which bizarre reports circulated.

LETTER 13

1. 'Do you want milk for your herds' is the literal translation of the accepted text, but milk is an odd thing to want for herds. It seems likely that an error has crept in, and that instead of '*du lait pour vos troupeaux*' the text should read '*du lait de nos troupeaux*' ('milk from our herds'), on the lines of the phrase immediately following.

LETTER 15

1. On this name, see note 1 to L. 97.

LETTER 16

1. A mullah is a man qualified in both sacred and civil law.
2. On Ali, see note 2 to L. 60.
3. The word has two meanings, both containing the idea of religious leadership. Here, the meaning depends on the Shiite belief that there was a succession of supreme leaders of Islam, called imams, going back to Mohammed and his son-in-law Ali. There had been twelve of these imams, according to the Persians, so that to call the mullah the thirteenth is in keeping with Usbek's flatteries. But the word also means religious leader in a more local sense, a leader in prayer, and it is in this sense, presumably, that the mullah himself uses it in L. 18.

LETTER 18

1. Montesquieu's story is not his own invention, but comes originally from a book of Muslim legends collected by Hermannus Dalmata (*Machumetis Saracenorum principis doctrina*, 1550). In the source the story is told of Christ, not of Mohammed (Vernière).

LETTER 19

1. i.e. the military commanders, or governors of a province, try to get their money back from the inhabitants.
2. The customary name, since 1530, when it was granted the island of Malta by Charles V, of a Christian military order founded during the crusades under the name of Knights of St John. They made the island into an outpost on the frontier between Christendom and the Turks.

LETTER 22

1. This letter was included only in the 1754 edition; a letter found among Montesquieu's papers (see Appendix, p. 289) must be a draft of it. The similarity of its date to that of L. 20 and L. 21 shows that the reason for Jahrum's return is the misbehaviour of Zashi.

LETTER 23

1. The first letter from Europe contains the first examples of the pseudo-naïve remarks about the strange civilization observed by the Persians – here they concern the liberty of Italian women – which are such a feature of their letters. For other examples cf. L. 24, L. 28, L. 29, and L. 32.

LETTER 24

1. Rica is referring to measures such as the venality of official posts and titles, the introduction of paper money, and the manipulation of values in the early years of the eighteenth century, when the Protestant powers were pressing France hard; the final remark concerns the belief that sufferers from scrofula (or king's-evil) could be cured by being touched by the king.

2. It is probably clear that the beliefs said to be inculcated by the Pope are the doctrines of the Trinity and Transubstantiation. This passage was arguably the most audacious of Montesquieu's ironies at the expense of orthodoxy (although some editions of Marana had gone further); it must have had a lot to do with the defensive 'Reflections' (see p. 283) which Montesquieu added in 1754.

3. The so-called Constitution, a papal decree also known as the bull *Unigenitus* (which would date from 1710 if Montesquieu's dates were to be trusted: in fact it was issued in 1713), was directed against the Jansenists (see the Introduction, p. 30), and especially against a book on the New Testament by one of their leaders, Quesnel, which said among other things that everybody, i.e. not only men, should be allowed to read the Scriptures. Rica's explanation of Jansenist recalcitrance is, of course, only a small part of the full story. At the end of the letter the Jansenists become Louis XIV's invisible enemies, while the 'dervishes' are the Jesuits (Barckhausen).

4. The subject of women and Paradise crops up later, in L. 125 and L. 141. The Koran says in fact that women go to Paradise, but to a different one from men (Barckhausen).

LETTER 28

1. The asterisks are presumably meant to indicate that the name of the addressee is unknown.

2. Rica misunderstands where the action goes on in the theatre, and treats the spectators in the boxes as actors (it was by all accounts fairly common for romantic incidents to occur there). The 'crowd of people down below' are the spectators in the pit, where there were no seats. As Rica implies, there was no love lost between the richer and the poorer in the audience.

3. The identity of these people is not very clear. Ozell suggests that they are '*petits-maîtres*', young men about town. If so, they are occupied in visiting their friends in different boxes, and their 'crutches' must be walking sticks or canes.

4. This is elaborate politeness in the foyer during intervals. The phrase immediately following, about two or three hours of fierceness, refers to the times when the actresses are on stage, playing heroic and virtuous ladies in tragedy.

5. The singers and dancers at the Opera had an unflattering reputation. As for the lover of this one, an abbé was an ecclesiastic who had taken the minimum vows necessary to qualify for a benefice, but did not have to perform any clerical duties. To be an abbé was a normal way of life for young men of noble family; the '*abbé galant*', i.e. gallant to women, was a standard figure in contemporary society and literature.

LETTER 29

1. Montesquieu's lack of respect was probably less surprising in 1721 than it would be now. An attitude of independence from Rome was traditional in the French Church; known as Gallicanism, it had been encouraged by Louis XIV, and was much favoured in the Parlementaire circles from which Montesquieu came.

2. Montesquieu may be referring to the fact that there had been not only a Pelagian but also a semi-Pelagian heresy.

3. Here the implication is that in order to satisfy the Spanish Inquisition it was sufficient for a Catholic to have observed certain purely formal religous duties: praying with a rosary, wearing a

scapulary, and making the pilgrimage to Santiago de Compostela, in Galicia. Similar views about Spanish Catholicism are expressed in L. 78. The details about Inquisition methods come largely from Marana.

4. This is derived from Chardin (Carcassonne).

LETTER 32

1. Rica has been visiting the blind people's home in Paris, the Quinze-Vingts ('Fifteen-Score').

LETTER 33

1. Seneca, whose influence during the seventeenth century had been considerable, wrote works of consolation embodying Stoic principles of the sort indicated here.

2. It is debatable whether Montesquieu means stimulants such as coffee, or drugs such as opium.

LETTER 34

1. In constructing this letter from his sources Montesquieu seems to have over-emphasized the unsociability of Persians (Adam).

LETTER 35

1. In Asia such an expression was apparently frequently used with reference to Jews.

2. In this semi-serious comparison between the two religions there is an error in that Muslims pray five times a day, not seven. The book on polygamy was *Polygamia triumphatrix* (London, 1682), by the Lutheran Johann Leiser.

LETTER 36

1. Coffee-houses were a new and important social phenomenon. Some among them were particularly favoured by intellectuals; Montesquieu may be referring to the Café Procope.

2. The dispute about Homer (which arose later than the date of this letter would suggest, La Motte-Houdart's translation of the *Iliad* having appeared only in 1714) is also mentioned in L.137. It was a late phase of the 'Quarrel of the Ancients and Moderns', a prolonged debate about the relative merits of classical and modern culture and civilization.

3. This refers to the controversies, in Latin syllogisms, of theologians, who were to be found in large numbers in the area around the Sorbonne. The nation mentioned at the end is said by Barckhausen to be the Irish Catholics who had come across to France after the English Revolution of 1688.

LETTER 37

1. At the date of this letter Louis XIV was seventy-four.

2. Editors suggest two names for the young minister: Barbézieux, appointed a secretary of state at seventeen, in 1685; and Cany, who held a similar post at eighteen, in 1708. The mistress, Mme de Maintenon (whom Louis had in fact secretly married in about 1684), was seventy-eight. The numerous other references in this letter are to Louis' combination of devoutness and hatred of Jansenism; his taciturnity and love of glory; his militancy and dislike of able men; his policy of ostentation and the poverty of the nation; and his policy of encouraging the nobility to lead useless lives at court. The jibe about the general who fled four leagues may refer to the incompetent and unpopular Villeroy, who was given a command in Italy.

LETTER 38

1. This, it is generally agreed, is likely to be the writer, wit and polymath Fontenelle (1657–1757), whom Montesquieu very probably knew before 1721.

2. They were a tribe which in classical times lived in what is now part of Russia, and was according to Herodotus descended from the Scythians and Amazons.

3. The precept is taken from the Koran.

LETTER 39

1. Barckhausen notes that the Koran does not prescribe circumcision.

2. A high mountain near Mecca.

3. In using this name for the name 'Isben Aben' found in the text I am following a suggestion made in Vernière's edition. The scholar Ibn Abbas was a cousin of Mohammed and the origin of legendary traditions about him. Montesquieu's material comes from the same source as L. 18, Hermannus Dalmata.

LETTER 40

1. This detail probably comes from Tavernier; the ceremony has continued down to modern times with the Aga Khan.

LETTER 44

1. Alexander the Great (Maccabees I, 1–8).

LETTER 45

1. This translation of '*aussi ne déplaça-t-il pas*' is strongly implied by the context; Carcassonne observes that he knows of no other example of the verb *déplacer* in the sense 'pay cash'.

2. i.e. the transmutation of base metals into gold, the aim of alchemy, which still had a sufficient following for Montesquieu's attack to have some point. Flamel (*c.* 1330–1418), 'reputed French alchemist and scrivener to the university of Paris' (*Encyclopaedia Britannica*, 11th edition), and Ramón Llull (*c.* 1234–1316), the Spanish mystic, writer and missionary, were according to legend 'adepts', as Rica's acquaintance claimed to be.

LETTER 46

1. No doubt it will be clear that the various rites referred to belong to Islam, Judaism and Christianity.

2. Brahmins usually forbid meat (Carcassonne); this one is alluding to the belief in the transmigration of souls.

3. The third of these notes by Montesquieu does not appear to have any basis in his usual sources. Perhaps he is practising a slight deception, and under the guise of Armenian religion is really satirizing the Christian prohibition of eating meat on Fridays.

LETTER 47

1. The *corrouk*, as can be inferred, prohibits anyone to come near high-born Persian women when they are travelling. The information about it, and the risks involved, comes from Chardin.

2. On the boxes, cf. the note to L. 3. Editors point out that there is no river of the kind implied by Montesquieu in the vicinity of Ispahan.

LETTER 48

1. The *ancien régime* method of raising taxes was by 'farming'; a tax-farmer paid for the right to levy taxes according to the law, and made his money by the amount he could extract above what he had paid. The literature of the time is full of tirades against rich and extortionate tax-farmers. It was commonly said that they were recruited from the servant classes and acquired enough money to buy their way into the nobility, as Montesquieu implies here and in L. 98.

2. This portrait of a fashionable confessor contains reminiscences of Molière's lecherous hypocrite, Tartuffe. Montesquieu's satire is less violent.

3. For Montesquieu's dislike of poets and poetry, cf. the note to L. 137.

4. This translation, for '*je ne vaux pas grand' chose*', follows the interpretation suggested by Adam, and also implied in Ozell's translation: 'I am a sad dog'.

LETTER 49

1. Chardin mentions a Capuchin mission, but in Ispahan.

LETTER 51

.1. No very clear explanation of this remark has been found.

2. The joke about Russian women was an old one. Montesquieu's note indicates that he did not believe in it.

3. Part of Peter the Great's campaign to Westernize his country was to discourage (by direct action) the wearing of beards, and other traditional customs; the changes caused some rebellion. The Orthodox clergy were allowed to keep their beards; Montesquieu's remark about ignorance may refer to Peter's educational reforms, education until then having been in the hands of the Church.

4. Peter had conquered territory belonging to Sweden; he also visited France in 1717, and Nargum is perhaps referring to this visit (despite the discrepancy of date).

LETTER 54

1. I have been unable to translate the pun; the proper meaning of the phrase is 'corporate spirit', e.g. of a regiment, but Montesquieu also takes the word *esprit* in its other meaning of 'intelligence' and 'wit'; the character will participate in the mental qualities of the body (the Academy) of which he will become a member.

LETTER 55

1. The time-lag was in fact rather long: Baghdad fell in 1638, Candahar in 1649.

LETTER 57

1. This translation of '*libertins*' is unsatisfactory in that the French word also implies the sense of 'free-thinker'; later in the letter the casuist's use of it inclines rather to the second sense.

2. Montesquieu presumably means that confessors encourage their penitents to make bequests to the Church.

3. The attack on casuistry contains many reminiscences of Pascal's *Provincial Letters* and Molière's *Tartuffe*.

LETTER 58

1. It may not be immediately obvious that Montesquieu is referring to the number of ecclesiastics intriguing to be given some lucrative appointment.

LETTER 59

1. i.e. he had not been brave enough to accept a challenge to a duel, and instead had got a beating – a punishment reserved for lackeys and the like.

LETTER 60

1. The Huguenots, who were Calvinists. They are mentioned also in L. 85, and in passing in L. 59. The Jews had been proscribed in Spain in 1492.

2. Ali was the son-in-law of Mohammed and founded the Shiite form of Muslim belief adopted by the Persians; Abu-bekr was Mohammed's father-in-law and first successor, although the succession was disputed by Ali. Abu-bekr, together with Omar, the second successor, was followed by the Sunnites.

LETTER 61

1. Cf. note 1 to L. 57.

2. This is presumably an elaboration of an incident following the Tatar conquest of China in the seventeenth century. The Tatar ruler aroused serious opposition by ordering the Chinese to cut their hair.

3. The reference is to the massacre in 390, by Theodosius I, of three thousand inhabitants of Thessalonika, after a riot. St Ambrose refused to meet him until he had done public penance. The other details, which are mythical, come from the historian Theodoret (Vernière).

4. This is milder than the early editions, which had '*un fanatique et un fou*' – 'a fanatic and an idiot'.

LETTER 63

1. At the time this was a favourite place for conversations, especially of a more or less amorous kind.

LETTER 66

1. This remark is directed against the view that religious truths must be accepted without question by an act of faith (fideism), while philosophical matters are open to intellectual discussion and doubt; the distinction between religion and philosophy was a major issue.

2. A common form of book production was to collect the best remarks of men of letters into an anthology, or 'ana'.

LETTER 67

1. The Gabars or Ghebers were a religious minority in Persia, followers of Zoroaster (Zarathustra), who in the seventh to sixth centuries B.C. reformed the ancient Iranian religion of the mages, sun-worship. Tavernier and Chardin depict the Gabars, on the whole, as virtuous agriculturalists (cf. the remarks about them in L. 85).

2. The names of the characters are derived from names in Chardin and the English orientalist Thomas Hyde, who wrote on ancient Persian religion; he also provided the elements of the religous argument between Apheridon and Astarte later (Vernière).

3. Herodotus records that Cambyses, the son of Cyrus, married his sister; according to Hyde the Gabars had once been allowed to practice incest, but not after the conquest of Persia by Alexander. It it is impossible to tell whether Montesquieu was inaccurate intentionally.

4. I use this word here, instead of 'seraglio', merely because Montesquieu unaccountably changes from '*sérail*' (his usual word) to '*beiram*' – which however does not mean 'harem' but 'public prayer'; he presumably confused it with 'haram', the word used by Chardin.

5. Vishtaspa or Gushtasp, in Greek Hystaspes, was the king who became Zoroaster's disciple and protector; Aurvataspa was his father.

6. The toman declined in value to about a shilling in 1965; it must have represented about £2 in English money of Montesquieu's time.

LETTER 69

1. Zeuxis (464–398 B.C.), who is supposed to have based a portrait of Helen – not of the goddess of beauty, who must be Aphrodite – on five young women of the town of Croton.

2. This last paragraph was added in 1754, and implies that the preceding arguments had gone too far in rationalistic speculation.

LETTER 70

1. This is the literal translation. However, its sense is inconsistent with the rest of the letter, all of which implies strongly that the girl is innocent and that the accusation is fabricated (because her husband was dissatisfied with the size of the dowry); that only 'some' maintain her innocence suggests on the contrary that it is she who was at fault. In my view this inconsistency indicates a defective text, and instead of the accepted reading '*Il y a des personnes qui soutiennent que* . . .' I would guess that Montesquieu meant '*Il n'y a personne qui ne soutienne que* . . .', i.e. 'There is nobody who does not maintain that' (the girl is innocent).

LETTER 71

1. Moses, who was then officially considered to be the author of the first five books of the Old Testament. The reference is to Deuteronomy XXII, 13–21.

LETTER 72

1. Jean Chardin (1643–1713), a Huguenot who came to England, to be knighted by Charles II and sent as an envoy to Holland, was a merchant traveller in the East; the first edition of his travels was in 1686. Jean-Baptiste Tavernier (1605–89) was also a Huguenot and a merchant traveller; his travels ('Six Voyages') were first published in 1676–7.

LETTER 73

1. One of the duties of the forty members of the Academy was to produce a dictionary. Its decisions, therefore, concern the correct usage of words; but usage depends on society, hence the Academy's difficulties. Its dictionary, or 'compilation', first appeared in 1694, having been commissioned by Richelieu in the 1630s. It was 'almost smothered at birth' by the greater merits of a rival dictionary, which had appeared in 1690, that of Nicolas Furetière, who had been expelled from the Academy when his intentions became known.

2. i.e. the abundance of ceremonial speeches, produced especially when a new member was introduced.

3. Various explanations have been given for this: that some Academicians were considered over-keen to obtain royal pensions, or to increase their income by frequent attendance; Ozell, who appears to be knowledgeable on the subject of the Academy, asserts that an academician named Granier had swindled an orphan out of an inheritance.

LETTER 75

1. Usbek is less pious than Rhedi had been in L. 31 with regard to the same point.

LETTER 77

1. This letter was added in the 1754 edition; Montesquieu's note-books show that at first he thought of incorporating it into L. 76. It was presumably designed to counteract any scandal produced by Usbek's defence of suicide, but a careful reading will reveal that it is an explanation of the laws against suicide rather than a retraction of L. 76.

2. The two elements are body and soul.

LETTER 78

1. Editors have established that this letter was put together from information taken chiefly from books on Spain by Mme d'Aulnoy (1681) and Vayrac (1718).

2. Commemorated in Camoens' *Lusiads*, Castro (1500–1548) was governor and viceroy of the Portuguese Indies. The anecdote is substantially true.

3. i.e. not descended from Moorish or Jewish converts.

4. It will be noticed that Montesquieu's arithmetic does not conform to what he presumably means, viz., 'twice as much respect'. The text ('*la moitié plus de considération*') seems to need emendation, the most obvious alternative text being '*deux fois plus*', 'twice as much'.

5. Cervantes's *Don Quixote*, which in outline is a satire of the romances of chivalry criticized by Montesquieu in the preceding paragraph.

6. The Batuecas are isolated valleys in Estremadura; why Montesquieu speaks of 'nations' is obscure. Nor has it been explained what he means by the reference to bridges.

LETTER 80

1. It should be noted that Usbek's question does not concern the constitutional form of government so much as the choice between harshness and leniency, as is shown by the sequel (although the two questions are of course related).

2. These were standard examples of dictatorship and republicanism at the time (cf. L. 136).

3. Osman II, deposed and strangled in 1622, was succeeded by Mustapha I, an uncle, who was of unsound mind.

LETTER 81

1. By 'Tartars' (an older and vaguer word which seems preferable to 'Tatars', ethnographically more specific) Montesquieu seems to mean a variety of Asiatic warrior nations. The letter appears to be his reaction to a book on Genghis Khan by Pétis de la Croix (1710) (Vernière).

2. The Mongolian 'Golden Horde', originally led by Genghis Khan at the beginning of the thirteenth century, conquered both China and Russia; the empire founded by Genghis Khan lasted, in a

more or less fragmented form, for centuries. But the second conquest of China is presumably that of another Mongolian nation, the Manchus, in the seventeenth century.

3. The Mogul Empire (the word is a form of 'Mongol') was founded by Baber, a great-grandson of Tamburlaine, in northern India, at the beginning of the sixteenth century.

4. Cyrus founded the Persian Empire in the sixth century B.C. On Vishtaspa, cf. L. 67, note 5.

5. The Turks are not usually considered to be of the same race as the Tatars.

6. This is presumably a reference to Attila the Hun, who invaded the Roman Empire in the fifth century.

LETTER 82

1. The Carthusians do not in fact have a rule of silence, but do not talk at meals.

LETTER 83

1. A. Crisafulli, in his article 'Parallels to Ideas in the Lettres Persanes' (Publications of the Modern Language Association of America, 1937), relates this letter to the work of Hobbes, Malebranche, Leibniz, and Shaftesbury. The definition of justice at the beginning is very similar to that of Leibniz, in his *Theodicy* (1710); some of the reasoning seems to come from Malebranche and Shaftesbury; and the argument that justice 'does not depend on human conventions' is almost certainly directed at Hobbes.

2. This rather obscure paragraph may refer to doctrines of pre-destination, according to which God punishes men for doing actions which are preordained (this would fit in with the arguments in L. 69), or to the portrayal of Jehovah in the Old Testament.

LETTER 84

1. The word means 'incapable of military service', through wounds or old age; the object of Montesquieu's praise is Louis XIV, who had had the Invalides built in the early 1670s.

LETTER 85

1. Suleiman III reigned from 1666 to 1694. Tavernier's account suggests that his favourite (not 'some ministers') was more interested in money than religion (Vernière). As with the Gabars later, Montesquieu uses his source so as to imply that the 'zealots' encouraged Louis XIV, and that the effect of the Revocation of the Edict of Nantes, in 1685, was to weaken the nation economically and militarily for the sake of dogmatism.

2. Shah Abbas I, the Great, the greatest Persian ruler of the seventeenth century (c. 1557–1628 or 1629).

LETTER 86

1. The Galerie du Palais, outside the lawcourts, was lined with shops.

2. The public test of a husband's sexual powers known as 'trial by congress' had been abolished in 1677, but in 1714 there had been a notorious trial concerning impotence, the accusation having been made by the Marquise de Gesvres against her husband (Adam).

LETTER 87

1. It was common to employ Swiss porters, guards, etc.

LETTER 88

1. Chardin says that there was no aristocratic class in Persia, the most respected members of society being the important functionaries.

LETTER 89

1. Presumably the *'tribunal des Maréchaux de France'*, the court of the Marshals of France, which had been established in 1643 as part of the campaign against duelling, and decided on matters of honour.

LETTER 90

1. To regard something as a point of honour meant being ready to fight a duel over it. Royal edicts against duelling, which caused a large number of deaths among the aristocracy, had been frequent since the sixteenth century. Montesquieu was to devote a notable chapter of the *Spirit of Laws* (XXVIII, 20) to the origins of the custom.

2. In 1627 Richelieu had made an example of two young men, Boutteville and Chapelles, who were executed; Louis XIV also took firm measures against duelling.

LETTER 91

1. The ambassador was a Persian official, Mehemet Riza Beg, who visited Paris in 1715 and was received by Louis XIV. Usbek criticizes him because the gifts he brought for the king were derisory and his behaviour appeared eccentric. On his return to Persia he committed suicide, apparently because he was long overdue and had sold almost all Louis' gifts to him (Adam, Vernière).

LETTER 92

1. The letter outlines the historical situation. The new king was Louis XV (cf. L. 107), his uncle Philippe d'Orléans (1674–1723), who used the traditional authority of the Parlements, much diminished under Louis XIV, as support in his manoeuvres to get power.

2. A clearer expression of favourable opinion towards the Parlements is to be found in L. 140.

LETTER 93

1. Literally a 'holy man', from the Spanish 'santo', 'holy'.

2. It looks as if the rationalistic explanation which follows is Montesquieu's own, since no source has been found for it.

LETTER 94

1. Vernière suggests that this is directed especially against Machiavelli.

LETTER 95

1. This passage must be a criticism of Louis XIV's foreign policy.

2. The kings were Amasis of Egypt and Polycrates of Samos, in the sixth century B.C. Montesquieu seems to have preferred a morally edifying version of the incident found in Diodorus Siculus, instead of Herodotus' more colourful account.

3. In the early editions, instead of the passage 'Conquest in itself ... of their despair', the text was: 'The right of conquest is not a right. A society can be founded only with the consent of its members. If it is destroyed by conquest, the nation becomes free again; it is not a new society, and if the conqueror tries to create one it will be a dictatorship.

'As for peace treaties, they are never legitimate if they enforce the surrender of territory, or payment of compensation, to a value higher than the damage which was caused. If they do, they are merely acts of violence, and can always be repudiated; except when, in order to recover what has been lost, it is necessary to resort to methods so violent that they produce an evil greater than the good which could be obtained from them.'

LETTER 97

1. The name of this mountain to the south of Shiraz is used in L. 15 as the name of a eunuch.

2. The laws of nature admired by Usbek are expounded according to the ideas of Descartes, in his *Principles of Philosophy*, which were superseded by Newtonian mechanics. Montesquieu's emphasis on order, regularity, and simplicity combined with 'fertility' is perhaps more characteristic of Descartes' follower Malebranche.

LETTER 98

1. See L. 48, note 1, on attitudes to tax-farmers. Montesquieu's remarks about their current situation concern the commission set up in 1716 to investigate their affairs. The witty minister is assumed to be Noailles, president of the Council of Finances from 1715 to 1718.

LETTER 99

1. The excesses of fashion were a favourite topic; Marana writes about it and La Bruyère's *Characters* contained a chapter on it. What Montesquieu says appears to be substantially true (for instance, about architecture).

LETTER 100

1. French law was a combination of canon law, Roman law and customary law, varying from place to place.

2. The reference is principally to Justinian, in the sixth century; at about this time the Salic law and other Frankish laws were being created. The democratic method of making these laws suggested here seems to be a fiction.

3. It is curious that Montesquieu should describe papal decrees so favourably (cf. L. 24, on the Constitution), and there is some reason to think that the text needs emendation.

LETTER 101

1. Cf. L. 24, note 3. The large man is a bishop in favour of the bull against the Jansenists, and the dervish a Jesuit who does his theology for him.

LETTER 102

1. Philip Augustus, in the twelfth century. It was said that Richard Coeur-de-lion, his rival in the crusades, had had assassins sent to kill him.

2. This is presumably a hyperbolical expression for the royal prerogative of pardoning criminals.

LETTER 103

1. Ravaillac, in 1610. In one of his notebooks Montesquieu relates an incident of 1719 when an Indian king was assassinated 'without any disturbance being caused'.

LETTER 104

1. It has been suggested in an article by Crisafulli (see note 1 to L. 83) that Montesquieu is here influenced by Shaftesbury's ideas on 'public spirit' or 'fellowship', but the resemblance is not particularly close. It would have been quite possible for Montesquieu to attribute his own ideas to an undefined English source.

2. Charles I. In 1649 the House of Commons declared that the king could be guilty of high treason.

3. An allusion to Romans XIII, 1: 'Let every soul be subject unto the higher powers.'

4. Barckhausen suggests that the prince is Edward, son of Henry VI, speaking to Edward IV after the battle of Tewkesbury; Shakespeare included in *Henry VI*, Part III, a scene of the sort implied by Montesquieu (Act V, sc. 5). It is not clear how Montesquieu knew of the anecdote.

LETTER 105

1. In his notebooks Montesquieu, writing of harmful scientific discoveries, mentions Greek fire and gunpowder (Vernière).

2. The reference is to the Spanish and Portuguese conquests in the New World (a recurrent theme in the latter part of the work – cf. L. 78, L. 118 and L. 121) and to the precious metals which were brought into Europe. In his notebooks Montesquieu says that Europe acquired smallpox from the Arabs, and yaws, a type of endemic (i.e. non-venereal) syphilis, from the New World.

LETTER 106

1. The editions from 1721 to 1754 have, instead of the passage 'there would be an end ... die of hunger', the following: 'that mutual exchange of money, and propagation of earnings, which derives from the dependence of one trade on others, would cease completely; each individual would get his income from his land alone, and would get from it exactly what he needed, and no more, in order not to die of hunger'. The phrase *'propagation de revenus'* in the earlier text seems to me clearer than what replaces it in 1758,

'*progression de revenus*'. At the beginning of this sentence, I am far from sure that 'economic relationships' is the precise meaning of the phrase '*relation de facultés*', found in all editions.

LETTER 107

1. Louis XV was seven years old at the date of this letter. His uncertain health made it seem unlikely that he would live long, and since there was no obvious heir war might easily have broken out if he had died. The international intrigue that went on in anticipation included the Cellamare conspiracy, which forms the subject of L. 126.

2. Montesquieu must be thinking particularly of Louis XIV. La Chaise and Le Tellier, his Jesuit confessors, had had great influence, as did the devout Mme de Maintenon in his old age.

3. The phenomenon described here was a well-known feature of the Ancien Régime.

LETTER 108

1. Literary journals at the time were more like books than magazines. They usually contained little else but summaries of recent publications, without much comment.

2. Writers ran the risk of a thrashing if they offended important people. It was to happen to Voltaire in 1726.

LETTER 109

1. The university claimed to have been founded by Charlemagne.

2. It concerned the pronunciation of Latin, and was started by Ramus (François de la Ramée) with his *Scholae grammaticae*, in 1559.

3. There is a note of the incident in Montesquieu's notebooks. The date he gives here is an error or misprint for 1510 (Adam).

LETTER 111

1. In the second edition of 1721 the letter begins differently (there are also several minor variants): 'The people is an animal which can see and hear, but never thinks. It is in a state of surprising lethargy

or of surprising fury and goes constantly backwards and forwards from one state to the other, never knowing where it came from.

'I have heard people in France talk of a certain governor of Normandy, who, wishing to enhance his standing at court, himself occasionally stirred up a few outbreaks of sedition, which he immediately put down.

'He had since admitted that the most serious of these insurrections cost him in all only half a toman. He would get together some of the riff-raff in a drinking-house; this would set the tone for the whole town and subsequently for the whole province.

'This reminds me of a letter written during the last disturbances in Paris by one of the city's generals, to a friend of his:

'"Three days ago I ordered a sortie by the city troops, but they were repulsed and suffered some losses; however, I am sure of easily making up for this setback . . ."'

Vernière has investigated the sources of this letter in the memoirs of the Cardinal de Retz, one of the leaders of the Fronde, and of Guy Joly, and concludes that the 'general' is Retz himself; the governor of Normandy is the Duc de Longueville.

2. The historical similarities between the regency of Philippe d'Orléans and that of Anne d'Autriche, during the minority of Louis XIV (1643–61), encouraged interest in the former period. This letter is a satire on the first part of the Fronde, the civil war of 1648 to 1653, and is based on the propaganda campaign against Mazarin, the leader of the court party against the nobility and the Parisians.

3. Montesquieu added a note in the second edition of 1721, about Mazarin's pronunciation: 'Cardinal Mazarin, intending to say "Decree of Union" ("*Arrêt d'Union*"), said, in front of the deputies of the Parlement, "Decree of Onion" ("*Arrêt d'Oignon*"); which became the subject of many jokes on the part of the people.' The decree was one made by the Parlement in May 1648.

4. According to Guy Joly, Mazarin's name was in fact used in swearing at animals.

5. This looks like an allusion to the stories that Mazarin was a pederast. The phrase 'original sin' may possibly refer to his country of origin, Italy.

LETTER 112

1. Rhedi's question, answered in the next ten letters, is based on ideas that were fairly common at the time. In 1685 the scholar Isaac Vossius maintained that the population of Europe had fallen to thirty million; his views aroused considerable debate. Chardin and Tavernier noted the desolateness of Persia and other eastern regions.

2. Circassia stretched from the Sea of Azov to Mingrelia, north-east of the Black Sea; Imeretia and Guria were small kingdoms between the Black Sea and the Caspian, and had sometimes been independent and sometimes incorporated into one or other of the greater neighbouring powers.

3. In editions before 1758, this read: '... that there is scarcely a fiftieth of the number of men on earth that there was in Caesar's time'. Originally Montesquieu had also put 'a two-hundredth part' of the number of inhabitants of America, and in his 1754 manuscripts he changed the figure for Greece from a hundredth to a fiftieth.

LETTER 113

1. Montesquieu presumably means the Black Death of about 1350.

2. No doubt this is syphilis, once commonly thought to have been brought to Europe from America (cf. L. 105, note 2); the usual treatment (referred to in the next paragraph) was with mercury.

LETTER 115

1. Roman slave marriages were not formally celebrated but recognized in practice.

2. This was the *peculium*, in law the master's property, but used by the slave for his own enterprises, which were sometimes on a large scale.

LETTER 116

1. Barrière suggests in his article (see L. 8, note 1) that Montesquieu was reporting his own experience; he was married in 1715.

LETTER 117

1. The Council of Trent had fixed the age at sixteen; it is not known whether Montesquieu had any reason for putting the lower age.

2. The *lex Julia* and the *lex Pappia Poppaea*, promulgated by Augustus.

3. These must be the words required to celebrate mass.

4. Estimates of the property owned by the Church in France range from a fifth to a third of the total; the clergy numbered about a quarter of a million in all. Property which came into the possession of religious communities, for instance by bequest, was thenceforward inalienable, by the right of '*mainmorte*'.

LETTER 118

1. Montesquieu's information comes from Frázier, *Relation du voyage de la mer du sud* ('An account of a voyage to the Southern Seas'), of 1717; but he apparently made a mistake in saying that imported slaves were used in the mines (Vernière).

LETTER 119

1. This is the doctrine of a Messiah.

2. Another reference to the Gabars (cf. L. 67 and L. 85); the source is again Chardin.

3. Montesquieu's interest in China apparently arose from personal acquaintance with the Christian convert Hoange, who was resident in Paris; he also used books by Kircher (1670) and Couplet (1687).

4. This concept of the ancient religion of China is similar to that of Heaven, seen as possessing and exercising divine power.

LETTER 120

1. This generalization was based on reports about Madagascar, where abortion was supposed to be frequent.

2. Montesquieu is referring to a law of 1556. The death penalty

could be imposed if, after an unreported pregnancy, the child died without being baptized. The law had been reiterated in 1708, but was repealed later in the century.

LETTER 121

1. This paragraph was added in 1754.

2. This practice was prevalent under Augustus and Tiberius (Barckhausen).

3. The information comes from Tavernier and Chardin. Gilan is a district on the south-west coast of the Caspian.

4. This comes from a basic source for information about Turkey, by Ricaut (1670); the same fact is mentioned in L. 114.

5. They had been expelled by Philip III in 1610.

6. Flacourt's book on Madagascar (1658) tells of some Frenchmen who, while on Reunion Island, suffered no illness; those who had been sick recovered.

7. This reference has not been explained.

LETTER 122

1. By the laws of 1688 and 1701, only unmarried men were to be enrolled (Barckhausen).

LETTER 123

1. Usbek means the victories of the Emperor Charles VI and his general Prince Eugene of Savoy over the Turks, in 1716 and 1717. The 'mufti' is generally taken to be Cardinal Alberoni, who was intriguing with the Turks in order to further Spanish interests against the Empire (cf. L. 130, note 2).

2. Cf. note 2 to L. 60.

LETTER 124

1. Indignation about Louis XIV's policy with respect to pensions was especially strong in 1715, and in the first edition in which it appeared, the second 1721 edition, this letter bore the date 1715. It

seems likely that Montesquieu later considered it prudent to transpose the letter to after Louis XIV's death, so as to make the criticism less pointed (Adam).

2. This remark is obscure in that there were apparently no laws about the age at which it was permissible or obligatory to marry, nor about anything similar in relation to dowries.

LETTER 125

1. This is the Hindu custom of suttee. One source is Tavernier; the author of another, F. Bernier, tells of having persuaded a widow not to burn herself (Vernière).

2. A bonze is a Buddhist priest; Montesquieu must have confused the term with that of Brahmin (Carcassonne).

LETTER 126

1. Montesquieu has slightly disguised an important incident in 1718, the Cellamare conspiracy. It involved the Spanish ambassador Cellamare ('the ambassador of the Grand Mogul'), who was arrested and expelled, and the Duc du Maine, the king's uncle. The conspiracy was based on the possibility that the king might die (cf. L. 107, note 1).

2. Quintus Curtius, in his life of Alexander, tells this story about Darius III, the king of Persia whom Alexander defeated (Barckhausen).

LETTER 127

1. Charles XII was killed in 1718 at the siege of Fredrikshald. The minister was the Baron von Görtz, executed in the following year.

2. The reasons for Görtz's trial were more likely to have been his foreign origin – he was German – and the financial expedients he employed in order to support Charles XII's militarism.

LETTER 128

1. The anecdote is told by Livy of Tarquinius Superbus, who cut off the highest poppies in a garden, so as to indicate the treatment he recommended for the leading citizens of Gabii, captured by his son.

2. Babylonian time was based on the duration of daylight, and in consequence, being variable, it would not have corresponded to the regular time-scale preferred by the mathematician.

3. This was a strategically important town, and was taken by Berwick in 1719 after a heavy bombardment.

4. The formula belongs to Cartesian mechanics, not Newtonian (cf. the science in L. 97).

LETTER 129

1. The criticisms which follow are too general for all the references to be tracked down, but the foreign language is no doubt Latin; the over-subtle laws may be those of Sparta, which Montesquieu describes in similar terms in L. 116; while in praising the institution of paternal authority he must be thinking of Rome, as is indicated by the end of the letter.

LETTER 130

1. Newsmongers, novelists, quidnuncs, or intelligencers (Ozell's word) were a recognized social group at the time. They had considerable importance, despite Montesquieu's jibes, as recipients of foreign news independently of the normally slanted government media. The most celebrated of them was the Count Joachim de Lionne, referred to here by his initial. They had meetings which were carefully organized and recorded.

2. The events referred to are those of 1716–18, as in L. 123, during the wars between the Austrian Empire and Turkey and between Spain and Austria.

3. I Kings xii, 8 says of Rehoboam, son of Solomon, that 'he forsook the counsel of the old men, which they had given him, and consulted with the young men.'

LETTER 131

1. The basis of these remarks seems to be twofold: (a) the ideal, mythical 'garden of the Hesperides', which however is not the same as (b) Hesperia, a name which indicates westerliness (from Hesper, the setting sun), and was used both by the Greeks, to denote Italy, and by the Italians, to denote Spain.

2. Editions before 1758 include the following passage after this paragraph: 'It would seem that freedom suits the character of the European peoples and servitude those of Asia. It was in vain that the Romans offered this precious treasure to the Cappadocians: this worthless nation refused it, and hastened into servitude as eagerly as other nations hasten towards liberty.' The king whom the Cappadocians preferred to liberty was Ariobarzanes I, in the first century B.C. (Barckhausen).

3. The passage is clearly an indirect criticism of the despotic tendencies within a centralized monarchial system, and implies that in origin the modern state was basically democratic; as such it is a brief early version of the final books of the *Spirit of Laws*. Some of the factual evidence is valid (the deposition of kings), some of it faulty (laws created at tribal assemblies).

LETTER 132

1. Montesquieu's first speaker is talking about the depression in agriculture which had gone on throughout the preceding century and was to be reversed only in the 1730s, and especially about the decline in land-values brought about by the rise in value of shares in John Law's company for the exploitation of the Mississippi; the second speaker, about the fall in money-values after public confidence had disappeared and the shares, together with the notes issued by the national bank directed by Law, became virtually worthless. There is considerable difference of opinion among scholars concerning the exact dates to which Montesquieu refers.

2. This man, having lent some money, has been paid back in notes worth less than the money he lent. The same idea is to be found in L. 146.

3. The general opposing Berwick, in the rather desultory Franco-Spanish war which ended by treaty in 1720 (cf. L. 128, note 3); he was threatening to invade Languedoc.

4. Even less was then known about sunspots than is apparently known now, but Montesquieu obviously regards this man's theory as a superstition.

LETTER 133

1. According to tradition, Montesquieu is describing the library of the Abbey of Saint-Victor, which since 1707 had been regularly opened to the public.

LETTER 134

1. This portrait may have been influenced by Montesquieu's friend and teacher, Père Desmolets, who in 1721 was put in charge of the Oratorian library in Paris.

2. The religious movement of the end of the seventeenth century, led by Mme Guyon, whose greatest adherent was Fénelon. Montesquieu's definition, in which the ambiguity of '*libertin*', meaning both free-thinker and libertine, is present, exemplifies the cynical belief that the emotional and mystical tendencies of the movement could lead to disregard for religious and moral conventions.

3. Montesquieu must be referring mainly to Sanchez's *De matrimonio* (On Marriage) (1637), which he mentions in L. 143. On casuistry, cf. L. 57.

LETTER 135

1. On alchemy, cf. L. 45.

2. Magic of all sorts had been prevalent throughout the seventeenth century. Judicial astrology is the art of prediction by the stars; Chardin wrote of its importance in Persia.

3. As the pun on 'system' makes clear, the reference is to John Law.

LETTER 136

1. The passage takes up the theme of L. 131.

2. i.e. the Roman; Montesquieu is referring to the use of the name

'Holy Roman Empire'. The idea behind what he says of its defeats is obscure.

3. The references seem to be to the establishment of the Merovingian dynasty by Clovis and of the Carolingian by Pippin the Short and Charlemagne, followed in both cases by increasing disunity, and then to the Capetian kings and the vicissitudes of the medieval monarchy up to the achievements of Louis XI in the fifteenth century.

4. From the eighth to the fifteenth century Spain had been gradually reconquered from the Moors by the Christian kings, who at one time were confined to the mountains of Asturia. L. 121 explains why the Spanish empire did not make the country great but weakened it; its prosperity was unreal because it was based on gold and silver, which, according to L. 118, are merely the signs of wealth.

5. Continental opinion generally viewed the English revolutions of the seventeenth century with anything from awe to horror. Montesquieu's remarks here are similar to those of Voltaire a decade later in his *Lettres philosophiques*. For a rather different approach to English politics, cf. L. 104.

6. Ozell says that the city was called 'Genoa the Proud'.

7. This no doubt refers to the decline of Poland and the Polish monarchy in the later seventeenth century, a decline which was by no means ended at the time of the *Persian Letters*.

LETTER 137

1. These views on poets, which may seem curious, were common enough in the extremely rational atmosphere of the time. Montesquieu makes an exception for drama because of the great dramatists of the preceding century, Corneille, Molière and Racine. On epic, the reference is to the Quarrel of the Ancients and the Moderns; cf. L. 36. The two epic poems are those of Homer and Virgil (the *Iliad* and *Odyssey* are presumably lumped together); many unsuccessful efforts to write a modern French epic had been made, especially in the years after 1650.

2. This theory about pastoral poetry is most probably derived from a work of Fontenelle's on the eclogue (Adam).

3. I translate the word '*roman*', which now means 'novel', by 'romance' because Montesquieu is apparently referring to the high-flown novels of chivalry which had remained popular for much of the seventeenth century.

LETTER 138

1. Editors have been able to distinguish, with some degree of certainty, four policies before 1721 – those of Noailles, d'Argenson and John Law, and the reversal of Law's policy. An entry in one of Montesquieu's notebooks (the *Spicilège*) supports this. However, the date of the letter, 1 January 1720, is just before Law was put in charge of financial policy, not after the failure of his System; on the whole it seems preferable not to take the dates indicated in this letter too literally.

2. These were the so-called 'givers of advice' ('*donneurs d'avis*'), private individuals who put forward suggestions for financial policy in memoranda, and who might be paid if they were accepted (Adam).

3. The committee system of government, or 'polysynody', inaugurated by the Regent, which was terminated in 1718.

4. N*** is Noailles, who pursued a policy of retrenchment; the foreigner is John Law.

5. The Rue Quincampoix was 'the Stock-jobbers' rendezvous in the Mississippi year' (Ozell).

LETTER 139

1. Following the death of Charles XII (cf. L. 127), his sister, Ulrica Leonora, had become queen, but abdicated in favour of her husband in February 1720.

2. The date was 1654; Christina was the patron of Descartes. In his comments Montesquieu appears to be unaware of her colourful private life, or chooses to ignore it.

LETTER 140

1. For a government decree to become legal it had to be registered by the Parlement. If for any reason the Parlement did not see fit to

do so it had the right to make representations ('*droit de remontrance*'); Montesquieu must be referring to this right in his comments at the end of the letter. On this occasion the decree was a Finance Council measure aimed at withdrawing a large amount of paper money from circulation. The Parlement registered the decree but with the observation that it had done so under constraint. Its exile (one of the weapons often used by the government when it came into conflict with the Parlement) lasted from 20 July, the day before the date of this letter, until December.

LETTER 141

1. This must be the grand vizir of Suleiman III (1666–94), Ali Khan (Barckhausen).

2. Cf. note 4 to L. 24, in which Rica had taken this view.

LETTER 142

1. Montesquieu may be thinking of a Roman road near his estate of La Brède.

2. The story is an allegory of Law's System. John Law was born in 1671 in Edinburgh. His father was a rich jeweller, his mother a Campbell.

3. A reference to Law's travels through Europe, during which he won a fortune by gambling.

4. This must be Louis XIV, since Law was in fact banished from France in 1708 because of the suspicions attaching to his success at gambling. Betica was originally the name of part of the Iberian peninsula, and Montesquieu used it in this sense in L. 131; it was also used as the name of an ideal country in Fénelon's *Télémaque* (1699), a book much admired by Montesquieu.

5. The balloons (or is it the air they contain?) sold by the son of Aeolus are bank-notes or shares, and later 'imagination' is the financial confidence on which the credit-system is based.

6. The current price of shares in Law's India Company (Barckhausen).

7. i.e. henceforward the value of notes and letters of credit will be fixed, not floating.

8. Measures were taken to prevent the use of possession of gold

and silver coin in the first half of 1720, in an effort to keep up the value of the paper money; bank-notes were to be used instead. Large amounts of gold were sent abroad, and purchases of jewellery made, by people hoping to protect their money.

9. This reference remains obscure.

10. A reference, according to Adam, to the preamble of the edict of 21 May 1720. The edict announced that the value of shares was to be reduced by nearly fifty percent; this caused much alarm, and another edict six days later annulled the first one.

11. Different explanations are given for this; perhaps the most straightforward is that it refers to the rapid fall in the value of shares following the edicts at the end of May 1720 (Adam).

LETTER 143

1. Amulets and talismans are worn to ward off disease or danger (as in battle). Chardin says that the custom was widespread among the Persians, after the fashion described by Rica.

2. Despite the emphatic phraseology it is not clear to which panic terrors Montesquieu is referring.

3. The name recalls that of a well-known bookseller-publisher, Anisson.

4. i.e. 'Knowledge of the Globe', on the assumption that the traditional explanation is correct and that Montesquieu's abbreviation '*La C. du* G.' means 'La Connaissance du Globe', some work of geography (but why should geography be particularly boring?), which has not been definitively identified.

5. A Reverend Father of the Society of Jesus.

6. Caussin and Rodriguez were religious writers of the seventeenth century.

7. The rest of the letter was reduced to the status of a note in the 1758 edition; Montesquieu's manuscripts show that he thought at one time of omitting the letter altogether, no doubt because of the scurrility and disrespect of the last part.

8. Following modern editors, this means 'Degrees of the Council concerning the Bank and the Company of the Indies', i.e. John Law's enterprises. The pun on 'confidence' supports this.

9. This corresponds to '*les J.F.*' ('*Jeux floraux*', Floral Games), the name of an Academy at Toulouse, dating back to the time of the troubadours, which gave an annual prize for poetry.

10. A writer who was expelled from the Society for defending, against the traditional Jesuit position, the rights of the Gallican Church; 'a pompous and prolix historian' (Vernière).

11. A prominent but undistinguished seventeenth-century poet, satirized by Boileau for his high-flown style.

12. The first leader of the Jansenist movement, in the 1640s, whose style was elaborate.

13. The last three 'prescriptions' are in Latin in the original.

14. Lallement, a Jesuit, wrote a book accusing the Jansenist Quesnel (cf. L. 24, note 3) of sedition, in 1704.

15. Another attack, as L. 57 and L. 134, on Jesuit casuists; the idea is presumably that they make sin easy.

16. Here the theme is sexual obscenity, and the references are to Aretino's *Sonetti lussuriosi* (Sonnets of Lust) which, with their illustrations, caused a scandal in 1525; and to Sanchez's *De matrimonio* (1637), which went into great physical detail.

LETTER 144

1. This letter appeared for the first time in 1754.

LETTER 145

1. The letter which follows must be based largely on the scientific activities at the Academy of Bordeaux, of which Montesquieu was a founder member. Meteorology and anatomy were both studied seriously. Montesquieu established a prize for the latter subject, and a Dr Grégoire was well known for vivisecting dogs.

2. Cartesian philosophy, which asserted that animals had no soul and were therefore automata, provided a justification for vivisection: despite appearances they were supposed not to be able to suffer pain.

3. Montesquieu may be referring to, or influenced by, a work by Gabriel Naudé, *Apologie pour tous les grands hommes qui ont été fausse-*

ment soupçonnés de magie (An Apology for all the great men who have been falsely suspected of magic) (1625).

4. Such accusations abounded. Montesquieu may have been thinking especially of Fontenelle, who was attacked in 1707 by a Jesuit named Baltus for works written in the 1680s.

5. Montesquieu's friend Fréret (1688–1747), a scholar and sinologist, was sent to the Bastille in 1715 for making politically controversial speculations about history; Montesquieu's own such speculations, as L. 131, were also on rather sensitive subjects.

6. It will be clear that the object of this attack is the activity of national and government propagandists (an example is parodied in the first newsmonger's letter in L. 130). I have translated the 1754 and 1758 reading '*l'Empire*', which would mean the Holy Roman Empire; it seems slightly more likely that the 1721 text '*des empires*', which would have no specific reference, is preferable.

7. The second 1721 edition includes the following passage at this point: 'But how shall I describe the present age, when I see a man of learning at the disposal of a publisher? when I see a man who deserves to have a statue put up to him compelled to devote his waking hours to making the fortune of a mere artisan? His works might have been useful to posterity, but are rushed through because of avarice: the end is entirely subordinated to the means.'

LETTER 146

1. An obvious disguise for John Law in France. In this letter the theme is the dishonesty of altering money values and the consequent debasement of public morality – it becomes possible to pay off debts in money which has lost its value (cf. L. 132, note 2).

2. A metaphor for, presumably, the notes issued by Law's bank.

3. i.e. an officer ('*huissier*') whose duty it was to see that official decrees were carried out.

4. The Duc de Bourbon and the Prince de Conti, related to the royal family, carried off large sums of money from Law; the Comte de Horn murdered a speculator for his money (Vernière).

LETTER 147

1. Montesquieu goes back three years from the date of the preceding letter, in order to make a connected story of the events in the seraglio, especially as this story depends partly on the time-factor involved in the delays in communication between France and Persia (cf. L. 149 to L. 152).

LETTER 157

1. This letter, like L. 158 and L. 160, appeared only in 1754. Zashi's previous misdemeanours are the subject of L. 20, and another is reported in L. 147.

LETTER 158

1. On Zelis, cf. L. 147 and L. 152. Earlier, in L. 62, she had seemed to be mainly concerned with her daughter (and cf. L. 71); however, the Appendix contains the draft of a letter from Usbek reacting to her request for a separation.

LETTER 161

1. She is referring to Usbek's remarks in L. 26.

SOME REFLECTIONS

1. The 'Reflections' appeared first in 1754. The last two paragraphs are a response to a pamphlet published in 1751 by the abbé J. B. Gaultier, *Les Lettres persanes convaincues d'impiété* (The Persian Letters Convicted of Impiety). Montesquieu's manuscripts show that the whole of the 'Reflections' was carefully revised; the two most important variants are given below. The Appendix (p. 285) contains two other defensive passages, one of which includes many phrases also found in the final version. The double emphasis on the ideas of religion and strangeness in these explanations suggests that Montesquieu is particularly concerned to defend L. 24.

2. There is a variant reading to this sentence: '... and this is one of the causes of the success of *Pamela* and the *Peruvian Letters* (delightful works which have appeared since).' The first is Samuel Richardson's

novel, translated into French in 1742, the second a novel by Mme de Grafigny, published in 1747.

3. This must refer to the fact that in 1744 fourteen '*Lettres turques*' (Turkish Letters), attributed to Saint-Foix, were published in an edition of the *Persian Letters*.

4. Among the many variants in the manuscripts, the following passage is found in one version, replacing the last sentence of the definitive text: 'Of all the editions of the book, the only good one is the first: it did not suffer from the audacity of publishers. It appeared in 1721 and was printed in Cologne by Pierre Marteau. The present edition is to be preferred to it, since the style of certain passages in the first edition, and some printing errors which had slipped in, have now been corrected. Such errors were multiplied without number in subsequent editions, the work having been abandoned at birth by its author. End.' The publisher was in reality Jacques Desbordes, Amsterdam: 'Pierre Marteau', like other imprints often used at the time, was a fake name.

APPENDIX

1. The manuscript has a note: 'I thought to continue the history of the Troglodytes, and this was the idea I had.'

2. This is yet another letter about Law's System. In the first paragraph the reference are to the decree of 21 May 1720, and in the second to that of 27 May – see note 10 to L. 142. Adam points out that Montesquieu's date is too early for the second decree.

3. The turban is a cardinal's red hat, traditionally the reward for churchmen distinguished in politics. Montesquieu is probably thinking especially of the abbé Dubois, the regent's minister, who became a cardinal.

4. The manuscript has a note: 'This letter could not be put into the *Persian Letters*, because 1. it is too much like the others, and 2. it merely repeats what is better said in them. I have put it here because there are certain sections that I might be able to use and a few striking passages in it.' Montesquieu used some of the same material in L. 15 and L. 22, where the name 'Janum' becomes 'Jahrum'.

5. It may not be entirely clear that this letter is a variation upon two standard jokes: that women who had passed their first youth

gave up love-affairs for piety, and that the world of the devout, which was a society in itself, was not as pure as it might appear.

6. It will be observed that the first paragraph of this letter is a version of the end of no. 19. Similarly, a version of the end of this letter is among the pieces found by Mme Carayol. It begins with what is here the third paragraph of Hadji Ibbi's letter, and continues as follows: 'Germany is torn by a multitude of troubles. The Catholic and Protestant mullahs have consciences delicate enough to spread fire and conflict everywhere. The best brains in Europe have been working for the last year to put an end to a dispute which in more peaceful times would not have required more than a quarter of an hour's attention.

'If the fundamental principles of the two religions were at stake, it might have been possible to quieten them. But the importance of the affair is of quite a different order: it is a matter of deciding whether six Jesuits, or six Protestant ministers, are to suffer a humiliation, and the whole of Germany is about to fight for the honour of the six ministers or the six Jesuits.

'What contributed more than anything else to the acrimony was certain words in the Protestants' sacred book which express hostility towards Catholics. The Catholics wanted them removed, the Protestants refused; both were equally foolish.

'It is extraordinary that the Catholics should have insisted on taking exception to these insults, which are so general that they cannot refer to anyone; but since they have in fact taken exception to them, it is even more extraordinary that the Protestants should have refused to remove them, it being contrary to natural equity and religious piety that anyone should be the object of insults which he finds offensive, and contrary to good sense that they should be said in the form of prayers.'

According to Mme Carayol, Montesquieu is referring to the religious controversy of 1719–20 in Germany.

7. An asper was a Turkish silver coin.

8. Mir-Vais was an Afghan leader who rebelled against Shah Hussein in 1713 and whose successful campaign led eventually, in 1722, to the Shah's defeat.

9. Nos. 17 to 20 were discovered by Mme Carayol in a shortlived

periodical of 1745 written by Thémiseul de Saint-Hyacinthe, who knew Montesquieu. The other letters published by him are variants of L. 91 and of nos. 9, 10 and 13 above.

10. The fact that this letter on prayer and sea-sickness is from Hadji Ibbi suggests, as does no. 8, that Montesquieu once thought of making him one of the Persian travellers in France.

READ MORE IN PENGUIN

In every corner of the world, on every subject under the sun, Penguin represents quality and variety – the very best in publishing today.

For complete information about books available from Penguin – including Puffins, Penguin Classics and Arkana – and how to order them, write to us at the appropriate address below. Please note that for copyright reasons the selection of books varies from country to country.

In the United Kingdom: Please write to *Dept. JC, Penguin Books Ltd, FREEPOST, West Drayton, Middlesex UB7 OBR*

If you have any difficulty in obtaining a title, please send your order with the correct money, plus ten per cent for postage and packaging, to *PO Box No. 11, West Drayton, Middlesex UB7 OBR*

In the United States: Please write to *Consumer Sales, Penguin USA, P.O. Box 999, Dept. 17109, Bergenfield, New Jersey 07621-0120*. VISA and MasterCard holders call 1-800-253-6476 to order all Penguin titles

In Canada: Please write to *Penguin Books Canada Ltd, 10 Alcorn Avenue, Suite 300, Toronto, Ontario M4V 3B2*

In Australia: Please write to *Penguin Books Australia Ltd, P.O. Box 257, Ringwood, Victoria 3134*

In New Zealand: Please write to *Penguin Books (NZ) Ltd, Private Bag 102902, North Shore Mail Centre, Auckland 10*

In India: Please write to *Penguin Books India Pvt Ltd, 706 Eros Apartments, 56 Nehru Place, New Delhi 110 019*

In the Netherlands: Please write to *Penguin Books Netherlands bv, Postbus 3507, NL-1001 AH Amsterdam*

In Germany: Please write to *Penguin Books Deutschland GmbH, Metzlerstrasse 26, 60594 Frankfurt am Main*

In Spain: Please write to *Penguin Books S. A., Bravo Murillo 19, 1° B, 28015 Madrid*

In Italy: Please write to *Penguin Italia s.r.l., Via Felice Casati 20, I–20124 Milano*

In France: Please write to *Penguin France S. A., 17 rue Lejeune, F–31000 Toulouse*

In Japan: Please write to *Penguin Books Japan, Ishikiribashi Building, 2–5–4, Suido, Bunkyo-ku, Tokyo 112*

In Greece: Please write to *Penguin Hellas Ltd, Dimocritou 3, GR–106 71 Athens*

In South Africa: Please write to *Longman Penguin Southern Africa (Pty) Ltd, Private Bag X08, Bertsham 2013*

PENGUIN AUDIOBOOKS

Penguin Books has always led the field in quality publishing. Now you can listen at leisure to your favourite books, read to you by familiar voices from radio, stage and screen. Penguin Audiobooks are ideal as gifts, for when you are travelling or simply to enjoy at home. They are edited, abridged and produced to an excellent standard, and are always faithful to the original texts. From thrillers to classic literature, biography to humour, with a wealth of titles in between, Penguin Audiobooks offer you quality, entertainment and the chance to re-discover the pleasure of listening.

Published or forthcoming:

Emma by Jane Austen, read by Fiona Shaw

Persuasion by Jane Austen, read by Joanna David

Pride and Prejudice by Jane Austen, read by Geraldine McEwan

The Tenant of Wildfell Hall by Anne Brontë, read by Juliet Stevenson

Jane Eyre by Charlotte Brontë, read by Juliet Stevenson

Villette by Charlotte Brontë, read by Juliet Stevenson

Wuthering Heights by Emily Brontë, read by Juliet Stevenson

The Woman in White by Wilkie Collins, read by Nigel Anthony and Susan Jameson

Heart of Darkness by Joseph Conrad, read by David Threlfall

Tales from the One Thousand and One Nights, read by Souad Faress and Raad Rawi

Moll Flanders by Daniel Defoe, read by Frances Barber

Great Expectations by Charles Dickens, read by Hugh Laurie

Hard Times by Charles Dickens, read by Michael Pennington

Martin Chuzzlewit by Charles Dickens, read by John Wells

The Old Curiosity Shop by Charles Dickens, read by Alec McCowen

Crime and Punishment by Fyodor Dostoyevsky, read by Alex Jennings

Middlemarch by George Eliot, read by Harriet Walter

PENGUIN AUDIOBOOKS

Silas Marner by George Eliot, read by Tim Pigott-Smith

The Great Gatsby by F. Scott Fitzgerald, read by Marcus D'Amico

Madame Bovary by Gustave Flaubert, read by Claire Bloom

Jude the Obscure by Thomas Hardy, read by Samuel West

The Return of the Native by Thomas Hardy, read by Steven Pacey

Tess of the D'Urbervilles by Thomas Hardy, read by Eleanor Bron

The Iliad by Homer, read by Derek Jacobi

Dubliners by James Joyce, read by Gerard McSorley

The Dead and Other Stories by James Joyce, read by Gerard McSorley

On the Road by Jack Kerouac, read by David Carradine

Sons and Lovers by D. H. Lawrence, read by Paul Copley

The Fall of the House of Usher by Edgar Allan Poe, read by Andrew Sachs

Wide Sargasso Sea by Jean Rhys, read by Jane Lapotaire and Michael Kitchen

The Little Prince by Antoine de Saint-Exupéry, read by Michael Maloney

Frankenstein by Mary Shelley, read by Richard Pasco

Of Mice and Men by John Steinbeck, read by Gary Sinise

Travels with Charley by John Steinbeck, read by Gary Sinise

The Pearl by John Steinbeck, read by Hector Elizondo

Dr Jekyll and Mr Hyde by Robert Louis Stevenson, read by Jonathan Hyde

Kidnapped by Robert Louis Stevenson, read by Robbie Coltrane

The Age of Innocence by Edith Wharton, read by Kerry Shale

The Buccaneers by Edith Wharton, read by Dana Ivey

Mrs Dalloway by Virginia Woolf, read by Eileen Atkins

READ MORE IN PENGUIN

A CHOICE OF CLASSICS

Francis Bacon	**The Essays**
George Berkeley	**Principles of Human Knowledge/Three Dialogues between Hylas and Philonous**
James Boswell	**The Life of Samuel Johnson**
Sir Thomas Browne	**The Major Works**
John Bunyan	**The Pilgrim's Progress**
Edmund Burke	**Reflections on the Revolution in France**
Frances Burney	**Evelina**
Margaret Cavendish	**The Blazing World and Other Writings**
William Cobbett	**Rural Rides**
William Congreve	**Comedies**
Thomas de Quincey	**Confessions of an English Opium Eater**
	Recollections of the Lakes and the Lake Poets
Daniel Defoe	**A Journal of the Plague Year**
	Moll Flanders
	Robinson Crusoe
	Roxana
	A Tour through the Whole Island of Great Britain
Henry Fielding	**Amelia**
	Jonathan Wild
	Joseph Andrews
	Tom Jones
John Gay	**The Beggar's Opera**
Oliver Goldsmith	**The Vicar of Wakefield**

READ MORE IN PENGUIN

A CHOICE OF CLASSICS

William Hazlitt	**Selected Writings**
George Herbert	**The Complete English Poems**
Thomas Hobbes	**Leviathan**
Samuel Johnson/	
James Boswell	**A Journey to the Western Islands of Scotland and The Journal of a Tour of the Hebrides**
Charles Lamb	**Selected Prose**
George Meredith	**The Egoist**
Thomas Middleton	**Five Plays**
John Milton	**Paradise Lost**
Samuel Richardson	**Clarissa**
	Pamela
Earl of Rochester	**Complete Works**
Richard Brinsley	
Sheridan	**The School for Scandal and Other Plays**
Sir Philip Sidney	**Selected Poems**
Christopher Smart	**Selected Poems**
Adam Smith	**The Wealth of Nations**
Tobias Smollett	**The Adventures of Ferdinand Count Fathom**
	Humphrey Clinker
Laurence Sterne	**The Life and Opinions of Tristram Shandy**
	A Sentimental Journey Through France and Italy
Jonathan Swift	**Gulliver's Travels**
	Selected Poems
Thomas Traherne	**Selected Poems and Prose**
Sir John Vanbrugh	**Four Comedies**

READ MORE IN PENGUIN

A CHOICE OF CLASSICS

Leopoldo Alas	**La Regenta**
Leon B. Alberti	**On Painting**
Ludovico Ariosto	**Orlando Furioso** (in 2 volumes)
Giovanni Boccaccio	**The Decameron**
Baldassar Castiglione	**The Book of the Courtier**
Benvenuto Cellini	**Autobiography**
Miguel de Cervantes	**Don Quixote**
	Exemplary Stories
Dante	**The Divine Comedy** (in 3 volumes)
	La Vita Nuova
Bernal Diaz	**The Conquest of New Spain**
Carlo Goldoni	**Four Comedies (The Venetian Twins/The Artful Widow/Mirandolina/The Superior Residence)**
Niccolò Machiavelli	**The Discourses**
	The Prince
Alessandro Manzoni	**The Betrothed**
Emilia Pardo Bazán	**The House of Ulloa**
Benito Pérez Galdós	**Fortunata and Jacinta**
Giorgio Vasari	**Lives of the Artists** (in 2 volumes)

and

Five Italian Renaissance Comedies
  (Machiavelli/**The Mandragola**; Ariosto/**Lena**; Aretino/**The Stablemaster**; Gl'Intronati/**The Deceived**; Guarini/**The Faithful Shepherd**)
The Poem of the Cid
Two Spanish Picaresque Novels
  (Anon/**Lazarillo de Tormes**; de Quevedo/**The Swindler**)

READ MORE IN PENGUIN

A CHOICE OF CLASSICS

READ MORE IN PENGUIN

A CHOICE OF CLASSICS

Molière	**The Misanthrope/The Sicilian/Tartuffe/A Doctor in Spite of Himself/The Imaginary Invalid**
	The Miser/The Would-be Gentleman/That Scoundrel Scapin/Love's the Best Doctor/Don Juan
Michel de Montaigne	**Essays**
Marguerite de Navarre	**The Heptameron**
Blaise Pascal	**Pensées**
	The Provincial Letters
Abbé Prevost	**Manon Lescaut**
Rabelais	**The Histories of Gargantua and Pantagruel**
Racine	**Andromache/Britannicus/Berenice**
	Iphigenia/Phaedra/Athaliah
Arthur Rimbaud	**Collected Poems**
Jean-Jacques Rousseau	**The Confessions**
	A Discourse on Inequality
	Emile
Jacques Saint-Pierre	**Paul and Virginia**
Madame de Sevigné	**Selected Letters**
Stendhal	**Lucien Leuwen**
	Scarlet and Black
	The Charterhouse of Parma
Voltaire	**Candide**
	Letters on England
	Philosophical Dictionary
Emile Zola	**L'Assomoir**
	La Bête Humaine
	The Debacle
	The Earth
	Germinal
	Nana
	Thérèse Raquin